English Settlement

By the same author

Fiction

Great Eastern Land
Real Life

Non Fiction

A Vain Conceit: British Fiction in the 80s
After the War: The Novel and England Since 1945

ENGLISH SETTLEMENT

D. J. Taylor

Chatto & Windus
LONDON

First published in 1996

1 3 5 7 9 10 8 6 4 2

First published in Great Britain in 1996 by
Chatto & Windus Limited
Random House, 20 Vauxhall Bridge Road,
London SW1V 2SA

Random House Australia (Pty) Limited
20 Alfred Street, Milsons Point, Sydney
New South Wales 2061, Australia

Random House New Zealand Limited
18 Poland Road, Glenfield
Auckland 10, New Zealand

Random House South Africa (Pty) Limited
P O Box 337, Bergvlei, South Africa

Random House UK Limited Reg. No. 954009

Papers used by Random House UK Limited are natural, recyclable
products made from wood grown in sustainable forests. The
manufacturing processes conform to the environmental
regulations of the country of origin

A CIP catalogue record for this book
is available from the British Library

ISBN 0 7011 3898 X

Typeset by SX Composing, Rayleigh, Essex
Printed in Great Britain by
Mackay's of Chatham, PLC
Chatham, Kent.

In memory of

Joseph Lloyd Carr 1912-1994
Jonathan Peter Warner 1959-1994

Contents

I began to brood on the complexity of writing a novel about English life, a subject difficult enough to handle with authenticity even of a crudely naturalistic sort, even more to convey the inner truth of the things observed . . . Intricacies of social life make English habits unyielding to simplification, while under-statement and irony – in which all classes of this island converse – upset the normal emphasis of reported speech.

ANTHONY POWELL – *The Acceptance World*

PROLOGUE

1

Pretzel logic

Have you ever nearly choked to death on a fragment of seafood? I did once: the incident is etched on the surfaces of my mind in plunging, ineradicable contours, something for ever stirring down there in the compost of memory. It happened in the most expensive fish restaurant in Manhattan, a venue of high, empurpled windows and sleek, executive heads. The immediate witnesses were neither friends nor relatives, in whose company this embarrassment might have been barely tolerable – a quaint footnote to the parchments of family history, say, a reminder of mortality sent to barb a de-energised acquaintance – but my employer, a man named Daniel J. Hassenblad, and two senior vice-presidents of the Chase Manhattan Bank.

Often thinking about this inglorious episode, piecing together sensation and detail in the quiet of the obsessive's mental cell, I have wondered about these two characters, encountered neither before nor since, and the reason for their attendance that lunch-time in the upper room of Balaraj's, with its noiseless waiters and its scintillating view out across the crowded Manhattan skyline. For these were august and venerable gentlemen, silvery-haired and shrewd, more accustomed to dining in private rooms accompanied by senators and fiscal regulators than in public with the proprietor of a nine-man computer consultancy and his personal assistant. My current employers, a by no means unrespectable international firm, would happily have given an arm – not their own, perhaps, but somebody's arm – to be able to say that they had entertained two Chase Manhattan top-dogs. They would have framed the check and hung it on the boardroom wall with the Rothko prints.

Looking back I can see that enticing them there, in the upper room of Balaraj's, marshalling them together on public display as it were before the silent fish tanks and the crowds of knowledgeable onlookers, represented the profoundest business coup of Danny's career, that in attending to these molten gods and their grave and almost professorial desires – the obscure brands of mineral water, the pernickety side-orders – he was a man defined, whipped suddenly out of the rut of prosaic humanity and framed within a rosy, ethereal glow. I appreciate, too, that if Danny was the impresario of this unlikely entertainment, the magician plunging his hands into a series of pocket kerchiefs to draw forth, and oh so effortlessly, coloured baubles, tricoleur flags and teeming wildlife, then I too had a role, if only that of the mute assistant, dutifully allowing himself to be cut in half, to have oranges extracted from his ears, admiring and complaisant. So it is a matter of regret, even now, four years later, that in Danny's hour of symbolic triumph I should so monstrously have failed him, so badly let him down.

With hindsight, too, I can see that Danny – poor Danny with his processed hair, the stretched suit proclaiming him a sartorial also-ran – was simply deluding himself, that in responding to his lunch invitation his guests were pursuing not the Hassenblad Consultancy's computing techniques, its network systems and treasury management add-ons, but the spirit of the age. This was the late summer of 1986, the wildest time. People were selling debt that year, grotesque, imponderable debt in six-figure bonds; there were lock-up garages on sale in Queens for forty thousand dollars, and adverts in the business press for Master's degrees in Creative Realting. I saw Michael Milken once, in that same restaurant in Manhattan as it happened, and as he stalked purposefully into the thronged lobby, the tribe of flunkies unregarded in his slipstream, the ellipse of faces gathered and then fell away with sacramental awe. It was this scent, I realised, that the Chase Manhattan pair had come in search of, this earthy yet enticing tang that had driven them down from Olympus to the bare level plains populated by Danny and his kind, the tang of money made without effort, through expertise, connection or simple bluff. It was this that had sent them in a gleaming stretch limousine to a distant quarter of their city, and persuaded them to approach the nervous, gesticulating figure of Danny Hassenblad – a man who, had he penetrated the sanctums of their wider corporate life, they would merely have ignored – this that informed their courteous but splendidly ironic conversation. They wanted money, they were prepared to allow you to make it for them, but their contempt, that fine old financier's contempt for the huckster tradesman, was infinite.

And so we sat, the four of us, at the table in Balaraj's, beneath the winnowing fans. Danny was jiggling with nervousness, despatching waiters on unnecessary errands and then recalling them, at one point going so far as to pour his guests glasses of mineral water with his own hand. The two august and venerable bankers and I regarded each other with a kind of amused complicity, a half-humorous recognition of the absurdity of the situation. None of this feeling, I divined, had communicated itself to Danny. Despite his nervousness, despite the patches of rank moisture spreading evenly across the frontage of his shirt, he was soaring into a private stratosphere of elation. Dazzled by the silvery heads bobbing before him, by thirty dollar entrées and mineral water at seven dollars the glass, he was convinced that the lurching juggernaut of his business career had broken through, pushed aside walls of rock and emerged finally into bright caverns hung with precious stones.

What visions Danny had contrived to sustain him in this condition, what Wall Street satrapies he saw himself a part of, I could only guess, but it was clear that they had blinded him to the incongruities of his current state, and the magnitude of the bankers' mistake. And it *was* a mistake, as the looks exchanged between me and the Chase Manhattan pair readily admitted. Somewhere in the long chain of whim, insinuation and strategy a link had snapped, somewhere in their patient accumulations of intelligence a faulty assumption had been overlooked, and the result was this numskull errand to Manhattan to meet a giggling computer consultant and his stooge.

How far Danny was aware either of his imposture or its exposure I have never determined. For an American business-man of the late twentieth century, he had a touchingly naïve belief in the probity of his fellow men; his assumptions about the people he did business with excluded the possibility of guile. An economic forecast or a Congress committee report on

5

technology had him nodding his head, unaware that his sobriety, his wholly antiquated straightforwardness, found no echo in a world of deceit and subterfuge. Even here, looking out over the Manhattan skyline and sipping Perrier at seven dollars the glass, he thought he was being treated as an equal, on some green and level playing field, unaware that such an attitude would lead him to make bizarre assumptions, encourage him to imagine that he cracked uncrackable codes. Trapped in this wholesale delusion, he missed the tiny signals that might have helped him to break free.

Thus, barely ten minutes into the meal, when the senior of the two Chase Manhattan senior vice-presidents, having established the meagre nature of the Hassenblad Consultancy's resources and the triviality of Danny's suggestions, turned to his companion and murmured, 'Well, we might as well eat while we're here,' Danny continued to smile, confident that somehow it was going to be OK, that there was a hidden kernel of promise somewhere in this put-down that could only work to his advantage. And so, perhaps, it was fortunate that what happened happened, that the cancelling out of Danny's dreams should seem to be effected by this immediate calamity rather than by some more sinister and external agency, and that I rather than incompetence or venal corporatism should emerge as a scapegoat.

It happened without warning. One moment I was eavesdropping on the quiet hiss of chatter – they were street-sharp, those Wall Street bankers, they talked not as you might imagine of fine porcelain and Balanchine but of the Superbowl, the budget deficit and Carl Lewis – the next I was aware of a gross and irregular constriction in my throat, of a reflex attempt to swallow fatally compromised by something coursing unpreventably downward to lodge deep in some forgotten laryngal cranny. Like a cork plunged into a bottle, I thought – and the image was actual, not retrospective – as I gulped a couple of times and wheeled round in my chair with the mute, imploring glance of a man who fears that some dark and determining structure has suddenly been placed over the pleasant randomness of his life, like a partridge chick nervously aware of the hawk's expanding shadow. Still innocent of the impending

6

horror – for there were remedies at hand, I thought, I would take a glass of water or plunge a finger down my throat as I had done when the deceptions of childhood required a factitious nausea – I tried to cough. Nothing happened (this, I later discovered from the medical textbooks, is a characteristic symptom of the choker, the victim wants to cough but there is no purchase, and in the absence of air no lubrication, nothing to cough *with*).

Uneasily conscious of the disquiet around me – Danny, to do him justice, had realised something was wrong and was making little fluttering movements with a short wooden stick pulled from a Florida cocktail – and also of mounting physical distress (a swimming sensation in my head, a second constriction, angry and deep-seated, in my chest), I staggered to my feet. Clutching at a chair-back, one arm making vague, imprecatory gestures, I gazed around me with a look that was alarmed but also mildly benevolent, caught up in the wonder of this eerie, sagging world that seemed to be curling at the edges, its light and shade bruising somehow into dull purples and yellows.

And while much of the wonder was levelled at the magnificent, fuzzy clarity – the bankers remote and inaudible but curiously defined, the silent fish tank all murk and moving shadow – I also saw again the girl to whom I had bidden farewell that morning at 7.30 and whose last action before my departure had been to disappear into the bathroom, tallowy breasts gleaming in the orange light, saw again the letter with my father's handwriting lying face-up on the mat. And thinking of all these things, of the silvery-haired manikins before me, the girl's receding breasts, a room grown suddenly fragmented and calamitous, I pitched forward to collapse head first on the table.

They moved fast, those Wall Street princelings. Calamity found them dextrous, resourceful, urgent. Scarcely had my head hit the deck – the flagons of mineral water foaming skyward, plates cracking underfoot – than the senior of the two had me folded over a chair-back and was administering the Heimlich manoeuvre. The look on his face, while still patrician and invulnerable, had been extended by other emotions, by a sort of Boy Scout eagerness, a complacency born of expertise and appropriateness to milieu. Even had I wanted to, I realised,

7

there was no way of ignoring those fingers probing into my diaphragm, no way of suppressing the cough or the particles of seafood sent skittering out over the tablecloth. I was in thrall to a superior intelligence, whose remit extended not merely to the tricky chicanes of high finance but to life and death itself, something to whom expressions of gratitude or resentment would be simply irrelevant, so much were actions of this type merely the furtherance of a gross personal satisfaction.

And so I sat on the expensive floor of the upper room at Balaraj's, dotted and furrowed now with fallen detritus, grateful but also distressed by the knowledge I had gained: that expertise is transferable, that it is a characteristic, a technique of the successful operator's life – distressed, too, by the consequences of this knowledge for my own life. Until once again physical reality supervened. Which is to say that I threw up, threw up good and hard over the vermilion carpet, while the two Chase Manhattan senior vice-presidents, being men of the world, conversed above my head about a summer cottage one of them was renting in the Hamptons, and the unreliability of the Chesapeake ferries.

It was at this point, too, that the Wall Street pair demonstrated another of their conspicuous abilities – the ability to delegate. Consequently it was Danny who shepherded me to the washroom, stood over me as I vomited a second time – on this occasion louder and more effortfully – proffered towels and deflected the stares of prurient fellow-diners. Throughout, his expression was one of intense and mournful reproach, the look, I thought – trawling back through my own childhood – of the mother who discovers her son's closest college friend in the loft gleefully clamped to the exposed thighs of her teenage daughter.

'Not a career-advancing move, Scott,' he said at one point, as I plastered my hair back into place with a borrowed comb. It was his only comment, either then or subsequently, on what had happened. Only then, too, did I appreciate the enormity of the hurt I had done him. Danny, I realised, had had high hopes for this meeting; its expenses and incidental humiliations – 'three hundred fucking dollars this is going to cost me,' he had exclaimed jubilantly during the two hundred yard cab ride from the office – were proud and necessary scars. Now I had blown them away. Worse, perhaps, was the manner of this demolition.

To Danny, I divined, the misadventure with the piece of seafood was more culpable than any professional inadequacy. He sympathised with me, he recognised the distress to which I had been subject, but I could not have offended him more had I been detected in passing a forged promissory note through the Hassenblad Consultancy's accounting system. For in choking well-nigh to death in front of two Wall Street bankers whom a cultivated delusion allowed him to think of as potential customers, in vomiting over the carpeted floor of the most expensive fish restaurant in Manhattan, I had been guilty not of professional negligence – something Danny could cheerfully have forgiven (what, after all, didn't the Hassenblad Consultancy know about professional negligence?) – but of social ineptitude. Retching over the floor, supine among the smashed crockery, I had infringed some wordless etiquette, its arbiters the glossy-haired duo at our table, of which Danny fancied himself the interpreter, and he would never forgive me.

Worst of all was that the bankers agreed with him and to a certain extent sympathised with him in his humiliation. This was clear from the moment we returned to the table which was pristine once more and covered with fresh foods and decorations ordered in our absence. Disapproval was apparent in their redoubled courtesy – always studied, now raised to an impossibly remote eyrie of irony and diffidence – in their reluctance to dwell on the enormities of the previous ten minutes, above all in their willingness to express this disapprobation by shifting allegiances. Previously, the meal's only collusion had involved the bankers and me; it was we who had cracked our little jokes and quietly mocked Danny's presumption, his naïvety, his inability to comprehend either the unseen protocols and structures of the commercial world or his own place within them. Now, I saw, those roles were reversed. In the spectacle I had created by puddling the floor with my vomit a new alliance had been forged, one so tenuous that it would vanish with the appearance of the check, but temporarily sufficient to drench me with shame.

Though no further mention was made of my misfortune – even Danny, in an unprecedented display of tact, contrived not

9

to refer to it – its memory hung over every subsequent exchange that I tried to become a part of, over every joke, smile or shred of badinage, so that in the end I ceased to snicker loyally at Danny's winded puns, ceased to display my not inconsiderable knowledge of computing techniques (in which the bankers might conceivably have been interested) and relapsed into silence. It was apparent, too, in the expression with which I found the senior of the two bankers – the one who had upended me over the chair – regarding me towards the end of the meal. It was not an unkind look; it contained no malice – and I am a management consultant, I know all about the turbulent eye-glint of wounded seniority – it was quite free of a resentment that would have been understandable in a man whose shoe leather still crinkled and stank under the flecks of vomit I had deposited there half an hour before. Yet the faint hint of contempt was unignorable. In doing what I had done, I had ceased to be a human being – if in fact I had ever been one in the eyes of this dollar god – and become simply material for an anecdote.

'I saved a guy's life this lunch-time,' he would say that evening to his wife, his children or to an identikit tuxedo'd representation of himself, the venue a thronged art gallery, a cocktail party, a Coney Island dinner party. Gradually, endlessly repeated at gatherings of this kind, mentally retold in a thousand pre-dawn reveries, the story would acquire embellishments – background minutiae, dialogue – I would become transformed into a figure of massive inconsequence and incongruity, until I finally became a vital and unavoidable part of the man's personality: the time 'Daddy', 'My husband', 'Old Ralph here' saved a man's life; the coda about the computer salesman who had a fucking nerve to intrude himself into that august presence would remain mercifully unspoken.

More so than Danny's silent reproach, or the aloof three-way alliance, it was this realisation that finally humbled me, so that weighed down both by self-knowledge and by perceptions of a wider and more ominous kind – knowledge of the abstruse codes and structures governing the society in which I laboured – I passed the remainder of the meal in sulphurous gloom.

10

The party broke up at three. This in itself was a bad sign. In these the wildest of times hospitality habitually telescoped, stretched out to cover great tracts of the working day, turned into seven-hour brunches, night-long festivals of amity and hope. For the record the Chase Manhattan senior vice-presidents ate a pair of seafood cocktails apiece, followed by grilled bream in hollandaise sauce and pan-fried monkfish with anchovies, followed by peach melba and coffee, the whole washed down by a truly noble Chablis and a bottle of Beaumes de Venise. The check came to three hundred and fifty dollars. Danny settled it with a wide-eyed simpleton's casualness.

After they had left we sat surveying the post-prandial clutter of three-quarter-full wine glasses and errant bagels, conscious of our failure to bring down our quarry, but also of a quaint, irrepressible bravado welling up within us, a complicity of spirit that led Danny eventually to order up a bottle of cognac and two plump glasses and permit us to make crazy, bombastic toasts to each other as the light fell and darkened over the room, the waiters roamed effortlessly around the adjoining tables and the last of our fellow-diners crept away. It was late summer now, with a wind drifting in off the Hudson and the first of the stiff September leaves flicking up against the high windows, the thought of the year's extinction lay everywhere about, but we didn't care: Danny because he knew no better; I because I was twenty-seven and imagined that I viewed the scene with a fundamental detachment. Yet we were aware that in however narrowly symbolic a way the afternoon represented some sort of climacteric in our lives. Later that day, aflame with brandy and the consciousness of how near I had come to death, I would return home and fall upon the girl with the tallowy breasts in a fury redolent of psychological terror rather than sexual desire. The rhythm of the age had altered and we had somehow failed to keep pace with it. The wildest times were at an end and we had nothing to show for our imbrication but bravado and a stack of restaurant checks.

The Hassenblad Consultancy failed for three million dollars in the spring of 1988. Danny, who had lunched regularly at Balaraj's and employed a corn-haired secretary from a Rhode Island finishing school to whom he was almost afraid to speak, now works as an operations manager for Coopers & Lybrand in Boston, and when I last spoke to him had received the lofty privilege of being permitted to stow his convertible in the underground car lot.

Me? Well, I had my own escape hatches out of this sink of blighted hopes and stalled aspirations. And though we could not foresee these destinies – far humbler than the splendid trajectories we had mapped out for ourselves in those bright, Reagan-sponsored days – I am confident that we had some inkling of them, were already conscious that when from the vantage point of later life we followed the trails back through nurturing moss to a seedbed of causality, we should return to that afternoon in Manhattan, with its cracked plates, its social insecurities, its behavioural gaffes, its silent, enveloping unease.

Though the memory of that incident at Balaraj's lingered on the surface of my mind, it took a little time for its resonance to become properly apparent, for the pebble wedged between sock and shoe of my interior landscapes to work itself into a position where it could push up into the overlying flesh and draw blood. It was only later, somewhere else – in Europe, maybe, on a train, in one of those aching pre-dawn mental shuffles – that I realised I already had a context for the data that afternoon had brought me, a framework that extended out beyond the narrow confines of fish tanks and New York skylines, out into the middle distance to take in upbringing, heritage, the eternal, unvoiced assumptions of caste, family and friends.

Like many exclusive groups my family had a number of pet phrases, stock expressions designed to swathe the incidental resentments and confusions of daily life in a blanket of consoling irony. But somehow these expressions, whether gnomic or aphoristic, differed from those I had heard at other tables, spoken by other fathers to their sons, let fall casually by other mothers to their daughters in kitchens or on back doorsteps: they were at once more oblique, more savage, more *exclusive*, incomprehensible, in fact, to anyone without a widescale understanding of our family and its traditions, and as such often used to introduce an element of tension into social events. None of the rare evening parties we gave – rare because my parents were silent, self-effacing people – was complete without its nonplussed guest and its sense of quiet embarrassment.

'Riding with General Gorgas', for example, more or less the exclusive property of my father, derived from a neighbouring family of ours which claimed Confederate ancestry, and indicated social pretension. 'Hoosier boy' – a branch of my father's family came from Indiana, three generations back – meant wild, louche, inelegant, and was capable of being used as an adjective, so my father would occasionally, as a joke, refer to a notably inoffensive member of our local church congregation as 'Hoosier boy Williams'.

The most resonant saying of all was one which seems to have been as much a part of my childhood as my mother's face rising up over the big boxwood table on the back porch of the old house in Margaretsville. I can recall its being applied to twenty different situations or contingencies. It came not from the here and now (or rather the then and there) but from way back, from a time when my father had not even known my mother, or that this lexical shorthand would play such a momentous part in his future life.

The expression dated from the early 1950s, a period in my father's career when he was living in the eastern part of Tennessee, and, so the story went, paying court to the daughter of a well-to-do local family. The girl's name was Charlotte, or perhaps Ella (my father's ability to remember people's names worked in inverse proportion to their closeness to him: thus he could recall the name of his grandfather's coloured chauffeur but not the name of his daughter's boyfriend), though the photograph of her in an old bachelor's album – a striking woman with blonde hair looking a little like Doris Day – is uncaptioned. As it happened, and despite conspicuous evidence of unreliability – the legal apprenticeship which had brought him to this part of East Tennessee was his fourth choice of career, and there had already been two broken engagements – Charlotte or Ella's parents rather approved of my father. They liked his formal, sobersides air – there are pictures of him from around this time in a neatly pressed Legal Eagle suit, his hair slicked back and wearing narrow, horn-rimmed glasses – yet at the same time, or so my father maintained, they detected in him a kind of insouciance that was in keeping with their own highly specialised notions of grandeur. For Charlotte or Ella's parents were – and here my father's memories were, for once, precise – grand people, a distinction that advertised itself not in rampant expenditure or display but in commemorating anniversaries of the battles of the Civil War, or looking down on prosperous Northern relatives whose money came from manufacturing or stock exchange speculation. And for a time it looked as if my father, with his severe hairstyle and his subfusc suits, the amused deference seeming to conceal an underlying fizz of exuberance and unpredictability, might fit into this curious and self-absorbed family circle, might indeed marry Charlotte or Ella, sire a brood of aristocratic, buzzard-featured Southern children and combine his legal career with dinner parties convened to memorialise the Battle of Gettysburg. As it was, in a gesture characteristic of my father's style and temperament, he blew it all away.

My father's crime was to arrive at the family house early one evening, still in his lampblack courtroom suit, his legal briefcase tucked under one arm, bearing in his outstretched hand a half-eaten pretzel. Having been admitted by the servant, he was confronted in the vestibule – a flaring, high-walled tunnel lined with wolf- and deer-heads – by Charlotte or Ella's mother, Mrs Frobisher. Recounting this anecdote in later years, my father made strenuous attempts to find words suitable to describe the bewilderment of Mrs Frobisher's eyes, the rictus of disbelief that contorted her mouth when she became aware of the semi-consumed biscuit and the off-white paper bag from which it protruded. 'Like a valkyrie'; 'like the girl in *Creature from the Black Lagoon* when she sees the water bubbling'; 'like Pat Nixon on her wedding night' – this is only a selection from my father's efforts to recapture the nuances of that doorstep encounter. Typically – and this was a sign, maybe, of the grandeur, a mark of the complicity that at this stage persisted between my father and his hosts – no word was spoken. In fact, so far as my father remembered, he was treated that evening with more than ordinary courtesy. But he knew, and Mrs Frobisher knew, and Mrs Frobisher knew he knew, that such a startling solecism could not go unpunished. Again, through the ensuing decades, my father tried to settle on an imaginary situation that would have produced the same bonfire of outraged social codes: 'As if I'd said my father was a Jewish insurance salesman from Chicago'; 'As if I'd been found screwing the black cook'; 'As if I'd walked into the house wearing a T-shirt with FUCK IKE written on it'. But I got the feeling that none of these lavish scenarios was quite appropriate to define the enormity of my father's offence. Although nothing was ever said, although my father's relationship with Charlotte or Ella persisted amicably for some months, and though Mr Frobisher even contrived to have my father elected to temporary membership of the vicinity's sveltest gentleman's club, everyone involved in the transaction from my father down to the Frobishers' gardener knew that he had slightly less chance of succeeding in his matrimonial ambitions than the chairman of the local Democratic Party, and that the half-eaten biscuit lay at the root of it all.

'Pretzel logic', my father called it, by which he meant a judgment based on quite arbitrary criteria, in this case his own appearance on the Frobisher doorstep, in defiance of their grandeur and all manner of silent warnings, with a pretzel. Lodged comfortably in the mines of our family life, the phrase proved itself resistant to the vagaries of time or happenstance. It was fireproof – you consigned it to the flames and it reared up at you, unscorched and gleaming. Deciding not to go to church because it was raining – that was pretzel logic. My mother's dislike of one of my sister's boyfriends on the grounds that his ears stuck out and that she had once seen him reading a copy of the *Harvard Lampoon* – that too could be referred back to my father and his experience on the Frobisher doorstep. Even then I wondered how my father felt about the continued exposure of what must surely have counted as a kind of humiliation to a steadily expanding audience.

It was only later that I came to appreciate that such memories, however sharply perpetuated, formed only a comparatively minor part of his contemporary life, and that he saw scant connection between the crop-haired young man in his attorney's suit and the person he was eventually to become, no link between Charlotte or Ella and the turbulent emotional life of his maturity.

Meantime, I had my own private vantage point on this family saw. Held up for the inspection of the two Chase Manhattan senior vice-presidents, I too had been found guilty, if not of an inability to perform the tasks for which these two hoary senators might conceivably have hired me, but of social ineptness, for having – to put it plainly – the colossal effrontery nearly to die in front of two people I was entertaining to lunch. Even at four years' distance the memory rankles, its legacy apparent not so much in rancour – though were I to encounter either of those venerable monsters again there are long conversations I could have with them, endless verbal humiliations to which I could submit them without batting an eye – as in lowered horizons, a solemn personal quietism. I go easy now, and take things slowly, go easy with food, go easy with the girls, with my father, Slater and Barry Mower – with anything that might disturb the smooth tenor of my existence, leave me vulnerable and distraught, just as I had been that afternoon in Balaraj's when the wild times came hastily to an end and the ordinary world, that grim, terrible ordinary world, spun up once more to take their place.

PART ONE

———◆◆◆———

As one of the UK's leading professional firms, KLS has
an unrivalled reputation for providing quality service.
With over 5000 partners and staff working from
offices throughout the British Isles, our aim is to bring
imaginative solutions to bear on key issues facing the
business community and to treat our clients' problems
as if they were our own.

KLS 1991: *A mission to serve*

2

In the City

I get up early these days – 6.15 finds me twitching aside the frail coverlet, moving out into stale, cold air, glancing disinterestedly across the ridge of pillows in search of the auburn crop or the blonde cascade, some Penny or Jenny to rekindle the memory of the bygone night. For some reason the girls from the Mirabelle fear the dawn: daylight finds them hours away, asleep in spinster beds. By 6.45 I'm prowling across the grey battlefield of the Fulham Road, with its rearing trucks and slim cyclists, to mingle with the early commuters, those white-faced dealers come from obscure suburbs at the end of the line, while above us the pale sky breaks in the east and the clouds shift. Thirty minutes later I emerge from the subway at Blackfriars, catch my breath for a second on the topmost step and steam south across the bridge. At this early hour the river falls silent, a police launch, maybe, chugging in close to the bank, mysterious little boats vanishing upstream. The mist hangs low over clustered tower blocks (lights in the distant offices have the sickly quality of yellow tinfoil) so that the bulk of the KLS building looms up out of the dense air like a ghost ship come to startle ancient mariners.

Unless you're an exceptionally acute reader of the City pages or have some professional lien on the workings of accountancy firms you won't have heard of KLS, though you might have heard about its predecessors, Savage Sullivan & McKay, and Kellogg Lansdorf & Powell; and you might conceivably have come across Lowndes & Trevithick, which was the name in which Savage Sullivan & McKay sold its computer consultancy services to ailing foreign banks shellshocked by the Big Bang. Accountancy these days is about mergers. Six months back, after Trelawny Morrison had climbed into bed with Munby Moore & Foster to the horror of *Accountancy Age* which had

19

forecast a liaison with Phillips Richards & Rowe, and Berkmann-Hislop had achieved a similar union with Mackesey & Thomas, the partners of Savage Sullivan and McKone met the partners of Kellogg Lansdorf & Powell in an upper room of the Savoy, whence they emerged, three days and several adjournments later, and minus Mr Sullivan, Mr McKay and Mr Powell as Kellogg Lansdorf & Savage. The resultant combine turns over £300 million in the UK alone – oddly there is money in filing other people's tax returns and approving their bought ledger accounts – and bills itself as the fourth largest professional services firm in the world.

Little of this sense of purpose, this communal resolve that animates groups of professional men in times of crisis, can be detected within Centaur House, the KLS headquarters. Three dozen Savage Sullivan & McKay partners followed Messrs Sullivan and McKay into leisurely home counties retirement, and even at this late stage the 'P' remains unchiselled from the raised exterior logo (the old Savage Sullivan & McKay offices in High Holborn are bare and tenantless now). At this early hour, bereft of all but a handful of its two thousand or so inhabitants, the place has a forlorn, faded look, the night security guard head-down over his paperback, the early receptionists voluble over their coffees and carry-outs but restrained by the greater silence, cigarette smoke and warm air mingling in the empty corridors. I nod my way into the foyer, past a couple of nervous partners gearing themselves up for breakfast meetings, sidle into the gaping elevator, press the button for the ninth floor, where the management consultants, us, the important, golden guys have their lair.

Coming out of the elevator area – a distant clock, glimpsed out of the far window, reads 7.30 – I find Slater loitering in the corridor. Five feet six, fiftyish, with a gnarled professional bodyguard's physique, Slater seems lost in some contented private world.

'Hey,' he says sternly. 'Guess who I've got booked in for the Sudebank presentation?'

'Andy McWhirter?'

'Are you kidding? Andy got fired last Wednesday.'

'Ricky Jordan?'

20

'Still suspended by the Institute . . . No, Jack Devoto!'

'Not . . . Not *the* Jack Devoto?'

Slater blinks proudly. For a moment he is not a senior management consultant in a sixth floor office near Blackfriars Bridge but the fatherly coach reaching up to pat the million dollar quarterback's padded shoulders. 'Sure. Says he's going to turn up this afternoon.'

'Mr Billings? Mr twenty-five per cent? The guy who . . . The guy *who ran the Cairo job*?'

Slater nods seriously. 'I was on the team. Not *that* week. The first week. And we're talking strict budgets, Scott. We're talking three-figure expense claims else the whole thing gets referred back to London. Well, you can take it from me the first thing he does is to book himself and Julie into the Nile Hilton.'

'He took Julie as well?'

'Research assistant. Naturally she had to sit in on a few meetings and so on, but . . . Look, I don't know if I should be telling you this, Scott, but anyway dinner the first night cost two hundred and eighty dollars.'

'He never . . .?'

'Sure. All of it. The expenses claim', Slater intones solemnly, 'came to seven thousand dollars. What's more, central accounts didn't even query it.'

I add this to the glittering mental roster of Devoto's achievements: the man who billed UNESCO sixteen thousand pounds for two days of lectures to their software staff; the man who was supposed to have invoiced a director of Citibank for a five-minute conversation at a cab-rank.

'So why is a guy like Jack Devoto interested in a training contract with Sudebank?'

'Jack?' Slater smiles. 'Jack says he's getting soft. Figures a bunch of know-nothing spick bankers is just what he needs to get started again.'

Back at my desk, the working day kicks soundlessly into gear. From my throne – a high-backed swivel chair tethered amid blocks of paper in a cubicle eight feet square – I make imperious telephone calls to the outer reaches of my empire, its remoter satrapies and distant sub-kingdoms. I telephone subordinates in

Hong Kong, Tokyo and Detroit. Nearer at hand I telephone the boys working on the telecoms project in Salford, and the oil refinery study in Aberdeen. I contact the two junior trainees engaged on the South Coast lighthouse feasibility survey and receive from their lonely eyrie the disquieting intelligence that it is snowing and no one has visited them in three weeks. 'Keep it up,' I tell them, 'keep it up,' and the urgency is unfeigned. As I dispense these terse, omnicompetent instructions last night's faxes are stacking up at my elbow: from Piotr in Bratislava, from Basim in Jakarta, from Pilau in Delhi. I amuse myself with the world standard time chart, pull Piotr out of his breakfast meeting, summon Basim from the squash court, wrench Pilau – so far as I can tell – from some early afternoon siesta. We don't stand on ceremony, us management consultants. We take a pride in the eighty-hour weeks, the vanished weekends, the black-hole public holidays. We don't make the fatal professional operator's mistake of assuming that we are somehow bigger than the job before us. I once conducted a twenty-minute conversation with Slater on the relative merits of IBM and Compaq desktops while a girl named Serena slithered expertly up and down my glistening midriff. Slater, a veteran of the bad old consultancy days before respectability, has a sheaf of stories of this sort. 'So then we had three hours to write a forty-eight-page report . . .' 'Only I was in Paris and he was in Berlin . . .' 'Took the next flight out, but the chairman had cancelled . . .' Somehow we survive, somehow the next assignment finds us, sleekly confident, here in the foyer of the merchant bank, there in the nerve-centre of the telecoms tower, articulate, companionable, direct.

Imperceptibly the hustle of the early morning settles down. The mail arrives, wheeled up on trolleys by burly grey-haired men, with its mournful cargo of requests to attend computing seminars (who goes to those computing seminars? I don't go, Slater doesn't go, nobody in this building goes), its head hunters' circulars, its fawning solicitations from less successful practitioners: 'Dear Scott, You may remember that we met on the Amex job . . .' 'Dear Scott, Now that I have been made redundant by Fishwick-Profitt . . .' All over England there are desperate out-of-work consultants looking to vault back on to this shiny conveyor-belt, hoary-headed fifty-year-olds who know all there is to know about Just-In-Time manufacturing, bright thirtysomethings with Harvard MBAs who've spent three years on water-generating projects in the Saudi desert and are looking to settle down. Don't they know what's going on, these boys, don't they read the papers? Don't they know there's a downturn coming, and that only the clever guys like myself and Slater will be left to deal with the mad computers and the coiled laserprint? Slater has a theory about the downturn – and it's coming, it's been coming for years. I could see it shambling into view that afternoon in Balaraj's fish restaurant back in 1986, see it in the Chase Manhattan vice-presidents' sneer. The theory is that in the good times everyone makes money – you, me, the little guy in the shoebox office in Lewisham. Come the downturn only a few people make money, but they make more money. Slater's theory – like nearly all his meagre cache of professional lore, monstrously prescient – has already been telegraphed in the *Financial Times* under the banner of 'Crisis Management – a solution for the '90s.'

The morning slows down now, chugs idly in mid-lane, turns back on itself, loiters by the sidewalk. Outside the clouds have settled low and angry over the huddled city. The wind lifts. Inspired both by the mail and the vainglorious comfort of offices in winter – the frail, pinkish glow emitted by half-open doors, the serious faces passing intently down the corridor – I dictate faxes to Hank in Toronto, to Sven in Copenhagen, to Mahmoud in Kuwait City. At intervals secretaries – Debbies and Clares, Mandies and Melodies – bear them away for typing, bring them back for stern fine-tuning. I marvel at these impassive young women. Back home the secretaries are all moonlighting Jewish princesses between modelling jobs who have stockbroker boyfriends and vacation in Europe, and in whose company you wouldn't dare wear a suit that cost less than seven hundred dollars. Here they're lumpen, adenoidal girls whose muscular calves have the texture of liver sausage. My own secretary is called Linda, comes from Streatham and has a boyfriend called Grant. There have been other boyfriends called Kevin, Gary and Jason, their white, stolid faces lingering for a month or so in cheap frames above the filing cabinet next

23

to Linda's desk before Grant came and stomped them. Looking up from the pale screen, tracking a path between the scattered coffee cups and the packs of Marlboro – management consultants smoke, you know, we're the only accountants who do – I notice her in the doorway, luxuriate in her aimless stare.

'Hi, Linda.'

Linda nods, chews on her lower lip in a way that would be well-nigh erotic if it weren't for the complete absorption of the gesture. 'Was there anything you wanted at all?'

Somehow it is that final 'at all' which saddens me, which serves to confirm the narrow patterns of Linda's life. You could fix it for her to have tea with Barbara Bush or arrange for her to sit in on one of George's clambakes with President Mitterrand and Mrs Thatcher and she'd still ask them if they wanted Sweet 'n' Low with their coffee at all.

'Linda,' I say urgently. 'What's the capital of America?'

Linda stares back, as if there's nothing even faintly unusual in her boss springing this trick geographical question, as if winter forenoons are habitually enlivened by this intellectual call and response. 'I don't know. New York.'

'Not bad. Who was the last Democrat president?'

'Ronald Reagan.'

'OK. If you left the US at the New Mexico border and headed south, which country would you come to?'

'Brazil.'

'Thanks Linda. I'll catch you later.'

Face down over the desktop, I apply myself with mock strenuousness to a pile of assignment reports. She watches me for a moment before taking off again, incurious and un-flustered, to the corridor. Sobered by the sight of her retreating ankles I remember other obligations, other promises. I call Jenny at Sothebys, I call Penny at the alarmingly exclusive PR agency where she feigns employment, I track down Perdita in the basement of her Bond Street palace, I have Henrietta hauled out of the photocopying room at her gentleman publisher's in Bedford Square. I suggest drinks, I propose dinners, I hint at tickets to 'Cats' and 'Les Mis', am rewarded with subdued and effortful chatter. What is it about these well-bred English girls and their telephone manners, their conditional clauses and their

24

edgy *hauteur*? Even in her modelling days, Sondra didn't have that kind of negative poise. Is it because I'm American? I think they treat English guys the same way. Listening to Henrietta descanting pitilessly on the *hice* that her parents are keen for her to buy, on the *trizers* that one of her female colleagues turned up to work in to general consternation, on her forthcoming weekend in the *cuntreh*, I am forced to recollect how much I know about Henrietta, how delicately – and approvingly – I could itemise her bulky anatomy (the solid shoulders, the splendid haunches, the classy, low-slung breasts), how thoroughly I could reproduce the punctilious order of her bedtime preparations: the clasp of pearls snug in its basket, the white underthings folded carefully across the chair-back, the serious shoes (they call them court shoes, my mother once told me) side by side at the door. She and her kind have no equivalent in the States. There are Vassar girls, there are heritage girls – East Coast sophomores whose ancestors signed the Declaration – there are Tennessee aristocrats whose great-great-grandfathers died at Vicksburg, but nothing like Henrietta. As our frosty exchange peters to a close – I extract the promise of a rendezvous later in the week – Linda edges back through the doorway.

'Uh huh?'

'Scott.' For once there is awe and even incredulity in her voice. 'Jack Devoto just phoned.'

'OK. Any message?'

'He said he was coming at three, and the car would be ready to take you to Sudebank.'

I nod modestly at this as the clouds rush and collide in the angry sky. The limo. Jack Devoto. Sudebank. Linda's authenticating smile. Somehow it is a triumph of a sort.

3

Things I carried

A question you'll want answered before we proceed very far: what kind of American am I? The answer is: *that* kind of American. The kind that stands ostentatiously in the subway train doorway, spruce and elegant against the rainy dawn, reading a copy of the *Wall Street Journal*. The kind that calls any man more than five years older than him 'Sir' and any woman more than five years younger 'Miss'. The kind that leaps up unbidden to offer his seat to old ladies. The kind that has all the principal Continental dialling codes filed in the back of his pocket book. *That* kind of American. Rather, that is, than the other kind.

Standing on station platforms, watching the Skips, the Dexters and the Lavernes frowning over their subway maps, eyeing the Chucks, the Francines and the Dwights manhandling their backpacks and their hulking cameras, I can see no connection between myself and these depraved emissaries of my race. Striding over Blackfriars Bridge towards the office, I take cautious detours to avoid the knots of highschool students in their stretch slacks and windcheaters staring out across the grey river, shoulder past the squat, camcorder-toting family groups, anxious to reach the southern side where the tourists never tread and there are only urinous walkways and winding streets.

According to a guidebook I once read, one of those strident and unspeakable productions in which West Coast actors are pictured arm-in-arm with unsmiling Beefeaters, there is such a thing as 'American London'. If so, I never found it. I found odd, vagrant Americans – academics here on exchange programmes to whom the British Museum was a source of archaic, Brobdingnagian terror, ironical bankers who thought little of driving to Exeter for a lunch date – but no greater national solidarity. In fact the expats I encountered – the nervous smile at the party, the too-eagerly proffered handshake in the corridor – were oppressed by their solitude, by their inability to stake out a patch of ground in territory for which nothing in their extensive reading (and Americans check out England in advance, the planes are full of college students reading novels by Evelyn Waugh and Anthony Powell) had quite prepared them. The new world had come to saunter round the interminably imagined pleasure parks of the old, come to frolic on its temperate uplands and linger around its sinuous rills, and discovered picketwire fencing and the gamekeeper's smoking gun.

This is not a fanciful analogy. I once spent a weekend at a country house in South Yorkshire in the company of a highly sober and punctilious baronet for whom KLS were doing some consultancy work, where the principal recreations appeared to be excluding other people from the estate and killing unwary fauna. And yet the baronet, six feet two, leonine hair, those *bruised* eyes – Hollywood would have fought their way to his door – was not an unfriendly man. Compared to West Coast hospitality, where you might in a forty-eight-hour stint glimpse your hostess once on the patio, or Southern hospitality, where your recitations of gratitude are not only expected but marked out of forty, so to speak, his was a pattern entertainment. Even so the sense of unease in that great grim house, perched athwart the still lucrative coalmines which had given the baronet and his half-dozen ancestors their money – was almost tangible: you could reach out and grab it along with the Sheraton footstools and the Rex Whistler firescreens.

Other Americans have confirmed to me the truly desperate feeling of exclusion that arises out of these encounters. Listen, we want to say, we admire you. We like the way your government nuzzles up to our presidents, we like your pungent disregard for world opinion whenever some towelhead from the oil country tinkers with his safety-catch, we like your books and your art and your films. Why, we are your degenerate children, your epigoni: respectful, emulous and conscious of our own inadequacies, our too-short heritage and miscegenated stock.

And for all our reverent overtures you despise us. You find us brash, ingenuous, complacent, too serious about some things

28

(money, power, religion), not serious enough about other things (movies, consumerism, politics). You find our leaders a subject for low comedy. You covet our money and our bombs, but you withhold your respect. And so, raking over our nervous early evening suppers in hired Chelsea apartments, frowsting in the cramped corridors of your overheated trains (perhaps, after all, there is such a thing as American London, united only by its distrust), we resent this. We find it, as the jargon goes, demotivating, a disincentive. We don't stay long, and we return full of the specialised bile that grows out of wrecked illusions and unreal hopes, back to the people who cultivated these dreams for us, who pointed us towards the ocean and told us what we might find on the farther side.

My father, to take a grotesque and radically unrepresentative example, was an inveterate anglophile, one of that substantial collection of Americans – and there were venerable relatives prepared to testify to this – who as a youngster had demonstrated against Charles Lindbergh and in later life would never vote for a Kennedy on account of old man Joe and what he told Roosevelt about England's chances of winning the war (to my father's unrelenting gaze the Monroe scandal and Chappaquiddick were minor peccadilloes – it was the old man he hated). Even as a kid, to whom England meant no more than my mother's rusty accent, soldiery in odd-shaped helmets seen in military drama docs and the Beatles wisecracking with Ed Sullivan, I found this obsession perplexing and, while it corresponded with certain other bizarre outpourings of my father's temperament, devious. There were other anglophiles at large in our West Virginia foxhole – stout insurance salesmen who had followed Eisenhower into Europe, who had even, some of them, brought back English wives and a taste for continental delicacies – but their interest was static, reminiscent, elegiac. They kept pictures of Churchill on their walls, razored from *Time* magazine or robbed out of books, they could remember, with an effort, the tiny English villages in which they had been quartered – and the incongruity of these squat, shirt-sleeved men performing such feats on sunny Cook County patios was massive and startling – but this was a lost world, a Conan Doyle theme park, maybe, yet with waxwork dinosaurs.

My father's interest was urgent, promiscuous, rarefied. He had subscriptions to English magazines – *Country Life, Tatler, Horse and Hound* – which arrived once a month in shiny blue airmail bags, and he was the only man I have ever known to read the meagre three line paragraphs at the back end of the Sunday newspapers where they capriciously recorded English sports results.

The result of this altogether studious immersion – there was a college boy's fervour in the way my father unwrapped his parcels of English books and English newspapers – was to give him an almost unique vantage point on this rival national life. His was a selective and discriminating lore. He could not, for example, have told you the name of an English government minister, but he could have spun you a fine line on ducal prerogatives; he could not have told you where the town of Grimsby was, but he would know that they had a soccer team that played in parti-coloured shirts.

At the age of ten, the time at which I took an interest in my father's obsessions, I detected something deeply bewildering in this painstakingly acquired and slantendicular view, which even with what little I knew of England seemed remote from any sort of quantifiable reality. The smart society magazines – not unlike the periodicals that more *soigné* cousins sometimes sent down from Washington, but at the same time both more amateurish and more confident – only magnified this confusion. From them I divined that England was a place where clear-skinned young women with at least two surnames constantly rode, contriving as they did so to look distressingly like the steeds that bore them, or attended social functions at which, decked out in weird tent-like appurtenances, they were fisted glasses of champagne by the young men in evening suits whom they would presumably marry. Their parents, I gathered, divided their time between maintenance of the ornate, formal gardens, on whose lawns they were languidly photographed, and race meetings.

And yet this evident splendour seemed always to be cancelled out by what to my juvenile gaze were insupportable privations, stranger still in that they were cheerfully acknowledged, regarded almost as a mark of status. English people, I supposed, lived in immense, rainswept castles, shorn of the most basic

30

necessities (*Lord Todmorden*, I would read, *an avowed traditionalist, has so far resisted the introduction of the electric light to his Scottish estate*), were compelled by dint of their poverty to shoot wild animals and birds for food (*the opening day of the season at Blairgowrie produced a splendid bag of 300 grouse*). How I pitied Lord Todmorden as I imagined him groping his way along the inky dark passages to his ancestral chamber, a candle clasped in his palsied hand! How I felt for the Earl and Countess of Blairgowrie as they picked over their feathery carcass! There was romance in this straitened pomp, glamour in this pinchbeck nobility, self-possession in those serried faces.

Those faces! Everywhere one looked in my father's English magazines, framed by the virid embroidery of an herbaceous border, beneath top-hats or behind binoculars in sun-lightened paddocks, the faces peered out. From the prows of sleek yachts, sliding on into the complaisant ocean, from the drivers' seats of frisky roadsters, from endless dining tables suffused in the dazzle of cut-glass, they stared into the middle distance: calm, commanding, omniscient. Each found its welcoming smile.

My father was not altogether a subtle man, but in the matter of England he displayed a rare and wholly efficacious delicacy. Saturated in England and Englishness, albeit of a momentously specialised sort, we questioned the incidental detail of this grand obsession rather than its wider architecture. Led into this ornate and shimmering palisade, invited to traverse its limestone walkways and inspect the exotic foliage that clustered beneath, we marvelled a little, tried to raise the odd, dissenting claw and found ourselves stuck fast.

Inevitably much of this baggage accompanied me across the Atlantic. Some novelist whose name I can't remember wrote a story about the preoccupations of a band of Vietnam grunts called 'The Things They Carried'. When I arrived here in 1988 the things I carried were strange and multifarious. An accent pitched midway between West Virginia and the North-East seaboard and a glistening fraternity tie pin, but also a precise understanding of the ancestry of the British royal family and a mental map of the old English county system; paperback novels by Bellow, Roth and Malamud, but also the *Collected Letters of Virginia Woolf* and the diaries of Parson Woodforde; caches of records by the likes of Captain Beefheart, the Residents and weird American fauna that you won't have heard of, but also bizarre recordings cut in studios overlooking the Vale of Evesham by the Incredible String Band.

I carried my erotic memories, of the Hollys and the Pollys, the Rhoda-Joes and the Patti-Sues over whose gladsome forms I had sweated and yearned in college rumpus rooms and motel back-lots, but also my aspirations, of the Henriettas and Alexandras, the Emmas and Rosalinds whom time would surely deliver up to my knowing embrace. I carried my pained recollections, of Sondra late at night in the loft overlooking the Hudson as cool Manhattan air shivered the Chinese lanterns that concertina'd from the roof, but also my softcore imaginings, of demure English girls, their crisp white underwear folded on bedroom chairs, drowsing in wide, ambrosial beds.

The things I carried included a copy of *Whitaker's Almanac* for 1969 and a set of *Saturday Night Live* tapes from 1975–8 including the famous 'Last Days In The Whitehouse' sketch with Dan Aykroyd as Nixon and John Belushi as Kissinger, the *Look and Learn* wall-chart of significant events in English history and the *Harvard Business School Management Consultant's Handbook*. I was at once grossly over-familiar with England and dangerously ill-informed. The things I carried included a detailed knowledge of the principal English landed estates and Lynyrd Skynyrd's greatest hits, a set of medals depicting the 1970 English World Cup squad, and an Eagle Scout's citation: the usual pious Yankee illusions, ripe for spoliation.

'And another thing,' Slater says, on the phone twenty minutes later. 'There's a problem about Gayfere-Japhet.'

'What sort of a problem?'

'I dunno. System's crashed or something . . . Seems they were loading all this stuff on to the new software and it disappeared. I got a call from this guy in settlements an hour or so ago.'

Gayfere-Japhet were a middling firm of stockbrokers of aristocratic provenance (there was an Earl Gayfere somewhere, and a standing City joke that if you went into the partners' suite and shouted 'My Lord!' loudly enough half the partnership would assemble on the staircase) in whom the prospect of the Big Bang and its transatlantic depredations had provoked a wholly reasonable terror. Four years later these premonitions of doom were well on the way to being realised. A US bank had arrived from Boston, wondered about buying the equity, looked at the investment figures, had a spat with the Earl or it might have been the Marquis of Gayfere which made the back page of the *FT*, looked at the investment figures again, thought twice about it and had gone elsewhere, leaving Gayfere-Japhet to get by on diminishing volumes of private client work and some government connection that was so secret nobody even talked about it. Our current deal with them, whereby half-a-dozen consultants sat in the back-office for a month playing computer golf, had been fixed by a non-executive director pal of the senior consultancy partner in return for a no-questions-asked audit sign-off. Or so the story went.

'If the systems are down I don't see how it can be our fault. The deal was to do nothing. Run a few tests maybe, but not load in software.'

'Christ knows what's going on,' Slater says truculently, Gayfere-Japhet plainly no more than a smoking dot on some vast, lava-strewn mental horizon. 'Only last thing I heard there was fucking shredded paper coming out of the printers and some partner with three names was ringing up Birningside to complain about it, so just get round there and fix it will you?'

Towards eleven the pace slows. Linda and the secretaries have disappeared to the smoking room on the eighth floor, doubtless to muse about oral sex and the executive mothers such as myself who make their lives hell. A graduate trainee or two saunters timorously by. Slater is locked in his office with two venturesome kingpins from the tax division. The light gleams off their bald heads like poolhall neon off billiard balls. Pale and solitary in my room, smoke curling beneath the stacked eaves, the piles of faxes in the in-tray reduced to inch-high respectability, I attend to the routines of the consultant's life, fix my expenses – a dextrous programme of larceny which even Slater would approve – and leaf through Birningside's latest bout of corporate philosophising. Printed on hard,

33

expensive paper and copied to all consulting staff, this proposes that *managers should concentrate on developing new business styles and shifting the organisation's centre of gravity from a fixed line-based structure towards a flexible prospect-based organisation. A what-*based organisation? *In 1991* Birningside gravely confides, *the challenge is to become a genuine enabler of people.*

What irks me about it, curiously, is the certitude of purpose, the absolute rightness and tightness of intent, like the poetry jag the old man had embarked on in the months before he walked out on my mother, when he spent days addressing verse to members of his family, sonnets TO JEANNIE, backyard eclogues TO SCOTT. Appalling and derivative garbage – the palest imitations of Hart Crane, the dimmest echoes of e e cummings – but, like Birningside's techno-vapouring, somehow buoyed up by the thought of its own invincibility.

There's no jargon like consultancy jargon, of course. Birningside's memo talks about *integrative proaction* and *consumer reorientation.* During a presentation at some Olympian big-boy get-together I once heard him pull a minion up sharply to remark that it wasn't the semantics he was interested in but the meaning of the words. Inevitably, such criminal assaults on the purity of language have an ulterior motive. This much Slater once ruthlessly divulged during a joint perusal of a two-hundred-page document put out by the American practice under the modest title *Sourcing the Millennium: Prospecting the Future.*

'Of course it's all bollocks.'

'It is?'

'Course it is. We're here to make our clients a profit, OK? Now, there's one guaranteed way of making a profit. Find out what people want and make them pay a proper price for it. The rest is just corporate paranoia.'

'And computers.'

'Sure.' Slater's eyes were gleaming by this time. 'And computers.'

And top-team add-ons and feasibility studies and performance improvement, all the quaint redoubts of that corporate fantasy theme park where *people empowerment* actually means giving the secretaries a choice of flavours at the vending machine and *proactive* is shorthand for calling in the receivers before the bank gets there first.

A veteran of the bad old consultancy days of the late 1960s, when teams of diffident guys in pinstripes loafed around doing time and motion studies, Slater had greeted the arrival of computers on this side of the Atlantic with unmitigated satisfaction. 'Of course, you're too young to remember it Scott, but . . . I mean it was like someone had turned up at Waterloo with an Uzi sub-machine gun or something.'

'It was that good?'

'Sure. One minute we're freezing our arses off outside some factory gate with a stopwatch, the next there's half a million quid's worth of circuit boards in crates in the basement and the client's desperate for someone to tell him how to stick them together.'

The traditional client/supplier relationship having been overthrown at a stroke, the average consultant's career fizzed off tornado-like into the corporate stratosphere: implementation jags, telecoms projects, bare, angular caverns beneath City dealing rooms stacked to the ceiling with seething machinery. Slater apparently spent the whole of 1971 sitting in an office in South Wales at three hundred pounds a week having secretaries fetch him coffee while sixteen floors below a dozen puzzled technicians assembled a Loewenstein Series II in much the same way as you or I might assemble an erector set.

'The CG job? They were great days, Scott. It took a year. I didn't know what I was doing. Technical knew fucking less than that. The day before we went I counted up the restaurant bills, and do you know there were two hundred and sixty-five of them?'

Beyond the door Linda and a couple of sidekicks – saucier versions of Linda with bubble cuts and pendulous lower lips – come waddling by, back from the smoking room, and I glance up at their grey, dogged faces. A tall, willowy guy called Grieveson – junior to me but with career-advancing tendencies – goes mincing back to his office along the corridor. Incandesced by a sudden flame of rivalry, I wait half a minute and dial his extension number.

'Hollo Charles Grieveson.'

Two things irk me about Grieveson's phone manner. One is his habit of saying 'Hollo' instead of 'hello' or 'hallo' or 'hi'. The other is his habit of running the words together as if he were actually greeting himself. On impulse I shift my accent half a key downwards and in the guise of a Wall Street head hunter gravely inform Grieveson of his apparent suitability for a Credit Suisse Boston IT analyst's job. Amazingly, it works like a dream. Lured by the growl of New World solemnities ('Mortified if I have . . . uh, inconvenienced you, Mr Grieveson'), enthused by the occasional hustler's imperative ('firefighters who can kick some ass'), intrigued by discreetly veiled largesse ('Let's say the rewards package will be . . . ah, superior') Grieveson chirrups and whinnies with acquiescence. 'Actually,' he says at one point, 'actually you know I'm reasonably happy here. I mean . . .' I cut in with some gruff promises of air miles, pension contributions, health insurance. 'Would I . . . I mean, would this be in *America*?' Grieveson asks. 'This is a multinational organisation, Mr Grieveson,' I tell him sternly. 'We think in terms of continents, not jurisdictions.' Grieveson undertakes to call me back in twenty-four hours. Further inspired, I give him the number of the Chicago Futures Exchange, which happens to decorate a wall-chart a foot or so above my head. I let a couple of minutes go by, and watch as Grieveson hurtles back down the corridor towards Slater's room, before I seize my case and descend in the cramped and rickety elevator to the distant streets.

Later, as the cab shoots northwards over the bridge, I gaze out interestedly at the wayside antiquity, the jutting buttresses, the cool green gardens glimpsed between crenellated surrounds. Even now London retains its fascination, its jumbled incongruities: the mysterious courtyard shut behind high, locked gates; the silent, sunlit square. Here, as a young woman, family legend maintained, my mother had spent a night sleeping on a street corner, the better to procure some coign of vantage for the next day's Coronation. 'Why did you go?' I asked her once. 'I don't know. I guess it was what you did.' 'You remember it all?' 'I suppose not. I remember the glass coach and the Queen. Not much else.' I was used to this smokescreen of silence which billowed up, unfailingly, over any discussion of her pre-American life. Years later when I saw the old black-and-white film, resurrected to garnish an NBC doc on the Bicentennial visit, the scene seemed to have regressed into antic period hokum, a series of archaic tableaux orchestrated by Cecil B. de Mille: the thousand peers and peeresses rising noisily to their feet, trumpets breaking on the ear like klaxons, the slight, stoical figure beneath the ermine cape, like a trapper, I thought, weighed down by surplus pelts.

The cab swings east on to Upper Thames Street, leaving the tall ships and the floating restaurants and the tourist honeycombs. Thinking about my mother invariably makes me conjure up the distant, passionless spectre of Henrietta, less through any similarities of temperament or physiognomy – though my mother's high, aquiline nose and popping blue eyes conformed entirely to the physical type – but owing to a roster of shared assumptions and behavioural tics. Twenty-five years of America, a decade and a half of my father, half a lifetime of shopping malls and redneck banter had failed to suppress these characteristics in my mother, tendencies that combined to produce a kind of seething stoicism, a vast, smoking resentment, intermittently breaking out into decisive exercises in superiority. Even at fifty she had the sharp English accent, full of flat diphthongs and neologisms like *lavatory* and *sofa*.

Once or twice a year perhaps, exasperated beyond measure, my mother would turn this freezing glance on some personal inadequacy – my father's postponement of a household chore, my brother Greg's late arrival at a family supper – and the effect was never less than devastating, the more so in that it was wholly unexpected. My father, in particular, never quite understood the magnitude of his failings in this area, how his inability to mend fences, ferry automobiles to service stations at the time promised and fix leaking water butts grated on my mother's nerves. Prostrate under her sarcasm, transfixed by some polite, admonitory thunderbolt, he had the look of a man who, reaching out to stroke the muzzle of a faithful hound, suddenly finds a razor-blade embedded in his finger-tip.

Once, years later, I asked my mother what it was about my father's procrastinations and deferrals that so enraged her, what exactly went to ignite a powder keg of displeasure characterised by Greg as 'Napalm on Laos': she refused to be drawn. 'Oh I guess he kind of irritated me once in a while,' she rationalised, and it was a measure of her desire to ingratiate that she said 'guess' rather than 'imagine'. 'Wasn't there a time when he took a week to fix some hole in the fence and I got a little cross?' Time had sanded away these abrasions, whittled down the knots of rage and anguish to a smooth, even surface. This cannonading volcano of temperament was another of the great, secret areas of my mother's life, like the mystery of her arrival in the States and the mystery of what she'd left behind, a remote, palisaded enclave inaccessible to members of her family.

In a subdued, less strident way, Henrietta has this characteristic, a kind of damped-down, residual hauteur, always liable to flare unexpectedly into life. Once, not long after we met, and in the role of dapper swain proudly invigilating his girlfriend's leisure, I escorted her to some jeweller's store in Chelsea, one of those absurd and dramatically English places known only to Henrietta and her kind where the staff enquire after the customer's grandmother and the check comes in handwritten italic. It took half an hour: ten minutes to reach the head of a silent and languorous line, five minutes to attract the assistant's gaze, another ten to run Henrietta's watch or bracelet to earth beneath a stack of brown paper bags, a final five to settle up. Only at the end, at the very door of the premises, did Henrietta snap, and the provocation was so painfully slight – something to do with negligent packing – that you suspected the whole thing was simple contrivance, like a Candid Camera TV show. Worse, perhaps, was Henrietta's elaborately feigned regret. 'Did I behave dreadfully?' she asked outside in the street. 'Dreadfully.' 'Well I'm sorry,' Henrietta said complacently, 'but the silly bitch should have known the thing was under the counter.'

I get lost in these labyrinths of outraged social propriety, I get squeezed in these laboured coilings of dignity and status, but mostly I survive. England. English marmalade. English girls. English pubs. English rain. Each carries its signature remark, its defining moment – the crimson grin, the smell of smoke – for us transatlantic connoisseurs to get a handle on. But I knew my quarry. Years spent riffling through my mother's stack of Anthony Powell novels in the sitting room at Margaretsville – those queer, dusty out-takes on life where every conversation is somehow encoded, every smile frozen at the edges – had sent the beast skittering into view – cautious, ironic, wise, inscrutable. If I could never drag it down – and these English things were elusive, dissolving into the glittering daylight, for ever wanting to turn tail back into the jungle – at least I could recognise and admire. Henrietta and Co. are still mysterious to me – the freezing silences, the mute ironising – but they aren't mysterious in the way they would have been to the old man or Greg. I had a terrifying vision, once, of Greg trying to sweet-talk Henrietta, Greg with his mooncrater complexion and his sloppy jock's grin descanting on Dan Rather's salary or the Oprah Winfrey Show. All down to my mother, I guess.

What would she have said about Henrietta? My mother had a number of enigmatic terms which she applied to the sirens of backyard Margaretsville society, Greg's girlfriends, say, or a neighbour's vacationing niece: *waitress service*, which meant conventionally pretty but mentally mundane; *high society*, which indicated social pretension, although it could be directed at girls who in my parents' phrase simply 'talked back'; *hotlips*, used ironically to mean a girl of exceptional plainness. But deep down I had a feeling that my mother would have greeted Henrietta with the words she had once used to criticise a Boston brahmin penfriend of Jeannie's who came to stay: *a nice enough girl if you take the trouble*. It was impossible to work out exactly what my mother meant by this phrase, impossible to separate out its contending nuances, its mingling of reluctant admiration and rebuke; impossible, too, to measure Henrietta by any effective yardstick, for Jeannie's penfriend was a plain but somehow formidable girl who remained sleekly silent during the whole of a ten-day visit. All the same, those are the words I calculate my mother would have used.

There are other Henriettas crowding the foyer of Gayfere-Japhet, when the cab drops me in Eastcheap: beaky thirty-year-olds in calf-length business skirts waiting angrily for limos or talking to slightly older guys in bespoke West End tailoring.

Gayfere-Japhet are one of the last City firms still to recruit on the basis of social provenance: honourable Georges and Jacks who can't settle to Sandhurst or estate management, splendiferously dentured Sophies and Alices down from Oxford who fancy being 'career girls'. I once attended a planning meeting here where, doubts having been expressed about the availability of some impossibly Olympian figure from the board, appeal was made to the fresh-faced trainee whose duty it was to bring phone messages and refill people's tumblers with Perrier. 'I'll just go and see if Uncle Toby's finished lunch,' he remarked as he quitted the room. It can't last, of course. One of the first casualties back in 1986 when the big money moved in and started moving the smaller money around was the airhead in the suit. Jonjo and Tim are back in Northamptonshire now, frowsting in the gamekeeper's cottage and pretending to manage the estate of some titled forebear, selling wine in St James's, or, alternatively, just sitting in sad repose in the Admiral Cod in Eaton Terrace.

Reaching reception, with its clutch of toothy, well-groomed traffic, I flick my KLS pass at the seneschal and waft by unimpeded. An element of surprise always works best in these circumstances. Legendarily, Slater had once turned up unannounced at a hotel in Nairobi, the better to monitor a laggardly finance project for the Kenyan government, to find one consultant drunk, another downtown visiting his venereologist and a third engaged in a poker game with the civil servant through whose auspices KLS had garnered the job. Within Gayfere-Japhet the discreet, soberly-carpeted passages roll by. Occasionally suave, silent money gods hove into view, but these are minor deities in the great pantheon of capital, lacking the poise and the security you feel on Wall Street or around the Long Island barbecue spits, cast down by doubt and haemorrhaging profits. I wouldn't care to be an equity partner at Gayfere-Japhet, not now, not with the bad times rolling in and no sign of a Yankee suitor. In a remote corridor at the back of the building, in among janitor's storerooms and stationery cupboards, I find the unmarked white door and whip it open without deigning to knock.

'*Fuck* is going on here?'

40

Two scarlet-faced twenty-five-year-olds spring up from their computer golf, one so violently that he spills a cup of coffee into his lap. While the second one is attending to the first one's scalded groin, I make a rapid inventory of the room, noting the strew of cigarettes, Coke cans and paperbacks and the two tenantless chairs.

'Where's Sillery and Blanchflower?'

'Sillery's off sick . . . Blanchflower said he was taking the day off.'

'Uh huh. You have his number?' They nod cravenly. 'Well, just call Blanchflower, OK, and tell him unless I see him here inside thirty minutes his career's seriously fucked.'

In the fizzing half minute while these instructions are carried out ('No Chris, he's really here . . . That's right, seriously fucked') I inhale a cigarette and ponder the images summoned up by the cab ride, Henrietta's hawk profile slowly replaced by my mother's softer but no less ominous stare, Slater, Devoto and the Sudebank job. Blanchflower's apologies having been humbly tendered ('There's a cab on the way, Scott, he says') I sit reverseways in a plastic chair, arms folded broodily across the back, and gravely disclose plans and contingencies. Later, as I make phonecalls, run software tests, summon all the sleek paraphernalia of the consultant's repertoire, they gaze at me with reverential awe. En route to our grail, encouraging and indulging their own timid suggestions ('If you stick the plug in there, the whole fucking thing will blow, OK?') I regale them with stories of my own early combats with machines, in the dark, shiny vaults of Manhattan and the Wall Street dealing rooms. Grateful and eager, they ferry me cups of coffee, relay instructions to admiring Gayfere-Japhet technicians who arrive from time to time. Half-an-hour later, about the moment in fact when Blanchflower stumbles through the door, one eye bloodshot, tie hanging down his shirtfront in a sad, pendulous knot, the situation is retrieved, and I'm tersely dictating a list of instructions to carry them through to closedown. Godlike and glowing, casting a final crumb of approbation over my shoulder ('Nice work guys!'), pummelling Blanchflower's quarterback shoulders with buddyish enthusiasm, I sail off again into the silent corridor.

41

Back in the foyer the Henriettas and their sleek attendants have all disappeared, the commissionaire is recruiting himself with tea out of a flask, and there is a faint air of elegy creeping up from the pot plants and the surrogate tropical shrubbery. Three years or even two years from now Gayfere-Japhet will have ceased to exist, or at any rate will have ceased to exist here. The last of the institutional clients will have gone by then, along with Uncle Toby and his fresh-faced nephew, the private client list bought up for a song by some smarter rival, and Gayfere House scythed up into a warehouse of offices peopled by import/export outfits, commission agents, metal brokers, a sub-traffic of lively parasites crawling over the old dead monsters of the forest floor. Here on the steps above Eastcheap, the wind gusts suddenly, billowing out my coat like Count Dracula's cape. Hailing a cab which has just deposited a watery-eyed old guy on the kerbside, I fling myself into the back seat and am borne complacently away.

Heading back across Blackfriars Bridge, my mother's spectre pushes into view once more between the jetsam of Mac screens and circuit boards. Who read English books – *Villette, The Tenant Of Wildfell Hall, Venusberg*, to herself on summer afternoons. Who said *'Remarkable!'* and *'Extraordinary!'* like a dowager in a play by Oscar Wilde. Who arrived on a boat in New York harbour in 1956. Who met the old man at some Washington clambake. Who said nothing about the whole sweep and prospect of her bygone English life. Ever.

4

Some statistics

Later, alone and nervous amid the lines of bowed heads, silent among the professional chatter, I take forty minutes over a lamb curry in the canteen on the thirteenth floor. There is a bad moment halfway through when a whisker of rice gets stuck in some crevice at the side of my throat, but somehow I manoeuvre it down, gulp back a tumbler of Coke and emerge, scarlet-faced and defiant, to stare once more at the tables of silent auditors, the subdued, fretful tax execs, the ominous corporate recovery specialists. Outside narrow striations of cloud pass over the spires and domes; helicopters buzz through the dense air; the river curls below. Over by the elevator there is a mild commotion, suggestive of bodies in purposeful collision: Slater surges out of a press of pinstripe suits in the direction of a glass case full of sandwiches and Coke cans. Shirtsleeved, braces constricting his squat, bulging torso, he is a tremendous figure, wanting only the peaked visor and the bow tie to turn him into a New York newspaper editor, the sub-machine gun to turn him into Al Capone. Seeing me he turns and glowers, waves a despairing hand over the cowed and unregarding throng. 'Accountants,' he says sadly. '*Fucking* accountants.'

Some statistics: the average UK turnover of a Big Six accountancy firm, in which category KLS indisputably reposes, is £250 million. In the States it might be five times that. The annual fee-income of KLS's US arm, the product of a hundred amalgamations, takeovers, shotgun weddings and corporate burglaries, exceeds that of many second-league manufacturing outfits, the difference being that there are few overheads, no unions, and the profit-share is nobody's business but the partners. This is serious: how did it happen?

You can read about accountants in Victorian novels. They

43

hung out in taverns near the insolvency court and got drafted in to advise creditors' meetings. The characters in Dickens who wind up in the Marshalsea on the upper rung of a step-ladder of debt whose lower bars have simply disappeared into quicksand, would have had their accountants, any landowner with a rent-roll would have had his eagle-eyed man of business, but it wasn't a profession for gentlemen, no sir, and there weren't any qualifications. But then, suddenly, in the wake of the mid-century's spectacular insolvencies, in the wake of the Merdles and the Melmottes and the ruined widows and the grieving vicarages, business became respectable. Governments weighed in with finance bills, there were City regulators nosing through the garbage in Lothbury and Finsbury Square, and before you knew it the inky-knuckled drunk whose descant note had been heard piping above the creditors' chorus had given way to a demure fellow in a frock coat who belonged to what he was proud to call the professional middle classes.

No one so proud of being a professional man as an accountant. Not a lawyer, not a medic, not a chartered surveyor with a slide-rule and a roll of cartridge paper. No one quite so well-heeled, either. Slater's time costs three hundred pounds an hour. Hire me out for the day to a bank with a beat-up mainframe and the software spewing out double-printed waste paper and it'll cost you fifteen hundred. Even taking on the two assistant consultants out doing the lighthouse study – rosy-cheeked twenty-three-year-olds with history degrees – will set you back a thousand or so a week. Each. This isn't the biggest money, of course – the biggest money gets made on the dealing floor, in share placements for privatisation schemes, in selling Eurobonds to the Finns – but it's big enough. The big money started in the early 1970s when computer technology came in. Until then accountants had fallen into three categories: auditors and taxmen, with the insolvency guys a kind of unmentionable extra you kept in a backroom someplace because the financial community looked on them as hoodlums, which of course they were. Computers changed all that. All of a sudden the banks were full of hardware which was supposed to produce year-on-year figures but didn't, the production lines were hitched up to CADCAM systems, double entry book-keeping (which had lasted

44

five hundred years) was going down before a tide of spread-sheets and printouts, and basements everywhere – in the City, under the big furnaces up north – were stuffed full of what looked like outsize freezer compartments, which nobody really knew how to operate and which cost an alarming percentage of turnover to maintain.

And so in the early 1970s management consultancy – which had previously meant time and motion studies and standing there with a clipboard figuring if three guys could unload a truck in twenty minutes – suddenly became talking to people about computers. Talking to people about computers, that is, at three hundred pounds an hour. Want some guys to fix those systems you thought would last five years but bombed out after two? We'll send you a roomful. Want someone to impress a board of directors that you aren't getting left behind in the technological revolution? We'll send you Jack Devoto, who's got a Yale MBA, a CV the length of an elephant's dong and who once, back in the Elysian days of the early 1980s, billed a U.S. bank for *half a million dollars* on a security contract. Keep on sending him too, because the wonderful thing about the Information Technology race is that it never slows down. No sooner have you got your word processor installed and the stenographer trained how to use it than everyone's talking about Apple Macs and Compaq desktops. The minute your new mainframe is puttering away in the back office then the word is that it's unwieldy, won't adapt, and the smart guys are favouring AS/400s anyway. One result of this breathless marathon in which nobody really knew what they were doing except the computer manufacturers was that whole tribes of consultants spent the 1980s camped out in their clients' offices, an entire extra labour force nervously kow-towed to by finance houses who wondered what would happen if their systems crashed on settlement day. This in an era where the mark of corporate respectability was not the size of your turnover or the frequency of your bonuses but the number of consultants you had working for you. Consultants to help you decide which stuff to install. More consultants to help you install it. A third lot of consultants to help the first and second lots decide whether the stuff installed was the right stuff. There were guys

45

working hundred-hour weeks around the time of Big Bang, sleeping on camp beds on the dealing room floors and writing strategy reports which new technology invalidated within a fortnight.

Take it from me, anything you ever heard about accountants is true. You might imagine, if you were the owner of a department store empire with, say, two dozen branches, that being audited would mean having your accountants look at two dozen sets of till rolls. You'd be wrong: they might see two or three. You might think, too, that 'corporate recovery' meant scooping ailing concerns out of the trash can, dusting them down and fattening them up again, whereas – as a corporate recovery specialist's first duty is to the bank that employs him – it means selling the thing off for the best price you can get. I once saw Slater filling out his expense claim form at the end of a particularly demanding week which had seen him dine thrice at Langan's, pay two visits to Royal Ascot, attend a party in Düsseldorf and supervise the installation of his current mistress, over on a shopping holiday from the States, at the Dorchester. Needless to say, Slater's principal client of the time, an Arab bank setting up in London the better to deploy the oil revenues, suffered a notably severe depredation. So far as I can recall, Slater's total callback on travelling time, meals in transit and accommodation came to £3,718, and I only narrowly dissuaded him – on the grounds that in smuggling livestock out of a zoo it is easier to conceal an elephant than a guinea-pig – from putting the hire of the Ascot morning suit down under 'research'. Inevitably, retrospect insists that in the course of these lavishly funded assignments – the discussion meetings for twenty at Mosimann's, the hire of a Booker shortlisted novelist, once, to write a deferential foreword to a proposal for computing services that Slater aspired to foist on a crumbling publishing house (as I recall, Slater multiplied his fee by the day's date before recharging) – it was possible to overdo things. Even Slater was once mildly reprimanded by a frankly awed senior partner after trying to attach the check for the divisional Christmas party to the account of a notoriously indulgent merchant bank on the grounds that it involved 'essential inter-personnel contact and strategy formulation'. The words 'Austen

Langdale' and 'Magivision' may not mean much to the workaday reader of the financial supplements but even now, five years on, the average accountant regards them in the way that Robert E. Lee regarded Appomattox. Austen Langdale was an engineering firm that collapsed six weeks after its auditors, a somnolent West End outfit named Simkins Pirbright had given it a clean bill of health. Magivision was a TV production company whose bankers diffidently suggested at a meeting one Thursday lunch-time that they might care to enlist professional help in dealing with some minor cashflow glitch. They approached KLS. Magivision were in receivership by Monday morning, on sale by Tuesday, sold off by Wednesday afternoon, and it was rumoured that the managing director, finessing his way into the barricaded office on the Friday to retrieve his files, narrowly avoided prosecution on a larceny charge. Mr Austen became a famous figure in accounting circles in the late 1980s – famous for not getting any of the trade papers to take up his cause, famous for not persuading the Institute to investigate, famous for not procuring any kind of enquiry into the circumstance of his personal bankruptcy. I saw a picture of him once in *Accountancy Age* and he looked like a man who, stepping out of his front door one fine morning in an Armani two-piece, suddenly finds himself coated in dung. Oh yes, they were great days.

But now it's late 1990 and the great days are gone. The map's getting smaller and there isn't enough work to go round, not for international firms who have to grow at ten per cent a year to stop the partners leaving for industry, not in a stalled economy, not in a saturated market where every yak farmer in the Gobi desert is down on the Price Waterhouse client list. There are MBAs working in corner stores now, and the pages of *Management Consultancy News* and *Corporate Adviser* hum with talk of 'downsizing scenarios' and 'reconstructing the client base', which means firing people. All across the City you hear news of black baggings (throw-outs handed a black rubbish sack before being told to clear their desks), the guy who came back from lunch and found that his department had disappeared, the guy who went to lunch and found the canteen had disappeared (the consequence of a dispute with the catering

47

contractor), the guy who arrived to work one morning – I can vouch for this one, he worked for a strategy outfit – and found the office had been shut down overnight. There must be an army of those guys out there with their pay-off checks, their outsize mortgages and their festering resentments. And where does that leave Slater, purveyor of consulting services to the embarrassed corporation? And where does that leave me?

Later, in a humid, windowless cavern somewhere under Finsbury Square, we sit facing the Sudebank team: three perspiring Argentinians in sharp Savile Row tailoring. None has so far spoken save to exchange the eager pleasantries of arrival. Three feet to my left, his eyes focused on a blank spot on the wall a yard or so above the heads of his audience, Slater talks relentlessly on. About the feasibility study we did for RKO, about the 'definitive' savings at CEG, the 'uncontested' fraud survey at HB&Q. The swart, mustachioed faces stare silently back. To my right Devoto is crosshatching in the corner of a scribble pad. From far away in the concrete distance comes the noise of traffic. 'And now I think I can hand you over to Mr Marshall here,' Slater says unexpectedly. On cue I lean forward in my chair across the shiny table, marker pen poised like a cutlass.

'Well gentlemen,' I say easily. 'As you know, I've conducted the preliminary investigations we agreed upon, and the results are pretty much in line with what I think I may say' – a nod to Slater and the head Argentinian – 'are *all* our expectations. Basically you have a problem with your mainframe. Now, I don't want to get over-technical, but it appears to me that the system module simply isn't equipped to handle the kind of software resources you're channelling through it. And, not to put too fine a point on it, everything's heading out of control.'

To my right Devoto has stopped crosshatching and is slotting dollar signs into a complex, imbricated spiral. Slater, eyes staring sightlessly in front of him, is nodding vigorously. The head Argentinian raises his hand slightly, but I chatter on.

'Way out of control. Now gentlemen, you have two options. Either you can downsize, or you can retrain your in-house people to deal with it themselves. We recommend that you do the latter, and I'm sure you won't regard it as bias' – another

48

craven nod to the head Argentinian – 'if I say that we recommend you to commission us to do it.'

There are some head-shakings and mutterings at this. The head Argentinian's sidekick, who looks as if he had recently cut short a career playing the maracas in Carlos Santana's backing band, furrows his brow. As each of us starts to speak simultaneously, both our voices are drowned out by Devoto's grim monotone.

'What he's saying', Devoto explains with startling off-handedness, 'is that your systems are seriously shafted. I mean *seriously*. Get some college kid with a grudge hacking in there and you could spend a year getting him out again. Speaking for myself I'd say you need a complete overhaul rather than a few seminars to teach your programmers which buttons to punch. Whatever, we're talking eighty, maybe a hundred thousand. And that is a conservative estimate.'

The dark, heavy faces coalesce and break apart. The head Argentinian smiles nervously. 'And when, Mr Devoto, do you think it would be convenient for your people to begin?'

Outside the city is sunk in late afternoon gloom. Across Finsbury Square there are giant excavators tussling like angry dinosaurs above the broken tarmac. Back in the car, purring sweetly along the grey frontiers of London Wall, the air is one of quiet satisfaction, pleasure in a job well done. Proposal document hefted across his knees, pen poised over the page like a stabbing machine tool, Slater makes calculations in a frail, minuscule hand. Sickly light from the streetlamps flares up unexpectedly from his half-moon glasses. Eventually he says:

'Two teams working a month. Add another fortnight to test the software. I make that a hundred and twenty. Plus an extra thirty if we can kid them they need a fraud study. Say a hundred and fifty altogether. What do you reckon Jack?'

Devoto stares out blindly into the dusk. He has not spoken, I realise, since his curt valediction to the Sudebank team. From time to time his hands clench and unclench. Slater goes on:

'The thing about these spick bankers is that they still respect anyone with a white skin. Sounds crazy but it's true. They think that because we invented computers we're the guys to come to when they go wrong. Basically you could send a couple of kids fresh off the Apple Mac training course and they'd still come out with a ten grand feasibility study.'

Nearing High Holborn the traffic thickens. Trucks rumble out of the Faringdon Road and idle in the central reservation. The sidewalks are clogged with courier bikes and their lounging mohawk owners. Taking the inertia as a personal offence, Slater beats his hands nervously on his thick accountant's briefcase. He says hoarsely:

'Ought to go and celebrate. A big job like this, a hundred and twenty, a hundred and fifty, we ought to go and celebrate. What do you say? Jack? Scott? Got an hour before the management council. Ought to go and drink a toast to those spick bankers. What do you say?'

Slater's celebrations of new work are a part of the KLS folklore. The average audit team, on learning of its ability to match the whims of some capricious new client, might nervously broach a couple of bottles of *vin rosé*. Slater's response to a lucrative commission of this kind would take in flying his entire support team to Paris for lunch or a day's grouse shooting in Scotland. A junior consultant once nearly died of alcohol poisoning at the conclusion of a day-long binge convened to memorialise the bringing down of some government contract or other.

'Let's go to Tarantino's,' says Slater wildly. 'Let's go to Tarantino's and drink a toast to those spick bankers.'

Veering left into Chancery Lane, the traffic thins out again into clumps of taxis, the odd limo carrying sleek, besuited finance house gods back to offices in Fetter Lane and Plumtree Court. Pale frontages of law stationers, brilliantly lit windows of sandwich bars huddle together behind the narrow kerb. On the corner of Carey Street a black sedan spins out lazily before us, the rear wheel conjuring up a spiral of dead leaves, like the opening shot of a movie. Slater leans forward interestedly.

'Jesus will you look at that!'

There is a brief vista of florid, shiny faces in uncomfortable proximity.

'Look at what?'

'Can you believe it? Butler-Stevenson are still using those shitheap Daimlers.' Butler-Stevenson are a medium-league outfit with a litigation problem. 'Now if me and Jack here turned up for a meeting with Lazards in a Daimler,' Slater goes on, 'ten to one they wouldn't let us in the car-park.'

'*I* heard', says Devoto, staring furiously around him and waving his hand at some invisible assailant, 'the senior partner was mortgaging his fucking *house.*'

There is something very peculiar, I realise, about Devoto, something strained and intransigent and somehow mournful: eyes set far back in his skull, foot tapping remorselessly against the door-frame. But these observations are lost in the swirl of bonhomie that accompanies this confirmation of our rivals' decay. Slater's courtroom eyes swivel crazily behind their frames, Devoto gives an eldritch croak of satisfaction, I snicker anxiously, proud to be a part of this convoy of regular guys, a small component in this fusebox of power, influence and intrigue. The car burrows west into the Strand, noses into a bolthole down along the crumbling streets that back on to the river, and deposits us in a back alley alongside scuffed, gloomy portals, partly blocked by a pile of refuse sacks.

Tarantino's is one of those typical English places where men of power go to converse in modest surroundings. I had lunch one time in a gentleman's club – Grey's or Huck's or someplace – with a potential client with three surnames who thought we might be able to fix the profit shortfall on his Scottish estate, and it was unbelievable, a sort of jokey canteen with ghetto food that would have disgraced the average high school. Tarantino's is much the same: a couple of oblong boxes and a pool table with a bar up the far end and a tremendous air of glory on vacation. I once saw the Deputy Governor of the Bank of England in the outer room swigging an orange juice with a fan of deferential cronies, and he looked like a kid from a Bronx urban renewal project set down in a Florida beach party. Inside, the light is dim and lazy, like a giant aquarium but with white, human faces staring up out of the ooze, the conversation simply a pop or two of exhaled breath. Devoto disappears somewhere. Slater nods at a couple of *convives* as he shimmies over to the bar.

'Hi Farq. Hi Quoodle.'

Another thing about these well-bred professional Englishmen:

their chronic absorption with nicknames. Six-foot butterballs whose suits sag unhappily over their quarterback shoulders are unfailingly introduced to you as 'Tiny'. I have a quartet of acquaintances – the corporate finance team of an A-grade merchant bank – known as 'Wombat', 'Boofy', 'Sprout' and 'Penis'. On his way back from the bar, fan of champagne flutes in one hand, bottle in the other, Slater nods again and there is a sudden three-way detonation of laughter before his squat, belligerent torso looms into view above the table.

'Someone say something funny?'

'Oh dear. Oh dear. Well apparently they appointed this female director at Citibank and . . .' Slater's eyes narrow. 'What happened to Jack?'

'Washroom.'

'Fair enough.' Slater looks flustered for a moment, the conspiratorial gleam denoting anxiety rather than triumph. 'You notice anything about Jack?'

I falter for a second. Suggesting that Devoto looks as if he's about to weird out on us might not be what Slater wants to hear: after all, this might be how the guy behaves in proposal meetings.

'Impressive. I guess he's kind of quiet though.'

'Quiet?' Slater ponders this tactful résumé of Devoto's volcanic unease, his shattered detachment, his voiceless gloom. 'That's *exactly* right. Quiet. Listen Scott. Between you and me' – he shoots a glance at the adjoining table but Farq and Quoodle are deep in some corporate glossy – 'between you and me, Scott, I'm worried about Jack. Look, I don't know if I should be telling you this but . . .'

I nerve myself for some unprecedented revelation, about the seven-figure transfer fee, say, Devoto has negotiated with Ernst & Young or the relationship lately contracted with the sexagenarian tea lady on the seventh floor. Instead Slater goes on seriously:

'I don't know if I should be telling you this, but the thing is, I know for a fact he's started sleeping in the office.'

'But everybody does that.'

'No, *not* in the executive suite. In the actual office. I went in there at twenty-past seven this morning with a stack of software prospectuses and he was lying down under the table wrapped up in his mac.'

'Perhaps he just got stuck in town the night before.'

'Maybe. But I'm telling you Scott, there was a tooth-mug and a packet of razors in his out-tray. Plus, have you seen any of those memos he's started sending out?'

'What memos?'

'Christ. Dozens of them. Tons. Senior partner. Management committee. "Strategy for the coming decade", that kind of stuff. But the weird thing about them, Scott, the really weird thing about them . . .' Forestalled by the sight of Devoto emerging furtively but with a certain intentness from the flapping door of the washroom, Slater lapses into gloomy silence. I scoop an olive out of the tray between us, think better of it, put it back. Outside the afternoon is dissolving away into blues and greys, the leaves dance up furiously against the window and it seems very *English* in here, very mellow and wound-down and inert. Farq and Quoodle have launched off into some rip-roaring anecdotes about what a chum of theirs said when presented with a Lloyd's cash call for three hundred grand. I stare as Devoto shambles over towards us. In the pale light of Tarantino's he seems a more solid and reliable figure, thinning hair slicked back over his scalp, hard bar-tender's face suffused with patches of ruddy, abraded skin. Slater says uneasily:

'Have a glass of champagne, Jack. Have a glass of champagne and let's drink a toast to those spick bankers.'

Devoto upends the bottle into his glass with a palsied action of the wrist, so that the liquid gutters down over the table mats. He says morosely: 'You know something? I was in this place the day before the 1987 General Election. Sitting right here with the whole of the front bench Treasury team. No bleeding nonsense about whether they were going to win or not. Just straight magnums all the way. They were great days.'

'That's right Jack. They were great days.'

Devoto sucks down the glass of champagne in one, a gesture so rapid that it scarcely punctuates the flow of his discourse. 'But it's all over now. You know that? All over. I saw one of those Treasury guys the other night. Minister now of course. Got promoted. And he said to me: "The old lady's sick, Jack.

53

She's not well at all." And I said: "What, you mean the Bank of England?" And he said: "No, I mean the old lady in Number Ten." Do you know AGB laid off a hundred and fifty consultants the other day? And these were, like, regular people. Strategy guys. Privatisation guys. They cleaned ten million off the wages bill in a quarter of an hour. Thought they'd be clever, diversifying and so on, but it's all over now.'

'That's right, Jack,' Slater says soothingly. 'It's all over.'

There is a sudden shifting of furniture as Devoto rises hastily to his feet. Bent over the chair-back, prehensile knuckles gleaming above the dull surface of the wood, he looks somehow dazed and sub-human, like an ape bundled into a suit and cruelly confused by these everyday chores of movement and response. 'I'm not feeling well,' he says sadly. 'You'll have to excuse me.'

In silence we watch him retreat once more. Slater frowns.

'You see what I mean? Between you and me, Scott, I've seen a lot of people crack up like this. Always consultants, too. You work hundred-hour weeks in some computer room or out in the jungle on some reservoir project and by the end the chances are you're just babbling. And then when the work stops it's like someone cut your leg off. I had this senior consultant once working on a CADCAM study in some factory who went crazy and ended up stamping his hand to a conveyor belt with an industrial stapler.'

Somewhere in the distance a clock strikes five. Tarantino's is filling up now, with heavily prosperous men in suits who lean carelessly across the bar to display plump calves and monogrammed socks. Corporate laughter punches out erratically through the dead air.

'Do you reckon he's right? That it's all over?'

'It's bad,' Slater says doubtfully, 'but it's not *that* bad. At least not yet. OK, the government contracts are drying up, and the World Bank's stopped throwing money at nigger dictators, but there's plenty of finance houses haven't got a clue how to manage their back offices. Plenty of rationalisation too. But, yeah, Jack's right. Basically, the bucket's threequarters empty and I can't see anyone filling it again for a while, can you?'

'What do we do?'

54

'What do we do? We sit tight. We lay inessential people off. We find some more spick bankers who still think hiring management consultants makes you respectable. Work it out for yourself.'

After this we sit in silence until Devoto reappears, drained and chastened, from the washroom, nod our goodbyes to the throng at the bar, saunter out into the darkening streets. Back in the car, cruising home along Upper Thames Street, the lines of traffic bump and concertina; ships' hulls loom up from the river. Devoto leans against the window, head averted, the rest of his body drawn up in shadow. Slater is lost in some penumbral private world of calculation and design: his lips move noiselessly in the half-light. Steaming across Blackfriars Bridge, the car is suddenly caught up in a coruscating naphtha glare; the humps of the distant towerblocks converge. Slater says:

'Come and see me tomorrow first thing. Got something I want to discuss.'

'Laying off inessential people?'

'*Fuck* no!' Slater whoops delightedly. 'Something that needs a safe pair of hands. Tomorrow first thing mind.'

The glass frontage of Centaur House, with its myriad lighted corridors, swings into view. Preening, I take a quick check on my surroundings, determined to frame the moment irrevocably in space and time. Slater, gathering up the papers from his lap, looks composed, ironical, dismissive. My own face, glimpsed at angles from the mirror, is excited, hectic, impressionable. Shoulder down against the window, chin sagging towards his chest, Devoto sleeps.

Oddly what remains of this episode is not the sight of Devoto, forlorn and reminiscent in Tarantino's, or Slater's weasel stare, but the memory of Farq and Quoodle quietly colluding in the corner. London is full of people like Farq and Quoodle. They sit on government advisory committees, they work as PR reality softeners to merchant banks or operate those Lloyd's syndicates that nobody is allowed into except the people who operate Lloyd's syndicates. Walk into a board meeting in EC2, a livery company dinner at the Guildhall or an Institute cocktail party at Moorgate Place and you can bank on finding Farq seated next to the chairman, Quoodle interrogating the warden about his grandson's education or the two of them questioning the president about the latest committee report on UK Generally Accepted Accounting Practice. There are female Farqs and Quoodles who live in Holland Park Crescent or Onslow Square, whose brothers are stockbrokers and whose fathers once helped run ICI and BP and now inhabit Berkshire manor houses, from which they still address caustic letters to the *Financial Times*. There are juvenile Farqs and Quoodles, too, at Harrow or Charterhouse or the expensive London day schools, proleptically exercising their charm on the colleagues of tomorrow.

When I came here from the States it took me maybe a week to appreciate the cliquishness of English business life, its picketwire fences of codes, passwords and ID cards. If the silences and restrictions reminded me of anything it was my mother talking about her early life or musing over the airmail letters with English franks that arrived in the house once in a blue moon. No presentation in those first days was complete, it seemed, without one of our guys sidling forward to nod at one of their guys, who would turn out to be his cousin or his room-mate from college or his godfather. Sitting down to fashion a proposal to a prospective client you began not on the basis of your suitability to do the job but on who you knew. Slater once obligingly quantified for me the sway exercised by a particular KLS audit partner over a blue-chip client whose audit fee KLS had managed to treble within three years: 'Now, let's see. The chairman, right, is his wife's cousin's husband. He used to play rugby with the finance director – or was it rugby? Could have been badminton now I think about it – when they were trainees. The chief executive still owes him one for some valuations we did years back. There's one director belongs to his Territorial Army regiment and another goes to his Masonic lodge, so I think you could say we were fairly safe.'

'What about the non-execs?' I asked, straight-faced.

'One's married to his mistress. The other used to work here. Like I said, it's not a problem.'

Searching for a context in which to settle this bright, breezy web of intrigue, I was sadly at a loss. This is not to say that

American business life has no connections: there are Ivy League networks, there are business school mafias, there are lodges full of elks and moose just itching to break out into the corporate water meadow and kick up a storm, but such conspiracies are either high-level or low-level; they take place on Olympus or in the boondocks, and there is no middle ground. If a single characteristic defined and marshalled the people with whom I did business in New York – and they were a sprawling, heterogeneous crowd – it was that they had no past. They existed not in the vanguard of an endless chain of relatives, friends and associates, but as dynamic solitaries. Like Farq and Quoodle they had most favoured nations, but transportation further back into the ties of family and schooling left them naked and exposed. Danny Hassenblad, to take a tiny remnant of the mid 1980s corporate jetsam, came from nowhere. Or rather from nowhere special: he was simply a figure moving single-handedly out of the empty mid-western glare. Even the molten monarchs of Balaraj's, pinned down and turned over in corporate handbooks, in *Emerson's Executive Profiles*, would prove to have no heritage worth speaking of. Their dynamic was interior and personal. In dealing with them, I divined – and this applied even to poor Danny Hassenblad – you bought a series of propositions. In dealing with Farq and Quoodle you bought an attitude or a way of life, you bought Mrs Farq in Onslow Square, Master Quoodle at Colet Court and old man Quoodle in his Berkshire grange. That is, if you were allowed to buy at all.

Curiously enough, Slater doesn't conform to this pattern. There are no infant Slaters romping in cerise blazers over the prep school asphalt, and Mrs Slater, encountered once or twice at corporate clambakes, has a ten-day set and what the society hawks courteously designate as a 'regional' accent. Slater's voice, too, is one of those raw, adenoidal barks come from out of the great urban wasteland. Searching for a frame in which to fix his relationship with Farq and Quoodle – a kind of mutual dependency undercut by resentment – I can only come up with the English Second World War propaganda movies which occasionally turned up on TV on Sunday afternoons when I was a kid and on which, needless to say, father doted. In black and

57

white, peopled by impossibly remote and seigneurial beings such as Noel Coward and Trevor Howard, in which plucky submariners tacked this way and that beneath the chill Atlantic, or bomber crews droned anxiously through the velvet sky, they were distinguished by the massive, phoney amity that existed between officers and their men. Watching them as a child, on my father's lap, sometimes, with the light fading away in the distance beyond Huntsville Woods I refused to be hoodwinked by this spurious confraternity. Staring at the lantern-jawed squadron leaders, with their pipes and their gorse-bush 'taches, as they discoursed to rows of fresh-faced grunts, I knew immediately that it was a fraud, a hoax, a put-on, that each side simply tolerated the other for harbouring a skill that they didn't possess. Half a century on in the boardrooms of London the same rules apply. Slater is the big-eared boy in khaki who doesn't like being bossed around but has a niggling regard for an Oxford accent; Farq and Quoodle are the blue-eyed exquisites in the officers' mess.

Prompted by some of these speculations, I once asked Slater about his early life.

'Yeah, well, you know how in big American cities they have what you call Projects?'

'Sure.'

'Hundreds of niggers living in a municipal barracks and getting free milk and welfare checks? Well, we have the same thing here, only they're called council estates. You know where Hackney is? Yeah? Well that's where I was born. I was four years old when the Blitz started. They pulled thirteen bodies out of a house in Mare Street in February 1941, and everyone I knew thought Winston Churchill was a lunatic. You ever been to Hackney?'

'No.'

'Well don't. I went over there a couple of years ago. See an old lady who was a friend of me mum's. Lives in a council flat now, there's dogshit all over the landing and every night the black kids come and hammer on the door. Made me sick just thinking about it.'

Gradually further details of Slater's career seeped out: the early departure from the educational process; the selling of false jewellery door-to-door ('they're called jargoons and everybody knows they're fake, but somehow they keep on buying the stuff'); a step up (selling dodgy insurance), a step down again (turnstile operator at Hackney dog track). By the early 1960s, though, Slater's restless track was running sweetly alongside the zeitgeist. Tin Pan Alley, night-clubs, corporate hospitality: in each of these burgeoning empires Slater seemed to have intervened to some purpose. Among many questionable accomplishments, he claimed to have organised the victory party after the 1966 World Cup Final ('Sir Alf, now he was sober as a judge, but some of them were well out of it') and to have driven the catering truck during the filming of *Magical Mystery Tour*.

And then suddenly at the end of the 1960s it all went wrong. There are rumours of CID investigations and poker debts, fast women and slow horses. Slater doesn't deny them: 'End of '70, '71 I was way down in shtook. Doreen' – Doreen was the first Mrs Slater, married at Hoxton register office in 1958 – 'had gone by then, there was two others doing me for maintenance, the housing contracts had dried and Frank Rosati' – I never worked out who Frank Rosati was, but Slater liked to talk about him in hushed tones – 'was leaning on me for four thousand notes.' A year or so later he emerged blinking into the light as a serious business adviser. ('Anyone could be a management consultant in the '70s. There were bankrupts setting themselves up as management consultants back then.') He caught the end of the time and motion boom. Then he did strategy consulting for nationalised industries, which basically meant telling them that they were overmanned and the incoming Conservative government would privatise them. KLS made him a director in 1979. The rest is history.

Traces of this spangled former life remain in the perky suits, the flaring suspenders, the feisty disregard for propriety and privilege. Watch Slater coming towards you down a corridor, prowling briskly by the doorway of someone's office, and you can see he doesn't fit. Not calm enough. Nor polite enough. Nor ingratiating enough. Oddly the clients *love* him.

What happened in the 1980s? What happened in the '80s was

that money won. Often it came disguised as something else – as politics, say, or economics, or personality, as Reagan, Thatcher or Kohl – but always in the end you could see the dollar signs rising to dominate the chatter about balanced budgets and fiscal prudence. Startling, in retrospect, was the speed with which money took over. In America this happened almost overnight. For half a century economic policy had been conducted on the back of the New Deal, and suddenly here was Reagan ushering in the Old Deal again, supply-side, trickle-down and goodbye to the welfare check. And all over America the effect was like a compressed spring suddenly being released. People had hated Jimmy Carter in the last days of the 1970s, hated him for his dog-faced preacher's guilt and for making them feel bad about their prosperity, and now here was Reagan, here was Ron, telling them that, sure, you couldn't spend what you didn't have, but if you did have it then what you did with it was your concern and *fuck* those Ricans on the benefit.

Over here, after a shaky start, money got its head down and rumbled forward, chewed its way through the miners and the nationalised industries. Increasingly in our dealings with the Iron Curtain bad boys, who after forty years were finding the ground shifting under their feet, what you dangled before them was not freedom or co-operation but money. Free elections don't mean free elections. They mean Coke dispensers and McDonald's and Amex Gold cards. A free press doesn't mean a free press. It means life insurance and real estate and dividends. Money broke down the Berlin Wall, not Gorbachev or George Bush, and the multinationals who're heading east of the Dnieper don't want to set people free, they want to buy them up and sell them off.

In the early '80s money won. By the late '80s, though, money would have been happy to sit on the bench, have the coach rub its knees with embrocation and settle for a draw. Only the game doesn't work like that. Wasted and wounded, bruised and rheumy-eyed, money will be brought out again for some further bouts of humiliation at the hands of those plucky Mexicans, those teeming Slavs, those seething Third World mobsters. Whatever happens, money looks set for a very bumpy ride. All the corporate reality softeners, all the add-on-benefit brokers and profit-redeployers such as myself and Slater, all the parasites who live off surplus, we're holding on to our hats.

The building is winding down now, it's 6.15 p.m., the secretaries are long gone and the footfalls in the corridor grow fainter. Somehow the sense of purpose survives these abandonments. Outer quarters plunged into darkness, the cluster of commissionaires and receptionists reduced to a single security goon, the KLS tower still glows with a faint, cosy heat, the heat of resolve, industry – and money. There are guys here – corporate finance gophers sprinting to beat deadlines, a tax team working on an evasion scam for a Kuwaiti prince in London for the week – will be working until midnight or beyond. In the basement, chugging away unmonitored behind closed doors, computer mainframes hum.

Up here on the sixth floor the passageways are dark and silent. Lines of light from the windows fall over the empty workstations and the humped desktops, and I pad undisturbed through a grey kingdom of silhouettes and half-tones, where there are ghostly piles of printouts drawn up in rows and Grant, Linda's boyfriend, grins hazardously from the filing cabinet. Slater and Devoto have disappeared, gone to a management council meeting on the thirteenth floor ('You want an aspirin or something?' I heard Slater anxiously enquire as he propelled his mentor into an elevator); the door to Slater's office stands open, advertising the velvet darkness within.

Back in my room, balanced on a crowded desk top, amid the guttering ashtrays and the stacked memoranda, is a sheaf of faxes, placed by Linda in a file helpfully marked *fax's*. Collapsed in the chair, one leg hooked over the other, I leaf casually through the pages of wavery type. Messages from Piotr in Bratislava, Basim in Jakarta, faint trails across the surface of the spinning globe, sober intimations of deadlines, backhanders – and money. Messages from the boys at work on the south coast lighthouse feasibility study, where apparently a force nine gale is raging and they're down to their last carton of milk. In the distance the great hummocks and vertebrae of South London edge up into darkness, given body by the firefly lights;

61

the debatable lands of Streatham, Norwood and Penge. Nearer at hand the files of autos crawl effortfully towards Peckham and Dulwich.

Brooding over Penge, Norwood and Streatham, over all that dampened suburban life, I try Henrietta's number in Bedford Square, but the gentleman publishers with their books about flyfishing and hardy perennials shut down at 5.30 and all I get is an answerphone telling me that the lines re-open at nine. I try Jenny at Sothebys and get a wheezing concierge. They leave work early, these English. In the States to stay tethered to your desk until the small hours is a mark of virility, and no wideawake business girl ever makes a date earlier than nine. Henrietta will be on her way to a drinks party in Cadogan Square by now, handing out canapés at a book launch someplace or drowsing in the bath as the water rises above her splendid breasts.

Coat slung over my arm I nix the lights, step out into the silent corridor where the shattered images of traffic swim across the perspex. On impulse I halt outside Slater's office, poke my head inside and breathe in the warm smell of leather and cigar smoke. There are framed certificates on the wall – Slater's membership of the Institute of Management Consultants, a fake MBA he bought from some mid-western bible college – and a Jackson Pollock print hung deliberately upside down. As I pause there the phone starts to ring. I pick it up: nothing, a faint hiss of faraway air and the click of the receiver being replaced.

On the long, solitary voyage over Blackfriars Bridge I stop and eat a Mars Bar. It takes ten minutes, each tiny mouthful graded and regraded, flicked cautiously to the back of my throat and tensely swallowed. The final gulp has to be helped down by a sharp, self-administered jab in the stomach. After it's finished I lean brokenly over the rail to stare at the grim, churning water. A promenading cop, chafing his hands together against the cold, gives me a sidelong look, and I feel like saying: *Look, I have a problem with food OK? Every time I eat something I have this morbid fear that I'm going to choke. Now how does that sound?* Instead I cough nervously and prowl on towards the subway. The moment leaves a sour aftertaste though. Would you like my life? Would you? *Really?*

Six hours later, staggering back into the apartment on a tide of brandy and bonhomie, there are other contingencies to consider. Mail with U.S. postmarks lies stacked up on the mat. The green light of the answering machine pulses on. The girl from the Mirabelle – not Penny or Jenny or Henrietta but a new girl – hovers uncertainly in the hallway, framed in bright, eerie light.

'Look, er . . .'

'Miranda.'

'Look, Miranda. Why don't you just go into the kitchen and fix us some coffee?'

Miranda nods, comfortably at ease with the range of nervous intonations and unconfident gestures that accompany the casual pick-up. Watching her through the doorway I marvel contentedly at women's efficiency, how they guess instantly which is the coffee jar, which mute, earthenware frontage hides the sugar. It must be something they teach them at college, along with keeping your legs crossed and smiling in bed. Outside the Fulham Road shrieks and judders. For some reason I flick the button of the answerphone. There is a pause, a rattle of machinery, a wisp or two of breath and then my father's voice, so long unheard, so perfectly remembered, comes pouring out into the empty air.

5

Model worker

Curiously the girl is still there in the morning. Waking up at six to the turbulent commotion of the alarm I find a pile of yellow-orange hair spilled out over the pillow beside me, the faint hum of breath. Henrietta or Perdita would have been long gone by now, back to their nests of Laura Ashley bedspreads and sprigged cotton nightgowns (I once asked Henrietta why she never slept naked and received the answer 'Because it would feel indecent.') Heading swiftly from bed to shower, from shower to kitchen, from kitchen out into the hall I listen out for intimations of movement: nothing stirs. Only when I pad back into the lounge for a second playback of the answerphone is there a far-off slither of bedclothes, the slap of feet hitting the floor.

'Hi. You want breakfast?'

What do you say in these circumstances? I never knew. Guys I remembered from college maintained that you had to play it super-cool, give the impression that this was such a routine contingency that the girl was lucky you even bothered to look at her. From the girls themselves one elicited a bewildering variety of response, ranging from hysterics to goofy complicity. Miranda simply gives a practised nod and starts pulling on her clothes, about as abashed by my presence as the ornament of a seraglio surprised in her bath by the chief eunuch.

Later, as we eat breakfast in the lounge – she muesli, toast, juice, myself a strew of cornflakes lightly drenched in milk – I conduct a swift, neutral inventory. Twenty-six or -seven, judging by the faint crevices beneath the eyes, the scaly traces on the wristbacks (and other, more intimate evidence which I won't go into here), which is, when you come to think about it, a tad old for this kind of thing, a tad old for cruising the Mirabelle, the bright light of alien bedrooms at dawn and all the rest of that cheerless singles package. Not English either, or not completely. In fact her accent has an American twang to it which sounds very like Upstate New York: the same adenoidal vowels, the same flattening down of sharper consonants (*godda, lodda, bedda*). Halfway through the muesli – and she eats with a kind of elemental rapture that fills me with ravenous despair – she says:

'You having trouble with those flakes?'

'I don't eat much in the morning.'

Or in the afternoons. Or in the evenings. We sit for a while as the grey dawn rises over the Fulham Road and the tops of buses slide by beyond the window, and I think for some reason of a girl called Jodie Summers with whom I used to share similar silences years ago in Vermont and who liked to beguile the time by recording her dreams in an exercise book. Miranda peers up again.

'That your dad on the phone last night?'

'Uh huh.'

'How long is it since you saw him?'

'Five years. Six.'

'You must miss him. Do you miss him?'

Do I miss him? Do I miss my childhood? Do I miss my mother's face? Do I miss the sun setting over Galveston Lake and the dappled backs of the fish brooding under the surface? But somehow I don't think this is a subject on which Miranda and I, whose only shared experience is a meal and a fuddled coupling, can talk with any seriousness.

'Listen, I have to go to the office right now.'

'The office?' To give her credit she looks disappointed. 'Where's the office?'

'Blackfriars Bridge. South side.'

'OK. I remember you telling me. And you're a . . . *management consultant*, right?'

Before I can agree she goes on conversationally: 'I slept with another guy who was a management consultant once, and do you know what he did? When we were in bed I mean?'

'Tell me.'

'He had one of those portable phones and he took it out of his pocket and hung it on a hook above the bed in case anyone wanted to get hold of him urgently. Can you believe that?'

All too well, as it happens. But the exchange comes as a nasty jolt, in which a demure compliance is suddenly replaced by the sharp tang of delinquency. Is this one of those pick-ups from hell you hear about, the kind who spend the first two hours after your departure holding a party for all their biker acquaintances and then, having changed the locks, move in with their six boyfriends? Something of this thought seems to have occurred to Miranda because she scoops an ashtray off the tallboy, flips it an inch or two in the air and then slides out another hand to catch it. I decide to live with the risk.

'Like I said, I have to go to work right now. Stick around though if you want. Use the phone. Whatever.'

She nods again. 'OK I'll do that.'

The last thing I see before shutting the door is her seated on a cushion rummaging through a pile of video tapes, her long legs unfurled across the carpet like giant scissor blades.

In any case I have other things to worry about: Slater and what he has lined up for me, and now, edging up effortlessly in the outside lane to overtake, this business of my father. Prior to quitting the apartment I took the precaution of pulling the tape out of the answer machine. Now, slinking along Fulham Broadway towards the subway, I snap it into the Walkman. The crackle and pop of rusty static gives way to late-night noises from the freeway diner three or four thousand miles away and finally to the sound of the old man himself breathing heavily over the wire. Actually there isn't a lot to it – a few sedate and slightly rambling formulations of the kind in which he rather specialised, drifting away into a backcloth of fraught hustler's chat and slammed-down side-orders. He sounds a little confused, a little remote, as if acknowledging that Jack's or Mac's or Hotburger, curled up under the arm of the freeway, gathered up in its din, wasn't quite the venue for confidences of this sort, but that there was nothing better, and somehow he had lost control of it all, the environment, and his ability to frame himself within it. The dense, eerie spaces between the words I fill with memory: dappled West Virginia lawns, my mother and her lawyer Mr Exley on the porch the day after he'd quit, the stacked airplane kits in the study a permanent reminder of his absence. I snap the tape out of the Walkman and plunge down into the subway mouth.

Briefless amid the unfurled tabloids, I peer over shoulders and beneath the wide arcs of outstretched arms. Today, like yesterday, the front pages are devoted to a murder in the West End, some guy in his twenties found dead in his apartment with . . . Well, even the tabloids are verging on the euphemistic to describe what happened to him, but it would seem that during the course of the attack the guy's genitals were hacked off. Rookie stuff, of course, if you come from where I come from, but I stare on – the *Daily Telegraph* has a particularly moving statement from an ex-girlfriend detailing his prowess as a lover – as the train rolls into Blackfriars and the cheerless ascent to daylight.

Back in the office I make calls, check in-trays, run my eye nervously along wallcharts. At this hour the place has a gaunt, ghostly feel, last night's comforting darkness replaced by mournful half-light. I stalk a corridor or two but find only a janitor swabbing the gloomy lino round by the coffee machine, hasten back to my desk where Slater – at least I presume it's Slater – has left a note simply stating *10 a.m.*, and yesterday's cigarette smoke sours the air. More letters, dozens of them. *The association of MBA tutors requests . . . Dear Scott, You may remember that we met at the . . . AS/400. A time to consider your software options . . .* I flip them into the can unread, haul an address book out of my slipcase, punch some numbers: the last number I had for the old man, my sister's apartment in Berkeley. But the Florida lines are down and my sister's number produces only an unidentified male voice briskly intoning above a Fleetwood Mac song, so I try my brother Greg's cabin in Montana. Amazingly the phone gets picked up at the second ring.

'The *fuck*?'

'It's me Greg. Scott.'

There is a brief flurry of movement. Greg says, calmer now: 'You know what time this is?'

'I don't know . . . Two a.m.? Three? Am I interrupting anything?'

'Are you interrupting fuck. You think I spend my time sitting in the woods round here having parties with the bears? What do you want?'

Greg has an office in Bozeman where he sells timeshare apartments to West Coast movie stars. I drove up there once, cross-country, and in one lonesome valley just over the Nevada state line went eighty miles without seeing another vehicle.

'Greg. You seen the old man recently?'

Greg's voice sobers down. There is a recognised Marshall code and volume level for discussing family affairs. 'Not so as you could mention. A couple of calls maybe a month ago.'

'Uh huh. How did he seem?'

'Seemed OK. Talking about buying shares in some condo development down in the Gulf . . . Why are you asking me this?'

'No reason. Did he say anything about coming to England?'

'Not that I remember. Mostly he was talking about Barbara-Jean. You know she quit on him again?'

'No?'

'Sure. Cruised off to Hawaii or someplace with a scuba instructor. Reckons this time it's for keeps too. Said he was trying to get back with Elizabeth.' This was a white-haired old lady named Elizabeth Schenectady, variously described by people who had met her as 'Little Red Riding Hood's grandma', 'Nancy Reagan with attitude' and 'the best wine last', with whom the old man had previously conducted an intermittent oldster's courtship. 'Look,' Greg goes on stolidly. 'Why are you so interested in Dad all of a sudden?'

Greg and I have never been big on fraternal confidences. When I was fourteen I once made the mistake of telling the hulking seventeen-year-old whose insouciant apeman's attitude to women I so much envied of the regard I bore for a girl named Anita Knoepflmacher whose parents played bridge with our mother. Unbidden, Greg devised an intercessionary letter, in a very passable imitation of my hand, which began: *Dear Hotlips, M'm I'd sure like to chew on you.* The letter was signed 'Ten Incher'.

'It's just I had this weird phone message the other day.'

'How weird is weird? Not the dianectics stuff again? Not the Buddhist church of the air?'

'No, nothing like that. Just about coming to England and seeing Pall Mall and Horseguards Parade . . .'

'And the little Queen with her white face and the stalwart

beefeaters. Forget it Scott. It's old news. My opinion is he stays where he is until he dies. It's just Barbara-Jean scrambling his head again is all.'

'Well, you're the expert.' I pause for a second, reviewing the various ways in which a chat of this kind with Greg might be concluded. 'How's Debbie?'

'Mindy actually, Scott. She's fine.'

'Business ticking over?'

'Sure. We had a call from Sly Stallone's office just the other day.'

Then I remember the question he really likes to be asked, alone amid the scorched, cattle-strewn plains of Montana. 'Hey, what can you see out of the window?'

'Long-horn steers,' Greg says proudly. 'Thousands of them.'

I put down the phone and wander out into the corridor where Linda, clad in a fun-fur and stack-heel boots, is unloading items from her handbag on to a desk. This glistening treasure trove includes three tangerines, a pack of sanitary towels, a Mars Bar and a paperback called *Having it All and More*. There is a raw, dirty bruise on the side of her forehead, imperfectly concealed with make-up.

'You OK Linda?'

Linda nods. 'Was there anything you wanted at all?'

Suddenly a thought strikes me, something left over from yesterday but still fizzing away through my head. 'Linda. You ever hear of a place called Penge?'

Obscurely her face brightens. 'Grant's nan lives that way. Beckenham, Bromley way. I never been there but Grant says it's nice.'

Somehow there is comfort in this intelligence, comfort in the thought of Grant's nan snug in her municipal shoebox down Beckenham, Bromley way. I look at my watch. Five to ten. Beneath the door of Slater's office, fifty feet along the corridor, pale light beckons. Time for the favour that every good boy deserves.

'Walham Town?'

'It's a football club,' Slater says uneasily.

'It is?'

70

'I thought you said you knew about football? I thought you said your old dad was nuts about English sport?'

'That's right. Manchester United. Chelsea. Nobby Stiles. Peter Osgood. But I never heard of Walham Town.'

Outside Slater's window, beyond the rooftops, the river drifts in and out of view. Further away, beyond the bridge, cloud hangs low over other spires and pediments. Caught between these two tides, marauding tugs move rapidly upstream. Slater adjusts the thick, spatulate fingers of his left hand with the thick, spatulate fingers of his right.

'OK. You ever heard of a bloke called Barry Mower?'

As it happens, I have heard of Barry Mower. Barry Mower turns up rather a lot in the raucous newspapers favoured by the kind of citizenry I sit alongside on the subway. Sometimes it's 'Big Bazza', as in *Big Bazza In Onscreen Shocker!* More often it's simply 'Bazza', as in *Bazza Wanted My Boobs: Vice-girl's Shock Confession!* Occasionally it's just a terse *The King Of Filth*. Best not to tell Slater any of this though.

'Barry Mower the pornographer, right?'

'"Successful businessman with media and property interests" is how I'd put it, Scott.'

'The guy who printed those shots of HRH? The ones where she . . .'

'It might interest you to know, Scott,' says Slater wearily, 'that Mr Mower is a *client* of ours.'

This piece of intelligence, it has to be acknowledged, is a modest surprise. Like many another major-league accountancy firm, KLS has worked for some scuzzbags in its time. Many a rapacious City shark has sidled off to the calmer waters of the Middle East or South America – friendly havens with deficient extradition treaties – under our auspices; many a rock star with a coke habit, a squandered advance and three years' unpaid tax has been wrenched out of the Revenue's grasp by our practised hands. But the Barry Mowers of this world tend to shy away from our awesome respectability: they favour two-partner firms in Shoreditch and complicated VAT scams negligently administered by their finance director's brothers-in-law.

'Barry Mower?'

'You'd be surprised,' Slater intones listlessly. 'Tax. Audit.

71

When he bought that soft-core cable channel the other month –
you know, the one the *Daily Mail* complained about, it was in
the papers – it was the corporate finance boys found him the
money. We had the whole of litigation support – Roger
McQuorquedale and five executive managers at two hundred
and fifty quid an hour – working on some copyright case he
wanted to bring against this Dutch firm he reckoned was
ripping off his schoolgirl mags. Anyway, he's a friend of John
Birningside's.'

'How come?'

'Christ knows. Masonry or something. Some livery company
in the City. Anyway, the thing is Barry Mower owns Walham
Town. Bought it for a song a couple of years back when the last
owner went broke. Now he reckons he wants it sorted, put on
a sound commercial footing and all that.'

'Where do I come in?'

'Piece of piss. You know where Walham is? West London.
Ealing way. You can hear the A40 from the terrace. You spend
a week, or two weeks, or a month there – full rate too, because
we're not doing Barry Mower any favours even if he does ponce
about in an apron with John Birningside – and see what the
score is. Income against expenditure. Where the slack is – if
there is any slack. How they might bump up the margins. Barry
Mower's happy, Birningside's happy and litigation support
carries on earning twenty grand a week for seeing if the tits in
some magazine in Leiden are the same as the ones in *Schoolgirl
Party*.'

Outside bright sunshine breaks suddenly through the cloud
and gleams beyond the window. Slater, caught up in the glow,
is instantly transfixed, a monarch visited by divine revelation. I
try again, a shade more cautiously.

'It's not really in my line, Tony. I mean, what sort of systems
do they have in place there?'

'Systems?' Slater snickers hoarsely. 'We're talking a secretary
with an IBM typewriter if you're lucky. This is the fourth
division of the English football league, Scott. They probably still
pull the tickets off a raffle roll.' Catching the furrow of
incomprehension on my brow, he pulls up. 'You know minor-
league baseball in the States? Well this is like that and then a bit

72

more. There'll be thirty players on the books because Mower likes to run a reserve team for the look of the thing. Another dozen staff. Groundsman. Club Secretary. People to lick the floors. Forty salaried employees, say. And all they're getting back is the gate receipts and whatever sponsorship deal they can fix with the newsagent round the corner. Might have a cup run once in a while, but the rest is scrabbling around for peanuts. Barry's probably picking up a half-million-pound tab just on staff.'

'So why's he doing it?'

'Barry? He's a local boy. Probably had a trial for them when he was a kid. You'd be surprised, Scott. Working-class tossers like that, when they make a lot of money first thing they want to do is buy a football club. And Barry, I mean they're hardly going to let him have Spurs or the Arsenal are they? So he has to settle for Walham, which basically means buying a million quid's worth of debt and then spending another hundred grand on paying somebody to sort it out.'

Still framed in the molten sun, Slater looks like a triumphant goblin king recently advised of the unexpected rout of the forces of light. I reckon I might be able to get away with a single entreaty.

'But why me? Why do I have to do it?'

Slater seems briefly chastened, as if for once in his magical career things haven't worked out, as if for the first time some superior intelligence has bitten him good and hard.

'Look, Scott. You know that management council meeting we had last night? Well, you'll get the memo in a day or so, but ... take it from me, the bad news starts here. *Lots* of bad news. Last year's fee income was down 30 per cent. Plus GEC are pulling out of that systems contract. A hundred and fifty, two hundred jobs. Across the board. And I mean across the board. Systems. Distribution. Strategy. There are guys been here twenty years'll be out on the street come the weekend. So when it comes to Barry Mower and Walham Town, let's just say that I'm doing you a favour OK? Get down to Walham this afternoon and see what he has to say, all right?'

'And what about you? What will you be doing?'

'Me?' Slater smirks. 'I'll sit here and fire some people. Hey,' he says cheerfully. 'Knew there was something I wanted to tell you. I had that poof Grieveson in my office the other morning. Know what he wanted?'

'Tell me.'

'Told me he reckoned he was undervalued and needed another ten grand a year to stay.'

'What did you say?'

'Told him there was an environmental renewal project on the go in the Sudan and he was booked as team leader if he didn't sod off. He shut up after that. You know how it is.'

I know how it is. As I get up to leave, the phone rings on Slater's desk. I stand and watch him for a moment as he bays wordlessly into the receiver, then press on into the stale headachey corridor.

Back at my desk, the door open to disclose the fretful traffic of the department, it becomes clear that the bad news has leaked. A couple of tearful junior consultants carrying plastic rubbish sacks are led haltingly towards the elevator. A bit later there is a distant explosion of shouting and shattered glass and a security goon goes galloping off down the corridor in pursuit. Enquiry reveals that a sacked systems analyst has elected to mark a stalled career by defenestrating his Apple Mac. But these are minor skirmishes, timorous engagements in the eternal struggle between ruler and ruled. I knew one outfit in New York in the mid 1980s where someone made the mistake of telling a roomful of computer consultants about their impending dismissal a good two hours before they were due to be escorted off the premises. What happened? Why, led by a mournful systems analyst who had been hired a fortnight before and was due to get married a week later, they locked themselves into the room and set about smashing up the hardware. Having wrecked seven out of the eight computer terminals beyond repair, they used the eighth to send profane salutations to the chairman of each of the firm's twenty-four largest corporate clients. Subsequently they took multiple photocopies of the firm's confidential strategy documents, which someone else had made the mistake of copying them on the day before, and faxed them to the marketing departments of every leading accountancy practice in America. Their final act, before a posse of security guards broke down the door, was to despatch a motorcycle courier with a plastic bag containing eight sets of car keys to a vantage point above the New Jersey turnpike and throw them in the Hudson. The whole episode was supposed to have cost the management three hundred thousand dollars. But this is England, where anger means a raised voice or a turn of the heel: in an hour or so the corridors are asleep once more and all that remains are the empty desks.

A bit later I settle down to some serious research for the Walham Town assignment. There are two principal sources. The first is the sports section of the *Daily Telegraph*. This informs me that, having played 17 games, Walham currently lie 17th in the fourth division of the Football League. They have accumulated 11 points, nine at home and two away, and their goals F are 6 (H) and 1 (A) and goals A 13 (H) and 24 (A). At this point I give up the search for a Walham player among the 'leading scorers' columns. There is, however, a mention of them in 'Last night's results', and the disquieting intelligence that in front of 1,327 supporters they lost 1-4 at home to Wrexham.

Source number two is a fat paperback entitled *The Rothman's Football Yearbook*, procured by Linda from a Fleet Street bookshop in her lunch-hour. Edging my way through the double-page spreads on Man Utd and Tottenham and the stern articles on 'Italia '90: the lessons', I come finally to:

Walham Town. Founded: 1923. Club nickname: 'The Squirrels'. Ground: The Dray, Walham Road, London W13. Strip: Black and white hooped shirts, black shorts. Manager: E. Bright. Major honours: none. Players achieving international honours: J. Murphy (N. Ireland) 1930. League position 1989/90: 21st. Leading scorer: J. Hood (6).

Legend has it that soccer has been played in this part of West London for 500 years. Historical documents show that the apprentice boys of Walham enjoyed 'foteball' as long ago as the 1490s. Sadly this tradition has been of little use to ailing Walham, whose occupation of the bottom end of the fourth division dates from the mid-1960s. A staple of the old Third Division South, Walham, led by their legendary manager 'Tusker' Holloway embarked on a famous cup run in the 1958/9 season, losing only in the semi-final. Having narrowly obtained a place in the recently-formed Third Division, they were relegated in 1961. Liverpool and England star Jimmy Satterthwaite spent five months on the books in 1971. According to colourful chairman Barry Mower: 'Walham have missed out on the action in the last few years, but we'll go on playing the type of football our fans have come to expect from us.' 1990/1 prediction: 22nd.

Later still, in the grey foothills of the early afternoon, the phone rings. The voice, slow, ironic, takes a second or two to locate.

'You know, I think I may have a problem with your CD collection.'

'You do?'

'Uh huh. Crosby, Stills, Nash and Young I can just about take, but when I hit Grand Funk Railroad I started to wonder what kind of '70s retro I was hitched up to.'

'Anything else you want to tell me about myself?'

'If you like. The only thing your apartment possesses an adequate supply of is coffee. You keep your condoms in a drawer by the bedside under a pile of handkerchiefs. There's half-a-dozen back numbers of *Playboy* under the bed in the spare room.'

'Fine. Is that it?'

'Oh and your father called again. He said to tell you same message as before.'

She rings off after this and I sit enveloped in the cigarette smoke wondering what all this portends, just what I may have let myself in for, as Linda cruises back and forth with the lunch-time mail. Outside in the corridor the huddled conclaves chatter nervously. Fired up by rumour, the faxes have been humming all morning: plaintive entreaties from unpaid suppliers, offers of professional assistance from outplacement agencies, paranoid enquiries from Piotr in Bratislava, Basim in Jakarta and Pilau in Delhi wondering if they should cancel the three-week vacation, the automobile purchase or the girlfriend with expensive tastes. I summon Linda back – an inert, uninquisitive Linda, in whom the events of the past two hours have apparently awakened not

76

the slightest concern – and dictate a terse circular informing interested parties of the sudden shift in my responsibilities and referring them to Slater. I take time out to mumble over a KitKat in a series of jerks and willed, tearful swallows, gulping down the last half-inch or so with furious bravado.

A bit later Henrietta calls: not, as it happens, to chide me for yesterday's abruptness but to invite me to a pre-Christmas drinks party some weeks hence. Henrietta and her friends specialise in old-fashioned entertainments of this sort, in drinks parties convened after work in rickety apartments in Battersea and Clapham, elaborate suppers served up to late-night assemblies dying of fatigue and stultification, country weekends at Henrietta's parents' place in Oxfordshire. Even now, as a two-year veteran of the social circuit so painstakingly traversed by Henrietta and her kind, I have trouble with Henrietta's parties: trouble with the milieu, trouble with the conversation, trouble with the people. The guys who turn up there repose in a social and professional category I haven't quite fathomed. Sometimes they're barristers or brokers or money men. On other occasions they follow weird amateurish callings like land agency or wine. Most of them have that look I always associate with up-market English colleges – high, beaky nose, blond hair cut in receding wings – others are simply dandruff-sprinkled fatties, but what distinguishes them is a kind of exotic nonchalance. They're so self-assured, these boys, that they don't even have to remind themselves of their invincibility. Whereas in New York the chatter is always about money or real estate – commendably blatant ways of impressing your superiority on the *vis-à-vis* – here it takes in absurd marginalia like sailing or skiing holidays – a more oblique but equally potent form of one-upmanship. Early on in my time here I made the fatal error of asking some blue-eyed six-footer with a Hitler Youth Movement crop how much he earned, and you could hear a horrified murmur rise up from the six or seven people in earshot and Henrietta wouldn't let me fuck her for a month.

I listen for a while as Henrietta converses formally about her sister's husband's job and a defective wristwatch she bought at Harrods. Henrietta's attitude to this surging throng of male

77

humanity is not indiscriminate. On the contrary, the Guys and the Gavins, the Ruperts and the Simons are subject to a subtle form of linguistic grading. Most of them are classified as *amusing*, which I take to mean loyal, discreet, affectionate and wealthy, but there are flakier categories such as *clever* (intelligent, over-talkative, unreliable, poor) and worst of all *funny* ('Gavin's a *funny* chap') which means cynical, peculiar, shiftless and immoral. Henrietta's female friends are ranked via an even more Delphic shorthand; *nice*, which means 'We were at school together'; *sweet*, which means 'My mother knows her mother'; and – a stupendous put-down – *I don't see much of her these days*, which so far as I can deduce means liable to steal money out of your handbag. What is it about these English girls? What do they think they're up to? Henrietta wouldn't last a minute at a New York party of the kind Sondra and I sometimes lazily attended in our early days before she was trampled in the rush of twenty-five-year-olds with MBAs and attitude snapping up the Wall Street lawyers. It isn't that she's dumb. Research discloses that she went to Oxford University, but as far as I can make out she spent the time there in punts and at balls alongside the Gavins and Ruperts, with the result that she's fit only for joke ladylike jobs at the gentleman publishers in Bedford Square. Not that Henrietta wants to work, dear me no. She'd rather be living in the Old Rectory someplace with a brood of hawk-faced children while Gavin or Rupert or whoever gets on with bringing home the bacon. But this is 1990, darling, and those days are gone.

And always, too, that high English frost, that upper society aloofness rising up out of the damp to chill your bones. I stayed a couple of days once at her parents' place in Oxfordshire, a weekend of ceremonial meals and crazed social ritual played out in draughty, high-ceilinged chambers and on smoky lawns, and on the Sunday afternoon Henrietta's father, who hadn't hitherto spoken a word in my presence, sidled across to enquire – jovially? inquisitorially? It was impossible to tell – 'And how did you and my daughter er . . .' What do you say in these circumstances? 'I picked her up in a bar and she came back to my apartment'? I muttered something about meeting at a party given by – and here I dealt out the names of the two most socially exalted of Henrietta's friends I could think of – and got a tiny, thawed smile, a sensation that one of the numberless barriers between us had somehow been broken down.

Poor Henrietta! Her attitude to sex is a kind of scandalised fascination, coupled with a faint bewilderment that this is how the girls of her acquaintance are expected to spend their leisure hours. I was conducting a particularly adroit manoeuvre once in the cradle of her thighs when I became aware of sharp, admonitory breathing from the region of the pillow. I glanced up to find Henrietta, wide-eyed and baleful, regarding me in what was, when all was said and done, a rather puzzled way. 'Actually,' she said, in the tone I remembered her mother used to bring a Labrador to heel, 'I'd prefer it if you didn't do that.' Not specially interested by this stage in what Henrietta preferred, I carried on doing it, all the while expecting some quite magisterial rebuke. Curiously Henrietta accepted these indignities with a weary resignation, long years with the Ruperts and the Simons presumably having warned her of the impossibility of tempering male desire.

Beyond the window mist hangs over the endless traffic that curls away towards Kennington and the Elephant. South London – Brockley and Brixton, Herne Hill and Tooting, Bromley and Petts Wood. Once in a while I take a train out to the coast and pass through this sad hinterland of railway arches, lock-up garages and toytown streets, broken up every now and then by patches of thin municipal grass, where Alsatians chained up in backyards bark at nothing and the wind chases torn paper over empty pavements. The boys who work in the mailroom here, the Daves and the Steves, the Winstons and the Leroys, the Ravis and the Iftaqs, big teenagers with a quarter of an inch of bristle doing service as hairstyles, come from South London, from Lewisham and Catford, Orpington and Denmark Hill. What kind of life goes on there? I can only guess. Back home we don't have anything like this. New York is built on a rock. Take a train out towards Albany and pretty soon you hit scrub countryside, those odd, pale cornfields with lean-tos and chickenwire fences and antediluvian cars drawn up in the yard, where people laugh at a city suit. Here you get fifteen miles of unbroken suburb, a down-market urban theme park, dense and impenetrable, crammed with smoky pubs and newsagents and breakers' yards.

Shifting the debris on my desk, I have an idea. Management consultants specialise in studies, surveys, research projects, *corporate analysis*. You're a finance director, say, with a six-figure R&D budget? Slater will help you spend it. He'll have two dozen consultants camping out in your factory for a week; he'll have twenty-five-year-olds who've never lifted anything heavier than a pen all their lives putting the fear of God into your management. He'll give you the works – markets, labour costs, efficiency, process innovation. And at the end of it he'll give you a nice little booklet with his recommendations in it and bill you for a hundred thousand pounds. Implementing the recommendations will cost another half million, and curiously the R&D budget all seems to be spent now, but thanks very much for your insights Mr Slater, and we're sure our shareholders will be delighted. Or something like that. One of KLS's recent clients in this line as it happened was a sporting charity who wanted advice on how to spend a million or so of government money on refurbishing a couple of hundred urban playing fields. The assignment was a joy for all concerned. 'Seventy grand just in fees,' Slater had crowed nostalgically, 'and a dozen site visits – I'll be going by helicopter of course.' Remembering this, I decide to call a guy named Terry Long, Slater's team leader on that job.

'Terry? How's tricks?'

Terry sounds subdued. 'Oh, you know. Ten assistant consultants went an hour ago. Plus there's a couple of execs in there at the moment trying to blackmail the management council.'

'Any grounds?'

'Threatening to tell *Accountancy Age* how we got that last defence procurement study.'

'What? The one where we had to . . . The one where Slater had to leave the MOD with his head under a sack?'

'That's the one. Birningside thinks he's going to be able to fire them. Between you and me I think he's going to have to keep them on. Anyhow, what can I do for you?'

'It's a long shot, Terry, but do you know anything about football?'

'A lifelong hobby,' Terry says simply. 'What do you want to know about it?'

'How long is lifelong?'

'Let's say thirty-five years. Saw my first cup final in 1959. Season ticket at West Ham in '62.'

'OK, I'll buy that . . . You ever heard of Walham Town?'

'The Squirrels? Barry Mower's black and white army? Sure. They're having a good run at the moment.'

'They're 17th in, what is it, division four.'

'Take it from me, Scott. 17th in division four is a good run for Walham. What exactly do you want to know?'

I explain about Slater's bargain, two hundred redundancies across the board and favours for the chairman's friends. Outside the dusk is deepening into dense blue-black pockets, bruising the pinker sky beyond the embankment. Terry listens interestedly, occasionally throwing in impossibly knowing statistics about gate receipts and FA commissions, and I realise that I've hooked up with one of those rapt English sports obsessives, the kind of guys you read about in the paper who spend their vacations touring rugby grounds in the North of England or postpone their wedding because it clashes with a reserve team practice. When I finish, Terry clicks his tongue a couple of times.

'Heard we were doing stuff for Barry Mower. This football thing is a new one though.' He fills me in on the Mower empire and our part in it. 'Actually Walham's tricky, Scott. Only thing anyone really remembers about them is the 1959 cup run.'

'Remind me.'

'What happened? Jesus, it was a dream. They were bottom of division three when it started, virtually bankrupt, hadn't won a home game all season, and suddenly in the third round they beat Everton at Goodison. The press took them up after that – they had this weird manager called Tusker Holloway who'd been an RAF fighter pilot – and they got as far as a semi-final replay at White Hart Lane.'

'And what about now? Slater says they're practically insolvent.'

'Yeah, well half the clubs in the league are probably trading illegally if it comes to that. Walham are just your average fourth division side, Scott. All right, your below-average fourth division side. They never win anything so nobody comes to see them, but the players still have to be paid. There'll be half-a-dozen of them on twenty, thirty grand a year. It all adds up.'

'Management history?'

'Pre-Mower? Usual bunch of locals. Small time: solicitors, small business, that sort of thing. The council ran it for a bit because they thought they could sell the ground for development, only they found someone had put a preservation order on the old stand. Then along comes Mower. I think he got it for a few thousand quid. There isn't anyone else. A couple of tame directors, maybe, and a company secretary out of Mower's dirty magazine business.'

'But Mower hasn't tried to do anything with it?'

'That's the funny thing. Normally when a rich bastard buys a football club he starts chucking money about. Get a new midfield for six million quid. Build a new stand. Mower hasn't done any of that. Two or three transfers from non-league clubs, maybe, and they wouldn't have been more than five figures.'

'Terry,' I interject, 'how do you know all this?'

'Like I said, it's my hobby. Come round to my house some time, Scott. I've got a complete set of football league scarves – all ninety-two of them, *and* the clubs that got thrown out. Accrington Stanley. Bradford Park Avenue. Would some programmes help?'

'Some what?'

'You know. Little booklets with pictures of the players and the team lists. They have them for the Superbowl. I've probably got some Walham ones if I look hard enough.'

He chatters on for a while. I light a cigarette and watch Linda moving heavily along the corridor. An English preoccupation of course. Henrietta's friends wax grim and serious over jibs and spinnaker cleats. At the other end of the scale I once witnessed a quite serious ruckus in the elevator here between two of the mail boys which hinged on whether some first division goalie or other was gay. Eventually Terry rings off, having imparted more authoritative-sounding statistics about attendance figures, backhanders, tax write-offs. Reverently I lay down the cigarette, struggle wearily into my coat as Linda clumps effortfully into the room – a kind of military gait that makes her look as if she were wading through shallows – bearing a large brown envelope.

'This just came. It says Urgent.'

I squint at the double row of *Private and confidential, open addressee only* stickers. 'Uh huh. I'll take it with me.' There is a pause. I reflect that Linda's life must be full of these pauses, pauses in the line at the newsagent, pauses in the slow, fractured converse of the family hearth, pauses with Grant or whoever as they try to articulate the dense rhythms of their desire (Linda's sex life, by the way, I find unimaginable, or rather all too imaginable – I see seals frolicking in mid-stream, furry limbs perilously entwined), that hers is more or less an existence lived out in parenthesis, spun out in looking and waiting.

'Linda,' I say, stone faced, 'who was Buzz Aldrin?'

Not a flicker. I used to find Linda's stare disconcerting, until I realised that it wasn't directed at me at all, that it was simply the long, slow English stare: lymphatic, uninterested, remote. Linda must stare at Grant like that while he does whatever he does to her, at her mother over the breakfast table. I stow the envelope away, move off into the silent corridor.

Later I take the subway west into the streaming darkness. Beyond Hammersmith the tunnel gives way to open track: wet parklands full of spindly trees winding down to distant asphalt, flat ponds with lamplight shining off the surface of the water. At this hour the trains are half-empty: a few guys in suits bunking off early, gangs of girls from the expensive London day schools – mini-Henriettas in candystripe blazers and designer jewellery who trade homework tips in the aisles or stand pressed up against the windows titivating their lambent hair. The boys, manikin Ruperts and Gavins, stand further off down the carriage swearing in faultless cut-glass accents. Picking up a tattered *Daily Mail* that someone has left on an adjoining seat, I stare randomly at the front page. The papers are still exercised by the West End murder – a definite case of mutilated genitalia according to a Home Office whitecoat – and now, as it turns out, by the discovery of another similarly mangled corpse down in Peckham. The guy was twenty-four, a loner, worked in a packing factory, no known vices. On this occasion, though, they found the letters RAM daubed on the bedroom wall – the report doesn't actually specify that they were printed in blood, but this is the popular assumption. An ID-style photograph of the guy shows neutral, worn-down features – at any rate not the kind of guy you'd expect to find belly up in a Peckham tenement with his dick cut off. I read on for a while, stuff about the guy's colleagues breaking down when they heard, a startled landlady swearing that no one ever came to call, the usual things. Then, shifting the paper to one side, I pull the brown envelope out of my bag and tear it across. I expect to find some software circular or expense claim knuckle-rap, but instead discover a four-page document entitled MEMO TO ALL SENIOR STAFF *from J. Devoto*, broken down into innumerable italicised sub-headings: *Macro-economic indices; total quality parameters*. It takes a paragraph or two to divine that the whole thing is meaningless, not meaningless in the way that computer guidebooks are meaningless – that is, without interest to any serious person – but literally without meaning. Bemused, I pick a sentence at random. It goes: *Pan-global factors may necessitate a total quality/value for money (VFM) interface – there are no quick fixes*. After this I stop reading, bitterly disturbed by the thought of Devoto composing it – no doubt on the floor of his office sometime in the small hours – alarmed by the fierce conviction of a mind twisted out of kilter.

Loud, unignorable voices a foot or so above my head march these demons away. Schoolgirls on the train have two topics of conversation. Either they talk about their boyfriends – public school Adonises with whimsical nicknames like 'Oofy' or 'Thumper' – or exotic foreign travel. These two are no exception: what Alexandra said when Hugo stopped seeing her; what Emma's mother said when she found the packet of condoms. Without warning fond, orgiastic reminiscence gives way to backpacking in Burkina Faso, chalet girls and Camilla being beastly about the rucksack. I look up to see a younger, svelter version of Henrietta strap-hanging over the *Standard*: corn-coloured hair in waves, Romanesque nose, plump, cantilevered breasts, the general effect like an impossibly sleek and well-groomed racehorse. What is it about these English girls? You don't see a skin like that in Milwaukee. I once caught sight of Henrietta through the crowd at a party, snickering in the midst of a brace or two of Guys and Simons at somebody's joke, and her face – frozen for a second between the periscoping foreheads – perfectly blended the characteristics of her kind: hauteur, massive, stoical unease, clannishness, and beneath it all a kind of residual panache. Whatever destinies you envisaged for her, whether prosaic (loafing in the Rectory, say, with Hugo or Rupert) or dystopian (the post-Holocaust soup-kitchen) it could safely be predicted that this tiny streak of self-preservation would see her through.

For some reason – I start thinking of Danny Hassenblad, whose dealings with women were, if in vastly different circumstances, a mirror of my own relationship with Henrietta and her friends. Danny Hassenblad's attitude to girls, though constrained by chronic nervousness, was governed by a conviction that they existed largely as social accessories and that the having of them was no more than a badge of approbation pinned by society on the shoulder of a particularly smart and successful male operator. He approved very strongly of the kind of photographs you saw in New York glossies where tuxedoed Joes in their fifties who had made fortunes out of computers or real estate or wood pulp were pictured arm-in-arm with Vassar heiresses or the ash-blonde daughters of cabinet secretaries. Such arrangements ministered to one of his most settled convictions – that the basis of human attraction lies not in looks but in real or imagined status. Evidence to the contrary – an actress setting aside her career to 'spend more time' with a middle-aged librarian husband – drove him to fury. 'Let's face it, Scott,' he would say, contemplating a magazine spread of Trump or Milken or some even less well-preserved male icon, 'the Errol Flynn scenario is dead. Sure, in a primitive society I can see attraction being purely physical. You stroll out of your cave and you're feeling fresh – ten to one you haul down the first pair of tits in view. But this is the eighties. There are musclemen sweeping the streets down in Long Island.'

Whatever one thought about this proposition – and Danny had a theory that the attraction of wealthy men increased in proportion to their ugliness – it was impossible not to believe that its source lay in his own utter physical anonymity. 'The basic thing about Danny,' a friend of his once confided with rather ominous seriousness, 'is that he needs to take a liedown every time he crosses the street.' Yet even these drawbacks – the swaying homuncule totter, the peanut-butter complexion, the steel-wool tufts of thinning hair – need not necessarily have inhibited the pursuit of some kind of romantic life. For there were any number of girls – secretary typists, designers who hung around the office – who would have been prepared to tolerate Danny Hassenblad's physical limitations in return for the benefits a relationship with the proprietor of a Manhattan computer consultancy might allow. In shunning them, in ignoring the Doloreses and the Rhoda-Joes who winked at him over the filing cabinets and stirred Sweet 'n' Low fondly into his coffee, Danny merely compounded his misfortune. Aiming high – he wanted the Studio 54 girls, languid but steely, he wanted the kind of women you saw stretched on davenports in *Vanity Fair* and *American Vogue*, he wanted women like Sondra, who always treated him as if he were some kind of pet troll – he somehow missed any sort of target at all.

The exception – and even with pitiful, self-absorbed losers such as Danny Hassenblad there is always an exception – was his secretary, a statuesque Aphrodite, hired by Danny at twice the normal salary simply because her mother was supposed to have been at Vassar with a Vanderbilt. It was possible to gauge the extent of Danny's obsession with this girl, whose name was Nancy and who sat outside his office for seven hours each day in a kind of disaffected trance, by the fact that he sidelined any discussion of her appearance – and Danny was a great one for appraising the secretaries' tits in after-hours camaraderie – in favour of awestruck gossip about her social connections. 'Do you realise, Scott,' he informed me seriously after a week of unanswered phones and haughty incompetence, 'that Nancy got asked to Jimmy Carter's inauguration party? And Claudia Goldstein is her fucking *godmother*?' Obscurely, these goggling admissions of social inferiority struck a faint, responsive chord. They had lunch a few times and took to arriving at work together, a manoeuvre in which Danny always seemed to resemble a harassed Victorian footman ground down by a severe and exigent mistress. Once in these early days I asked him how it was going. His face brightened immediately out of its usual hang-dog furrow. 'Uh huh. Had dinner with her the other night.' 'Go OK?' 'Go OK? The bill was two hundred and seventy-five bucks,' Danny said reprovingly. 'So what does she talk about?' 'Oh, you know, her parents and that. Europe. You ever been to Florence, Scott?' 'Sure Danny.' 'Uh huh.' And for a moment Danny looked wistful, sad and extraordinarily like the diminutive, untravelled, Jewish proprietor of a minor-league New York computer consultancy. 'I just wondered.'

It went on like this for a month or so, the tokens of Danny's regard growing steadily more unignorable: daily flower deliveries, afternoon excursions into town. There was a picture of them once in one of the New York social papers, taken at some gallery preview: Nancy sleek and invulnerable, Danny's face a fuzz of mingled pride and social insecurity. Not long after this, on a morning when Nancy's desk lay bare and untenanted, he summoned me into his room and stared at me through hard, sleepless eyes. 'Listen, Scott, I don't know if I should be telling you this, but . . . Thing is, Nancy finally came across last night.' 'Uh huh. How'd it go?' I was expecting some rapt account of smooth, pitiless congress. Instead Danny looked incurably shifty and hopeless. 'Look, Scott. I can talk to you. Not like those creeps in the office. I . . . It was her parents' place, OK, out on Staten Island. They're in Europe or someplace, some three-month vacation. First time I'd got asked to dinner. *Do you realise, Scott, they have actual servants*? Two maids and a negro cook. So anyway, I'm all fired up because, you know, it's been three months and I'm thinking tonight's the night, tonight's got to be the big one.'

'What happened?'

'What happened? She just lay there. I'm telling you, Scott, it was like screwing a corpse. And when I'd finished, do you know what she said?'

'Told you you were her dream lover? Said it didn't matter you were five six and Jewish?'

'You're not taking me seriously Scott . . . No, when I'd finished she rolled over and said: "I'd just like you to know that I've never been so insulted in my life?"'

'Those were her exact words?'

'Sure. I couldn't stay there after that of course, I've got my pride Scott, so I got one of the maids to call me a cab.'

'What did you do?'

'Jesus! I hardly touched her. No hardcore stuff. No sword-swallowing or anything. I even managed to come outside her for Christ's sake.'

Even in his hour of doom, I noticed, Danny's social antennae had not entirely deserted him: he had still retained an exact impression of the Staten Island mansion's decor and furnishings. Details of these embellishments were occasionally toted out to impressionable clients. But what gaffe he had blown, what unlooked for sexual calisthenics he had forced upon his unwilling partner, what revelations from his personal life he had flourished as a bedroom gambit, I never found out. Nancy never came back. In her place Danny hired a Puerto Rican girl named Maria, who word-processed his letters with unfeigned devotion, pined for an opportunity to sleep with him and was rewarded for these overtures by an unswerving contempt.

The schoolgirls disembark at Ravenscourt Park, go scampering away into the twilight, that after-hours upper-class teenage world of geography prep, pastel chambers and the callow attentions of Oofy and Thumper. I sit in an empty train thundering west through the alien suburbs. At intervals the river slides up between the gaps in the houses, beneath rickety footbridges carrying intent, hurrying men, dull and heavy, like oil puddling the city's concrete surface: borne away downstream, tiny craft with winking firefly lights vanish into obscurity.

At Walham there is a sudden rush of unearthly light, a debouch through subterranean walkways into grim, silent streets. Westward, beyond grey, descending parkland, I can make out the subdued glow of floodlights. Beyond the bandstand and its asphalt surround the road picks up again: past tall mansion blocks, high yellow-grey walls ghostly in the naphtha glare. Here the graffiti stretches out in twenty-foot scrolls: MILLWALL BUSHWHACKERS; VOTE PAT ARROWSMITH; TOSH MULLIGAN IS GOD; MOWER IS SATAN'S SLAVE! I make a mental note to ask Terry about this. The Millwall Bushwhackers I can make a guess at, but 'Vote Pat Arrowsmith'? On the left-hand

88

side, where the park railings come to an end, patched red brickwork extends a hundred yards down the street. A single car parked negligently at the roadside turns out to be a Jaguar with the registration MOW 1. All at once I feel kind of sad, lost and disinherited. I shouldn't be here. I should be somewhere else, far away from the streetlamps and the stadium shadow, courting Henrietta or reassembling the fragments of last night, listening again to my father's voice and its disquieting news. Not here. The mist comes on now, drifting across from the dead park, hanging over the grey pavement. I hunch deeper into my coat, move on towards the bright, unwelcoming foyer.

PART TWO

HAROLD 'BIDDY' BIDDLECOMBE (b. 1935): A legendary wing-half of the old school, 'Biddy' was an ever-present in Squirrels' line-ups of the early 1960s. Remembered above all for his last-minute equaliser in the tumultuous 4-4 draw against Aldershot that rounded off the 61/62 season and saved Walham from re-election. Biddy's subsequent career took him to Hartlepool, Stafford Rangers and Wisbech. Present whereabouts unknown.

from *Walham's Glory Years: A history of Walham FC*

6

Not one of your glamour clubs

'Of course', Barry Mower says seriously, 'we're not one of your glamour clubs. No one could say that.'

'Naturally.'

'I look round sometimes, and I think, there's people who'd come in here and spend two, three million quid just like that – a centre forward, say, and a couple of defenders – but where would it get them?'

'I see.'

'People don't seem to realise you have to build a team from its foundations. That's what Sir Matt did, that's what Shankly did. You didn't see them arriving at Old Trafford or wherever and chucking money about like Co-op stamps.'

At right-angles to The Dray's meagre executive lounge, beyond a wall of photographs proudly titled *Walham's Hall of Fame*: Barry Mower's office. Here, as well as the sporting memorabilia, there are intimations of other existences: a picture of Barry Mower in evening dress shaking hands with minor royalty; another picture of him presenting a grossly enlarged charity cheque to a Radio One DJ; portraits of Barry flanked by busty models underwritten with prurient captions – *Barry with hugs from Babs, For Barry – it's what you're right arm's for*, that kind of thing. In each case the other person looks hugely discomposed or affronted or scared. Barry, on the other hand, is perky and ebullient: baring his teeth obsequiously at the minor royalty, smirking at Jimmy Smash or whoever, snaking out a fat hand to encircle Babs and Dolores.

'There's some people', Barry goes on, giving a faint impression of having rehearsed the words, 'think all you need to buy a football club is a wallet and a copy of the *Rothman's Football Yearbook*.

Seen at one remove from the tuxedoed and dinner-jacketed

93

splendour of the charity reception and the motor show preview, he seems a slightly diminished figure. Grey hair, cut short and thinning, rises above a seamed, weary face. Beneath, burly shoulders and a massive, rhomboid torso fall away to short and curiously dainty legs. The general effect is to make him seem top-heavy, a single push or incautious step liable to send him crashing to the floor. For all the familiarity of the get-up – flapping, fat man's suit, florid tie – the result is oddly un-English. Badger-headed, worn down, morose, he could be an elderly relative in a French comic film, Uncle Pépé, say, reluctantly agreeing to supervise a brood of noisy children.

'And of course there are your other business interests as well.'

'That's right,' Barry agrees affably. 'I can see you've done your homework, young man. Can't be in three places at the same time, which means there's blokes running round here like they owned the place without me to keep an eye on them.'

'That must be a problem.'

'Breaks my bleeding heart,' says Barry sincerely.

Beyond and slightly above the level of our heads, where fog hangs low over the pallid arc-lights, a ball rises suddenly into view, lingers for a second in the drifting vapour and then falls away. Faint cries mark its descent. Barry stares at the window.

'"A" team game. Between you and me nobody comes except their dads. We're losing money just opening the gates.'

A memory of the walk from the underground station bobs back into view. 'Who's Tosh Mulligan?'

Barry shrugs. 'Played left back in the 'fifties.'

'And Pat Arrowsmith?'

'Some old girl used to put up for Parliament. Ban the Bomb and all that.'

'Sure.'

I wander over to the low, rectangular window and gaze out. At ground level the mist lies in thick, rolling striations, so that a defender forced suddenly to back-pedal will disappear altogether, re-emerge a moment later several yards away, separated from his colleagues by a dense grey cloud. To the left bare, empty terracing rises sharply to the perimeter wall. On the far side of the ground a cavernous grandstand is sunk in darkness. The whole feels at once too vast and too gloomy to

94

have anything to do with sport. You could imagine an evangelical mission taking place here, or a public execution: a football match seems way too frivolous.

'Why carry on? Why open the gates when you're losing money?'

Barry glares at me fondly. 'Ah, you're an accountant ent you? No, don't take it the wrong way. It's tradition, isn't it? Do you know, there's been a soccer team here seventy years? First team, reserves and "A" team. Jesus, time I used to come here when I was a kid they had a "B" team as well. Fifty players on the books at least. Now, if I said I was going to stop the "A" team there'd be pissheads demonstrating in the road and old boys chaining themselves to the railings.' He claps me on the shoulder. 'Come on. Seeing you're going to be spending some time here, I'll show you round.'

Ah, that English tradition. You get a lot of this here in London, from the Bank of England with its swaggering flunkies in damask tailcoats, down to KLS where the annual results are communicated to partners behind closed doors in a private room at the Guildhall to the accompaniment of thimblefuls of sherry. In the summer I can miss seeing Henrietta two or three nights a week because of Ascot or Henley or the Chelsea Flower Show or some other engagement in her archaic social calendar. Barry Mower, too, is drifting off down river, borne away on this thin tide of sentiment.

In the corridor, werewolf's paw angled over my shoulder, he says shrewdly: 'You an American or something, son?'

I explain a bit about that odd sequestered childhood in sight of the tumbled West Virginia hills, George Eliot and Angela Thirkell on the shelf, the old man conning over the English sports results in the paper. He listens vaguely. 'Yeah? Well, I daresay you'll pick it up.' From beyond the window a few scattered handclaps drift away into the night.

We set off through Barry's domain, pausing for a moment by the Walham Hall of Fame and its pictures of square-jawed guys from the 1930s with brilliantined hair, ignoring the executive lounge (empty) and the trophy cabinet (also empty). Outside, the game has come to a temporary halt and the players stand around with hands on hips or jog sedulously to keep warm. The empty terraces and bridleways beyond them are caught up in shadow. Sprung from the confines of his lair, at large in his mazey private fiefdom, Barry looks appreciably more at ease: avuncular, proprietorial. Descending frail, rickety steps towards a warren of bootrooms and tiled passages reeking of disinfectant, where defunct lightbulbs hang in rows like straps on the underground, he gamely consents to answer questions on the club's sporting and financial health: 'A mistake to think you can buy your way out of trouble. Look at Chelsea . . . Tottenham . . . Palace . . . Plenty of talent, just a question of developing it. Not our fault if we don't win matches. Look at Norwich . . . West Ham . . . Millwall . . . Told the FA it ought to make help for the small clubs a priority . . . No question of trading illegally. Got the money to cover all outstanding liabilities, not like some I could mention. Look at Tranmere . . . Maidstone . . . Aldershot . . . Fucking idle bastards in the reserves . . .' The high, sober cadences rise and fall. Rounding a corner in the passage we come upon three pale, bovine teenagers listlessly punting a ball against the concrete, whereupon Barry jolts instantly out of his reverie.

'Here. Stop all that. Go on. Fuck off out of it.'

Meekly the pale boys comply. One of them even says 'Sorry Mr Mower.' Receding down the passage, the light glints off their cropped, bony heads.

'Fucking apprentices. Think they own the place.'

Beneath the stand, where the tunnel opens out into a spacious cavern with whitewashed walls, shuttered confectionery stalls and stark urinals, good humour returns. Jauntily pacing the asphalt floor, he settles into a gruff tourist guide. 'That's our pisser . . . Burger bar . . . Programmes . . . Club shop.' Here there are older echoes, of baseball grounds in the South visited with my father in childhood, families picnicking on the mound, grandmotherly women selling fries, dust rising with the clamour of the square.

'Been coming here since I was a kid . . . Dad used to bring me up on the train . . . Always had this dream, ambition really. Happens a lot in football . . . Plenty of other clubs desperate to sell. Look at Barnet . . . Scarborough . . . Crewe . . . Question of loyalty . . . Remember my old dad standing on the terrace in the pouring rain . . . Idle old sod.' Drenched in this opulent coating of nostalgia, Barry's account of how he came to buy Walham Town has all the paraphernalia of some epic myth, a series of dramatic oppositions each cancelled out by his sterling qualities of endurance, zestfulness, pertinacity: 'The league weren't happy . . . "Not a fit and proper person to have charge of a football club" . . . Bollocks . . . Had to stop the last lot calling in the receivers . . . Five hundred thousand *in notes* down on the table . . . Stood in the foyer at Lancaster Gate and told them to fuck off . . .'

Somewhere in the distance a whistle blows: there is a faint drumming of feet, a dutiful handclap or two. The noise has a desolate, perfunctory quality. Watching Barry prowl beneath the naked lightbulb, hunching his shoulders into the stiff carapace of his suit, I revise my opinion slightly. Not so much Uncle Pépé, or some put-upon relative out of a Gallic comedy, as Big Vern. Big Vern turns up occasionally in an adult comic that I buy sometimes at subway stations: the ex-con restlessly caged behind dark glasses and a teddybear coat. Big Vern's comic dysfunction is his inability to separate *agents provocateurs* from the rest of sentient humanity. In this way busloads of innocent shoppers are routinely mown down by Vern's retributive shotgun, Vern's companion Ernie is invariably rent in twain with a meat cleaver, and each instalment ends with Vern, despairing of his chances of keeping out of the pen, sternly resolved that 'No bastard coppa's gunna take me alive, Ernie', turning the gun on himself. Barry reminds me of Big Vern. There is the same slightly predatory grin, the same deep, unyielding suspicion, and beneath the stage moroseness, and half-a-dozen other comic appurtenances, a faint air of unease. I'd reckon that if you lived for very long in Barry Mower's orbit you wouldn't care to offend him, and if you did offend him he'd make it pretty hot for you, that's what I'd reckon.

'Get a few drinks inside us first, then we can talk business.'

In the executive bar, which Barry refers to without shame as the Barry Mower Lounge, a handful of middle-aged men and women sit watching a fizzing TV. Their faces have the worn, anxious look of people keeping intense personal sorrow at bay through concentration on some arduous, mundane chore. Frowning seriously, Barry moves among them diffusing bonhomie. It's quite a performance in its way, names accurately recalled, interests indulged: intent, unsmiling. The TV watchers, fists grasped over their lager-shandies, gaze at him with parched, grateful faces. Prodded and harassed by a pair of women with hair the colour of barley sugar, an elderly man is sufficiently emboldened to ask for Barry's autograph on the back of a beer mat. Peering uneasily at the proferred biro, Barry obliges.

On the wall nearer the bar there are more photographs. Players with wiry, razored hair, ballooning shorts, hard, eager faces. Captions in faded type run beneath: *Tosh Mulligan, Biddy Biddlecombe, Les Parrott*. Those English names! My mother's relatives, those dead ghosts she never talked about, had names like Jefferies, Anstruther, Borthwick. Pride of place is given to a picture of the 1958/59 cup team. Drawn up in descending rows, the turf before them taken up by a grinning, cardboard squirrel, they seem grim, serious men. Standing a little apart, but regarding them with a kind of wary suspicion, is an extraordinary figure. Immensely tall, saturnine, trilby-hatted, high shoulders like up-ended champagne bottles, he has both hands plunged deep into the pockets of what might be a service greatcoat, and a look of massive ill temper. As I stare at him Barry lurches over to the bar, still carrying the biro in his outstretched hand.

'Marvellous old boy . . . Been coming here since 1936 . . . Friend of me dad's as it happens . . . Always happy to oblige.' He lowers his voice. 'Between you and me it's not worth keeping the place open for the pensioners' club. Come in here and spend three hours with the fire on over a half of lager.' In sight of the bar, with its neat rows of Walham F.C. ashtrays and its nervous teenage barman, he grows newly expansive.

'Yer look pale, Scott, lad. Need building up and that. Give him a glass of champagne, Glenn.'

This, it transpires, is a piece of vainglory. Neither, Barry having subsequently demanded some whimsical cocktail, is there any vodka. In the end we settle for whisky. In the background the TV rasps and whinnies. Barry peers up, sober and interested, nods interrogatively at the barman.

'What did Doreen do when she found out Ron was fucking Charlene?'

The barman shrugs. 'They never said. Anyway, Ron had his leg blown off when the gas main went up.'

'The fuck he did . . . ? So what happened when Ron's sister got back from the States?'

'Last thing you saw they were still searching her case at the airport.'

I twitch at Barry's billowing subfusc elbow. 'Who's the guy in the hat?'

'Him? That's Tusker Holloway.'

'Tusker?'

'Actually his real name was Archibald. They called him that because . . . Some nickname he got in the war, I dunno . . . The thing is, Scott, Tusker Holloway epit . . . epit . . . Tusker Holloway represents the spirit of this club all right? I mean, do you know what happened one time in a game the season after the cup run? No? Well, they were 3-0 down at half-time, against Brentford it was, big local derby, and Tusker thought they weren't trying. Do you know what he did? He only substitutes the centre forward and puts himself on doesn't he? And this is a man who was fifty, fifty-five years of age. He put himself on against a load of twenty-year-olds.'

'What happened?'

'The crowd went wild. They were baying for him.'

'No, what really happened?'

'He dropped dead of a heart attack in the 57th minute,' says Barry coldly. 'Like I said, Tusker Holloway represents the spirit of this club.'

After this there is a silence. Barry treats himself soberly to another whisky. Above our heads the light dims for a second and then revives. Barry stares at the TV again with dead, unforgiving eyes.

Speeding eastwards through the dark, he grows confidential. 'Naturally, Scott, I'm as concerned with the bottom line as the next guy. Old days when you could run a club for the fun of it, they've all gone. Dead as Accrington Stanley, they are. Twenty, thirty years back any tinpot scrap dealer with a bank account

99

could run a football club. Not any more. Players' wages'll see to that. I've got kids of twenty, twenty-one, come up from the Diadora and the Conference, on fifteen, twenty grand a year. All with *agents* in C&A suits going on about long-service bonuses and my client just wondered about an upgrade on his fucking Mazda . . . Your average chairman, I mean he's not doing it out of charity is he? I mean, look at Ron Noades at Palace . . . Robert Chase at Norwich . . . Thing is, Scott, this place costs me half a million a year. Say six hundred grand in a bad year. TV revenue is a few quid. Haven't had a club sponsor in three years. The last one made condoms for God's sake. Got two local papers and a greengrocer from up the Walham High Road pay for half the first team's kit, that's it.'

I tote out some of the management consultant's nonsense that garnishes our proposals to down-at-heel London boroughs.

'Couldn't you diversify?' The dullard's stare impels me to elaborate. 'Couldn't you, uh . . . You've got a site standing idle say twelve days out of fourteen. Couldn't you do something with it?'

'Tried that. Last summer. Fixed up with this music promoter to do a rock concert. The Pixies and Carter the Unstoppable Sex Machine. Fuck knows who they are, but Ron says the tickets'll go. What happens? Two hours after the first ad goes in the paper I get a phone call from the Residents' Association. Two hours after that someone layers my motor with paint stripper. Next morning I get a court injunction. Bloody bitches in that mansion block over the way with nothing better to do and all got bloody brothers who're QCs.'

'Nothing else?'

'I've got the Walham senior citizens have their bingo night every other Thursday.'

The car slews right into the Brompton Road, where torn plastic sacks, like cowled monks, lift in the wind and expire on to the empty pavements. Even at this stage, I realise, I have no illusions about Barry Mower. Lovable cockney vulgarians, East End nabobs, nature's gentlemen, Ronnie Kray and George Cornell. I learned all that out of the old man's magazines, but I never believed in any of it. Barry Mower isn't a lovable cockney vulgarian. Barry Mower is a mean-spirited little hoodlum to whom someone has given an absurd sum of money and who is

100

allowed to wander around in ridiculous clothes. Somehow the contrast between Barry and his American equivalents – the fat Joes on the sidewalk in their seersucker suits, white midriffs guttering over their waistbands, is yet more depressing still. The American Barry Mowers know that money is all they have, that they got where they are simply through money, that if you took the money away they would merely relapse into the primordial ooze. The real Barry Mower, however, sees money as a vindication of what was already there, a confirmation of some innate, ineluctable quality deep within him, the stamp on his passport of dignity and self-esteem.

'Who handles all the club's financial affairs? Day-to-day, I mean.'

'There's the club secretary, used to work for me on *Cunning Stunts*. He's a good kid, Darren, but . . . I mean, it's all signing cheques isn't it? Like I said, Scott, this lot is costing me five, six hundred grand a year. Might as well chuck it down the crapper for all the good it's doing me. Now, how much do you think I paid your mob last year?'

I essay a rapid mental calculation, based on what Terry Long told me. Audit fees on three companies, plus tax work, plus fighting the VATman and the Customs and Excise, plus some corporate finance three-card trickery on a crashed video concern Barry wanted to asset-strip. Not to mention some investigations stuff of such an abstruse and confidential nature that Terry wouldn't even talk about it.

'A hundred and fifty?'

'A hundred and ninety. I'm not complaining Scott, I mean, if you want an accountant you're not going to go to the Paki in Walham High Street are you? But that's a lot of money. And I reckon, don't you, that it's time somebody done me a favour in return?'

The restaurant is in Knightsbridge, halfway along a gloomy sidewalk, at right angles to a dreaming mews. Like the car and the suit, it too seems an oddly flagrant extension of Barry Mower's personality, combining maximum ostentation with a kind of bedrock furtiveness, the thought of a flamboyant and exacting lifestyle lived out for some reason behind closed doors.

The kind of place, queerly enough, where I used to come with the old man in the early 1980s before the loan bank crash stifled his taste for high living. A dozen or so tables are jammed together beneath garish lights and extravagant decor. The general effect is not prepossessing.

Reaching the dowdy vestibule, where hoards of expensive-looking coats lie flung over a table, Barry waits for a moment, taking several deep breaths and letting his eyes adjust to the light. Here too, I note, his temperament has undergone a slight but salient transformation, has so to speak moved up a gear, the better to contend with more demanding circumstances. At The Dray he had posed as the convivial host; in the car he had appeared in what were presumably truer colours, those of the shrewd and censorious businessman. Now there is a kind of studied aloofness in the way he hands his Aquascutum to the attendant and remains staring coldly through the fishbowl glass at the doorway: suddenly he has become the successful man on public display.

In a recess to the side of the cloakroom there is a beat-up phone booth. I go over and dial the apartment. No one answers. Cheering at first, the knowledge soon hardens into a kind of cautious disappointment.

'Phoning your bird, eh?'

'You could say.'

'Well give her one for me, eh, next time? If there is a next time.'

'Sure.'

Seen at closer hand, the restaurant's interior confirms earlier suppositions: showbiz, but the wrong kind of showbiz; money, but the wrong kind of money – loud, obtrusive and ultimately evanescent money. On the wall hang framed photographs of TV comics and talkshow hosts of the kind whose liaisons occasionally figure on the inner pages, rarely the covers, of the *News of the World*. Several similar people, their faces vaguely recognisable, all with that tanned, smoothed and slightly featureless look of the minor celebrity, sit about eating. Giving occasional nods and straining after acknowledgment, Barry plunges past them. Here, at a table set a little way apart from the others, the restaurant signals, with dogged finality, that it is Barry's kind of place. Unusually for anywhere outside the Soho stoat-hatches, the joint has topless waitresses, great flame-haired Amazons with breasts like giant seed pods that quiver despairingly as they mumble over the order pads. In New York, of course, such things are *de rigueur* – Danny Hassenblad, for example, used to lunch at Di Maggio's on 53rd simply so that he could have the pleasure of hurling his napkin on the floor and asking the waitress to return it – but there is a strange sense of faded recognition in finding a tit diner in Knightsbridge.

'You hungry son?'

I murmur something about having eaten earlier. Oblivious, Barry's thick, frankfurter fingers hover eagerly over the foot-high card. He dines hugely: three prawn cocktails, a plate of roast beef, amply renewed, numberless depredations on the sweet trolley. I trifle with a slice or two of Melba toast and some pâté, coughing strickenly whenever anything brushes against my epiglottis. The flame-haired waitress looks impassively on. Her right breast is flecked with pointilliste vermilion splashes.

Obliquely, throughout the meal – and Barry is a shrewd customer OK, not prone suddenly to unburden himself to a management consultant encountered only three hours before – I get a glimpse of the darkling commercial empire whose potentate this is: the top-shelf absurdities of *Dirty Girls* and *Hot Talk*, the phone lines, the mansion flats in South Ken, the credit companies operating out of high street sites in the East End. Barry's latest scheme, it transpires, a tar barrel flung on a highly flammable ego, is the forthcoming renewal of the commercial TV franchises, and the chances of a consortium led by Barry and a few fellow-vulgarian money men.

'Thing is, Scott, that there's no such thing as adult entertainment on TV. Just soaps and cop serials, and a load of women waiting to press the panic button every time somebody says "fuck". Now, I'm not talking about anything extreme. I mean, not beaver shots on Jackanory, but . . . Put it this way, the people of this country have a democratic right to see the kind of entertainment they want to see, OK? And not just films. Comedy. Current affairs . . .'

Barry has it all planned, of course. Bernard Manning and Roy 'Chubby' Brown hosting a talkshow; quarter-famous actresses presiding over 'Guess the weight of my boobs' competitions; a

103

version of *Blind Date* where the contestants actually get to screw each other. Inevitably it won't work, not so much because of Bernard Manning and Roy 'Chubby' Brown, but because it's the wrong sort of people. TV franchises go to well-heeled accountants with City money and Treasury connections, not to Barry and his mates and their hilarious suburban largesse.

Nearly 11 p.m., the cargo of fellow-diners reduced to half-a-dozen middle-aged men with their trimmed, tucked, professional golfers' faces. The waitresses loaf around in exhausted resentful knots. Incidental highlights of the past two hours have included the arrival of a quite well-known American TV actor and his boyfriend (Barry, predictably, had never heard of either of them) and the departure of a minor TV comedian on the grounds of credit unworthiness. The lights flicker.

The last of the customers slip away. Barry goes on to drinking brandies, downing them in single gulps and jabbing the tumbler back at the waitress for a giant refill. Watching the odd juxtaposition of ballooning translucence and the girl's breasts, a candle not far away in the background, I suddenly remember an old illustration in a nineteenth-century medical textbook of a surgeon cupping a patient.

Decanted on to Fulham Broadway by a cab at 1 a.m. I get back to find the lights on and music blaring from the stereo. She sits cross-legged on the floor of the lounge wearing, some suitable words for the garment might be *otiose, exiguous* or *superogatory* – and flicking through a magazine of questionable legality (at any rate on this side of the Channel) entitled *Color Climax*. She doesn't look up as I enter.

'You're late.'

'Taking care of business.'

She twitches the magazine across. 'Do you think what they're doing there is physically possible? Or is just trick photography?'

I shrug. 'Some people will do anything for money.'

I don't get to work the next morning. Or the morning after that. Occasionally we wake simultaneously, creasing the ridges and inclines of sheets. Once she sends out for pizza and we eat it sitting up in bed, throwing broken-off fragments into the trashcan by the door.

7

Thronging, baleful clusters

It all starts to go wrong, supposedly, when they bring on Jimmy Hood. Until then – about ten minutes into the second half – nothing very much has happened, at least nothing much that would arrest my untutored eye. Drawn up across the rear of the midfield in thronging, baleful clusters Walham's inelegant defence has done what it has to do. Seen from my remote quarter of the stand, the action has all the predictability of some children's game, played out on a rectangle of green baize with strictly demarcated pieces, the rigid alignments allowing only the faintest variations of movement and design: a lofted high ball dropping on to the centre spot, a tangle of vengeful feet, a punt upfield, the process repeated as before. Variations have been provided by the stretchered removal of the opposing captain and a colossal fistfight in the Walham penalty area involving perhaps seventeen of the twenty-two players and ending, obscurely, in a round of hugs and fierce handshakes. ('They're good lads', the Walham coach told me at half-time, 'but that free kick was just diabolical.')

Now, however, there is a mild hint of drama, the thought of fresh strategy brought to illumine some arid military stalemate. The crowd, knots of middle-aged men with white, excited faces assembled behind the goals or high up on the terraces by the pie and Cola stands, are chanting *There's only one Jimmy Hood* to the tune of 'Guantalamera'. Trapped in the floodlights' glare they resemble some turbulent and despotic mob, itching to storm the palisade fences of the arena and put its protagonists to the sword. In fact this possibility is remote. 'Haven't had a pitch invasion in ten years,' Barry Mower will remark nostalgically when questioned on the likelihood of crowd trouble. 'Not since the Orient game in 1979 when they tried to do the ref.' The Orient game! It was the last big cup derby played at The Dray, apparently, with two thousand fans kept apart outside the ground by a line of police horses, and they were still clearing up the broken glass in Walham High Street two days later. But those days are gone now, replaced by a lower-key, more amiable belligerence. Jimmy Hood, a fraught, nervous manikin with a shock of red hair, catches something of this as he stands twitching on the touchline having his studs examined by the linesman, looks up towards the stand, crosses himself with a quick, perfunctory dab of the fingers and then scuttles out on to the pitch.

High above the stand, distantly outlined between the lights and the purple sky, rain is falling, fine, misty drops that hang lazily above the worn grass before moving towards the river. The players scarcely notice. The sturdy teenagers with huge calves, the bullet-headed guys in early middle age, hulking goalkeepers – all have seen much worse than this, will tell you tales of cloudbursts, goalmouth scrambles in three inches of water and referees struck by lightning. Curiously the rain seems to heighten the faint unreality of the proceedings, its arbitrary surges and doubling backs, framing the whole within quaint, otherworldly borders.

Down beneath us Jimmy Hood collects the ball as it cannons off someone's outstretched leg, jinks with it for a second or two, collides with a looming defender, is flung into touch, where he sits with his hands on his knee for a moment before jogging unconcernedly back into the fray. There is a choreography about this, a warped synchronisation of glance and gesture that is oddly comforting, like one of the *Saturday Night Live* 'bad ballet' sketches of the late 1970s in which Dan Aykroyd and John Belushi, dressed as milkmen or *condottieri*, would lumber round the stage in a clumsy, elephantine tread. Two minutes spent tracking Jimmy Hood's progress around the pitch confirms this air of stylisation: the wistful glide through the midfield, the check, the hands-on-hips pout when the decision goes against him, the remote, guiltless stare as a free kick sends the ball high over his head, the resigned lope back in the direction of the game's fulcrum – back, that is, to the second third of the Walham half. It is painfully apparent by this juncture that it isn't working out.

106

Subdued by Jimmy's effortful sauntering, and by the absence of Big Ashley Flack, whom he was brought on to replace, Walham are back-pedalling. Disturbed and frightened by a fizzing, knee-high cross, the line of mammoth backs wavers and collapses. The ball, whipped up by some unremarked foot, crashes harmlessly into the side-netting. The Walham goalkeeper, a bullet-headed guy with sad eyes, picks a defender at random and starts shouting abuse at him. The crowd murmurs once more and then falls silent.

'Lose this one and the bleeding season's over,' Barry Mower has obligingly confided in the Lounge before the game. A glance at the match programme, a vilely printed pamphlet in canary yellow entitled *News From The Dray* abets this prognosis. Tonight's encounter is not a league or an FA cup game (Walham are out of that already, humiliated 3-1 by a bunch of non-league part-timers) but something called the Rumbelow's Cup, of which this is the third round. If they win they book a place for the fourth and a date with one of the big clubs. That, at any rate, is how Barry Mower sees it. If I look up and squint to the left I can see him outlined against the flaring glass of Walham's sole executive box, a portly, gesticulating figure, intermittently turning away to study some distant outrage more closely on the video monitor. My being here tonight is Barry's idea, as it happens. 'Ought to stay on and see the match,' he remarked archly as I was loitering past his office this afternoon. 'Big cup game and that. You might learn something.' There is the additional obligation that Barry wants a confidential parley afterwards on 'how things are going.'

How things are going. I've been here a fortnight now, two weeks of interminable subway rides through the cheerless suburbs, fraught sandwich lunches in chill, airless cabin offices, two weeks of interviews with Barry's dim, know-nothing myrmidons. Financially, everything is much as I anticipated: horrendous overdrafts at the bank, implacable creditors, the whole sustained by ad hoc capital injections from the chairman's purse. There are wads of unpaid bills in duplicate and triplicate in Barry's office going back three or four months. The administration took me half-an-hour to elucidate. A tense twenty-four-year-old named Darren, who goes under the title of

Club Secretary, sits in an office down the corridor signing cheques and not picking up his phone; there are a brace of secretaries who alternate duty in the main office, and a promotions manager, as yet unseen, currently on extended sick-leave. Mower makes occasional grandiloquent appearances, sweeping in after lunch in the company of gnarled acquaintances with names like Lennie and Maurice, stopping by in the early evening to check the mail before proceeding to dinner in town. The playing staff – unhealthy-looking twenty-year-olds with shoulder-length hair, grim, older men with picturesque ailments – inhabit a warren somewhere under the grandstand or, more usually, are confined to the training ground a couple of miles away in Greenford.

What else to say? The profit and loss account exhibits the same ominous disparity as Terry said it would. There are about twenty-five professionals on the books, some of them, such as Jimmy Hood and a character called Neil Paragon at present sidelined with a long-term knee injury, on as much as twenty thousand a year, others allowed an humiliating fraction of this amount. A handful of apprentices don't seem to be paid anything at all. The weekly wage bill, what with Ernie Bright the manager, his two sidekicks and a number of hangers on of indeterminate status, is around forty thousand pounds. Set against this are the gate receipts, an infinitesimal sum of League TV revenue (the Squirrels were last on TV in 1985) and a few derisory kit sponsorship deals. At a rough calculation I'd say they were losing a million a year.

Back on the pitch a kind of mêlée has broken out above the inert form of a Walham defender, requiring the muscular intervention of both linesmen. The referee, menaced by two burly opposition forwards, blows for a free kick. Around me the cognoscenti of the grandstand – old guys in overcoats smoking hand-rolled cigarettes, a few balding creatures with pre-teenage children – stir and whinny. 'He's a fucking *cunt* that ref,' an eight-year-old three seats away comments conversationally to his father. Twenty-five minutes left. The rain is diminishing in volume now, just a few drops gliding gently downwards on the far side of the ground. Twenty yards below, Ernie Bright and his assistants have left the shelter of their

108

dug-out and are standing on the touchline exchanging sema-phore messages with various of their charges, while the second Walham substitute, a monstrous defender named Rickie Weller, stares seriously out into the distance.

In the lull before the game restarts I take another look at *News From The Dray*, a principal source of my intelligence-gathering here. *News From The Dray* ('A must for Squirrels fans') is an extraordinary production. For a start, Barry Mower's personality infects it like a kind of distemper. There are pictures of him everywhere: leering up from the inside cover together with a couple of bosomy charmers in swimsuits, handing out raffle prizes to crowing pensioners, gazing levelly from above a column in which 'Chairman Barry Mower takes a hard look at the new offside rule controversy and asks: could a fourth division club ever make it to Europe?' Ernie Bright's 'Manager's Notes', meanwhile, can be found towards the back, next to the 14-clue crossword ('Ground where finals are held (7)') and an appeal for kit sponsors. Elsewhere, however, freed from Barry's constricting embrace, the tone is determinedly downhome. A 'Captain's Logbook', garnished with the frail signature of Ashley Flack, candidly tackles the question of the team's consistent loss of form by way of a match-by-match analysis *(Rochdale (A) 1-4: One of the worst defeats I remember in my time at the club. A big thank-you though to those supporters who made it there to cheer us on)* and supplies uplifting despatches from the field hospital of broken limbs and groin strains *(Andy has now resumed light training, but it will be some time before we see him back at peak fitness)*. Then there is the inspirational 'Great Walham Victories' series, invariably topped by a black-and-white photograph from thirty years ago and a caption reading: *The Scunthorpe game also brought a fine performance from legendary right back Tosh Mulligan. Regrettably this was one of Tosh's last performances for the club as his career was ended shortly afterwards by permanent injury.*

Beyond, the quiet sussuration of noise rises suddenly to crescendo as Jimmy Hood, dispossessed on the edge of his own area, chases back after his challenger, clatters purposefully into him and falls over. The ball bobs clear, evades a scything

109

interception from a defender, is flicked up by a person or persons unknown, lingers for a long time in the empty air above a forest of periscoping heads and then descends gently into the back of the Walham net. Immediately the proceedings take on the outlines of some elemental tableau: virtue, represented by the triumphant opposition forward, arms upraised, borne aloft by his exulting team-mates; injured innocence, conveyed by the Walham goalkeeper dejectedly fishing the ball out of the net; wounded pride in the form of Jimmy Hood, who lies in torment near the penalty spot with his head in his hands. From the terrace a deep, angry ululation rises to quell the lesser protests: *Jimmy Hood is a homosexual, Jimmy Hood is a . . .* Amazingly, for reasons I can't begin to fathom, the goal gets disallowed.

Already, you see, I am learning the language of the game, even now I have some faint grasp of what the college kids back home would call its semiotics. The semiotics of football, so far as I can deduce, consist on the one hand of wild hyperbole – 'That kid'll play for England' (of a minimally competent trainee) – on the other, an equally lavish understatement. In Mower-speak 'Got a few money worries' translates into 'bankrupt'; 'taken a bit of a knock' means out for the rest of the season. Or perhaps this is not so much the difference between hyperbole and understatement as the difference between public and private discourse. One of the truly startling things at Walham, for example, is how much everyone hates the players. Trevor the groundsman won't have them in his hut, the pert assistants toss their heads if some mohawk from the lower depths so much as passes them on the stairs, while Barry shakes his head sadly over their want of finesse. 'They're good lads, Scott, but they've got no education. I mean, some of those apprentices, they leave school at sixteen, they can barely sign their names. You wouldn't believe it. Was a kid in here the other day signing schoolboy forms, had to have the contract explained to him clause by clause.'

The game is slowing down now, quietly fading away into late-period stupor. There are long periods of what is known as 'possession football', which involves someone conducting the ball over towards the corner flag, shielding it with his body and then awaiting developments. Players in the midfield, excluded

110

from these stalemates in distant parts of the terrain, jog diffidently up and down, rubbing their hands against the cold. Jimmy Hood stoops to retie an errant shoelace with calm, unhurried twists, one eye cocked to the ebb and flow. Jimmy Hood. Age 29. 'A popular and respected member of the first team squad, now in his 10th season at The Dray . . .' Happily I have acquired another source of information about Walham, quite apart from Barry's distortions and the monomania of the programme notes, a fat volume entitled *Walham's Glory Years*. Privately printed, dedicated to 'the illustrious memory of Archibald 'Tusker' Holloway', this is a lavish enterprise, complete with an introduction by Jimmy Satterthwaite, 'the only Walham player in modern times later to represent his country'. Most of *Walham's Glory Years* is given over to quaint accounts of the cup run games – *As the final whistle loomed, tragedy struck the Walham defence which had endured for so long. With goalkeeping stalwart Derek Strangeways the victim of a broken collarbone, it was left to his valiant team-mates to stem the tide* – along with endless, brooding facsimiles of Tusker Holloway in the manager's dug-out. In one shot a small boy is pictured asking for his autograph. Tusker looms over him like some gaunt, rapacious child molester. In another he stands alone on the margins of the pitch, remote and preoccupied, trilby hat tipped back above death's-head skull, teeth bared. Behind him crowded terraces rise steeply to the pale sky. There is even a picture taken a few moments before his death, in which he shakes hands with an anxious-looking official. Grim, with wispy legs protruding from outsize shorts, he seems wholly resigned. Later there are potted biographies of the 'Walham stars':

Les Parrott b.1946. An inventive and reliable full back, Les joined the Squirrels from non-league Kidderminster Harriers in 1967 and immediately established himself in Reg Simmonds' promotion-chasing squad. At this time there was talk of a Welsh cap for The Dray's talented crowd-pleaser born in Llanfair Talhaiarn. Sadly it was not to be, and after several seasons at right back partnering the legendary Billy Strivvens, Les departed to wear the player-manager's shirt at

Kettering Town. Les's current whereabouts are unknown. When last heard of he was working as an insurance salesman in the West Midlands.

I wonder sometimes about Les Parrott. Is he still alive? Does he enjoy selling insurance in the West Midlands? Will he riffle excitedly through the inside back pages of his tabloid tomorrow morning for the Walham result? Intrigued by these intimations of bygone glory, I once asked Barry about him: 'Nah, I don't remember. Full back was he? Well, there's been a few of them. Late 1960s anyway, wasn't it?' The late 1960s were one of Barry's busy times. He was away on the building sites then, or supervising his tenements in the East End, and he didn't get to see so many matches. Predictably Barry views the old-style reverence of *Walham's Glory Years* and its stern warnings about commercialism and 'the administrative strife that has bedevilled the club in recent years', with wild contempt: 'Silly old sods who tried to buy the ground last time it came up for sale. I had them in my office up in town just before the bid came in, told them if they had a million notes they were welcome to it. Didn't hear a dicky bird after that.'

Two minutes to go now, and the flotsam of the stand – the red-eyed dads with their children, the venerable gents with their roll-ups and their Thermoses – are on the move, drifting out into the gangways, craning back reluctantly over each other's heads or surging on into the gloom of the stairwells. I watch them with the complacent stare of the guy who knows he's going home to a heated apartment and a warm, occupied bed. Behind us Barry glares belligerently through the glass of the executive box, making feints and jabbing motions with his plump little fists. The rain has ceased, gone to fall over Pinner and Harrow, leaving only clear, empty air. I scoop up the programme, secure it in my inner pocket next to the fat wad of US airmail letters, edge sideways past the rows of tip-up seats. The debris of cigarette ends, torn paper and half-eaten burgers twists and turns beneath my shoes.

Walham score in the 90th minute: one of those high, drifting crosses that everybody assumes somebody else is covering. The ball drops into empty space midway between a scandalised goalkeeper and an indifferent defender, twirls off Jimmy Hood's rising forehead and falls over the goal line. I hear the noise from the stairs, a ghostly drumming of feet on concrete, like cavalry moving towards the guns, echoing and re-echoing above my head.

Half-an-hour later, back in the Barry Mower Lounge, the atmosphere is still narrowly exultant. Adrift on a tide of well-wishers, mottled and excitable, Barry is bawling terse instructions at Darren, the Club Secretary: 'Go and get the ref and tell him to come up here. Tell him I'll make it worth his while – well, tell him we'd like to see him then. Other lot are already on the coach? Well tell them they're missing the bleeding party.' Lennie and Maurice, business associates of Barry's from way back, in box suits and kipper ties, stand slightly to one side, regarding him indulgently. Here and there pink complexions and washed, steaming hair betray members of the victorious team.

Smoke rises vertically above the thronged heads. From a TV set secured to a wall bracket a disembodied voice is intoning other results to intermittent cheers. Dismissing Darren with a seigneurial wave, Barry launches into another of his Gatling gun monologues: 'Look on this as a significant victory . . . Proud of the lads, very . . . Start of a new era in a way . . . Plenty of clubs like to be in our position . . . Look at Wrexham . . . Chester . . . Scunthorpe . . .' The silent heads bob respectfully. Even here, though, in a private sanctum, hedged about by cronies and hangers on, there is an edginess about Barry, a kind of inner dishevelment, that pokes up unexpectedly like vertebrae under a sheet. Not long afterwards, with Lennie and Maurice showing no signs of faltering in their pursuit of endlessly fisted trebles, I watch him expounding some abstruse tactical point to the impassive figure of Jimmy Hood. The tone is kindly, if didactic.

'You see, Jimmy, the point about those crosses that Phil sends over is that there's nobody underneath them right? Now if you and Andy were to li . . . li . . . , if you and Andy got together down the right, then . . .'

'That's right boss.'

'Which would mean, if Darryl was doing his usual with the

113

centre back . . . I mean, you'd be straight through wouldn't you?'

'Sure Barry,' Jimmy Hood shrugs incautiously. 'I'll remember that next time.'

Barry's features drop like a stone. 'Mr Mower to you son.'

'I only . . .'

Jimmy Hood slinks away. Barry stares stroppily after him, as if he fears this might be only the first of many assaults on deeply cherished personal protocols. Then, turning neatly on his heel in that characteristic fat man's jink, he catches sight of me through the crowd.

'Nice party, Mr Mower.'

The joke misses its target by a yard. Barry shrugs. 'Load of cunts I never saw before drinking my drink.' He looks more than every like Big Vern: moody, fearful, minatory, the slightest provocation enough to have him extricate a sawn-off shotgun from the folds of his jacket and convert the room into a pile of bloody debris. 'Listen Scott, why don't we . . .' The earlier grievance strays back into his consciousness. ' . . . Fucking substitutes walking around as if they *own the place* . . . Why don't we go back to my office? Go back to my office and have a chat?'

Back in his office there are copies of Barry's porn mags – *Bouncers, Cunning Stunts*, that sort of thing – strewn across the desk, and a tray of fluted champagne glasses. From the window, empty beneath frosty darkness, the pitch looks remote and ghastly, like some deserted moor of legend endlessly traversed by loping behemoths. A few lights wink away in the distance. Here, unexpectedly, Barry's personality undergoes another of its lightning gear changes. Having masqueraded for a moment as an exacting Victorian employer alarmed by an excessive familiarity on the part of the staff, he emerges as a lofty footballing savant, the enlightened chairman anxious to consolidate his achievements through foresight and strategy.

'The right result, but what we want is better resources . . . Jimmy Hood, he's a good lad but . . . not a class player . . . Don't mind how much it costs . . . Important to bring in talent when you need it, not when you can afford it . . .'

I let him run on for a bit. It is impossible, in any case, to

114

establish just how much of this monologue Barry believes. In the past fortnight schemes involving the construction of a new stadium, the purchase of Paul Gascoigne and a Stock Exchange flotation have all been advanced with apparent sincerity.

'A team wants to work as a unit . . . No sense in changing direction because of a couple of poor results . . . Got to have faith . . . Feel like I'm wasting my time sometimes . . .'

Admittedly brief experience has shown me that the 'wasting my time' passage is a good place to interrupt. 'With respect Mr Mower, I appreciate your concern, but I think there are more important things to discuss.'

Barry approves of this deferential but no-nonsense style in his advisers. His face clouds over with florid gravity. Looking at him, framed in the luminous rectangle of the window, flanked by his showbiz knick-knacks – the starlets' good wishes, the Variety Club citations – I get an inkling of the camouflaged redoubt of English culture in which Barry and his kind repose. I've breathed that scent before, rising up off the page of the magazines my father ordered from England, am familiar with its outlines and personalities: the *Carry On* films, the Lulu Show, Dick Emery, stand-up comedians in evening suits – a pungent whiff of late 1960s vulgarity finding outward expression in the banana skin, the pratfall, Sid James's toilet-flush laugh. And behind it, something nastier. Once, early on in our relationship and seeking to verify a few inchoate presumptions, I asked him to tell me an English joke. Barry readily obliged:

'There was this darkie, see, walked into a pub with a parrot sitting on his shoulder and ordered a pint. So the barman says, "Where did you pick that up then?" And the parrot says, "There's hundreds of them in the jungle in Africa."'

There is no precise equivalent to this back home. There is racist humour, of course, the groaning bigot's vocabulary of shines, boogies and coons – and even Sondra, raised in an exemplary tradition of Massachusetts liberalism, used to talk about spades – but nothing with such technical pizzazz. A racist joke as conceived by Dexter or Skip, hunkering down on my parents' porch in the West Virginia sunset, would consist of an exaggerated sniff and a remark to the effect that 'you could

115

smell the wind from Johnston'. There was a small negro community at Johnston.

Barry nods. All right son. So tell me, how much am I losing on this outfit? How much a year, say?'

I take a deep breath. 'You're losing a lot of money Mr Mower. A million. A million two maybe. It depends. There are players' bonuses that probably – I'd take a chance and say definitely – won't come through. Money for scoring goals, or making sure goals don't get scored. That sort of thing. Then there's the dispute with the council over unpaid rates. That could cost you another fifty thousand. Say a million three in a bad year.'

'Football,' Barry solemnly intones. 'I mean, that's what it's about isn't it? Paying for what you believe in. And do you know there are people, there are people right here in this club, think I do it for me. "A million notes a year to stay chairman of some poxy fourth division club" – it's all right son, I'm only joking – "that couldn't win a game if the other sods didn't turn up": that's what I'd like to say to them.'

'It's a lot of money.'

'It's a *fuck* of a lot of money.' Barry smiles unreliably. 'So where's it all going?'

A tricky one. Who can tell, given Darren's vague superintendence of the coffers and the benign lethargy of the chairman, where the money is going? There are secretaries vacationing in Key Largo out of the petty cash for all I know. However, it won't do to tell Barry this.

'Salaries, mostly. There are half-a-dozen of the first team on five hundred pounds a week . . .'

'Bleeding incentive that turned out to be. Go on . . .'

'Then there were the court costs from the time Ashley Flack had that fight in the night-club.'

'That Ashley's fucking *dead* . . .'

'But there are some other . . . discrepancies I'd like your opinion on.'

'Try me son, try me.' For perhaps the first time in the conversation, Barry's air of ceremonious buffoonery is replaced by the glint of shrewdness. 'What discrepancies? If that Darren's been putting his fingers in the till I'll rip his legs off.'

116

'Nothing to do with Darren. At least I *think* it's nothing to do with Darren. Put it this way Mr Mower . . .'

'Barry.'

'Put it this way, Barry. The losses which you're sustaining are in excess of those I'd anticipate from the volume of transactions. Now I need to know where that money's going. Or rather why it's going.'

'Such as?'

Raucous laughter floats up from the corridor and is summarily extinguished. 'Well,' – and for some reason I hesitate before framing the sentence – 'you're spending a lot of money on promotions. Advertising, publicity, that kind of thing. I think this is an area that needs looking into.'

'It's all in the bank statements, isn't it?' Barry sounds bored.

No it isn't all in the bank statements, but this isn't something I can tell Barry, or not now at any rate. 'Let's say there's a certain amount of doubt over the sums expended, and to whom. What sort of promotions has the club been commissioning?'

There is a faint gleam of interest in Barry's otherwise torpid eye. 'You might not think it, Scott, but promotions is real bread and butter for a club like us.' He tells me a bit about the school visits, the ads in *Cunning Stunts*, the phone lines run out of a local radio station, the discount ticket offers for the senior citizens' groups. Smoke from his cigar hovers and eddies around his forehead. Outside the floodlights snap off, one by one, and the pitch slips away into shadow.

'And all this is handled by your promotions manager Mr Wilcox?'

'Stanley? That's right. Got this trouble with his waterworks. Back next week.' Barry stirs restlessly, a gross, truculent manatee rolling in the watery vegetation of the shoreline. 'OK son, that'll do for the moment.' He flicks me another glance from beneath the stage heavy's eyebrows. 'You reckon I could make a profit out of this outfit? You reckon I could make it work?'

Sure, I feel like saying. Halve the playing staff, fire Darren and the other retards and persuade another five thousand people a fortnight to watch the matches. I grin back. 'Well, there are various . . . economies you could institute. Not to

117

mention more efficient administrative procedures. Give me a week.'

Barry nods. 'OK, I'll buy that.' The phone rings, as if on cue, and he cradles it uncomfortably in the curl of fat between ear and collar. 'Yes? No, I've got someone with me just now. No, no one important . . .' He signals desperately. 'Nice to have talked to you, Scott.' Watching him crouched over the receiver, becalmed amid the hilarious paraphernalia, I get a glimpse of something petulant, something permanently unsatisfied by the casual palliatives of money and outsize cars. I pad away through corridors grown empty and tenantless, through the Barry Mower Lounge, deserted now except for the solitary barman stacking glasses, out into the freezing air.

Sometimes, convulsed perhaps by some notably flagrant inanity, I wonder what my parents might have made of Barry Mower. It was not that they lacked the experience necessary to determine what kind of man Barry Mower was, or even that they might have felt somehow embarrassed or ineffectual in his presence – for the West Virginia patios of my childhood abounded in embryo Mowers, in stolid, desperate fatmen with trackless and unfeasible schemes in their heads – merely that they would, I suspect, have been unable to conceal their distaste. At the same time, determining the aspects of Barry Mower's temperament and personality in which this distaste resided would not have been as simple a business as it sounds. My parents were not guileless people. They knew – or it seemed to me, as an observant child, that they knew – that the world contained an irreducible complement of deceit and subterfuge, of sharp operators and wanton liars, and that a certain type of civilised life was perhaps unsustainable without moral evasions of this kind. Though, for example, the old man detested Richard Nixon, he was only mildly discountenanced by Watergate. It was 'what any president would have done', 'what Jack Kennedy would have done', 'what *I* would have done'. This hitching of his own scrupulousness, his own transparent willingness to see all sides in an argument, to flit in conciliatory fashion between opposed or complementary points of view, to condone what seemed to me an indefensible abuse of power,

118

was revealing: it implied that he was wholly devious or wholly naïve.

Neither, though they were themselves subdued and unobtrusive characters, did my parents resent flamboyancy, for my father at least had been hatched into a world – that old, faded, genteel Southern world – which was itself a little larger than life, in which the grotesque, the overblown, the excessive was nearly always assimilated into softer and more familiar patterns of existence. My childhood was littered with family connections who had somehow exceeded the boundaries of acceptable behaviour: rambunctious grand-uncles who had ridden their chargers up the oakwood staircase of the family mansion – the hoof marks still to be seen, thirty years on – distant female cousins, crossed in love, who departed to smoke pipes and, it was thought, cast spells in the solitude of the Tennessee mountains. Such people were there to satisfy an almost primeval yearning for anecdote, for affectionate and nearly mystical reminiscence, rather than to provide a moral lesson.

Still less did my parents disapprove of the material extravagances that, here in West Virginia in this forgotten part of time, necessarily accompanied a flamboyant temperament. They realised – and here it seemed to me that they displayed a quite exemplary and unprecedented maturity – that there is a certain kind of ostentation that means no harm, a certain kind of exhibitionism that proceeds out of naïvety and delight rather than psychosis. In Uncle Waterman, who spurred his horse into the master bedroom (a location from which it could only be removed by means of a winch) and Cousin Eulalie, who was supposed to have sat in a log cabin on Mount Vernon for a quarter of a century crooning over a photograph of her lost love, my father detected not narcissism but the fulfilment of a necessary personal myth.

Undoubtedly, remoteness played its part. Even as a child I had the impression that though Uncle Waterman might have galloped happily enough through family legend, my father would have found his presence in our own front room a piece of desperate effrontery, that a quarter century's sequestered pining might have suited Cousin Eulalie, but would scarcely

119

have done, say, for his own jilted daughter; that in fact these were merely agreeable and mysterious ghosts to be taken or left on a whim, plundered when convenient, bearing no wider relation to our lives. Nevertheless these attitudes were not merely theoretical. Which is to say that my parents were tolerant people – a type less rare than might be imagined among the descendants of old Southern gentry – people who believed very genuinely in such things as human goodness and reciprocated kindnesses, who in their dealings with their fellow citizens expected honesty and fair treatment and were disappointed, though rarely scandalised, when such qualities could not be found. They were the kind of people who hesitated – out of scrupulousness, but also out of politeness – to regard charity or fellow feeling as an entry in a moral ledger. What dismayed them was not malice, or the casual disavowal of some principle that they held dear, but duplicity.

I can remember, from early childhood, an occasion on which my mother was duped out of a few dollars by a fraudulent vacuum cleaner salesman. The sum was unimportant, the demeanour of the salesman so comically unreliable, the fraud so spectacular – a matter of an almost non-existent interior – my mother's behaviour so pitiably ingenuous (so far as I remember she did not even ask the salesman to remove the casings or demonstrate the machine) that it was tempting to write the whole episode off as a huge joke, an event that would translate instantaneously into family history, be brought out and reassembled in a few allusive phrases: 'ten dollars for an empty shell', 'didn't even ask him to switch it on', 'easiest sale that guy had that year'. This, however, my parents resolutely refused to do. In fact they were gravely and shockingly angry, outraged that their good nature had been met with deceit, that what they regarded as a kindly act – my mother admitted that she had bought the machine because she felt sorry for the salesman with his scuffed suit and his flat panhandle accent – had been so slyly disparaged. 'How could he do that?' my mother demanded when the true extent of the deception had been revealed, 'how could a man do a thing like that?', and it was not the grumble of violated propriety but a cry of genuine despair. My father was largely silent, but I sensed that the vacuum cleaner salesman

120

could not have infuriated him more if he had shunted his pick-up into the family Studebaker as it lay in the driveway, insulted Winston Churchill or defecated on the front lawn.

And it was here, I realised, that my parents and Barry Mower would have fallen foul of one another. My father would have been amused by Barry's accent and charmed by the cultural baggage that came strapped across his shoulders, but he would have divined – and divined it instantly and irrevocably – that Barry meant no good. And having established that any dealings with Barry would be compromised by this chronic moral fallibility, he would have regarded him not with contempt – for my father was not a contemptuous man – but with distaste. And distaste was a word that meant something to people of my parents' generation and sensibilities, the understatement somehow confirming its potency. My mother had a *distaste* for Vietnam; my father had a *distaste* for Barry Goldwater, George Wallace and Abbie Hoffman. Transfixed beneath this moral glare, Barry Mower would have scorched, disintegrated and shrivelled away to nothing.

Or would he? Even then, I believe, I could have told my parents that it is impossible to conjure up shame in certain hearts. Even at the time I was confident that could the vacuum cleaner salesman have been returned to the scene of his crime and made to confess his iniquity, he would merely have laughed. My parents were not moral arbiters – I am certain that they saw themselves only as the mundane representatives of pattern humanity – but nevertheless there was about them a detachment that I and, I suspect, the rest of the people they knocked up against found wholly unsettling. They were people who watched TV series in which small-time crooks bumbled cheerfully through careers of petty theft and moral evasion with a kind of fascinated displeasure, unable to believe that folly could be so persistently and uncritically exposed. They were people who believed the stories of life, love and ambition told to them on back porches beneath mellow West Virginia sunsets by people whose own scrupulousness was only approximate. And they were also people – a much more important and wounding extrapolation – who believed, or at any rate did not seriously question, the statements offered to them on TV

121

screens and in newspaper columns by politicians and other professional communicators. And to their children, inevitably and, I presume, dangerously, such integrity was both deeply heartening and deeply suspect. As a child I admired what I took to be my father's moral superiority (though moral superiority was never a quality that my father would have claimed for himself), I appreciated the fact that he differed from certain other fathers who got drunk on Saturday nights at the Stonewall gentleman's club in town and who appeared in church on Sunday mornings red-eyed and restless, or were thrown out of their jobs for pilfering or inertia. But at the same time it occurred to me that this scrupulousness was a form of dissociation, that in unobtrusively separating himself from the bustle and inanity of more random existences, he had somehow separated himself from life. Remembering past connections I invariably picture them in terms of milieu: Sondra posed between her parents, Henry and Myra Greatorex outside the Baptist church in Pittsfield Ma: Danny Hassenblad surveying the Hudson from Balaraj's tower. With my parents, wider context falls away, and there are only figures defined merely by attitude: the two of them standing in the dead centre of the front lawn beneath the twisted trees, remote, preoccupied, aloof; my mother in the kitchen, chestnut hair hoisted up in a bun, brooding over an empty table; frail lives caught for ever in the startling West Virginia light.

There are cabs marshalled on the rank beyond Walham park, but I decide to take the subway. There are things I need to think about. On the seat next to me a newspaper headline scorches up. Another guy got murdered in London last night. Most of the papers have spreads. A merchant banker in his thirties inhabiting a penthouse in the Barbican, pieces of whom were found by his cleaning lady littering the passage in the ghastly dawn. According to the police reports, the links to the West End and the Peckham cases are conclusive; mutilation, limbs arranged in a particular way, and the letters RAM daubed over the adjoining surfaces. Nobody seems very sure what this acronym designates, although the *Sun*, which now has some excitable clairvoyant working on the case, reckons that it stands for Rape and Mayhem. Various theories are boiling up to explain it: S&M sessions getting way out of hand, satanic rites, Manson-style political statement. As usual the current victim is a bachelor. Sober workplace testimony reveals an industrious money god with an eye for the ladies. An ex-girlfriend has penned a tearful column in the *Star* headed HOW COULD THEY DO THIS TO MY SWEET LOVER? The *Independent*, which has its own theory about a vengeful psycho on the loose, carries an editorial lamenting the failure of the government's community care initiatives. Meanwhile the customary tribe of fantasists, ego-junkies and low-key delinquents has presented itself at police stations across the capital to confess.

The first of the things I need to think about is Miranda.

This thing with Miranda is fast becoming, as my compatriots would say, quite a thing: blazing away for a fortnight now and showing no signs of ceasing. At the same time, it seems a mysterious and, for reasons I haven't yet properly assimilated, slightly alarming thing. For a start, I know literally nothing about her. Not strictly true, perhaps – through a mixture of low cunning and persistence I've found out one or two choice items. More accurate to say that none of the things I know about her has been voluntarily disclosed. And these are not brutal, interrogative enquiries, but simple casual questions thrown out in the course of post-coital stupor, or wherever, each met with quite masterly evasion or diffidence. 'Where did you go to college?' 'Oh, back on the West Coast someplace.' 'You have many boyfriends?' 'A few.' 'How long are you intending to be over here?' 'It depends.' 'You have a job?' 'I work in a store.' 'Which store?' 'Oh, up Oxford Street someplace.' Contradictory diffidence, too. Thus far in our conversations, apart from the business of the store, Miranda has claimed to be doing post-graduate work at the LBS, working for a US senator over here on a research trip ('Which senator?' 'Oh, one of the obscure Southern Democrat ones, you wouldn't know.') and modelling clothes for Vivienne Westwood. All this I could take if it were presented tongue-in-cheek, spun out on the 'Why are you so *inquisitive*?' maxim. As it is, such shards of intelligence as she vouchsafes are transparently the first thing that comes into her head. All else is deep, inscrutable throwaway. Like this:

'What's your post-grad course at LBS?'

'Economics.'

'You heard of a professor there called Barrett?'

'I heard of him.'

'Does he teach any of the post-grad courses?'

'Not any of mine.'

All purest corn, incidentally. By chance the LBS frontage appeared on the TV news that night in a story about educational cutbacks, and she didn't even stir: in any case I know some of the guys who teach economics at LBS and there isn't anyone called Barrett. Consequently, the mental dossier that one invariably constructs around each new relationship is in this case simply composed of first-hand observation. I know, for example, that Miranda is five feet eight inches tall and has bobbed, flame-coloured hair. Though I haven't been told, I'd put her age around 28: boy's figure, scant but alluring torso, legs like a pair of scissors. In bed formidable and demanding: out of it aloof and preoccupied. I know she likes taking long, extravagant baths, and I suspect that she likes telephoning people – though I haven't yet found out who – and I presume she likes take-out pizza and Mars Bars, this being practically our sole diet over the past two weeks.

The rest is a catalogue of assumptions, stray hints and allusions woven into a chain of probability, a footprint in the primordial mud painstakingly built up into the mastodon who left it. *Place of origin?* Not too far from the north-eastern seaboard I'd say, but with excursions westward, and the accent is that faintly clipped Kansas meets City sophisticated drawl. I mentioned that I'd been to Chicago once and there was a faint elevation of the head, just enough to indicate that something had stuck. *Knowledge of environment?* Superior. Not in my class, perhaps – who could be? – but superior. She knows about popular TV programmes. She knows about the bar licensing hours, and she can talk with reasonable confidence about the political system. She knows enough about the newspapers to appreciate that you don't scan the *Daily Telegraph* for reasoned left-wing critiques of monetarism or the *Sun* for theatre reviews. *Job?* No firm clues. She goes out a lot – she isn't there if I call home during the day, or if she is doesn't answer the phone – but

124

it isn't to a store. Stores don't let their staff roll out of bed at 10 a.m. The LBS we can safely discount, but if pressed I'd lay my money on something semi-academic. She discusses TV soaps in vaguely structuralist terms – did I hear her calling some low-life in *EastEnders* a 'protagonist signifier'? – so it could be media studies. *General opinions*? Hard to tell. She won't laugh at my jokes about Bush and Quayle. I never heard her express a view about a book or a film. The minor irritations of living in an English city occasionally irk her, but not in the soul-consuming manner of those a week off the plane. *Family*? Not a whisker. None of the 'My father is such an asshole/My father is such a great guy – I love my folks/I hate my folks' badinage that characterises female colloquy. A reference once to a grandfather – parenthetic, non-committal. I was hardly listening at the time. *Interests*? Beats me. Sex. Staring out of the window. She watches gridiron games on the minority channel without being able to identify the players or the teams. A book or two: *Dombey and Son, Middlemarch*. Nothing you could base a psychological assumption on.

But this lack of candour would be less startling if it weren't coming from an American woman, and, more important, an American woman in London. US expatriates in England *talk*. Meeting each other at parties, in galleries or at restaurants they hustle off into corners, trade gossip, snicker about the food and vouchsafe halting facsimiles of upper-class English accents. They invite each other round to their apartments ('I guess Earls Court is a good area, but there's Arabs all over'), make long late-night phonecalls above the bump and grind of the city's traffic and sleep with each other simply for company. Miranda eschews this collective solidarity entirely. I never hear her mention another American's name. Neither – and this is unprecedented in my experience – does she want to talk about our relationship.

The distinguishing mark of American girls, as opposed to English girls or Continental girls, is their chronic absorption in relationships, so much so that you occasionally suspect them of conducting relationships merely for the pleasure of being allowed to talk about them. In retrospect the time spent with Sondra seemed like six months on an analyst's couch. The first night I made it with Henrietta, beneath chaste muslin bedlinen in her apartment at South Kensington, with Domingo crooning respectfully in the background, and the answerphone primed to instruct callers that Henrietta Wriothesey-Taggart was not at present available, scarcely a word was said. Next morning I sent a dozen roses to the joke gentleman publishers in Bedford Square. The day after that I got a thank-you letter written in crisp italic on watermarked notepaper. An American girl would have been on the phone twenty minutes later ('*I'm so glad that we . . . So sorry that I . . . We need to make space for each other . . . Try really hard to work this one out . . .*') and spent the rest of the day calling her friends in Manhattan to tell them about it.

The conversations I have with Miranda about our relationship, on the other hand, go something like this:

'Do you like me?'

'Sure. I like you fine.'

'Do you want to talk about it?'

'Do I want to talk about what?'

'You. Me. Us. Our relationship. How it's shaping up.'

'It shapes up.'

Infrequently – three or four times in a week – she talks about old boyfriends, sad, pitiable characters with names like Brad and Jeff, guys with spectacular hang-ups and complexes, who were, for example, fixated on their mothers or on other guys, or bi-sexual, or non-sexual, who were too macho or too effeminate, who wanted it too often or not often enough. There is a familiar ring to these exhumations of past dalliance, these emotional autopsy rooms streaked with gore and splayed limbs, the thought of late-night American TV: '*Was the time when he started dressing up in leather that I began to realise . . . Decided that I ought to make a commitment . . . A kind of old-fashioned person about these things . . . Guess he reacted negatively to that . . .*' Curiously I like her best at these times – self-absorbed, intent, pitilessly anatomising Brad's search for a mother substitute or Jeff's inability to pass his librarianship exams; a recognisable and consoling scent.

A couple of nights ago, taking care to wait until she was in the tub with the door closed, I ransacked her vanity case. If I was expecting a Pentagon ID card or a CIA name-tag I didn't find them, but I turned up one or two things. Most of them were routine – a couple of rolls of contraceptive pills, a bottle of Tuinol on a three-month-old prescription, a clasp of old subway tickets and cab checks – but there were a handful of eyebrow-raisers. Her name, supposedly is Miranda Hudson, but there's a postcard from Paris, courtesy of someone called John, mailed to someone called Abbie Chambers at an address in Notting Hill. Abbie Chambers, too, is the name on a London Library card that falls out on to the floor during this sifting process. Of course, Abbie Chambers might be some close personal friend who lets out her correspondence and her library cards. (Henrietta's reticule, I should add, is awash with other people's business cards, and multi-addressee letters from friends in Gstaad with weird little addendums for 'Hetta'.) Of Amex cards, bank books, IDs – anything truly incriminating – there is no sign. Hearing the noise of sharp, vigorous towelling from the bathroom I junked everything back in the bag and replaced it on the davenport, but the name Abbie Chambers stuck in my head.

The second thing I need to think about is my father, a subject that, like Miranda, is growing steadily less ignorable. After a week or so of leaving telephone messages – some from freeway diners or clamorous pharmacies, others from more muted environments such as guest-house reception areas or motel bedrooms – the old man finally got round to writing a letter. It arrived yesterday, postmarked Wheaton Illinois, which I wondered about until I recollected that a distant Marshall cousin had retired that way, a voluminous document, extending to six closely-written pages and providing in effect a chronicle of his life in the seventeen or so years since he and my mother had parted company. Most of this is familiar – the mobile home excursions on the Snowbird run, the loan bank crash, Elizabeth Schenectady, Barbara-Jean and the scuba instructor. There are other bits – the wine-growing in California, the religious jag – that no one had ever told me about. The final paragraph, though, is unambiguous. He's coming over here and he wants to see me, or rather he wants to see me and he's coming over here. There are flights booked for early in the new year.

What do I think about this? I don't know. I haven't seen him for seven years and I just don't know. Why now? Why the six-page recapitulation of his life and times? There was a weird side to the old man, a side of fierce, ungovernable whims, that when we were teenagers had manifested itself in cheek-igniting birthday presents – a package containing seven pairs of scratch 'n' sniff strawberry flavour split-crotch panties for Jeannie, a gross of hard-rider condoms for Greg. In search of answers to these and other questions I called Greg in Montana. Two calls got a ponderous answerphone, but on the third he picked up.

'Greg. It's Scott. You busy?'

'Sure I'm busy.' Greg's voice sounds infinitely remote and disconnected. 'What do you want?'

I explain about the week of phone messages and the letter. Greg whistles. 'Uh huh. I don't know. Maybe he's serious. Didn't sound like it, though, when he last called me.'

'When was that?'

'A week . . . Two weeks back. Back then it was still Barbara-Jean and the scuba instructor – she's not coming back by the way. Plus, you heard he was ill?'

'What with?'

'He won't say. Well, not properly. Henry – Henry was the distant cousin in Illinois – reckoned it was something to do with his chest. Said he had to go for an X-ray someplace, take a lung-function test.'

'Serious?'

'How serious is serious? He was OK when I spoke to him.'

Throughout our conversation I can visualise Greg sitting there in the pinewood chair in his upstairs workroom, smirking beneath his fake rancher's tan, plaid shirt rolled up to the elbows; beyond, the lip of the unravelling desert.

'OK. You have a phone number?'

'Do I fuck. He was staying with Henry last I heard, but that was a fortnight back.'

'Uh huh . . . How's business?'

'We thought Ted Turner was going to make an offer on a plot along the ridge but he pulled out.'

'Uh huh. And Mindy?'

There is one of those anguished pauses familiar to all who pursue such enquiries with Greg. 'I'm afraid that Mindy and I are no longer together Scott . . .'

'That's too bad. Hey, what's happening outside?'

Greg cheers up on the instant. 'You wouldn't believe it,' he says proudly. 'A fucking *timberwolf* just headed on up the trail. We're supposed to waste them on account of the cattle, but, shit, I just let the critter go.'

The third thing I need to think about, quaintly enough, is Barry Mower. I do this for half a minute or so with my back wedged sideways against the armrest as the tube rushes eastward towards Hammersmith, and graffiti shines palely off the tunnel wall. My need to think about Barry Mower stems from a conviction that I have not, in my recent dealings with him, been entirely honest. Nothing new in this of course. Management consultants are rarely honest with their clients. Slater and I once got called in to advise a clothing company, the decision of whose East End workforce to strike had coincided with the bankruptcy of its distributor. We spent four weeks in there at £200 an hour scrawling out reports on process improvement strategies and logistics management before the bank foreclosed on them, and even then Slater had contrived to get his bills settled in advance. After which he advised the extended family of harassed Bengalis who constituted the company's technical staff that their wiliest response would be a management buy-out, introduced them to the firm's corporate finance arm, watched Barclays lend them £5 million and KLS run up a six-figure adviser fee. You couldn't do it now, and you could scarcely do it then. As it was Slater emerged unscathed from the deliberations of the Institute's ethics committee, but then he is rather a genius in his way.

So I hadn't been quite straight with Barry, more out of genuine uncertainty than prospective self-aggrandisement. The financial situation is much as I outlined it: fifty or sixty thousand a week going down the can in wages, overheads, kit and so on; the shortfall generally, if not consistently, made up out of Barry's current account. Darren, the Club Secretary, takes his orders from Barry and wouldn't sign the tab for a six-pack without authorisation. However, even my limited experience proposes that fifty or sixty thousand a week is too much. Way too much in fact. In particular, Walham are spending thousands of pounds a week on what the books vaguely call 'promotions'. Darren's being shifty or plain incompetent about letting me view them all but in September, for example, they spent three thousand on a series of ads on West London radio stations, sponsored a 'Community sports day' on Ealing Common and paid for a junior basketball team to go on a tour of Bulgaria. The Bulgarian trip seemed so flagrantly disinterested that I asked Barry about it.

'Five K to send a teenage basketball team to Varna for a week. That's a lot of money.'

'That Bulgarian thing?' Barry's face assumed a look of pious conviction. 'Ah, that's just me being soft that is. Approved school down Northfields way they are. Can't get the sponsorship. So I says to their headmaster, dress them up in black and white shirts and take a couple of Squirrel mascots with you and the money's yours.'

'Any other benefits?'

'Mention in the local paper,' Barry said stiffly. 'What more do you want?'

A commendable gesture, no doubt. Anxious for a third party opinion, I put in a call to Terry Long at KLS. He sounded more chipper than of late.

'Terry. How's things?'

'Scott! OK mate. Can't complain.'

'Still in one piece?'

'They found us a leisure and amenity study for some London borough that wants to blow its budget before the end of the tax year. The trick is deciding if we can get away with recommending a marina complex or just leave it as an ice-rink.'

Those leisure and amenity studies. As a mid-level consultant in the early days, grandiloquently inducted beneath Slater's wing, I was put to work on leisure and amenity studies. East End councils, awash with tenement blocks and arterial roads, loved them for some reason. A brief inspection of the site – arid municipal parklands, grim sports grounds, the uncompromising ooze of Thames tributaries – would be followed by a report advocating a tourist trail. Patches of waste ground became nine-hole golf courses in our perfervid imaginations; threadbare libraries gamely metamorphosed into museums of local culture. Slater, so far as I remember, once canvassed a scheme to convert an area off the Bow Road into a kind of East End theme park with pearly kings, pubs doing cockney knees ups and courses on how to talk rhyming slang. Nothing ever happened.

'. . . About Walham is it, mate? I see things are looking up at last.'

'The third round of the Rumbelows Cup is looking up?'

'Seriously Scott. If they win, and get a home tie in the next round to a big club. They'll get pulverised of course, but the gate receipts and the TV money will be worth sixty, seventy thousand.'

I tell him a bit about the promotions money, Barry Mower, Darren and the cheques. Terry clicks his tongue over the wire.

'You think there's anything there?'

'I don't know Scott. The basketball thing . . . Well, let's be charitable and take it at face value. I suppose you could just about justify the radio ads . . . Is there any pattern to it?'

'What sort of pattern?'

'Any particular line they keep plugging? Are they buying space in newspapers? Throwing kit away to the local schools? Actually I wouldn't worry about the details, Scott, there's definitely something going on.'

'Too much money going out?'

'Way too much. Think about it. You're a small club with a smallish catchment area. People don't come and watch you. But it's not that they don't come and watch you because they don't know you're there. They don't come and watch you because you aren't any good. What use is a run of radio ads? "Come and see Walham Town and watch some exciting football." Everyone knows it's going to be crappy football played by a bunch of people nobody else would have, so why bother?'

Why indeed?

Fulham Broadway is near-deserted: a few late-night delinquents shuffle by in the shadows. I open the apartment door to the blare of amplified TV. Miranda comes through the lounge smoking a cigarette, something I haven't seen her do before. The accumulation of primary colours – red shirt, yellow surfaces, the royal blue of the carpet – is faintly disturbing.

'Good day?'

'So so. Any messages?'

'Some girl called Henrietta a couple of times. I said you were out.'

There are more airmail letters strewn over the floor. I scoop them up and pinion them across my torso in a fan. Miranda stares back. The noise of the TV crashes around us.

Later, poised expertly above her in blueblack darkness, I ask: 'Who's Abbie Chambers?'

'What?'

'I just wondered.'

'You ask too many questions.'

'It's a habit.'

'I'll tell you if you want.'

'Ok then.'

The light flicks on. 'She just a girlfriend, Scott. Just some fucking girlfriend OK? Like fucking Henrietta I suppose. Just some fucking girlfriend OK?'

There is silence for a bit. Then the light flicks off.

Everywhere things are changing. Within and around. I haven't seen Henrietta for a fortnight, or Jenny, or Penny, or any of the others. I haven't been inside the Mirabelle either, or the 301, or Lefanu's. They leave messages on the answerphone sometimes, haughty, low-key messages that I don't return until such time as I know that they won't be there. I still figure on going to Henrietta's party though, maybe even with Miranda. The weird thing is that Henrietta probably wouldn't mind. For all their vague, companionable humour, Henrietta and her kind lead callous, desensitised public lives. I once ended up at a dinner party in the midst of a quartet of solid middle-aged Englishry consisting of a man whose wife had left him, the wife, the wife's best friend, allegedly the cause of the separation, and the wife's best friend's husband, supposedly enamoured of the wife, and they spent the evening talking about sailing. But would Miranda like it? I don't know. As yet I don't know very much about what Miranda likes.

Everywhere old habits are dying down while new ones are coaxed into life. For some reason the eating thing is becoming less of a problem. I noticed this last week when I realised that I'd eaten a pizza without being aware that I'd eaten it.

132

Emboldened, I strolled into a restaurant in Walham High Street a day or two after and strolled out again an hour-and-a-half later having consumed a dish of whitebait, steak tartare with French fries and two helpings of Mrs McCallingham's olde English apple pie. It's quite something, this food thing. It reminds me, in a warm though mercilessly elegiac way, of winter afternoons in the loft overlooking the Hudson when, with Sondra out on one of the analyst's jobs she did to fill in time between assignments, driven by some unguessable hormonal frenzy, I would negotiate my way through, say, two packs of See's chocolates, a quart of loganberry sundae and much else that was neither nourishing nor sustaining. Yesterday I even found myself thinking, not uninterestedly, of what I might be having to eat later that night.

Somehow, out there, the pulse is quickening. Somehow the noise from beyond the window is a little more restive. There are streets full of houses down in Docklands that they couldn't give away, and the smart money is leaving town, going to Tokyo or Geneva or Frankfurt. Boom-time is over, and so, mysteriously, is Mrs Thatcher. I haven't checked out the guy who's replaced her, but nobody seems to know much about him. What my compatriots will make of this I can only surmise. It is not uncommon back home to meet people who think that Mrs Thatcher actually rules Great Britain. The Queen they regard as a faintly sinister feudal appendage: the real action is in Downing Street. Actually I watched Mrs Thatcher on the TV conceding defeat and the light was suddenly weirdly overemphasised, the faces curled and awful, blinking out into cancelled futures, the whole spectacle unreal, like some age-old landmark crashing down into dust and debris, like – to give it a McLuhanesque transatlantic context – Elvis dying.

I eat. I listen for the phone. I watch the silent screen. Wondering all the while what will happen next.

8

How Barry does it

A beguiling but manifestly insoluble question is: how do Barry Mower and his kind do it? Where did they come from, this race of troglodyte and slightly sinister fat men with their flamboyant suits and uncouth table manners? Or were they always there? Back home sometimes, out on the margins of my parents' social world, I have encountered transatlantic versions of Barry Mower: third-generation fall-out from freebooting dynasties that had started out marketing bath-tub gin during prohibition or sold fatigue pants made of ersatz cloth to the Government in the 1917 panic. The dynastic element was important: it gave context, pattern, connection. Invariably when some emulous Bart or Homer brought a scented soap baron or patent pill magnate – some cousin, usually, or elk confrère – to stand for an hour or so on the dappled West Virginia lawns under the wavering cypress trees, you could descry a trail leading back through dense undergrowth to a speakeasy or a whisky still, to some hoary grandparent who'd sent backhanders to Hoover or supplied synthetic vodka to Tammany Hall.

Here, so far as I can tell, the catalyst was the 1960s. Raised in some joyless suburb – their old men ran pubs or worked as news vendors, and they made their first money out of misappropriated stock – Barry and Lennie and Maurice and the others arrived in the capital at the time of the municipal property boom. Barry talks about it sometimes, scarcely able to believe his luck even now, a quarter of a century on: 'Incredible really. I mean, LCC developments down in the East End. Old bombsites down in Poplar and Shoreditch where the council was putting up flats and that. Lennie must have made half a million quid out of a fittings scam. Doing up houses at a hundred quid a time and he was getting the materials for six and seven. Me and Maurice, we were into electrics. Fit a block of flats with duff circuits, say, and fix a maintenance deal with the council. It's always buggered, and they're always having to call you in, but if there's any trouble, well, you just blame your suppliers.' Lennie and Maurice turn up in the Barry Mower Lounge sometimes after matches: great sweating hoodlums with faces carved out of teak. They belong to a category of Englishman with whom I remain grossly unfamiliar: the entrepreneur of humble origins, the self-made thug. Each list in their conversation, each nervous social gambit – Lennie's signed photographs of Mrs Thatcher, Maurice's memories of his days as mayor of Walthamstow – still has the capacity to startle. Traces of their early triumphs linger perilously. Barry still owns a couple of mansion blocks in Kensington where the trashcans lie unemptied for weeks, cockroaches swarm in the hall and shellshocked old dowagers are charged two thousand a year for porterage.

In the 1970s, of course, they diversified. The public funds that built the towerblocks were exhausted now, and Lennie's uncle, an East End Labour mayor, was out on a corruption charge, but there was always space for people with money who didn't mind getting their hands dirty. They went into import/export from crowded hangars on south-coast airfields; they managed dog tracks. In the guise of suavely publicised credit companies, they lent money to prospective homeowners and clawed its fabulous interest payments back by way of County Court writs and personal visits. In the mid 1970s, chancing his arm in a spare and exhausted marketplace, Barry even backed some films: *Barbiecutie, Manhunter* and so on. But whatever career he might fondly have envisaged as an impresario vanished after a solitary morning filming *The Great Rock 'n' Roll Swindle* at Shepperton ('I'm not going to tell you what happened, Scott, but you can take it from me they were raving nutters, the lot of them.') Barry belongs to an older world, alas, that measures out success in suits and pneumatic girlfriends.

Such activities were and are, everybody is at very great pains to stress, narrowly legitimate. Barry's always kept his nose clean, right back to the old Hillingdon days ordering up the supplies in his dad's pub; Maurice's brother-in-law works in CID anyway; Lennie once spent three months in Pentonville on a fraudulent trading rap, but everybody knew it was the company secretary's fault. (What happened to the company secretary? Ah, nobody knows.) Barry explained it to me once: 'I don't want no trouble with the law, son, and they don't want no trouble with me. England's a small country, Scott. Say I started bringing in hardcore mags on the Continental run. Ten to one some Customs nark at Gatwick says to himself, 'That's Barry Mower. Reckon I'll just have a squint inside this crate.' And then where are you? Up the Bailey on an intention to deprave and corrupt charge and paying some poncey lawyer five grand a day, that's where you are, and I don't need that at my age. Load of filth it is anyway . . .'

It is here in these incidental remarks that the enigma of Barry and his *convives* resides. For guys whose living is made through the exploitation of human frailty, they are ominously indifferent to its symptoms. You might expect a guy who runs a finance company to approve of credit or a guy who prints pornographic magazines to approve of promiscuity: in each case you'd be wrong. No, Barry, Lennie and Maurice might make money out of degeneracy but they don't *like* it. Barry on mortgages: 'Living on tick never got no one nowhere.' On some televised sex romp: 'Disgusting rubbish. Someone ought to ban it.' On teenage pregnancy stats: 'Makes me sick down to my stomach. Some little girl who ought to be tucked up in bed with her teddy bear.' At first I assumed that this stolid refusal to examine deeply held convictions about personal behaviour in the light of what he did for a living was simple hypocrisy – like a preacher connection of my father's who, famously, used to declaim sermons against adultery before driving to the home of his sister-in-law to commit it. It took me some time to establish that Barry genuinely saw no link between the piled copies of *Girl Crazy*, and the trumpery rubbish he unloaded on supermarkets in the guise of kids' toys and his choicer remarks about private morality. For Barry and his kind 'business' existed in some remote, hermetically-sealed container on the ocean floor: no seepage would ever be allowed to foul the surrounding water.

The fundamental question remains: how does Barry do it? And how does he get away with it? Notoriously, money in

England hides behind palisades; it sits tight beyond high walls in Belgravia; it goes on discreet outings to grouse moors north of the Trent. It doesn't career down Walham High Street in a Jag wearing a suit that no person of taste would consent to be cremated in. The States are awash with butterball millionaires, lunkhead Republican hayseeds from Wisconsin or Idaho who've made a fortune out of real estate or patented a new kind of suspender fastener, flailing across golf courses and gorging half-pounders in the window of Fatburger, and no one gives them a second glance. In England money still arrives in a Savile Row suit with Mrs Money, splendiferous teeth and pearl choker, hanging on its arm. Discovering Barry, Maurice and Lennie – the bare, level plain suddenly descending into a lost world of circling pterodactyls – was disconcerting. They were not even – and this was a category anyone in the States who kept his finger on the money pulse through the 1980s knew of and venerated – Thatcher's entrepreneurs. I knew about Thatcher's entrepreneurs. They had MBA degrees, plundered the money market or made a fortune in hi-tech. Barry Mower and his friends lend people money at extortionate rates of interest or sell them rubbish.

The City loves them, of course. KLS, I have since discovered, is wildly enamoured of Barry Mower. There are two audit partners back in Blackfriars do nothing but sell him add-on services, and the tax department makes £30,000 a year fighting the VAT inspector on his behalf or devising PRP schemes for the surly teenagers who pack his porn mags. The City loves Barry because it feels safe with him. He's not in property, so he won't go bust owing them hundreds of thousands: he prints magazines with authenticated circulations, and he lends people money at stated rates of interest with cast-iron guarantees. Farq and Quoodle love safe money. But this doesn't stop them regarding Barry as a throwback, a delicious atavism. Briefly, Barry is one of those people who have money but don't know what to do with it. Muddling around with football clubs; buying up restaurant franchises at the dogs – that isn't where the smart money goes, not any more, if it ever did. Barry and Co. get their share of the social rewards associated with money – they're allowed to join Masonic lodges, and Barry even sits on the council of a livery company, some stockbroker pal might slip them a couple of Centre Court tickets. But that's as far as it goes. You won't see Barry at Ascot, or on the Sovereign's lawn at Cowes, or leering at you out of the *Tatler*. He was on TV the other day, guesting on one of those afternoon talkshows, in a kipper tie and one of his suits, looking as stylised and as out of place as a pearly king or a morris dancer and sending the other guests into skirls of laughter every time he said 'pardon' or called the female presenter 'darling'. Barry's park, his pleasaunce, where he felt at home, was a picture-postcard landscape of wide-assed women and cheery vulgarity, stack-heeled shoes and mini-skirts. Poor Barry! He knew Tony Hancock once, back in the days of Goldwater and Kennedy, and he had a seat at Wembley for the 1966 World Cup Final. But these are ghost dances in the old, dead world.

9

Real nice gal

'Anyway, by the time the chairman asked if there was any other business, the guy was practically foaming at the mouth, all right?'

'And then what happened?'

'Well the first thing he does is to tell John Birningside to fuck off. Not nonchalant like but, you know, *fuck off*. And then – get this Scott – he starts throwing the 1991 brochures we'd been looking at on the floor.'

'He was definitely tearing them apart?'

'I was round the far side of the table so I didn't get to see, but, yeah, they were in pieces . . . And then finally, just as someone was phoning for security, he falls over a chair and bangs his head on a crate of Perrier bottles.'

'It sounds terrible.'

Slater pauses dramatically. 'That's *exactly* what it was. Terrible. And what makes it worse is that he was a friend of mine. Much worse.'

The news of Devoto's collapse, though not unexpected, had achieved wide circulation. Coming as it did in public, at the end of the management council meeting and involving a range of insult and gesture, the event had seized the imagination of the KLS staff to the extent that half-a-dozen versions competed for precedence. Among other exploits Devoto was supposed to have head-butted the managing partner, assaulted a waitress and sent faxes of his genitalia to several blue-chip clients. The truth, as I now discover, is more prosaic.

'What happened to him?'

'Jack? He's in a nursing home down near Brighton. On indefinite leave. Which between you and me means under sedation until they work out what to do with him.'

Hands clenched, face strangely contorted, Slater is clearly in the grip of some violent emotion. I haven't seen him so moved since the occasion when a fellow partner with whom he enjoyed chronically strained relations had been arrested in the KLS foyer in what, as it later turned out, was a case of mistaken identity. I listen idly as he carries on talking in a desultory way: 'And after he'd been cleared out of the meeting they went back to his room, and you're not going to believe this Scott but there were all these proposals for jobs which we hadn't actually been asked to offer for . . . I mean, he'd been quietly going bananas for weeks and none of us had noticed . . .'

Outside traffic lurches over the bridge towards the City. Things have been happening here in the fortnight or so of my absence. Oh yes. For a start, last week they sacked another hundred consultants – a fact of which Slater has not so far chosen to apprise me – and these weren't retards hired to do the filing but senior guys, executive consultants and above. People like me in fact. Plus there was a story in the *Age*, about another firm trying to buy out the whole of the consultancy practice. I fix Slater with a wide-eyed grin.

'So how are things?'

'Things are bad.' On the desk the phone rings twice and then falls silent. Slater stares at it angrily. 'I keep transferring this through to some secretary and it still won't bloody . . . You know we lost the Sudebank job?'

'No?'

'It wasn't their fault. Well, not really. Some spick back in Buenos Aires decided to pull the plug on consultancy work. Plus Torrington Construction's blown up again.'

Torrington Construction was a defunct insolvency client dating back to the early 1980s whose directors, careful scrutiny disclosed, had misappropriated the pension fund. Unhappily the sums recovered from this embezzlement had proved to be substantially less than the seven-figure fee charged to the creditor bank by the KLS receiver, a legendarily rapacious partner name Sammy Baldwin.

'Can't Birningside use his tame M.P.?'

'It's too late for that. Way too late. Sammy's up before the House of Commons social services committee tomorrow morning. Plus there's supposed to be a pensioners' lobby of

Parliament this afternoon. We should be all right though,' Slater ventures doubtfully.

Though fretful and a little subdued, Slater seems unabashed by these revelations. In fact, knowing him as I do, I'd say he was definitely up to something. I don't quite know what, but something. There are a few more despatches from the consultancy battlefront – late-night boozing sessions with Farq and Quoodle, from whom Slater currently seems to be inseparable, and the executive manager who on being informed of his dismissal burst into tears and insisted on showing Slater photos of his wife and children, before we come, finally, to the matter in hand.

'So. Walham Town. Barry Mower. Where are we Scott?'

Where are we? Deferentially I chronicle a few of my researches into the tangled labyrinths of SquirrelCorp, which is the name Barry operates Walham under, its frequent dealings with Dray Holdings, through which the bail-out money is channelled, and its precarious relationship with the two high street banks where Barry keeps current accounts. Slater listens disdainfully.

'Nearly bankrupt and the admin's a disaster. OK, I'll buy that. The question is, is there anything anybody can do about it?'

Through the elliptical window in Slater's door I watch Linda float vaguely down the corridor. Her face is gathered up in an outlandish, beatific smile.

'Short of laying off half the staff and selling one side of the ground off for real estate development, probably not.'

Slater smiles. 'Between you and me, that's where Mower's come unstuck. Forget all the bullshit about lifelong support for the club. When Barry bought it the first thing he figured on doing was to sell it on to some developer he'd hooked up with – you know how Mower made all his money in property. Only then the bottom starts falling out of property and he finds out there's an old shed round the side which the council's only gone and put a preservation order on, haven't they?'

Naïve incredulity seems the safest response. 'So in fact it's just, what's that phrase you have . . . a white elephant?'

'Pure albino.' Slater taps his fingers carefully together. 'You'd

143

better do a consulting report. You know, stuff about volatile trading environments, scope for economies, diversification opportunities.'

'What diversification opportunities? They're a football club.'

'How the fuck should I know? Say they ought to put a ten-pin bowling alley in there over the summer. Anything that'll make Mower think he hasn't wasted ten grand.'

We nod sagely at each other, a synchronicity of gesture that takes me four years and three thousand miles back across the Atlantic to the memory of Danny Hassenblad plotting to unload some defective software on an over-trustful client.

'Hey,' Slater demands. 'What do you reckon about the RAM murders?'

That's what they're calling them now, by the way, even the proper newspapers. No more victims have been added to the original roster of three – but the paraphernalia of blood, mutilation and daubed insignia continues to inflame the media. Current opinion inclines towards a female psycho – favoured career that of ex-hooker – probably on a religious jag. No one has yet established what RAM means.

'You know what I think?' Slater enquires. 'I think it's a bloke.'

'A guy?'

'Sure. Forget the date-stamper from the tenement. Rich bachelors in penthouse apartments. I'd say it was a faggot blackmailing syndicate.'

'You would?'

'Sure. Or someone with AIDs getting his own back. Some rentboy on the killer trail.'

Slater maunders on in this vein for a moment or two while I stare out of the window. As it happens, he's left his trump card until last.

'Hey,' he says again as I get up to leave. 'Hey there. Something else I meant to tell you. Had Barry Mower on the phone the other day. They've only gone and drawn Liverpool in the Rumbelows. They'll get stuffed, of course, but they'll get some money out of it for once. Anyway, Mower reckons he can't handle the admin, so he wants you to stay on for a fortnight or so.'

144

'That's what he said?'

'*A nice geezer for a Yank*. Those were his exact words. Anyway, I'm putting you on full secondment as of now.'

No point in complaining about this, even if I felt like it. A guy I knew was once despatched on a three-month electricity generating project in a remote Middle Eastern caliphate at twenty minutes' notice. Still, for form's sake I venture a polite enquiry or two about the projects notionally under my supervision.

'The Salford telecoms thing? Forget it. They all got fired a week since. The oil refinery boys came home a fortnight ago. Christ knows what's happened to the lot on the lighthouse, but they haven't rung in. So you needn't think you're missing anything here.'

Back in my office there is dust over the scattered files and mould growing in the neglected coffee cups. Pale, unwelcoming light shines over the ghostly cabinets and the stack of unanswered phone messages. Atop one of the files is a photo of my mother, which I found in a shoebox of Yankee paraphernalia the other night: the only one of her pre-American life I possess, aged around 25, in the company of a couple of grave, tall English guys in military uniform, with slicked back, 1940s movie-star hair. Like the Jefferieses, the Anstruthers and the Borthwicks, I knew nothing about them, who they were, whether they were alive or dead. I light a Marlboro from a half-empty packet on the desk and lean back in my chair, contemplating the mournful surround with deep unease. The Salford telecoms team got fired, and the oil refinery boys came home a fortnight ago, and I'm a nice geezer for a Yank. Indulged by some flaw in the ventilator system, cigarette smoke hangs in the air: I shoo it away with my hand. Wordlessly, Linda moves through the half-open door and hands me a fax. From Piotr in Bratislava, it contains the predictable intelligence that he is now driving a cab.

There are other messages piled up on the desk. Still taking stock, still filing away the information about nice geezers and full-time secondments, I junk them heedlessly into the can. At the same time there are other puzzles that demand elucidation. Glancing out into the computer-fenced secretaries' palisades in the corridor, I deduce that Linda's goofy benevolence is the result of some revolution in her personal life. From the photo frames above the Mac station Grant's fuddled glare has yielded up to a cross, rabbity-looking guy in a bomber jacket. Thinking to explore the turbulent switchback ride that is Linda's emotional career, I lie in wait for her as she swings past on her journey back from the Ladies.

'How's the boyfriend, Linda?'

Absurdly Linda bridles, turns and stares helplessly at the photo. I decide to help out.

'Too bad about Grant, eh Linda? But now you've got someone else huh?'

Nearly all my conversations with Linda demand the use of these queer, rhetorical dog-leads. She beams woodenly again as I hold up another well-worn prompt card.

'And what's this one called?'

'He's called Dalton. He's a . . .' A taxi driver? A shop assistant? A contract killer? ' . .. *A freight forwarder*.'

I think about this for a while, game Dalton forwarding his freight someplace, sending out little parcels, say, from a shack somewhere in Silvertown or Denmark Hill, while Linda dithers coquettishly against the side of a desk.

'OK Linda, who was Neil Armstrong?'

'I don't know.'

'Fair enough. Which one was the Democrat presidential candidate, Al Smith or Al Capone?'

'What you said second.'

She drifts off towards a gaggle of silent accomplices. There is a lunch-time *Evening Standard* lying unclaimed on a chair. I scoop it up, go back to my room and close the door. Sure enough, on the bottom left-hand side of the back page is a headline that reads SQUIRRELS IN CUP DRAMA. I scan it cautiously. 'People can say what they like about our league form,' Barry Mower is quoted as saying, 'but we'll be out to silence the doubters once and for all.'

The cassette tape sits in my inside pocket. It came this morning, with a New Jersey postmark, hand-addressed in my father's rolling scrawl. No message. Remembering it now, I pluck the

146

black rectangle out of my jacket, plunge it into an old, stenographer's dictaphone that lies on the desk. The room is suddenly irradiated by cheerless winter sunshine. I flop down in the chair again and switch it on.

Not much happens for a while, but finally swishes of static are overlaid by a limping acoustic guitar, the whole suddenly drowned out by a jaunty, quavering tenor.

I know a gal, real nice gal, down in Wroxham way
She were wholly nice to me back in the owd school days

A faint gleam of recognition enlarges slowly in my head, like stumbling over a twenty-year-old photograph and poring, first with mild interest, then with mounting certitude, over the upturned faces. The Singing . . . ? The Singing Cowboy? The Singing Ploughman? The Singing *Postman* . . . By this stage the song has whirled on to its refrain:

Molly Windley, she smoke like a chimbley
But she's moi little nicotine gal.

The Singing Postman was by some way the most outlandish product of my father's obsession with Norfolk. Oddly enough he really was, or had been, a mail delivery man – there were promo shots of him setting out on his rounds on an elderly push-bike, and the peaked, government-issue cap, perched above dense, aquarium spectacles, never left his head. Plaintive, wistful, as sad and self-engrossed as any Country Crooner out of a Nashville rehearsal studio, he sang about following the combines over wheatfields in the tail-end of summer, picking jetsam off the Norfolk beaches, hopeless bucolic love affairs.

Then one day she went away, I don't see her no more
Till one day I see her down along the Mundesley shore . . .

My father must have come across the Singing Postman in the mid 1960s in one of his English magazines, *Titbits* perhaps, or *Country Life*. His sympathies were immediately engaged. The butt-head grin, the gappy teeth, the lofted acoustic guitar. In

147

each of these trademarks my father detected the stylisation that he demanded from Art. He obtained his records by mail-order, listened to them soberly at the kitchen table, an imported Ordnance Survey map of Norfolk to hand to help with the geographical references. The Postman came from somewhere called Sheringham, whose population apparently referred to themselves as 'Shannocks': you got the impression that it was a grim kind of place, fenced in on the cliff-top by wind and rain. But when he sang that he was always thinking of a seaside town and wishing he was there the effect was wholly irresistible: more than comic, less than tragic, a kind of halfway house of suppressed emotion and raw English eccentricity.

Raising the volume slightly so that the dictaphone vibrates on the desk-top, I listen some more. The Postman has moved on to a sedate little number called 'Following the boinder round', which I imagine has something to do with harvesting, full of quaint feudal references to poachers and 'old Squire Knowles'. Why has he sent me this? It must be twenty years since the Singing Postman last strayed into my consciousness. Around 1970 the records dried up and the newspaper references faded away, and though my father sometimes looked out back numbers of the English *Melody Maker*, which a friend of his had on subscription, he never found out what had happened. By this juncture, in any case, my father had other English interests to pursue – pigeon-racing and morris dancing were two fixations from around this time – and so the Singing Postman fell away, slipped out of our collective life until he became nothing more than a handful of EPs in the record rack and the memory of a guy in a peaked cap and wire-rimmed spectacles singing about a girl on a nicotine jag.

Eventually I locate the off button, grab my Burberry, slip out into the corridor. Here silence reigns. Orange light seeps under Slater's door: within, subdued voices fretfully discourse. A couple of junior consultants – wary twenty-five-year-olds from Oxford or Cambridge or wherever – edge silently past. Christmas decorations, fronds of scarlet bunting and green creepers, garnish the secretaries' consoles. Linda has disappeared somewhere. I steal over to her tiny crib, where there are some early Christmas cards – *all the best from Toni*

148

and Jason, Hoping Your's and Dalton's is a good one, love
Maxine – and a stack of women's magazines – *Sophisticate,*
Urban Babe – with brazen shout-lines: HE WANTS TO FILM US . .
. HAVING SEX! WHY SIZE *IS* IMPORTANT. SUCK IT AND SEE – THE
NEW RULES FOR ORAL SEX! Their juxtaposition with the
paraphernalia of Linda's domestic life – a line of Dayglo
hippopotami on the desk-top, a knitting primer and a clutch of
peppermint Aeros – is painfully ironic. But then this is England,
where the contrast between private and public discourse,
between reality and the perception of reality, say, never ceases
to astound. Linda can't speak a sentence or write a line without
gravely offending the lexicon, can't communicate with another
human being without her face contorting in embarrassment,
and yet, seated demurely at her desk, poised chastely over her
knitting patterns – which are all baby clothes, by the way,
stitched for some infant nephew – she knows the new rules for
oral sex.

I glide downwards in an elevator crammed with other, stolid
Lindas, a crop-haired postboy and his trolley. In the lobby the
crowd divides suddenly and the commissionaires come grinding
to attention as, oblivious to the security gates and their harassed
operatives, a quintet of molten monarchs comes stalking
through. Two corporate gods, avuncular in neat pinstripes, a
pair of nervous boardroom flunkeys, and behind, gathering
them up somehow in his own private trajectory, steering them
forward in harness to his own desire, a tall, authoritative figure.
I never look at John Birningside without experiencing a faint
pang of envy: bulging forearms testifying to a hundred pre-
dawn workouts, tanned skin redolent of a thousand hours
under the lamp. He must be fifty or fifty-five now, but only a
tinge of grey on the broad, cropped skull betrays him. Even
Slater goes in awe of John Birningside who, legend has it, once
summoned him to a strategy session by the Olympic-size pool
on his back lawn, swam a hundred lengths while Slater rewrote
a proposal document at his dictation, and then did press-ups for
an hour on the patio while Slater read it back to him.

Watching Birningside and his cortège depart makes me think
of Danny Hassenblad, whose aspirations in this rarefied
promontory of corporate life were legion. Delusorily fixated on

boardroom satrapies, a subscriber to *Corporate Director* and to more specialist magazines with titles like *Executive Style*, Danny had embraced at one time or another nearly every aspect of the corporate mogul's lifestyle package: the processed hair, the punishing workouts in exclusive Long Island gymnasiums, the sunlamp romper-rooming, the martial arts coaching. The effect on his appearance and, more important, on public perception of that appearance was negligible. Once, returning to the office from some gruelling session on the mat, some stakeout under the lights, Danny asked me how he looked. What would you say? He looked like the puny, etiolated, Jewish proprietor of a nine-person New York computer consultancy. Once around this time, attending some corporate beanfeast or charity cocktail schmooze – Danny was a great one for paying two hundred dollars for the privilege of being able to say that he had dined in the same room as a Democrat senator from a white trash Southern state – he actually got to shake hands with one of the money monsters, if not Milken then some famous steel-nosed arbitrageur from the broking rooms. Impressed in spite of myself, I asked him what this brief five seconds of manual contact had been like. 'It was like kissing God,' Danny said simply.

At Westminster, three stops down the line, the gnawing at my stomach becomes too much, and I get out and head for a burger bar. Here – and this eating in public thing is still a radical departure for me – I halt and order a brace of McChicken sandwiches and a Coke. They taste like cardboard, or like the styrofoam cartons in which they languidly repose, but I wolf them down regardless. Fat Yankee tourists mill around the serving points as I eat, the guys wondering where has Jim-Bob gone with the subway map, awright, the girls yelling that there'd better be a john someplace or I'm gonna bust myself OK. Later they sit in ragged, unselfconscious knots, gorging heartily. Suppressing a desire to go to the booth at the side of the bar and call Miranda, I start thinking about Slater. The suspicion that Slater is up to something is reinforced by the repeated mention of Farq and Quoodle. Slater has been up to things with Farq and Quoodle before: a futures scam a couple of years back; little bits of corporate restructuring that no

150

boardroom or City page bloodhound ever knew anything about; that sort of thing.

Noise from the street hastens this reverie away. On the far side of the road a collection of elderly men and women proceed slowly from the subway station steps towards the square. There are perhaps fifty of them, a few carrying placards, the majority swinging their arms in an exaggerated military step. The men look bashful, resigned, unhopeful; the women belligerent, minatory. Collectively they project an air of self-conscious suffering, beaten-down humility, parched, resentful faces unconfident of redress. As the procession loiters slowly towards Westminster, ragged and indistinguishable chants borne on the air behind it, I realise that these are the Torrington Construction pensioners, come to lobby the House of Commons. Snug among the Jim-Bobs and the Gabrielles, hunkering down here in the heat and tumult of the burger bar, I watch them disappear.

That afternoon Sammy Baldwin spent three hours in front of the House of Commons Select Committee on Social Services – grim and, as it turned out, televised hours, large portions of which were subsequently beamed out on news programmes and financial chat shows. It was, Slater conceded, a bravura performance. Harried by the committee's ascetic Labour chairman, insulted at every turn by colluding Tory backbenchers, adrift beneath the TV lights and the stenographers' clatter, Sammy stared back impenitently into the camera. '*Mr Baldwin*', opined a parliamentary sketchwriter in one of the liberal newspapers, '*gave the impression that he could not imagine why he had been summoned to appear before the committee, that he regarded the proceedings as irrelevant, and the questions a gross affront to his own dignity.*'

Let Slater take up the story: 'Sure, Sammy had it all planned. They can't make you say anything in front of those committees – it's not a court of law – so what does Sammy do? He just clams up. He's got two QCs at a grand an hour on either side of him, so he lets them get on with it. OK, shouting at the chairman was a big mistake, but you've got to remember Sammy's a sensitive man. Plus he's one of this country's leading insolvency

151

practitioners, and how would you like to be insulted for three hours on TV just because a few old grannies don't understand how business works?'

Some more jottings from the Miranda file.

Fortuitously – at least I think fortuitously – I've found out where she lives.

It happened last Thursday night when, having inveigled her out of the apartment for practically the first time in our relationship – the apartment looks kind of worn-out and used up now, like the apartment in 9½ *Weeks*, arid scenery behind foregrounded tumult – we ended up eating late at a restaurant near Notting Hill.

'You want to take a cab home?'

'We could go back to my place if you want.'

'Back to your place?'

'Sure. It's not far away.'

The cab left us outside a grey barrack of flats at the far end of Lancaster Road. Here, amid signs of large-scale dereliction – boarded-up windows, patched exteriors – a few lights burned. Within, beyond silent corridors strewn with uncollected mail, a staircase rose steeply into darkness. I knew already what I might find. Occasional friends of Henrietta's, thrown together by chance or poverty, lived in places such as this: decaying mansion blocks with rank, overgrown gardens where it was not unusual to find syringes littering the ground and vagrants emerging from the grass at dawn. Some kind of comment seemed called for.

'I expect it looks better inside.'

Miranda shrugged. 'It's a dump,' she said with feeling.

The staircase ran on endlessly. Below, the lights grew faint and then receded into a mild, penumbral glow. We ascended in silence, each footfall raising a tiny spurt of dust. Eventually the stairs gave way to a high, circular landing, cluttered up with decorating materials: tins of paint, a trestle table or two. In the half-light these were sinister outlines: ghostly contraband, perhaps, the trestle tables unspeakable instruments of torture. Negotiating her way around this obstacle course of stacked lumber, Miranda pushed open a door whose outlines had

152

previously been lost in shadow. The impression that we had travelled along some cavernous, underground highway, were now forcing a passage into its splendidly habitable core, was renewed by a splash or two of graffiti. This, I dimly divined, was some Tolkien-like entrance hall, its portico engraven with silvery runes, the interior doubtless crammed with capering elves and goblins, awash with other-worldly light.

Within, a bare, angular passage led into a gloomy interior. The walls, unadorned except for the occasional gallery poster, smelled of paint. Somewhere towards the back of the apartment music sounded faintly. Miranda stood irresolutely by the door. Her face seemed oddly animated. Clearly the thought of inviting a friend back to this shady tenement sharply disturbed her.

'How many of you live here?'

'Four. There's a guy called Dan has the back room, but he isn't around much.'

'The others are girls?'

'Uh huh. Roz and Nancy. Roz works in a record store someplace.'

'And Nancy?'

'Guess Nancy just sits in her room all day and listens to the radio.'

Curiously she did not seem put out by questioning of this sort. In fact her description of Nancy listening to the radio carried a noticeable relish. We wandered on down the corridor, half-open doors leading away to the kitchen and sitting room, to a large, untidy bedroom, barren of decoration, containing bookcases and an unmade double bed. Miranda made a perfunctory dab or two at various stray items which lay across the pillow and then sat down heavily on the dishevelled sheet.

'I'm pooped. Stay up if you like though.'

Later, when she disappeared to the bathroom, I made a lightning inventory of the room and its contents. The bookshelves harboured scuffed English classics of the kind my mother read – *The Mill On The Floss*, *The Diary of a Nobody*, *Villette* – and some marketing textbooks. Of bank books, address cards, letters, all the incriminating rubbish of personal life, again there was no sign. A heavy, black, accountant's briefcase, of the kind seen a hundred times a day at KLS, sat on

153

a chair next to a rickety bedside table. I pulled out the topmost drawer and discovered a pile of chaste white panties, half-concealing a folded wad of hundred dollar bills. There might have been twenty or thirty of them. I shut the drawer hurriedly as footsteps sounded in the corridor.

Miranda's bedroom routine is as unselfconscious as any girl's I've known. A bored peeling off of stockings, a casual shedding of underthings, a nude stalk or two around the room straightening objects and searching out dental floss. By contrast, Henrietta's preparations follow a lavish, stylised pattern: the protracted, scarlet-faced strip-tease, the hastily-donned Laura Ashley nightgown, the stern surveillance before the mirror in quest of blemishes and skin-roughening. I once made the mistake of stealing in on Henrietta as she lay in the bath, and her consequent irritation might have been a rebuke to a prurient butler.

Far below in the street there was a faint clatter of noise. Miranda slept soundlessly, one forearm pressed deep into the pillow. I reckoned up the perplexities that life with her entailed. She has three thousand dollars in her bedside drawer but lives in a Notting Hill bedsit. She won't tell me what she does for a living. I know no other person who knows her. I have no means of verifying any fact that I believe to be true about her. Intriguing initially, then a halfway irritating quirk, these were turning into serious considerations. Most women in Miranda's position talk *all the time*. In the days after Sondra walked out, the loft buzzed with a tangible, foregrounded silence. What did Miranda want? What did I want? What was Slater up to? And Barry Mower? Sleep came at last.

Dawn came finally. Miranda slept on. I went and stared out of the window where, far below, a few children circled on mountain bikes. It was bitterly cold. Grey clouds moved in hurriedly across the western city. At this height familiar landmarks were visible beyond tower blocks: church spires, in the distance the Telecom tower. I turned back.

In the kitchen there was utter devastation: an intent, purposeful chaos giving the impression of being carefully designed by some avant-garde artist. Plates lay upturned on the floor; a teetering stack of crockery hung over the lip of the sink.

154

I boiled water in a filthy kettle. Apart from a few tins in a cupboard beneath the sink, there was no sign of any food. Later I hovered for a while in the bedroom doorway: no movement came from the bed. Turning to go I came upon an alcove by the door. Here lay matchboxes, old subway tickets, packets of aspirins, a square of yellow card with a pair of phone numbers traced lazily across it. I put it in my jacket pocket, smoothed down the lapels of my suit and slunk away.

That Sunday we took a boat along the river to Greenwich. Here in mid-stream, Westminster receding into grey, sunless skies, an older London reasserted itself: ancient warehouses, like bombazine-clad old ladies, their greenish skirts hanging over the water's edge; high, distant spires; rotting timber above the tidewall. There were barely a dozen passengers on the boat. On deck two Americans in plaid jackets argued noisily over an aerial map of the city. The rest kept sensibly to the glass-framed interior.

At Greenwich we disembarked into slow drizzle: in the distance, towards Dartford, lights broke occasionally out of the shadow. The passengers hastily dispersed in a hangdog way towards the town. I was immediately oppressed by a sense of history. Here jaunty English sailors had set out to subdue and regulate their Empire, red-jacketed soldiery had drawn up in files along the grass to the blare of trumpets, tall-masted frigates had lain silently in down river. We moved on slowly towards the high street, the trail marked out by the bright anoraks of the tourists.

On the boat, huddled into a leather jacket on a rickety bench, Miranda had not spoken. Now, imperceptibly, she became less remote. We had lunch in a pub on whose walls hung etchings of the sailing ships of legend: the 'Cutty Sark', the 'Golden Hind', H.M.S. 'Victory'. Later, as we strolled through a park where the Americans capered and skipped and took photographs of each other posed coyly beside the statues, she grew talkative.

'Don't you think English people are patronising? I mean, don't you always get the feeling they think they're doing us a favour instead of the other way round?'

'Naturally.'

'I mean with defence and everything. Don't you think it would serve them right if we just got up and walked away?'

'Of course.'

'My dad used to say that Lindbergh was an American hero and it was a shame more people never listened to him.'

The Americans had gone now, in search of camera shops and bureaux de change. Walking back up a slight incline there was a moment when the horizon suddenly lay exposed before us as a forest of masts and sailcloth, cut off from the river below. Miranda said:

'And of course this is nothing. Not like Cape Cod or Nantucket.'

Something in the intonation, the gesture – head thrown back against the wind, stern eyes, the thought itself – made me turn and look at her.

'Are you OK?'

'Sure,' I said. 'Sure I'm OK. It's just that you remind me of someone.'

Oddly, the person she reminds me of is Sondra.

10

This is a low

On long summer evenings, back early from the Mirabelle or Tarantino's, I used to amuse myself by listening to the long-range shipping forecast. Begun by chance, this recreation had swiftly grown into a settled habit, whose interest lay in its novelty. There was no American equivalent to these sombre yet comforting recitations. Regional radio stations might occasionally offer weather reports or storm warnings, but the great divisions of marine geography lay far off, a mountain range dark beyond foregrounded hills. For some reason, as the months passed, these prognoses – which appeared almost fortuitously, jammed up between garrulous actors' monologues and books at bedtime – grew and expanded in my mind until they took on the form of incantations, mantras almost, from another world, shining uplands glimpsed narrowly through fog. 'Dogger, winds backing westerly, seven . . . Cromarty, fair, six . . . Shannon . . . Biscay . . .' There was something elemental about this ghostly roll-call, something serious and profound in the thought of waves breaking on remote Scottish beaches, crofters huddled in their huts against winds moving south from the polar cap. Its effect was wholly fabulous, so that for a long time Dogger, Moray and Shetland seemed at best glittering and elusive threads picked out of a giant mythical tapestry, distant sequestered kingdoms, dormant in the mist, whose frontiers I could never hope to cross.

All these sensations, even down to the sonorous voice of the radio announcer, were knocked to the surface by the occasional visits I paid to Henrietta's apartment. Inconveniently situated, halfway between South Kensington and Gloucester Road, on the topmost floor of a redbrick mansion block, it was an unlikely cornucopia. But I was used to unprepossessing frontages of this kind yielding up unlooked-for treasure trove.

157

Like the locked trunk in the attic of my Marshall grandmother's house outside of Baltimore which opened to reveal old militia uniforms and cavalry harness from the Indian wars, Henrietta's apartment contained a great deal behind its prosaic exterior. Exact connections, in the shape of an Edwardian yachting map of the Irish coast borrowed from her parents, gave way to milder echoes: photographs of strange English people with fierce blue eyes and jutting chins bending over dogs or standing uncomfortably on terraces, pictures of Henrietta at various salient points in her career – dazed and sleepless in a ball gown, with fat white shoulders, on an Oxford bridge at dawn; reclining in a punt; in subfusc outside the Senate House accompanied by slim, saturnine dandy swains. Somehow my mother is there in these *Brideshead* reveries. Once, squiring Henrietta to a drinks party thrown by some high-born pal of hers (Felicity? Camilla?) in Cadogan Square, I turned to stare at the line of photographs on the gleaming mantel and there she was, almost, dressed in riding gear and standing on a gravel drive in front of what looked like a castle's worth of turrets and terracings.

It wants a week until Christmas. Standing rigidly in the doorway between hall and lounge, I can command a cheering prospect of the twenty or thirty upper-class young Englishmen and women who constitute Henrietta's most intimate circle: the Sophias and Charlottes, the Ruperts and Jonjos. And not so young either. There are forty- or fifty-year-olds, younger friends of Henrietta's parents who still have a house in town and like to keep some lien on the doings of what they call the younger set. Some of the guys I know from previous socialising here: blond giants who work as stockbrokers at Flemings or Smith New Court, with names like Hamish and Jeremy. The girls are the usual dinner party fodder, but more differentiated, ranging from slips of things in party frocks to rollicking Fergie lookalikes in yards of plunging taffeta. Some of the guys are in evening dress, with even a wing collar sticking out here and there, but for the most part it's a city suit bash, with a few ne'er-do-wells in greenery-yallery occupations sneaking in shame-facedly in cords. Henrietta reserves her sweetest smile for the dinner-jackets: in an ideal world she would spend her time

158

attending those gatherings where the invitation simply says 'Black Tie'.

What do I feel about this rapt inspection of Henrietta's friends, this anthropologist's corner on Hector, Rupert and Jonjo at play? Envy of course, and not just personal envy; envy on behalf of my compatriots. I envy them their physique, their mountainous shoulders and tyre-rubber necks, but also their poise, the way they continue to look and behave like jocks ninety per cent of the time while always retaining some golden kernel: the brick-red face surmounted by pale, delicate hair, say, the construction-yard forearms tapering off unexpectedly into sensitive concert pianist's fingers. As I watch, a guy with a perspiring, bovine face who might be called Fruity or Bobo is easing the cork out of a bottle of champagne while talking loudly to anyone within a range of eight or nine feet about his plans for Cowes Week. I couldn't do that. No American I know, apart from a handful of Admirable Crichtons from Harvard, could do that. They'd grasp the components, but the expertise – *the twisting the wire cage without looking at it* – would be beyond them.

Even more than the hulking quarterbacks' frames and the poise, though, I envy them their unselfconsciousness, so blatant and practised that it is almost a form of insouciance. A collection of Americans of similar age, income and status, would be talking about their jobs, about how they intended on making partner the fall after next and were kissing goodbye to this year's vacation, with maybe a little discreet sexual banter thrown in as filler. Rupert and Jonjo talk about rugby, about practical jokes they played on each other at school, about weird, luminous acquaintances who never turn up at gatherings of this kind but whose presence is endlessly resuscitated by anecdote. Above all, perhaps, I envy them their ability to handle women.

Watching the Sophies and the Charlottes exchanging small-talk with their Gavins and Williams is a sobering experience for us East Coast sophisticates. Gavin and William have no conversation, no real strategy. They simply stand there and guffaw, turn red-faced in the heat and watch the sweat course down their wrists in runnels. But somehow Sophie and

Charlotte love it. Somehow they bask wide-eyed in these unreflective stares, throw back their heads delightedly, show their fine white teeth when they laugh. As a bargain it seems criminally inadequate. At one of Henrietta's dinner parties I sat opposite an ox-backed twenty-four-year-old whose real name was Christopher or Roland but who was of course addressed throughout as 'Tiny'. Ponderous, chronically restrained in speech and gesture – there was a running joke, I gathered, about the number of times he'd failed his 'A' Levels – Tiny spent the negligible portion of the three hours in which he wasn't shovelling food talking about his stamp collection. When, at a late hour, he lumbered off from the table to another part of the room, the girl who sat alongside him and whose conversation had been, if anything, even more limited, murmured with unfeigned sincerity, 'Tiny's a *scream* isn't he?'

Tiny is here tonight, of course, guzzling smoked salmon in a corner and being chaffed by three or four of his intimates before an audience of squeaking girls. Back down the hall several more arrivals are entering through the front door, among them Quoodle, which is a mild surprise until I remember that he's a friend of Henrietta's dad from someplace. Quoodle, smoothing down his coat and hanging it gracefully over an exposed hook, looks faintly pleased with himself. I watch him greet Henrietta, who fairly bounces into his arms, at the same time sending out one of those gimlet English glances that identify immediately the half-dozen or so people he knows and feels like recognising. The English guy with whom I've been schmoozing desultorily for the past ten minutes or so, a beaky specimen of about my own age, says unexpectedly:

'Don't you think they've made a terrible mistake in getting rid of Mrs Thatcher? Don't you really think so? Made a terrible mistake, I mean?'

I feel mischief stirring within me. 'It depends what you mean by a mistake.'

'I don't know. Of course you're an American. You're bound to see things differently. It stands to reason. I was working late at the bank when the news came through on the screens and I don't mind telling you I had to go out and have a stiff one. And my mother, who isn't a political person or anything – I mean she

160

votes Conservative but she isn't political – my mother said when she saw the paper next morning she *burst into tears*.'

This seems as fine a time as any to tote out what was known in our family as Hervey's Creed. My Uncle Hervey, a famously extreme redneck, had stopped voting Republican at around the time Goldwater failed to carry the South in 1964. He believed, to name only a few hotly-desired expedients, in segregated schooling, Vietnam, and training nuclear warheads on Russia – all the good brave causes, in fact, which even the amateur politicans who loafed around my parents' backyard had grown chary of proselytising now that they were playing soul music on the local pop stations and Martin Luther King had made civil rights respectable. Uncle Hervey gave politics up for lost when Nixon won the nomination in 1968, contenting himself thereafter with fitting each twist and turn of US foreign policy into the pre-ordained checker game by which the West was to be surrendered up to Communism by its elected leaders. To Uncle Hervey, needless to say, Reagan was a closet pinko and Mrs Thatcher his unquestioning stooge. I spin out a few of the less contentious elements in this, such as the bitter legacy of the Falklands (dangerously de-stabilising to friendly South American regimes), the necessity of helping the Chinese with their nuclear technology, Bush's criminally reduced defence budgets, the fellow-travellers in the Pentagon and so on, and get rewarded with an interested stare.

'Do you really think that? Do you know, I hadn't thought of it like that. Of course, here one just assumes that American interests are our interests. I had an American girlfriend once, and she said it was a well-known fact that Reagan had Alzheimer's disease and his public performances were all done by a stand-in.'

I glance back over my shoulder to where Quoodle is proceeding slowly through the throng. Another thing about these upper-class English guys is their capacity for self-preservation. At fifty, Quoodle looks forty, just a badgerish speckle in the regular dark hair, a line or two on each side of the aquiline nose. At forty he probably looked twenty-eight (at eighteen though – and this is the weird thing about the Farqs and Quoodles – he probably looked twenty-five). All of it done,

161

too, without apparent effort. Back in the States Quoodle's corporate equivalents are all furiously working out during their lunch-hours, essaying cholesterol counts and contemplating lipo-suction. Quoodle spends his time boozing with Slater at Tarantino's and comes out lean as a rake. Wandering, or rather gliding past (I once got talking to a guy who worked in his office and he volunteered that Quoodle's nickname among the boys was 'Rollerskates') he nods very slightly and passes on into a swirl of people that instinctively widens to accommodate him into its centre.

The English guy says, 'I expect you know Hetta from work. She's a darling isn't she? I was talking to some people the other day who live near where her parents live and they were saying what a darling she is.'

This evening, it should be said, is not without its cargo of frets and anxieties. For a start, Miranda may or may not join me during its course. Then there is Henrietta. Henrietta knows, or has guessed, about Miranda – several weeks' silence has done that – and the result is, not recrimination, but a volley of sorrowful looks. Henrietta can't bring herself to ask me why I no longer call her up or come round here to burrow gamely under her Laura Ashley counterpane, which would represent a fatal abrogation of the code by which she lives, but she can still look at me. I catch her looking at me now – a level gaze in which bewilderment, peevishness and resignation are uncomfortably mingled.

The English guy, to whom someone has clearly given the lowdown on me in advance, says, 'I expect you must find your job pretty exciting just now. It's not my game, of course, but you can't help noticing it in the paper. I expect it must be pretty exciting down there.'

To this opinion I have humbly to defer. Two nights ago, at a ground called Anfield somewhere in the north of England, in front of 35,000 anguished spectators, Walham beat Liverpool by a goal to nil. I wasn't there myself, but Barry Mower's vainglorious recitation, which exploded over the phone an hour after the game ended, made clear the seismic nature of the event. 'Of course, between you and me it was the bugger of a fluke. They had seven of the first team out injured. The keeper slipped in the mud in the second minute and bust his ankle, so they brought on the substitute keeper, only he took a swing at Ashley Flack right under the ref's nose and got sent off. You never saw anything like it. And then ten minutes from time Jimmy goes and falls over in the area – nowhere near the ball or nothing – and the ref only goes and gives a penalty.' I saw the penalty half-an-hour later on *Midweek Sports Special*. Taken laboriously by Phil 'Razors' Smallweed, 'the Walham spot-kick specialist' as the programme put it, who could clearly be seen to stub his toe on the iron sod before making contact, the ball trickled forward lazily to a point midway between the yawning goalposts. Unhappily by this time the third-choice goalkeeper, a blanched eighteen-year-old apprentice plucked that morning from the youth team, had already flung himself instinctively to one side. The wrong side. As the ball rolled on he crawled back gamely on all fours, got a hand to it, but only succeeded in diverting it into the corner of the net.

Next morning the media storm broke. Under headings of MINNOWS BITE and WALHAM NO-HOPERS FIGHT ON the tabloids printed outsize pictures of the Walham team, Phil Smallweed's glare of misery as he mishit the spot-kick, Barry Mower flicking V-signs in the direction of the Liverpool bench. '*After years on the sidelines England's most unfancied club are going places,' says chairman Mower . . .*' Our share of the gate receipts is expected in a week or so. Barry reckons it can't be less than seventy grand.

'And then of course there are these dreadful murders . . .'

As it happens, the RAM atrocities have been given a new and apparently definitive twist by a letter printed in yesterday's *Guardian* under the signature of something called the 'RAM Collective'. RAM, it transpires, is short for 'Revenge Against Men'. A faxed letter, later bulked out by a stack of ghastly and corroborative polaroids, several of which the *Guardian* charitably forbore to reproduce, acknowledged responsibility for the killings, spoke of 'symbolic attempts to redress the male/female imbalance' and warned of future depredations. The fax was eventually traced to an open-access machine in Camden public library. I wheel out Slater's theory about the whole thing being a gay blackmail scam, the *Guardian* letter simply inspired camouflage to draw the cops off the scent. But the English guy merely looks interested.

'I say, do you really think so? Think that it's all done by men I mean? I must say, I think that's a really clever idea. I was talking about it to Marianne the other night and we both said, the idea of taking some girl back home and then . . . That last chap, it said they found a piece of his, a piece of his . . . Well, apparently it was sort of *sellotaped on to the wall*!'

The English guy has backed away for a moment, giving me a chance to infiltrate the main body of the room. Here there are further signs of the care that Henrietta has lavished on this gathering of her oldest and closest: plates of smoked salmon, little bowls of Oriental finger-food. There are even a couple of Filipino girls in black cocktail dresses flitting about with trays of canapés. Watching Hugo, Jeremy and the rest receiving this humbly proffered bounty is a chastening experience. They don't need to look up from their high-octane chatter: they know instinctively that the food is there. Long years of exposure to evening parties has taught their hands how to select items from a platter and convey them upward without reference to hands or eyes. The Filipino girls, presumably inured to this blind patronage, stand deferentially by. Without warning one of them surfaces in front of me bearing a plate of tiny pastry schooners topped with prawns: unthinking, I whisk one away and fit it between my jaws. This is a bad move as it turns out: swallowing incautiously, something sticks in the back of my throat. I steer clear of any real damage by the simple expedient of hawking up everything that happens to be in my mouth, but the effect is spectacularly unbeautiful, an eruption of half-chewed prawns and spittle-flecked mayonnaise, and a coughing fit that leaves me doubled up at knee level above the carpet gazing desperately at the rows of solid black brogues and the lines of court shoes.

Everyone behaves impeccably, of course. Henrietta brings me a tumbler of water and pats me dutifully on the back. Quoodle himself leads me to a davenport away from the throng and leaves me to recover from the shame. As embarrassments go this is minor-league stuff. I once watched some dinner-jacketed money god hit the parquet at a city reception, proved in the end to have dropped dead of a coronary thrombosis, and his

164

collapse was greeted with the most regal disdain, as if by dying so flagrantly and unapologetically he had somehow cancelled out the achievements that had caused him to be invited there in the first place.

As I lean back against the davenport, Miranda's spectre rises unbidden to disturb me, not so much the immediate problem of her possible arrival – and I don't imagine she'll come, not for a moment – but the wider mysteries that have occupied me since we met. As it happens, over the past few days the veil has turned out to be a little less opaque than it seemed. For a start, prompted by wary yet persistent questioning, she has unbent sufficiently to tell me about her family. A litany of misfortunes, as the weeks of reticence had led me to expect: parents dead in a plane crash over the Gulf, sister married to some psycho inebriate, brother disappeared into East Coast lowlife. Towards the end, in a hitherto unprecedented display of emotion, she started crying and I comforted her for a moment: twin heads touching over the gas-fire glow. Still nothing about what she does for a living, though.

Meanwhile, despite the pressing attentions of Barry Mower, who's now arranging with Slater to have me on long-term secondment (thanks a *lot*) I've been following up a couple of other leads. Of the phone numbers I purloined from her room, one produced nothing other than a crackle of static. The other was more promising, in fact an answerphone belonging to somebody called William Coe. One of those elaborate performances in which an immensely svelt-sounding dude regrets that he is not at present available, expects to return shortly, and begs you to leave a message, which he will return as speedily as possible. William Coe sounds English, patrician, decisive and faintly professional – an analyst, some kind of doctor, maybe? Whatever, you get the feeling that William Coe stands to benefit financially from the call. After considerable thought, I simply left my name and the Walham number with a request to call. So far he hasn't got back.

Providentially, my relations with Darren, having first looked set to founder on mutual suspicion, are beginning to prosper. Darren's chief characteristic is his awe: of the players, of me, of the middle-aged secretary who brings us morning coffee, and especially of Barry Mower. Profiting from Jimmy Hood's experience he calls Barry 'Mr Mower', even in the latter's absence, and looks alarmed whenever anyone ventures even the most anodyne remark about him, presumably on the grounds that Barry has the room wired or can somehow detect stray converse passing through the ether. He lives on some teeming estate under the Westway and was working as a pallet-stacker in Barry's porn warehouse when the master's seigneurial eye picked him for advancement, put him in a suit and stuck him in a tiny office at The Dray. Poor Darren! He has some joke accountancy qualification, the first rung on one of those interminable ladders that promise you an ACA at forty, and an unquestionable reverence for the circumstances of his ascent. Darren's other characteristic is a sweetly naïve interest in the States. Returning to the office on Monday mornings after a weekend in front of the VCR he invariable locates a meeting point between the turbulent intimations of celluloid and looser reality beyond.

'This tape I saw the other day all right? Set in Miami it was. You ever been there?'

'A little. My mother lived there a while.'

'All right mate. This guy goes insane with an Uzi sub-machine gun. Does his girlfriend, his mum, his dad, houseful of black blokes he's got a grudge against on account of he's secretly a grand vizier in the Ku Klux Klan. Takes three dozen policemen and a load of state troopers to catch him, and even then he's boobytrapped his body armour – he's got all this commando gear in his loft OK? – with Semtex. I mean, is it really like that?'

'Pretty much.'

But I mustn't be cute about Darren, who is proving invaluable in expanding the Barry Mower dossier. So far he's shown me the stack of hardcore tapes that Barry watches in his office on dull afternoons and a pile of bank statements that had mysteriously disappeared from central filing. I even have hopes of enlisting him in the promotions investigation, but it's early days yet and he still has the underdog's loyal habit of referring every question back to the throne. ('You know anything about last month's petty cash receipts Darren?' 'Oh Mr Mower'll tell you about that mate.' 'You remember the last time you had a get-together with the bank Darren?' 'It's Mr Mower that goes to the business meetings.') So I mustn't be nasty about Darren and his weekend stake-outs with *Miami Inferno* and *Urban Commando* and the pale girl in clattering high heels he sometimes goes off to eat his lunch-time sandwiches with.

Now it's 9.30 p.m. By this time some of Henrietta's friends are starting to get restive, talking loudly about supper dates elsewhere and the whereabouts of taxi ranks. This, too, is an upper-class English trait, the habit of standing on your host or hostess's carpet staring peevishly at your watch while someone calls a cab. I get the feeling – relief mingled with very faint disappointment – that Miranda isn't going to show. In the far corner of the room, wedged up behind Henrietta's piano, upon which repose photographs of Henrietta's mother as a debutante and Henrietta's father arrayed in the uniform of the Honourable Artillery Company, Quoodle stands caught up in a knot of people I vaguely know from the City, ornaments of stockbroking firms in Eastcheap, bond dealers from Leadenhall Street. Sparse, buttoned-down, resembling in fact a more genial version of Laurence Olivier, he looks every inch the successful City guy. There was a kind of English novel, very popular with Americans of my parents' generation, in which a cast of bankers, parliamentarians or clergy – the members of a gentleman's club, say, or a professional society – acted out some ethical or, more usually, social drama: a blackballing, the ostracism of an unpopular neighbour, an election to the mastership of some Cambridge college. These were Byzantine intrigues requiring tact, diplomacy, a precise understanding of shades of moral difference and, characteristically, an unhesitating ruthlessness. Without corresponding in any particular to caricature notions of *éminence grise*, Quoodle, when I first came across him two or three years ago, looked to have sprung directly from these pages. It did not take much imaginative licence to visualise him manipulating an election by committee, or skilfully promoting his own candidate to an assortment of interested parties in some boardroom tourney. In fact, according to Slater these were precisely the attributes by which Quoodle had established his career. Remembering all this, I watch as Quoodle detaches himself from the group by the

167

piano and comes gliding across. He looks – well, without labouring the point, Quoodle looks *English*, by which I mean amused, reserved, secretive, oblique, polite, faintly inquisitive.

'Speaking professionally,' he says, 'we've missed you at Tarantino's. But then your energies have been, shall we say, redirected elsewhere?'

'Speaking professionally' is an old accountant's joke, dredged up from some primordial creditors' meeting or waterlogged rights issue. I shrug. 'You know Tony. He never lets you stay too long in one place.'

Quoodle smiles back in a way that suggests the subject of Slater needn't be approached with complete seriousness, while hinting that the standard proprieties are still in place. 'As you know, Tony and I burn with a hard gem-like flame. A marriage made if not in heaven then certainly in Threadneedle Street. How is the old boy? Has he bought Mrs Slater the new patio surround we hear so much about? You wouldn't credit it, perhaps, but we hear a great deal about Mrs Slater. They must be a very devoted couple.'

I love it when Quoodle talks like this, like the butler in some Hollywood comedy, all ironic gravity and secret contempt. The stuff about Mrs Slater in particular has to be a try-on.

'I don't see too much of Tony just now. Too busy redirecting my energies.'

'Splendid. Good man.' Quoodle looks suddenly sharper now, as if he feels a shaft of irony flung back at him. Behind, the Filipino girls are collecting glasses and emptying ashtrays into Henrietta's kitchen refuse bucket. At an early stage in my dealings with Quoodle and Farq and various other of the guys introduced to me by Slater I realise how egregious, how misguided, how stupendously foolish it would be to underestimate them. This, it goes without saying, is something a great many of my compatriots did in the airy days of the Big Bang. Flown in by Yankee proprietors to supervise the take-over of blue-blooded broking firms where the average time of arrival was ten and the average time of departure was four and the partners' dining room boasted a wine list, introduced to Farq and Quoodle with their charm and their silences, they assumed, not unreasonably, that they were merely merger fodder, tedious obstructions whom persuasion and disgust at the new order of things would swiftly superannuate. Well it's 1990 now, and Farq and Quoodle are still stalking the boardrooms while Hank and Beauregard are back in Milwaukee telling everyone that London's full of prissy fruits who never work out and take three-week vacations.

'Tony's got a lot of administrative work on at the moment,' I say with that bright firmness of manner people apply to senior executives involved in shoring up some disastrous managerial crisis. Quoodle nods unhurriedly at this, plainly caught up in some private calculation of how much or how little to reveal. Then his manner changes abruptly – not in the cataclysmic Barry Mower fashion, whereby a raging euphoria is transformed immediately into grinding despair – but sharply enough to suggest a deliberate shift in gear.

'I should keep my eyes open there.'

'You would?'

'Definitely.'

Out of the tail of one eye I can see Henrietta dealing with a pink-faced youngster holding a half-empty champagne glass. Her firm cadences of remonstrance float up above the room's thinning conversation. Searching for something to say that will maintain the momentum of the previous minute, still looking for clues, I chip in:

'I saw John Birningside the other day.'

Quoodle's gaze narrows. 'Birningside's in California.' He says this with faint irritation, as if courtesy demanded that any alternative travel arrangements ought to have been cleared with him in advance.

'Perhaps he was on his way?'

'Now I come to think about it,' Quoodle says pacifically, 'Birningside told me he had to go and see one of your senior people in hospital. A nasty case of overwork and nervous breakdown. We had one ourselves not long ago. Chap working on a takeover defence, whose marriage was breaking down at the same time. In the end he just disappeared. Took a lot of valuable documents with him as well. We found him eventually in a hotel somewhere on the south coast. He'd been living there quite happily for a week, even joined an aqua club and so on.

The firm had to threaten legal action to get him to come back.'

This is the reddest of red herrings. Quoodle, like Slater, and probably with Slater, is up to something. Something to do with KLS and probably even involving John Birningside. Something, even more to the point, in which strict secrecy is inadvisable. If Quoodle hadn't wanted me to know about it he would have spared me the hints and the flagrant smokescreen. I wonder about this for a moment until someone shouts Quoodle's name, a high ululation, *Quoooooodle*, like a hunting cry, from the other side of the room, and he looks up, bobs his head slightly, as if to suggest that this formal audience, granted out of sheer good humour but serving no particularly useful purpose, is at an end, and moves away.

There are maybe fifteen or twenty people left in the room, which seems full of heat and cigarette smoke. Miranda is definitely not going to show. I thread my way along the side wall, where Tudor maps of the English counties hang, along with more photographs of Henrietta's father standing in front of a troop of Gurkhas and at the wheel of a yacht, and into the kitchen. Here Henrietta and the Filipino girls are purposefully sluicing glasses. Henrietta looks uncharacteristically subdued. On impulse, and not imagining anything will come of it, I ask: 'What's Quoodle up to? With my boss, I mean.' Unexpectedly Henrietta bursts into tears. The Filipino girls look knowingly at one another. 'I'm sorry,' she says. 'It's all been rather a strain this evening. No, I don't know what Quoodle's up to with your boss.' She pronounces Quoodle's name in a leisurely way, as if it were some kind of endearment. 'Nothing at all?' 'It's top secret,' Henrietta unhappily concedes. 'Tell me.' 'No, I can't.' 'Yes you can.' The Filipino girls are stacking tumblers now, venturing little giggles when the rims crack together. 'It's something about a buy-out,' Henrietta says reluctantly. 'What sort of a buy-out?' 'I don't know.' 'Go on, tell me.' '*Pas devant les domestiques*,' Henrietta hisses. The Filipino girls move off in search of further plunder. 'Look, I'm really sorry about all this,' I tell her. 'It doesn't matter. Honestly it doesn't.' 'No, really. I'm truly sorry about it.' 'Look,' Henrietta says, raising her voice for the first time. 'Will you just be quiet please and go away?' A plate fractures suddenly on the linoleum beneath us, the tears course down Henrietta's plump, handsome face, and I retreat into the drawing room worrying about Quoodle, Slater, John Birningside's alligator tan and management buy-outs.

A year or so back I enlisted Henrietta in the quest for my mother's past. She took it up enthusiastically, dealing out copies of *Who's Who* and *Burke's Landed Gentry* in which we searched for likely-looking Jefferieses and Anstruthers, even riding shotgun, once – vigorous in hacking jacket and cotton jeans – to a country house in North Yorkshire called Borthwick Hall. Recalling it now, and also the succession of dead-ends – the Jefferieses and Anstruthers all know-nothing investment bankers living in retirement in Lincolnshire, Borthwick Hall a moss-covered ruin where fox cubs tumbled in the sunshine – I remember how much I *like* Henrietta, her lack of calculation, her want of guile, the way she bit her lip over the road map, light coming off her glasses on the road out of York, and regret that this is gone.

Below uncurtained windows cabs slither by in the darkness. Back on the davenport, not wanting to be disturbed again, I pull out the latest communication from my father and subject it to perhaps its fifth bout of scrutiny. Not a letter, as it happens, but a press clipping, and from an English newspaper, the *Eastern Daily Press* or the *Eastern Evening News*. Christ knows how he came by it. Headed TV AD BRINGS WINDFALL FOR '60S STAR, it describes nothing less than the discovery of the Singing Postman, run to earth in a Salvation Army hostel in a place on Humberside called Grimsby by a brace of reporters anxious to acquaint him with some hot news. Strange as it may appear, impelled by some ineluctable whim, a creative director went rummaging through the tape vaults one day searching for something to play over the top of an ad for Ovaltine and came up with 'Have yew gotta loight, boy?' There is a photograph of the Postman, dressed in those anonymous Old Englishman's clothes, leaning on a stick and looking slightly lost and vacant. Now in his late sixties, he summons up a few halting sentences for his interlocutors. Apparently he is 'happy with anything they give me' (the ads, the paper proudly informs us, are expecting to bring in 'nearly £2,000!' in royalties). His living expenses are in any case 'modest'. The Salvation Army captain

171

weighs in with the sad intelligence that no one has been to visit the old guy for seven years.

There's some other stuff too, mostly about the slide in the Postman's career, how in the late 1960s it all went wrong, how he ended up in a court after slugging his step-father, a botched operation on his guitar-hand. Best of all ('*a flashback to the mid sixties when Allan's voice and guitar were heard all over the nation*') is a row of photographs from the early days. In one of them a row of chorus girls dressed in bowler hats and wantonly short skirts are tootling away on miniature trumpets while the Postman, seated on a chair before them, one leg hoisted over the other, applies himself with an intent seriousness to his guitar. In another, mouth open, teeth appearing to spring from his gums at forty-five degree angles, he cheerfully inspects the *décolletage* of a bare-shouldered woman in evening dress.

As I fold the clipping into a square and slide it back into my jacket pocket, Miranda comes into the room. Memory, replayed an hour or so later, preserves some faint recollection of her arrival – a stir of chatter from the hallway, a door slamming shut – but at the time she seems simply to materialise before me. It is immediately apparent that something is badly wrong. This much is clear less from Miranda's appearance – chalk-white and unsteady – as from the facial expressions of those around her. Henrietta wears a look of exaggerated horror; Quoodle glances shrewdly and dispassionately up from a soda-siphon; the Filipino girls gape. Curiously, what wells up in my mind is the thought of other entrances at other social gatherings: a jock's convention at highschool broken up by a slighted girlfriend wielding a fire-extinguisher; Danny Hassenblad confronted by a deranged secretary he'd made the mistake of firing. At the same time I take in background detail: Quoodle replacing the siphon deftly on a table; one of the Filipino girls rubbing her apron over her thighs in an odd, sensual movement; fir cones piled up in the empty grate. Miranda by this time is making fretful little scrabbling gestures with her hands. Her eyes swing crazily. Drink? Drugs? Drugs and drink? I pull her hands gently towards me, as one might greet an elderly relative of questionable sanity, but she ducks under my grip, spins round and, impelled by some sixth sense, fetches up a foot or two short of Henrietta. I wonder about intervening, then pull myself up in the consciousness that, whatever the potential embarrassment, Henrietta is perfectly able to cope with situations of this sort. Something of the kind seems to have occurred to Henrietta for, tapping Miranda brusquely on the shoulder, she indicates a tray of glasses on a nearby side-table. 'Would you like a drink?' 'Thanks,' Miranda says. She inspects Henrietta for a second or so in what is actually a very English way, her eyes eventually coming to rest at about the level of Henrietta's neck. 'Hey,' she says abruptly, 'we've got something we ought to talk about, you and me.' Henrietta, I notice, seems faintly mesmerised, like some small creature of the forest cornered by a silent, luxuriating snake. Quoodle, emerging by her shoulder, looks amused and intrigued. 'That's right,' Miranda goes on. 'Him. That's what you and me've got to talk about.' 'Actually,' says Henrietta, 'I don't think there's anything that you and I need to talk about.' 'Actually,' Miranda shoots back – and the imitation of cadence and pitch is quite flawless – 'why don't you go fuck yourself, sweetheart?' At this a minor tumult breaks out. A middle-aged chum of Henrietta's, who plainly sees his destiny as pacifying situations of this kind, leaps forward and says 'Easy now, easy now' a couple of times, as if he were quietening a horse. Henrietta bursts into tears. Miranda shouts *fuck* again very loudly to no one in particular, follows this up with a request to know if Henrietta takes it up the ass and stops to stare as the rest of the room descends on this single point of action. From somewhere near at hand comes the sound of breaking glass, later identified as the contents of the drinks tray hitting the floor, a gesture for which hindsight suggests Miranda to be only partly responsible. As I grab her by the waist and shove her in the direction of the door she starts screaming wordlessly. In the hall, where we struggle for a while like two pantomime actors bidden to mimic extreme but uncoordinated violence, cold air rises suddenly from the gaping door. Looking back, the last thing I see is Henrietta frozen at Quoodle's side by the entrance door to the inner room, following our clamorous exit with wounded eyes.

11

About personality

'I love these boys,' Barry Mower says expansively, 'like they was . . .' He stops in mid-sentence, glares fondly at the photo of Tusker Holloway in the Walham Hall of Fame, flourishes a fat, knuckleless hand in front of him to give the simile full weight . . . 'Like they was my own kids.' The players, drawn up in a line at the bar, gawky and silent in their double-breasted suits, look sheepishly at one another. No one dares laugh at this proud comparison, for the very good reason that Raymond Mower, Barry's elder son, is currently concluding a six-month sentence in Pentonville for possession with intent to supply. Of Barry's other progeny, Shane is a burly oaf who works on one of the dirty magazines, while nobody knows what became of Natasha after she stole the five hundred nicker out of her dad's wallet – Barry tells this story a lot to me, ever more disquieted – and disappeared to the continent with the thrice-married staff photographer from *Cunning Stunts*.

'Go on,' Barry enjoins. 'Ask 'em what you like. They're good boys.' He hesitates again, looking for some wrap-up line that will clinch the argument. 'They're good boys, 'cause they do what I tell 'em.'

The press, a gaggle of middle-aged guys with parched, unhappy faces, grin appreciatively at this. They know Barry from way back, back from the property scams and the import/export exposés of twenty years ago. In the early 1980s, when Barry had one of his run-ins with the Obscene Publications Squad, they staked out his house for a week, directed telephoto lenses along the blameless sweep of his conservatories and opulent bed-chambers, and printed the results as VICE KING'S DEN OF SHAME. Oddly enough Barry harbours no malice over these intrusions. 'They're good boys. Got a job to do like anyone else. They was coming down the

175

drive dressed as milkmen at one stage: one of them even put on a dog collar and pretended he was the vicar. You had to laugh. Was only at the end when they started following Nerys round the supermarket I had to get the lads down to sort them out.'

I watch him now as he advances on the bar, pausing dutifully each time a flashbulb goes off, staring solemnly at the row of players that opens up anxiously at his approach. Massively ill at ease in the company of the Walham team, members of his family or employees, Barry is surprisingly adept at dealing with journalists. The consequence is that media treatment of him during the Walham run has been profuse and admiring. This morning, for example, finds him in the *Mirror* warning against the dangers of the long-ball game, and in the *Sun* protesting at the power of footballers' agents (MOWER SAYS SHAFT THE SOCCER SHARKS). There is even an irregular column in the *Star* (GIANT-KILLING WALHAM CHAIRMAN TELLS IT LIKE IT IS), ghosted for him by the sports editor's PA, in which Barry furnishes breathless résumés of recent games ('I saw then that only a determined effort by all eleven players could save us . . . My heart went out to those lads.') Naturally Barry's picture is omnipresent: Barry wrapped in his Aquascutum trenchcoat sighing from the touchline, Barry draping a matey arm around the drooping, disconsolate shoulders of Rickie Weller on the occasion of the latter's sending off for violent conduct ('Give him violent conduct,' Barry remarked shortly afterwards, prior to fining him a week's wages), Barry posed soberly next to a TV set in the Barry Mower Lounge waiting for the cup draw. He gets fan mail now, sacks of it, from teenage boys who want to be apprenticed to the Walham staff and girls pleading for him to keep Jimmy Hood, with whom he recently had another well-publicised dressing-room spat, in the team.

From my vantage point just inside the door I stare out at what, for all Barry's bonhomie, is a sharply regulated throng. The players – Hoody, Rickie Weller, Flack, Keith Thomas the little Welsh seventeen-year-old pulled out of the reserves a couple of weeks ago and deposited in the midfield – loiter uneasily, hands in pockets. Ernie Bright, more lugubrious than ever, stands to one side talking to Darren. There are rumours about Ernie in the sports pages, murderous rumours about how

Barry wants a new manager to carry Walham through to the end of the season, and how Ernie will be shipped out to Colchester as reserve team coach, rumours that even a loyal press release from Barry ('Mr Bright, with whom I have worked for many years, has my fullest confidence') have somehow failed to dispel.

The 'meet the press' event is Barry's idea, and with good reason. Two nights ago, in front of a capacity crowd, with two thousand ticketless fans milling retributively in the street outside, they beat Aston Villa 2-1 in the quarter-final of the Rumbelow's. The semi-final, another two-leg affair against the likes of United or Wednesday, beckons. I was there. Even now, thirty-six hours later, having read the guy in the *Independent* and watched Barry Mower's specially commissioned camcorder footage, I don't know how they did it.

The Villa players treated the occasion with the iciest disdain. It was later calculated that their substitute goalkeeper, a nineteen-year-old lately risen out of the Vauxhall Conference, was worth more than the market value of the entire Walham team. Trundling efficiently over the bare turf of The Dray, deaf to the lavish taunts of a wildly partisan crowd, they contrived to prevent a Walham player touching the ball for the first five minutes of the game. Their goal, scored in the eighth minute, seemed a Disney animator's parody: a tiny, furious Villa forward jinking his way through an obstacle course of outstretched legs, failed shouldercharges and slomo dives, finally to deposit it between the legs of an imploring goalkeeper. At half-time, with the transistor radios in the stand all tuned to the BBC sports programme buzzing about Villa's measured and impressive performance in difficult conditions, it began to rain. The Villa players re-emerged on to the pitch with puzzled, slightly hangdog expressions. Plainly bemused by a surface that had already begun to deliquesce beneath his feet, their centre forward began the half by stroking the ball elegantly towards the wing. Rolling uncomfortably from one moistened divot to another, it eventually came to rest in a two-inch deep puddle of water. The future pattern of the game was established. Peering uncertainly into the downpour, essaying passes that stuck in liquid mud or skidded yards past their

177

destinations, Villa gifted the equaliser with a defender's flick that bounced off the rim of an imploding crater before squirming from the grasp of a rain-blinded keeper. Jimmy Hood settled it a minute before time with an heroic lunge on the edge of the six-yard box as the bodies crashed and tumbled around him like felled forest oaks.

I watched the game from the corner of the dug-out. Warned into silence at an early stage by the referee for his repeated touchline interventions ('You fucking short-arsed pansy!' he had yelled affably after the opening goal went in) Barry passed the remainder of the game in a state of silent exultation.

'I'd just like you to know, Scott,' he said quietly when the final whistle went, 'that this is the happiest day of my life.'

'As good as that, huh?'

'The happiest *ever*. Better than first fuck. Better than first million, day they sank the Belgrano, anything.' He was serious, too. The morning after, he summoned the team into his office. One by one he handed them each a thousand pounds ('Bleeding *notes* as well') before arranging a squad pre-semi-final bargain break to the Bahamas.

January rain dribbles over the windows. Phantom shafts of sunlight glint off the distant tower blocks. The pitch, quiescent in the background beneath the perspex of the Barry Mower Lounge, looks scarred and churned: a tractor and a couple of shire horses would not seem out of place on its cragged surfaces. Within, cigarette smoke rises vertically into the stale air. The journalists cluster round the bar. I watch as Barry detaches himself from the press and stumps heavily back across the ash-strewn carpet. He looks weary and faintly exasperated.

'Lucky if we get this load of pissers out of here by dinner time . . . You know, Scott, I done a wrong thing just now.'

'You did?'

'That's right. A wrong thing. Talking about my kids like that.'

Genuinely upset, Barry gazes levelly over the unpromising, populous terrain of the lounge.

'I shouldn't worry about it.'

'No, you don't understand. It's all right, Scott, you're a good lad, but . . . The thing is, well, I lie awake at nights sometimes

178

thinking about Raymond stuck in Pentonville with a load of criminals. I mean, he's not some smackhead, not like these kids you read about in the papers, he just . . .'

Barry rambles on like this for some time, random and maudlin, about the time Raymond won the 100 metres at his school sports, the time Natasha scandalised him by returning home with a Levantine boyfriend ('I mean, I'm not racially prejudiced or anything, Scott, but an actual towelhead!'), the ransacked wallet and the moonlight flit ('So I went into her room and it was clear you know? Even the teddy bear from when she was a kid.') Wondering how to cheer him up I try commending the soundness of what remains.

'Never mind Barry, you've still got Shane.'

Barry's seamed, petulant face brightens immediately.

'That's right. He's a good lad, Shane is. I mean, he's never going, he's never going to . . . pass an exam at Oxford University, but he's a good lad.' I look pleased and supportive at this, while Barry frames a lavish encomium to Shane's dart-playing ability, his ladykilling accomplishments ('Shane and the birds . . . You never saw anything like it.') and general acquiescence to parental design. Poor Shane! Darren, whose habitual deference to Barry strangely ignores his children, filled me in on Shane. Superannuated from the educational process at the age of sixteen, he was initially put in for the Post Office entrance test (Darren: 'You have to be pretty thick to fail the Post Office exam. I mean, not knowing where places are and that.') before proceeding to short-lived careers in hypermarket shelf-stacking, warehouse security and refuse collection. Finally Barry broke one of his cardinal personal rules – the Richard J. Daley routine in reverse – and gave him the job on *Outsize*. (Darren: 'They let him answer the readers' letters and that, straight up.')

In the far corner of the lounge, where they stage the pensioners' bingo sessions, hired waitresses are laying out the cutlery and glasses for lunch. This is another of Barry's innovations, a further demonstration of his belief that Walham are going places: hospitality suites, match-day diners, watch the game from the table, all that razzamatazz. Straightening up, he surveys them benignly for a moment and then demands:

179

'You seen Melanie around at all?'

'Not since everyone arrived.'

'Well if you see her just send her along, OK?'

I nod. Melanie is a recent addition to the Mower entourage. Recent from my point of view, that is. When I first saw her – blonde, late twenties, fresh-faced – I assumed, not unreasonably, that she was some model girl from one of Barry's magazines lately promoted to the role of fake, wife-deceiving PA. This assumption was apparently confirmed by her habit of prinking down the Walham corridors in vertiginous high heels, pouting when spoken to and waxing unnecessarily demure in the presence of her employer. In fact it transpires that Melanie has a BA in Psychology from the University of Durham, an ACA and three years' work experience at Coopers & Lybrand and a seat on the board of Barry's holding company. Moreover, her embroilment in the Mower empire is, as I discovered during an after-hours drink one evening last week, decidedly practical.

'You mean you supervise all the porno mags? *Outsize* and *Cunning Stunts* and so on?'

'That's right.'

'What? Right down to the . . . right down to the filming?'

'Why not?' Melanie pouted reflexively, took a quick, wristy little gulp of her vodka-tonic – her third – and stared unwinkingly back. 'It's not as if it's penetrative. This is England. They don't allow hardcore, in case you didn't know.'

'But doesn't . . . Don't they . . .?'

'Get embarrassed? Why should they? They're professional people. They take their work very seriously.'

They're professional people and they take their work very seriously. Any hope of persuading Melanie to impart a few bristling revelations about Barry Mower died then and there. Curiously, though, she seemed faintly sympathetic to the predicament in which I now find myself.

'So what do you think – professionally speaking – about the financial situation here?'

I provided a sanitised version of Walham's melancholy fiscal state, but with a few unignorable hints about the promotions budget. Strangely this didn't produce quite the defensive reproach one might expect from one of Barry's boardroom

180

bashaws. Instead Melanie furrowed her brow, pouted again and gulped down the rest of her vodka-tonic.

'I'm interested to hear you say that. I've been warning Barry about bad accounting practices here for months. It wouldn't surprise me if there's a lot of money going astray. But then you're from the same firm as our auditors, aren't you? What do they say?'

'Oh they say pretty much as I say,' I told her blandly, not wanting to give too much away at this stage and swiftly steering the conversation round to another vodka-tonic. Thereafter, I kept a watchful and impressionable eye on Melanie's doings. At present she seems to spend two or three mornings a week here at The Dray, arriving around 11 a.m. in a nippy little BMW and spending a couple of hours closeted with Barry in his lair before departing to lunch in the company of some sporty-looking hunk left to kick his heels for twenty minutes in the foyer beforehand. ('Oh Gavin,' I heard her say to one of them last week as she tripped through the door, 'you're so *importunate*.')

Here in the present Barry shifts uncomfortably from one leg to the other like some fat cartoon-book rooster, his gaze drawn back unerringly to the groaning trestle tables.

'What are you giving them? To eat, I mean.'

'To eat?'

He weighs one pudgy hand uneasily in the other's clutch. 'Prawn cocktail. Veal escalope. Sherry trifle.'

'Will they like that?'

'I dunno. It's free innit? Anyhow, come the semis we'll have a proper restaurant up here. Menus and everything. "A pre-match cocktail or a light luncheon",' he extemporises manfully. '"Dine in style the Walham way."'

Something seems to strike him and he reaches up to claw it down. ''Ow them tapes going?'

'They'll be here by Friday. At least the first two thousand will.'

'Okey dokey. And the mugs?'

'Next week . . . They said they were having trouble screen-printing the picture of Tusker Holloway.'

Barry nods soberly. 'OK I'll buy it.'

In the wake of the quarter-final win, merchandising has

181

begun to feature largely in the Mower scheme of things. In fact most of my time in the last couple of days has been taken up in commissioning and supervising additions to the burgeoning pile of Walham memorabilia: videos of the cup games, a WALHAM HEROES commemorative beer mug. There are inflatable plastic squirrels on sale now in the club shop, which has been newly refurbished and moved from its former site near the urinals to a superior coign inside the foyer, and a broken-down old sports journalist who owes Barry a favour is hard at work on a paperback provisionally titled *Walham's Glory Road*.

All this – plus the sackfuls of illiterate ticket requests, brought in hourly by the three YTS trainees graciously employed by Barry to expand the administrative staff – has necessarily impeded my investigation of the promotions budget. None the less a little faltering progress has been made. In particular I took the radical and unprecedented step of calling the audit partner. Audit partners in Big Six accountancy firms? I leave the taxonomy to Slater, as related to me on the occasion of my joining the firm. 'Audit partners? There's two, no three – all right, let's call it four – sorts. First there's the old buggers who've been here thirty years: you know, joined the firm when it was called some name nobody can remember. Then there are the young old buggers: you know, thirty-five but they act as if they're fifty. Sort of people' – Slater sniffed disgustedly – 'who call the senior partner Sir until he tells them not to. Then there are the spivs.' '*Spivs*?' 'Wide boys. Used-car salesmen. The ones with the flowery ties and the flash suits. Talk about providing the client with creative solutions and get to audit dodgy ad agencies.' 'That's only three.' Oh yeah. I forgot the girls. And you won't hang around with *them*, Scott, if you've got any sense. All schoolmistresses or career dykes.' 'Is that right?' 'And do you know the one thing they have in common?' 'No.' 'They all hate management consultants.' They did as well. Derek Cochrane, lead audit partner on the Mower group of companies for the last five years, turns out to be one of the oldest of the old buggers. I took the precaution of checking him out in *Who's Who in the City* prior to commencing operations. Late fifties. Private school (or rather public school, as you say here) and Oxford. Articled clerk back in the days when the firm – his part of the firm – was called Murgatroyd and Smithers. Made partner in 1961 when according to Slater the entire partnership could have been accommodated in a bathroom. Then I tried to get hold of him. It took a week and seven calls. Two calls to get his secretary to return my initial call. Two more calls to get her to remember my name. Another call to persuade her to ask Cochrane to call me. Three days waiting for a further call to be returned. Finally, at the tail-end of Friday afternoon, in desperation, I called the switchboard, pretended to be the vice-president of a Swiss bank and demanded to be put through direct. Several minutes later an impossibly suave and languid-sounding baritone began:

'Cochrane here.'

'Scott Marshall. It's about the Walham Town audit and I . . .'

He cut straight in in that mild, expostulatory way they have. 'I don't think I . . .'

'Scott Marshall. Executive consultant on Tony Slater's team and I . . .'

'Oh, from MCS are you? I really think that one of my senior managers . . .'

'They're all on vacation . . . The Walham Town audit. There's some things I need to talk to you about.'

He listened a bit after that while I tossed over a few anodyne statistics from the profit and loss account. Only when I reached the question of the accounting black holes into which Barry's promotions budget seems to be plunging did he turn nasty.

'I really don't think I need to hear any more. In fact if you're suggesting . . .'

After that I turned nasty. 'What I'm suggesting is that there's something weird going on. Never mind, we all know that. Well, maybe the management committee doesn't know. Would you like to tell them or shall I?'

Thirty seconds or so of conscientious huffing later, Cochrane admitted that there might have been a few 'irregularities'; a minute after this that the irregularities might be attributable to the promotions budget; two minutes after that that they might just be having a look at year-end. An inevitable question lingered in the air between us.

'What did Barry . . . What did Mr Mower say when you told him about this?'

'I don't think . . . Do you know how much Mower Holdings is worth to us as a firm?'

A fairly clear picture of the KLS audit of Walham Town had begun to emerge by this stage. Cochrane probably hasn't visited The Dray in a couple of years. Two audit seniors spend the week there, with an occasional manager to jolly them along. All awkward questions grandly dismissed by Cochrane, who signs off the accounts after lunch with Barry at Boulestins. The whole no more than a single rotting log artfully concealed amid the burgeoning foliage of Barry's commercial empire. Other than confirming what I already knew, there's wasn't much Cochrane could tell me. After slipping in one or two censorious remarks guaranteed to give Mrs Cochrane and all the little Cochranes a hard time of it over the weekend, I rang off.

Back in the Barry Mower Lounge the morning drifts away on a fog of smoke and laboured conversation. The crowd has begun to thin out now, the players disappeared to clamorous backstreet pubs, the journalists in convoy through the park to Walham High Street in search of cabs. A dozen or so figures lounge over the tables, where the prawn cocktails are giving way to the veal escalope. Barry hurries off to superintend a monosyllabic interview that Rickie Weller is conducting with an obsequious teenaged trainee from the *Walham and Hammersmith Gazette*. Snatches of it float back through the heavy air: 'So what's your reaction to these transfer rumours Rickie? Would you say you were happy at Walham?' 'I . . .' ''Course he's bleeding happy!' Barry intervenes. 'Give him a thousand pound bonus yesterday didn't I? Why don't you write that down in your notebook?'

Out of the tail of one eye I watch Melanie come into the room and stand indifferently eyeing the proceedings. Today she's squashed into a kind of black cocktail dress, not unlike the vestments the waitresses in Balaraj's used to wear, set off by giant handcuff-like wristbands and felt bootees, but the effect is ominously businesslike. You come across this type all the time on US cable network business programmes: twenty-two-year-old waifs in Calvin Klein slacks who've just voted themselves president of their own software companies but don't have a serious boyfriend; twenty-five-year-old elves who've made a fortune via the prudent deployment of their first divorce settlement and are now promoting how-to books entitled *Your Guide To Creative Realting*. Trailed by an admiring glance or two, Melanie glides across.

'Thought you'd be out lunching . . . with Gavin or whoever.'

'Gavin's on the back-burner just at the moment,' Melanie pouts. 'You don't have people like Gavin in the States do you?'

'We have prissy fruits from Ivy League colleges, if that's what you mean.'

'It isn't actually.' Gratifyingly she seems stung by this piece of calculated effrontery. 'I know all about them. They're quite sweet if you can stand the talk about how they're collateral descendants of someone who signed the Declaration. I mean people like Gavin.'

'He seems harmless enough to me.'

'You still don't understand. Shall I tell you about Gavin? He's thirty-three. Do you know what he's done with his life so far? He went to Oxford and got drunk a lot, but everyone liked him because he was so charming. They gave him a pass degree in Classics – I don't suppose he even knew what the set books were. After that he went into the army. Can you imagine that? A grown man sitting in an officers' mess writing pompous letters to his friends full of slang about COs and RAMCs. Only then when he realised he wasn't going to be a Field Marshal he thought he'd go into the City. They like ex-army officers in the City – they think they're reliable. Only the City didn't want Gavin, despite him having some uncle on the board of a building society practically bribing whichever merchant bank he wanted to work for. So now he's an estate agent. Rather a good one. He could sell a first-time buyer a pigsty with a leaking roof through sheer charm.'

'But he still doesn't cut the mustard?'

'Poor Gavin. You see, charm's all he's got. That and some stupid father who likes him because he does all the things he did only even more self-indulgently. And it's worse than that. It's his motivation. He thinks *because* he's charming and was in the army and sells houses to people who let themselves be taken in by him that I ought to go to bed with him.'

185

Tonally, this is Henrietta-land: the confidence, the certitude, the dispassionate demolition of third party characters. There's something more though, a disparagement that is not merely moral (and Henrietta and her pals relish a high moral tone every now and then) but rooted in class. Melanie dislikes Gavin, I surmise, because she sees him as a gilded drone, someone who gets by on accent whereas other people have to rely on ability. In fact I have a suspicion that Melanie, with her cocktail waitress's outfit, her bangles and her fearsome judgments, reposes in a category of English society of which I have lamentably little experience – what my college textbooks used to call the aspiring middle classes.

Melanie gazes over at the tables. Dripping with phantom bonhomie, Barry is conducting a pair of journalists along the Walham Hall of Fame. Their eyes are shuttered with boredom. As the voices move, or rather as a single voice moves into earshot I note that Barry is recounting his famous eyewitness account of Tusker Holloway's funeral, when Walham High Street was cordoned off to admit the cortège and two thousand fans stood with bowed heads on the silent terrace while they scattered the ashes over the goalmouth.

Melanie says: 'I told Barry this would be a mistake.'

'They all came. They'll all write it up.'

'Yes, but they'll do it in the wrong way. Barry wants to come across as sweet and cuddly and user-friendly. Only trouble is, the players are scared of him. Everytime they answer a question it's as if they're looking at Barry to check everything's OK. It shows in the coverage. As far as the public's concerned, Walham Town is Barry. It might as well be him out there on the pitch playing Spurs or whoever we get in the semi-final.'

'Does that matter?'

'Soccer's about personality,' says Melanie gravely. 'Find some player with an old grandma in a nursing home that he bought a TV for so she can watch him on *Match of the Day*. Some Jack the Lad with three children by different mothers, but they all love him because of his cheeky smile. The papers love that. Not some megalomaniac chairman taking time out from his porn empire.'

If you asked me, I'd say that soccer was about lack of

personality, about lumbering twenty-year-olds basking in their collective nullity, their inability to do anything except coax a football into life, but there you are. Such is my irritation with Melanie by this time, a kind of gloomy distaste for all this omniscient shrewdness, that I can't resist chewing back.

'Don't mind my asking, Mel, but how did you get this job?'

'I . . .'

'No, how did you get it? I mean, you've got Barry sewn up. You can read him like a book. Did you model for one of his magazines? Does he owe you some favour you couldn't even bring yourself to tell me about? Go on. I'm interested. Tell me.'

Unusually enough, Melanie laughs: a silvery laugh that removes her once more into Henrietta-land. 'It's OK,' she says. 'I mean, I'm on your side Scott. There's no need to take everything personally. Now, do you really want to know how I got the job?'

'Tell me.'

'I'm twenty-eight years old, Scott. I took a first-class honours degree in Psychology from Durham. Then five years at Coopers & Lybrand. But you know about that. Did you know about the Plender Prize for Auditing? That ought to mean something – even to a management consultant. I could have made partner at twenty-six, but actually I got bored with accountancy firms. That's why I went for the job with Barry. There were thirty-seven other candidates by the way. Does that answer your question?'

You have to hand it to these career girls. How did you get your job? Oh, I'm a genius, Scott. For a moment I felt a faint pang of fellow-feeling for Gavin who, with his charm, his toothy public schoolboy's smile and his career in estate agency, was clearly steamrollered into the asphalt by this pitiless intelligence. Unobserved, I steal a glance back to determine whether in this efficient recitation of personal excellence there is a trace of vainglory. Nothing.

Down in the compost of memory something stirs. Danny Hassenblad, among countless improbable and unfeasible aspirations, had a hankering after what he called 'executive babes'. The proprietor of a fledgling computer consultancy wedged into the basement area of a Manhattan skyscraper

187

whose landlords charged him eighty dollars per square foot in rental and whose turnover in a good year might have shaded the seven-figure mark, Danny was convinced that his operations lacked glamour, that only a want of style inhibited a lightning ascent through the New York business community. 'What we need', he would say as we shouldered our way out of perilously expensive restaurants into the grey late afternoon of a Manhattan winter, 'is to bump up on the sales side. Get some really shit-hot salesman out there in the dealing rooms. Easterhouse' – Easterhouse was a much-married forty-year-old analyst from Des Moines who doubled as Danny's sales executive – 'is dead meat. Guys at Morgan Stanley and Trumpelwinters'd piss their pants if Easterhouse tried to sell them a fraud survey. Fucking *class* is what we need, buddy,' Danny would say, 'if we're gonna arrow the bigtime.'

Class. In these the wildest of times there was class everywhere in New York City: clamouring up from the street corners and imploring from the sidewalks, class strewn over the personal columns of the *New York Times* offering CalTech PhDs and Apple vice-presidencies. Bent over this cauldron of style and prowess, Danny was frankly contemptuous. 'Small change, Scott. Basically it surprises me these retards even bother. Just no-hopers chasing the break. Guys mostly, too. I been thinking about this' – his eyes took on a glimmering, pentecostal fervour – 'and what we need is a chick.' 'A chick?' 'That's right. You seen the papers lately? There's a business revolution going on out there. Tits, Harvard degrees and a grand's worth of designer pinstripe: that's what's jerking off the corporate hard-on.' Emboldened by these decorous ideals, Danny approached the most prestigious firm of executive search and selection consultants in Manhattan. Turned down on the entirely foreseeable grounds that he was Jewish, he switched his pursuit to the second most prestigious firm of executive search and selection consultants in Manhattan. These, less fastidious, furnished him with a sheaf of biographical data. Danny returned to the office in a state of tremulous excitement and threw them on my desk. 'You busy at the moment, Scott?' While I outlined the afternoon's tasks Danny tapped his fingers impatiently on the proud, perfect-bound folders. 'Lose all that.

188

I want you to take the next two hours out and go through these OK? And I mean *really go through them*, right? Then pick the best three and come see me.'

Seated in the gloomy basement, as Easterhouse and the others made timid phonecalls and played computer ice-hockey on the Mac screens, I flicked through the CVs. They were terrifying documents. Their subjects had names like Sondra J. Karpfinger and Alicia Reeferfort, had graduated *cum summa laude* from the Yale humanities school, and turned down the chance of graduate work in critical theory with J. Hillis Miller and Frank Lentriccia to take jobs in the dealing room at Shearson Lehman or the Chicago exchanges. Staring out from their photographs, demure beneath sober designer cuts, calmly baring their level, perfect teeth, Sondra, Alicia and the others listed their hobbies as waterskiing, ecological preservation and oceanic carto-graphy, and their ambitions as 'personal fulfilment within the context of a progressive commercial operation' or 'an organic contribution towards positive growth'. I picked the best three, the least objectionable and immodest three, and took them in to Danny. Peering enrapturedly over the A4 sheets with a gaze I had occasionally seen him bestow on high-grade pornography, Danny sighed with exultation. Eventually we settled on a tall twenty-seven-year-old named Anastasia Mendoza, whose qualifications took in a Princeton MBA and a Rhodes scholarship, and whose sponsors included a vice-president of the World Bank and a senior executive from the International Monetary Fund. 'It's gonna be tough, Scott,' Danny reported after their first lunch-date at a restaurant that advertised twenty dollar *hors d'oeuvres*, 'but I think I can nail her.' 'How much are you offering?' 'We're talking ninety g's and a healthcare package.' 'The *fuck*?' After a fortnight's haggling, Ms Mendoza settle for a hundred, the healthcare package and an open-top Mazda. Subsequently, delivered to the office in her boyfriend's BMW, she consented to tour her new demesne. Twenty minutes later, after she had departed in a cab in the direction of Queen's, I asked Danny how it had gone. 'It went fine, Scott. That is one professional lady . . . Actually we got a problem.' 'What sort of a problem?' 'She wants Jackson's office.' No?' 'Yeah. Plus the lady's bathroom'll have to be redecorated.' Implausibly the deal

189

was struck. Jackson, Danny's senior analyst and a man whom he had previously held in the same awe as the molten gods of Balaraj's, was summarily relegated to an alcove near the fire-exit, and the lady's bathroom subjected to a switchback two thousand dollar refit. In his memorandum to staff apprising them of these new arrangements Danny also impressed on them the need for rigorous standards of personal hygiene. 'The last thing I'm gonna have, Scott,' he confided, 'is her screwing up her nose all the time over Easterhouse's body odour.'

Ms Mendoza lasted a fortnight: two weeks of occasional sightings in the late-afternoon twilight, hasty departures in search of cabs and downtown meetings. In a two-paragraph letter of resignation she spoke of her 'inability to develop any of the strong interpersonal relationships essential to marketing activity'. Subsequently some evil genie prompted me to run a computer track on her phone: eighteen hundred dollars' worth of calls to destinations as far apart as Lima, Edinburgh and Delhi. The cab account weighed in at seven hundred. Predictably Danny blamed himself. 'I blame myself, Scott,' he remarked, evidence of this spectacular financial recklessness having been tactfully presented to him. 'Somewhere along the line, I don't know, I guess I just fucked up.' 'Forget it,' I reassured him. 'So she was a con-artist. How were you supposed to know?' Instead of mutely accepting this charitable gloss on his idiocy, Danny's face cragged over. 'No, you don't understand, Scott. We employ this lovely . . . this talented, lovely girl. Someone the world's . . . someone the world's gonna hear about, and she walks out on us. Well you might be happy with your conscience, Scott, but I'm sure as hell not happy with mine.'

Glancing back at Melanie's cool, impassive stare, I get the impression that she could teach Ms Mendoza (last heard of heading up a Wall Street insider dealing commission) a trick or two. She pouts reflexively somewhere into the middle distance and says:

'What do you think of Darren?'

'He's a nice kid.'

'Of course he's a nice kid. Jimmy Hood and Ashley Flack are nice kids, though you wouldn't want to have dinner with them or find them answering general knowledge questions on your behalf. Do you think he's good at his job?'

I hesitate a little at this. Darren, hitherto a deferential if unforthcoming minor ally, is a Mower protégé. Not knowing Melanie's views on Darren, but suspecting – given the earlier chatter about accounting irregularities – that they might not be favourable, I decide to temporise.

'Let's say he's a bit . . . overwhelmed by the volume of material.'

Whatever code Melanie is operating by seems to have been safely encrypted, as she beams back. 'Like the promotions money you're having such trouble accounting for?'

'That's right. Like the promotions money.'

In the centre of the room the party is in the process of breaking up. A few of the journalists sit sorrowfully over guttering ashtrays. Barry stands at the bar, Rickie Weller and Keith Thomas on either side of him, arms clamped round them in a fervent bear-hug. Pale, smoky light bounces off the walls. 'You staying to eat?' Melanie wonders, and I shake my head. The food's OK at the moment, in fact the food's going down a storm, but there is such a thing as tempting fate.

Dipping and weaving through the plumes of smoke, I head back to the high, angular loft Darren and I now inhabit up beneath the eaves. Here the YTS trainees – beefy teenagers with catastrophic skin problems – are gamely punting a tennis ball back and forth in the shadow of a vast cardboard box. Barry's souvenir mugs, I surmise, hot from the kiln. Catching sight of me the kids straighten up, their motive less respect than a kind of surly, fretful resignation. The ball trickles away into a corner. I flop down into a chair and wave them sadly away.

'It's OK guys. Afternoon off. Come back in the morning.'

Gary the head trainee, singled out for advancement on the grounds of being able to read unaided, looks mildly upset. 'Mr Mower reckoned we ought to unpack all them mugs . . .'

'Mr Mower's in no condition to appreciate whether the mugs are unpacked or not, so beat it.'

They disappear after this, shuffling down off the staircase to do whatever it is that bored teenagers do in West London on a rainy afternoon in January, and I sit staring at a wall calendar featuring Miss Gayna Golightly, one of Barry's model stable, and outside at the scarred terrain of the pitch, over whose inclines and deltas labours the beaten and bewildered figure of the groundsman. (Barry currently has big plans for The Dray's disappearing topsoil: to re-lay it, maybe, sod by sod, with turf brought in from the Welsh hills, or put down one of the new plastic surfaces.) Darren comes back from lunch ('Cheers mate') with a copy of *Empire* tucked under one arm and falls asleep at his desk in a strew of candy wrappers and computer print-outs, curly head pillowed on his forearms. I light another cigarette and settle down for some serious thinking.

This thing with Miranda is becoming, as my compatriots would say, even more of a thing. A deeply disturbing and problematic thing, that is, driven by behavioural excesses that it pains me to itemise. Three nights ago, propelled by who knows what stirrings of intimacy and reconciliation, we dined at Boulestins. Sullen at first, remote and distant under the spectral lights, she warmed to the lure of company and conversation. By the time of the main course, our fellow-diners regarding us with indulgent smiles, we were laughing and talking like people who have not only spent the last seventy nights recumbent in the same bed but are gladly anticipating the seventy-first. As we reached the end of the dessert, a mound of strawberries which I greeted with cool imperturbability, she said pleasantly: 'What would you do if I threw my plate on the floor?' Thinking this to be part of the general air of wisecracking and come-hither levity, I deadpanned back: 'I don't know. What would I do if you threw your plate on the floor?' There was a split second, a tiny frozen fragment of time, a freakish recollection of the old, dead-eyed spats with Sondra, before I saw her face crease over, then a stretched, ominous silence, and then one of the bowls of strawberries went skidding over the tablecloth, its contents cartwheeling and skittering over the carpet. A moment later she started shouting: high pitched ululations of reproach whose purport largely escaped me in my anxiety to get her outside. Eventually, abetted by smirking waiters, the ring of faces behind us stuck in horrified freezeframe, the check settled in a breeze of twenty pound notes, I managed to hustle her into her coat and out into the street, where she stood staring at me – not sullenly or hysterically but in the slightly guileless way of a kid who has done the worst thing it can think of and, while fearful of the consequences, is rather interested to see how its parents will react.

'What the *fuck*?'

A shrug. 'I wanted to see what you'd do.'

'What I'd do?'

'Sure. How you'd react. How you'd deal with it.'

'In a restaurant surrounded by forty people. You think that's a good place to lay on a behavioural test?'

'It's as good a place as any. I mean,' she said, 'you're lucky really. Do you know what I was planning on doing?'

'Tell me.'

'I had three deals. One I was going to take my dress off. Two I was going to blow you under the table. Not really blow you, but make it look like I was and see how you'd handle it. Three was the plate. In the end I decided on three.'

I hit her then. Just a slap round the face, born of frustration rather than a wish to do her harm: she didn't seem to notice.

'Why?'

'I don't know. It just seemed like a good idea at the time.'

For a second I reviewed my own options. One was to get a cab back to Fulham, pitch her clothes out into the street, bolt the door and go to bed. Two was to take off somewhere myself and lie low for the night. What do you do when your girlfriend sets out to humiliate you in public? Naturally, as the former escort of a number of hawk-eyed and temperamental paramours, I hadn't altogether been able to evade the public rebuke and the bar-room explosion. But these had been low-level escapades: a raised voice, say, puncturing the serenity of a Manhattan parlour, a steely glance at the dinner table to intimate that the goddess was displeased or bored or pre-menstrual; nothing like this. Eventually we shared a cab back to the apartment, where she promptly fell asleep on the davenport while I brooded on into the small hours.

What do you do? I haven't seen her much since. Waking at dawn, a line of pattern enquiries running in my head, I found the lounge empty and the coop flown. (She came back that night, as it happens, icily nonchalant, and we had a painstaking

193

conversation about supper.) It takes an incident like this to bring home to me the extraordinary and labyrinthine distance that separates Miranda from anyone else I've ever known, her absolute dislocation from the serene and placid highways of ordinary life. Even going back to the New York girls of the early 1980s with their impatience, their sulks and their withering self-absorption I can find no connection, no past paradigm to explain a current disturbance. Those Manhattan babes, those ornaments of Long Island supper tables, had been venal, spiteful and indifferent, but you knew what they wanted, and those hankerings, whether translated into the medium of sex or money, could usually be reduced to a single desire: the reassurance of their own divinity.

I remember once waking up in a loft on Staten Island late one sepia-tinted Sunday afternoon to find a girl named Tulia Schindler, a girl of breathtaking and vertiginous beauty, weeping serious and genuine tears into the pillow beside my head, and discovering that the reason for these lacerations of misery and self-doubt was that the boyfriend of Tulia Schindler's best friend, a blond thirty-year-old recently elevated to the position of junior partner in a Wall Street law firm, had diffidently wondered whether Tulia Schindler's nose might not be a quarter of an inch too long. That was how seriously Tulia Schindler took herself, there in her half-acre loft on Staten Island, Klimt and Kroposchka on the walls and a baby grand dominated by a framed photograph of her sitting next to George Bush at the 1980 Republican convention.

But who knows what Miranda wants? The tutors at the LBS I can't identify might, the people at the end of the phone lines I can't get through to might; I don't. To the other questions that have to be asked, I can supply only cautious denials. Is she on drugs? I'd say the chances were about seventy per cent on the negative side. You can tell when people are on drugs, divine it from the paraphernalia of papers, vials and spoons, not to mention their egregious and quite stultifying discombobulation. On the occasions on which Tulia Schindler took sulphate, for example – Tulia was one of those grave, impressionable girls who would sometimes intimate that she thought drugs 'brought out the best in her' – her face turned puce and her conversation became narrowly infantile. Is she clinically insane? Again, I'd say that the chances were about seventy per cent on the negative side. In my experience the deranged or even the ordinarily neurotic tend not to go in for premeditated public humiliation, their solace, on the other hand, being found in bizarre and ineluctable patterns. I had a college acquaintance who passed, not unwillingly, into the psychiatrist's sedative embrace, and her specialism was hoarding burnt match-stalks: they lay around her apartment in taped bundles like miniature cigar drums.

Not chemicals. Not snapped nerve-ends. And so I brood on as the day fans out into its mid-afternoon sprawl, gone in a spiral of cigarettes and Coke cans filched from the big hospitality pack outside Barry's office along the way. A gaggle of apprentices in jogging suits loiter on to the ruined pitch. Beneath the backdrop of the stand they seem tiny, scurrying homunculi, their progress random patterns in the mire. Darren raises his head from the desk and burrows into the henge of papers at his elbow in a single movement, smiling dreamily. Barry Mower's voice booms in the tunnel underneath us and then falls away, and I stare at the debris, the strew of coffee cups, Darren's clutter of tabloids, the cache of three thousand Walham Town complimentary biros knocked up by some novelty manufacturer who owes Barry a favour and never distributed, wondering at the strangeness, the quiet desperation of it all.

To break the spell I try phoning Slater, but there is no answer from the high, shadowy room looking out over the Thames at Blackfriars. I try the gentleman publishers in Bedford Square, only to be told that Henrietta is in a sales meeting and can't be disturbed. Darren, meanwhile, head cradled into a telephone receiver, is contentedly chasing balances at the bank (' . . . It never? . . . *Whoops*! Cheers then mate.'), his left hand doodling vigorously on a scribble-pad. When he stands up to broach the filing cabinet, I take a look: a vast Gothic castle, crenellation upon crenellation, endless battlements rising into the distance. At five, when I get up to go, Darren puts one hand over the receiver, slaps the other down on his thigh in mock-exasperation, rummages confidently in his desk drawer and brings out a thin brown folder.

'Here. I was cleaning out one of those cupboards at the back there, old statements and that, and come across this. Thought you might fancy seeing it.'

'Thanks Darren. I'll take a look at it on the way home.'

''s a pleasure.' He claps the receiver back to his ear. 'So correct me if I'm . . . *Whee*! Cheers then mate.'

Coat flapping in the currents and eddies of Walham's unheated corridors, I descend the staircase to the Barry Mower Lounge. Melanie, deep in some conversation with the nervous teenage barman, looks up and waves. In the half-light she seems remote and conspiratorial. I wave back, the gesture alerting me to the fact that I'm still clutching Darren's thin brown folder. Idly I flick it open, nod slowly for a moment or two at a page of fascinating ciphers and a heading, laboriously printed in Barry's thin, sloping hand that reads: *Promotions Account 1989/90*.

Some more data.

Item one is that I've finally obtained conclusive proof of what it is that Slater's up to. I did this by the not unreasonable expedient of asking Slater himself point-blank, late one afternoon in his office as the dusk closed in around Big Ben and we sat examining the shoal of redundancy letters intended for the oil refinery contingent and the lighthouse team. Prised from an activity in which he took keen aesthetic pleasure ('No . . . put "reluctant as we are to dispense with your services." Sounds better doesn't it?') Slater proved surprisingly amenable to discussion of his future plans.

'Let's just say that it's going to be like McCormack-Wheatcroft, only different, shall we Scott?'

I had to think a little about this remote exemplar from the bygone world of management consultancy. McCormack-Wheatcroft were the consultancy arm of a middlingly successful top twenty firm, bought out by two or three of their directors with funding from an impressionable merchant bank sometime in the early 1980s. Their speciality was selling systems strategy advice to Lloyds syndicates, a lucrative line unhappily laid waste a few months after the buy-out when their biggest client had to be bailed out by the Lloyds council and three others went down in a bogus reinsurance scam. McCormack-Wheatcroft hung on for a while – they tried to do Big Bang strategy planning and computer-aided design, but their clients were all gentlemanly English broking firms about to be swallowed up in the wave of American depredations, all with bigger advisers in tow. McCormack-Wheatcroft failed for £10 million. One of the directors was supposed to still be working in the City, that is if you counted selling insurance from an office in Shoreditch High Street.

'Like McCormack-Wheatcroft only successful?'

Slater grinned. 'Got it in one. Farq's lot are raising the capital; Quoodle's got a couple of City PR agencies ready to massage the clients – Christ, they're already buying up boxes at Wimbledon for the next three seasons. I've got six, seven directors in on it. Meeting with the management council next week to settle final terms.'

'What's Birningside think about it?'

'John? He'll be happy to pick up his pension and walk. Between you and me that last lot of cosmetic surgery was a mistake – something about the knife slipping. In fact if you want my opinion, Scott, his brain's gone.'

'But what about the council? They won't want to say goodbye to a £40 million turnover.'

'Thirty million. You've seen this year's figures. They're auditors, Scott. They think we're all wide boys from the business schools in stupid ties . . .' Doggedly Slater extemporised on. 'Would have been all right four years ago, what with Big Bang. Would have been all right two years ago, even. But not now. The money's all gone. Or nearly all gone. Won't be back for another three or four years. Better off on our own out there than tied up with some auditor stiffs who can't see the point of us.'

There was a pause. Far away, beyond the river a light winked on and off. Londa, a bolstered shape drifting in the corridor, put her face against the door, gazed stolidly for a few seconds and wandered away.

'What do you think?' Slater asked.

I thought. The financial press, when they found out about it, would favour adjectives like 'bold' and 'audacious', which it was. Timely as well. In the 1980s boom management consultants made their money by doing everything, some of it quite badly – systems, treasury management, tourism and leisure. There were even individuals who lingered in expensive offices writing corporate brochures under the guise of 'internal communications consultants'. Now in the 1990s slide the idea was to do only a few things, all of them well, what the US management glossies called 'niche consulting'.

'Specialising, huh?'

'That's right. None of this advising leisure centres in Bridlington how to clean out the pool, or telling some East End council it ought to put in a marina. Software packages. Telecoms. All that advanced IT crap they keep buying in from the States. The banks are wild about it.'

'That won't be work for two hundred people.'

'I know. So we're only going to take a hundred with us.'

Smirking, Slater outlined his plans. A management buy-out. Fifty per cent redundancies. New offices someplace, probably Docklands ('There's great barns full of desktops down there at nothing a square foot), continental tie-ups with the French software houses. Licensing agreements with the US techno-labs, the approbation of the City, Slater, Farq and Quoodle controlling the board. I hadn't seen him so excited since the time Birningside had tripped and fallen, fully clothed, into twelve feet of water during a pool-side seminar at the Institute of Practitioners in Management Consultancy's annual convention.

One question, though, stays outstanding. Where do Slater, Farq and Quoodle's grand designs on the KLS management consulting arm leave me? Answer: Slater wouldn't have blown his mouth off if he hadn't wanted me to know. Therefore . . . I took the hint and diverted him into an account of Walham Town's improving financial position, which he listened to in a kindly way while the dark closed in around us and in the fuzzy distance beyond the frosted glass Linda's bulky raincoated figure, shopping bag clutched purposefully in each plump claw, could be seen proceeding to the elevator.

Item two presented itself midway through yesterday afternoon when the phone rang.

'Scott! How you doing man?'

It was Greg: sturdy, triumphalist tones presaging the

198

revelation of some dramatic adjustment to his personal circumstance. As the line popped and crackled and his voice disappeared momentarily in a fizz of static, I thought of other similar conversations extending deep into the 1970s: Greg, out of his head on mescalin, calling up one Christmas from somewhere near the border, on the occasion of his third marriage to a Tex-Mex night-club proprietress; from Dallas, another time, just after he had enlisted in the marines.

'Greg. What's happening?'

'Hey . . .' Greg's voice petered out again in self-wonder. 'I just sold a bungalow out on the mountain to Dr Cube.'

'Dr what?'

'Guy that sings lead with that black rap band Niggahboyz. You ever heard of them?'

'It's three years since I was back, Greg.'

'Well they're pretty big over here right now, you can take it from me . . . Anyhow, it was a steal. Cube drives up here in an army truck with some other guys from the band and puts a hundred grand down in cash . . .'

I listened on for a while as Greg outlined the vagaries of Dr Cube's entourage ('and these are heavy motherfuckers, Scott. I mean, there's *a fucking assault rifle on the dashboard right*?) and the reaction of his client's scandalised Montana neighbours, who apparently had him busted on a Grade A controlled substances abuse charge within 48 hours, until finally vagrant reality supervened.

'Sorry about all this, Scott, but y'know this is a big day for me, and well . . .'

'Sure Greg. Your biggest client just got busted on a narcotics rap and the IRS will probably pull the money back on a laundering charge.'

'The *fuck*?' Greg sounded genuinely alarmed by this humble piece of badinage. 'You reckon it's drug money?'

'Has to be . . . Anyhow, how's the old man?'

'That's why I was calling . . . Thing is, Scott, he really is serious. About the trip I mean.'

'How serious is serious?' Twenty years ago my parents had had sly, bantering conversation about 'going back', but the tour agents' brochures with daffodils blowing in St James's Park and worn Cumbrian crags on the covers lay around the house unopened.

'Plane ticket serious. He's booked on a flight from JFK in ten days.' Soberly, Greg deals out flight details and times. 'You reckon you can look after him?'

For a moment I try to remember the last time I saw the old man, tracking it eventually to a mid 1980s weekend spent in a trailer park near the Everglades, interminable hours of take-out burgers and watching re-runs of *Double Your Stake*: I'd left a day ahead of my schedule.

'Sure. I'll take time off . . . I'd kind of like to talk to him before he gets here though.'

'He says he's writing.'

'Wow.'

Greg's breath echoed supernaturally down the wire in sympathy. The Marshalls were idiosyncratic correspondents. My mother had never written at all. Jeannie communicated each Christmas: careful, formal letters, patiently chronicling her professional tourneyings with the works of Kristeva, Greenblatt and Stanley Fish and her chances of departmental advancement, with occasional homely interludes on the welfare of her lover Maddox, a grizzled fifty-year-old with a plate in his head from Vietnam and a Quaalude habit. Greg confined himself to postcards, mostly from West Coast vacation resorts, their frontages exclusively peopled by *Baywatch* clones, their messages wise-guy one-liners of the *I just made out with the one on the right* variety.

'What's his state of health right now?'

'The old man? Uh . . . he's OK. Well, uh, he's not *that* OK actually. Time I spoke to him on the phone he was coughing some.'

'OK. What about his, ah, personal situation?'

'Barbara-Jean? She's in Hawaii right now. They were supposed to be getting back together but it didn't work out.'

'Thanks Greg. I'll keep you posted. Love to . . . uh, who is it?'

'Actually,' Greg says shyly. 'I've been meaning to tell you. Bobbie and me are thinking of getting married.'

'That's great news. Congratulations!'

'Thanks Scott,' Greg says with really fatuous sobriety. 'I knew you'd be pleased.'

I get home to find the apartment empty and the radio on full-blast. Odd pieces of jetsam – a hank of tissues, abandoned album covers, tangerine peel – lie over the floor. From the mat gleams a letter with the familiar crookbacked handwriting, or rather not a letter but an envelope sheltering more pictures of the Singing Postman cut out of some twenty-year-old newspaper. I take them into the kitchen, where half-empty cups of coffee pattern the draining board, and inspect them cursorily while toast flares under the grill and the rain drips against the window. On the radio the pert inflexions of a lady newscaster give way to the shipping forecast. Winds light to moderate in Dogger, gales force seven to eight in the Faroes, cloud hanging low over the Irish Sea. Such is the spell cast by the reserved yet friendly voice that the toast chars, but I eat it anyway, grading and re-grading each mouthful before daring to swallow, staring at the plate in the hope that the contents will somehow reduce themselves of their own accord, that I could miraculously ingest those precious calories by way of osmosis.

Later on I crouch in a chair by the TV and think about the old man. Where am I going to put him? What am I going to do with Miranda (an ornate and terrifying vision of my father and Miranda trading small-talk over the breakfast cups)? Does he expect to stay here? Finding no answer to these and to other enquiries, I steal over to the desk and rummage for a photograph of him I keep there in a little pile of memorabilia – postcards from Knoxville, Chattanooga and Columbus, pictures of my mother, alone and austere on the porch, the old man fidgeting in the doorway. An old one as it happens, taken back in the Tennessee days in his natty lawyer's suit, hair combed reverseways over his scalp, eyes subdued behind outsize horn-rims. It is then that I realise – the knowledge suddenly flowing into my cerebellum like warm liquid oozing to the utmost perimeters of a plate – that *I know nothing about him*, not any more, never did perhaps, even back in the old West Virginia days of porches and sunlight, Artie Tripp sending down his pitches on next door's lawn, the white birds hanging in the dead air. Like my Pederson cousins, like so many figures out of past time that had once glowed with accumulated legend and recollection, he seems no more than a face, kept alive only

201

by hearsay. Staring down at him, it would be impossible for me to put into words the emotions that his face conveys. Is he shy now? Rambunctious? Cagey? Proud? Noncommittal? I don't know; and I never did know; and perhaps I never will.

I put the photograph back in the desk, down among the residue of these English years: the subway passes, the bank books, the coins with that dainty royal head. In a succession of coffee cups, cigarettes and TV the evening passes. She doesn't come back.

Once, years after the event, I sat down and tried to work out what had triggered my parents' separation, where amid the years of protracted, low-level bickering you could find the flashpoint, the warning sign. There wasn't much. The garbage can poetry, maybe. And Artie Tripp.

'Real weird kid,' Greg used to say whenever the name came up. In fact, obsession at the level embraced by Artie Tripp wasn't uncommon back in the West Virginia hills. Single-mindedness was rated as a virtue: a spurned boyfriend, say, camping outside his ex-fiancée's bungalow or pursuing her doggedly through a morning's shopping and social calls tended to get applauded for, at any rate, 'not being a quitter'. Even the old man, a tolerant and easy-going guy who mistrusted obvious extremes in human nature, had been known to approve of this kind of tenacity. And so Artie Tripp, the son of the whey-faced and anonymous family who lived next door, became a great favourite of his solely on account of his determination to play major league baseball. To his kids, the old man's absorption in a gangling fourteen-year-old who, as Greg once sagely put it, had as much chance of realising his ambition as he, Greg, had of counselling Norman Mailer on his prose style, seemed seriously misconceived. Watching Artie Tripp at practice, pitching strenuously against a crouched human outline chalked on the wall of his father's garage, essaying endless physical jerks in the shadow of the cypress tree that drowsed over our two gardens, we felt nothing but contempt, the contempt that cruel and clear-sighted people have for the delusions of the second-rate. We knew that Artie Tripp would never play for the Reds or the Pirates, and so we despised him not for his shortcomings as a baseball player but for his reluctance to acknowledge them.

202

To the old man, on the other hand, such constancy was a sign of moral salubriousness, and for quite a long time he flew the flag for Artie Tripp, even going as far as to drive him once to a trial game at a minor league ground seventy miles away at Beckley. Here, though his protégé's failure was absolute – as far as I can remember. Artie managed to connect with two out of the ten balls that were launched at him – my father approved the spirit in which it was accepted. Six o'clock the next morning found him out there again in the shadow of the cypress tree grunting rhythmically over his back-curls, his press-ups, his squat-thrusts, gestures that seemed so futile to me that I wanted almost physically to assault Artie Tripp, to hang a sign out of the bathroom window that said ARTIE TRIPP IS A FUCKING NO-HOPER. Fearing the old man's anger, I chickened out. To him the early morning calisthenics confirmed what he had already detected; an indomitable spirit, inviolable, unquenched by this momentary reverse. But my own mute reservations were as nothing compared to the scorn lavished on Artie Tripp by my mother. 'That boy', she would pronounce, delving deep into her memory bag to produce a word since known to me only from Victorian novels, ' is a *flat*.' 'But honey,' the old man would gently remonstrate, 'you have to give him credit for perseverance now.' 'That's as maybe,' my mother would retort. 'But if any of my children' – and it was a measure of her anger that she substituted 'children' for 'kids' – 'made fools of themselves like that I hope I'd feel ashamed.'

A kid who yearned to be a baseball star. A hundred and forty mile round trip to Beckley. The silent figure in the shade of the cypress. They were weird things to fight over.

I get in early the next morning – 8.45 finds me parked in the loft, coffee and cigarettes to hand, staring out across the arid wastes of The Dray, pondering yesterday's discoveries. Darren won't be around for an hour, shy Darren with his packet of sandwiches and the tape boxes awaiting lunch-time conveyance to the video store in the High Street. Barry, driving up through the East End and the City, caught up in the snarl and choke of the Westway, rarely shows until mid-morning. The only sound comes from far below: faint janitorial scufflings floating upwards from the foyer and the Barry Mower Lounge.

It takes no more than half an hour with Darren's sheets of paper and their fascinating lines of ciphers and a sheaf of bank statements robbed out of the file in Barry's office to establish – or come close to establishing – what Barry has been up to over the past year and a half. Barry has been feeding money – large sums of money, well over a quarter of a million I make it – into a couple of agencies called Starscene Promotions and Mediafile. Quite a lot of this has been done by cheque and as such turns up on the statements. But there are other payments marked down on Darren's sheet which have disappeared entirely. It takes a quick scan down the page to establish that each of the sums whose destination eludes me is marked with an asterisk. This leads me to suppose that they were paid in cash.

By now the quarter-hour is striking on the church clock hard by in Walham Park. Silently I steal downstairs and place the bank statements back in Barry's cabinet. Then I sit and think about it all. A quarter of a million pounds, cash and cheques, to a couple of promotions agencies whose actual labours for Walham Town in terms of legitimately billed hours – there are invoices winging around to prove this – can't be more than a tenth of the total. What is Barry up to? A good preliminary move would be to find out who runs Starscene and Mediafile. For a moment I wonder about going down to Companies House, but there are easier ways. A search through the phone book turns up no trace of Mediafile, but Starscene have an address somewhere near London Wall – an odd hang-out for a promotions agency, but there you are. On the thirteenth ring I get a tired-sounding female voice. Here, in the guise of an Inland Revenue official about to issue a new notice of coding, I ask it to confirm the names of the directors. There is a certain amount of equivocating and mention of a manager who hasn't arrived yet, but I brush this peremptorily aside.

'That won't be necessary. Just read me the names off the bottom of the notepaper.'

'M. E. Machen and L. S. Sullivan. Are you sure you don't . . . ?'

Maurice and Lennie, inevitably enough. After this I don't bother to continue the pursuit of Mediafile. Instead I sit and think about what the previous forty minutes have turned up. The news that Barry is diverting large amounts of capital to companies administered by two of his close friends in return for grossly overbilled promotional services or simply out of the kindness of his heart is scarcely surprising. A little more surprising, maybe, is the fact that he's doing it in cash. Wondering about this, and bewildered by the wider etiquette of what English soccer club chairmen can legitimately do with their money, I decide to put in a call to Terry Long at KLS.

'Terry? Scott. How's it going, dude?'

'Not so bad. We're just finishing off an activity-based costings job for ICI.'

'Activity-based costings?'

'Charging back your overheads,' Terry says laconically. 'Means the department ends up leasing their office space off the management. It's all the rage. Now what can I do for you?'

I explain about the morning's discoveries as the sounds from below grow more obtrusive. A few gulls hang low over the further goal post. Beyond, the ziggurat formation of the away terrace rises into a wintry sky. Throughout the recitation Terry whistles intermittently through his teeth.

'What do you think?'

'I dunno, Scott. Well, I could make a pretty good guess but . . . The payments to Maurice and Lennie sound like a deliberate tax scam. And maybe a whole lot more. Maybe they get the money back to him somehow, I don't know. From Barry's point of view it makes a lot of sense. You buy a dodgy football club thinking you can sell the land and then when you can't you start using it to fool the taxman.'

'Is that illegal?'

'I think the Revenue would like to know about it, don't you? And the Football League would definitely be interested. But it's the cash payments that worry me.'

'Go on.'

'You can't fool the Revenue with cash payments. At least not the way Barry's trying to fool them. Cash payments means laundering. What sort of business is Barry into these days anyway?'

I mention a few of the better-known outposts of the Mower empire. The porn mag offices in Lewisham. The warehouses in Silvertown. The casino-cum-fun pub in Leyton. The property interests – not as flourishing as they were, but still serious enough to demand a management team and a suite in City Road. Terry clucks his tongue interestedly.

'All sounds pretty legitimate. Not much spare change floating about in property. And you can bet the Revenue's keeping an eye on that casino; they always do. Don't see Barry pulling any security van heists either, despite his upbringing. I'd say it was drugs.'

'But Barry's high profile. TV docs. Picture in the papers. Jesus, his kid's inside at the moment for peddling smack.'

'Doesn't matter. It's what people like Barry do these days. Where the money is. Low overheads. No, I'd say it was drugs.' Terry sounds unusually pleased as he reaches this alarming conclusion, careless of the consequences for my own state of mind, livelihood, personal security and so on.

'But hang about. If there's money going out, there's probably money coming in as well. Any idea what the cash receipts for the Villa game were?'

'A hundred and fifty, Barry said. A hundred and fifty-five.'

'Way too much, Scott. About fifty grand too much, looks to me like there's some extra being sprinkled in from somewhere.'

'So what do I do?'

There is a longish silence. 'It's a tricky one, Scott. Never mind laundering, tax dodges tend to mean poor auditing, so no one in-house is going to thank you for pointing it out. Let's face it, you're not going to talk to Barry about it. Slater's not going to be interested: he's in the middle of buying us all out – some of us, that is – so far as the rumour goes. You could try the Inland Revenue. You could definitely try the police. Put it this way: how badly do you feel about Barry Mower?'

How badly do I feel about Barry Mower? From below comes the sound of footsteps. A second or two later and Darren's curly blond head rises from the ladder into the doorway.

'It's a tricky one, Terry. Thanks a million.'

I flip the phone back into its cradle as Darren slowly ascends into view: blond hair, anxious expression, copies of *Radio Times, TV Quick* and *Cine Sensations* wedged under his arm. Outside the gulls have disappeared. In the distance pale yellow sun glints on the surface of the water, and I wish I were a thousand miles away.

12

Orange claw hammer

It happens without warning.

Slowly the long night unravels. At eleven I go to bed to find her already collapsed beneath the sheets. The room is dark except for the purplish glow of the gas fire. Burrowing into the warm nest of the bedclothes I try not to wake her, try very hard to ensure that no prying finger or intrusive foot wrests her from her slumber; solicitously I curl up in a remote cranny of this smooth, penumbral terrain. Beyond, the outlines of the room, extinguished with the light, re-emerge; clumps and patches of darkness unbend to reveal chairs and cupboards, heaps and tussocks of discarded clothing. Sometime after midnight – the alarm clock's luminous dial is a foot away – I awake to find that nothing in this silent landscape has changed. In the distance the faint susurration of traffic ebbs and flows. I fall asleep again almost immediately, deep down in my warm, inviolable burrow. Rising at 2 a.m. from remote, sunless caverns beneath the rush and swell of the ocean, moving amid the fluorescent shoals of fish up to the far-off light, I notice that several of the essentials in this calm, somnolent world have changed: the huddled form at my side has gone; soft light coming from the open door falls over the carpet. Following its contours and traceries, I stare out over the room towards the source, charmed and fascinated by the way it colours Miranda's dappled flanks as she squats by the gas fire. Still half-conscious I look on in a kind of approving stupor as Miranda continues unobtrusively with whatever it is that she's doing, rummaging in her handbag, apparently, fingering something in its innermost recess. There is a faint slither of a zip, a hand scuffing leather, as she stands and half turns towards the bed. An affecting sight, this, one rosy haunch outlined in the firelight, a breast lobbed deftly into view. Whatever it is that she grasps gleams palely in the darkness near her waist, vanishes for a moment into shadow, reappears with a silvery glint at the level of her shoulders. It could go on for hours, this tableau – the quiet hiss of the fire, light drenching the doorway, the poised figure a yard or two distant – were it not for the fact that she suddenly leaps up, springs forward on to the bed and smashes down whatever it is she carries on to my skull. Or rather, on to the pillow three inches to the left of my skull. Alerted by some faint indication of trouble in store – a creak from the floorboards as her foot presses down, the expression on her face as she whips into view, the whole sensation of sharp, purposeful movement – I've already started shifting as her fist scythes forward through the gloom. Even so, something hard and ominous brushes against the side of my head as it thumps down into the pillow. As I lunge up in riposte the hand goes back again, but this time both my hands are clasped around her wrist. We stay locked in this position for a couple of seconds – her eyes expressionless sockets – before whatever it is in her hand clunks down on to the carpet and she's tearing away at my face with her fingernails. What surprises me – along with all the other things that are surprising me, all the alarm bells and panic stricken 'I told you so's' ringing in my head – is how strong she is. At the start I hefted her a couple of quick, dispassionate blows in the mouth, but it could be some scared, indifferent challenger vainly trying to impede Tyson's oncoming surge. Sure her face goes down for a second, but next moment my balls are wrenched halfway out of my scrotal sac and I have to squirm tortuously to one side to evade her. We hit the floor simultaneously but she hits it the harder, the back of her head wallops against the bed castors and before she can regain her balance I have one hand round her throat and the other scrabbling for the light switch that hangs down from the bedside lamp. Even then it's far from a straightforward war of attrition. I nearly lose an eye in the upward rake of her fingers. Several handfuls of hair come out during the course of her last, faltering assault. But finally it's all over and she lies silently and sullenly on the floor, one hand shielding her head, the other pawing furiously at the carpet. And that is the curious thing: the silence. Throughout the previous sixty seconds or so she hasn't spoken. I, meantime, have produced an alternative dictionary's-worth of abuse, screamed *fuck* very loudly when the first blow came down, shouted *shit shit shit* in a kind of mantra while we were grappling on the floor, fired short sharp bursts of *you cunt you cunt you cunt* when I eventually managed to clamp my arms round her. A minute later, when my pulse rate is down to a steady hundred and the breath has ceased to rasp terrifyingly in and out of my lungs, I say:

'Why did you do that?'

No reply. I let go cautiously and take a look at her. She lies twisted to one side. There is warm, fresh blood coursing down my chin, which turns out to come from my nose. The thing she tried to hit me with is revealed as a steel claw hammer, maybe a foot long and weighing four or five pounds. Try again.

'Why did you do that?'

She doesn't answer. I stand up, carefully avoiding all contact with the recumbent figure on the floor beside me, and examine the room's curious devastation: the ruffled sheets, a trail of blood darkening the pillow above them, alarm clock and bedside appurtenances thrown all around. The bag she was delving into lies by the gas fire. Suspiciously I kick it over. Painfully my foot connects with something hard and metallic. For some reason this is the final, authenticating terror, and I start shrieking: 'Why did you do that? Why did you do that? I ought to break your fucking neck. Maybe that's what I'll do. Break your fucking neck. Who the fuck are you, anyway? Just who the fuck?'

She doesn't answer. I turn the bag out over the floor. A kitchen knife – the kind macho chefs use to cleave steaks in two – clatters forth, along with a tide of pocket books, scuffed photographs, sheets of grey-white paper. On impulse I pick up the nearest photo. It turns out – and the shock is visceral, sickening – to be a picture of my wedding. Me. Sondra. Aloof, frowning Greatorexes. Greg and my mother. Hangers on, familiar and unknown.

'Where did you get this?'

She doesn't answer. I root through the surf of paper and come across more weird stuff, a letter signed by me on KLS stock replying (in the negative) to some job applicant, a sheet torn from a KLS in-house directory with my name picked out in pink marker, a photo of myself – dim, shadowy, but me without a doubt – emerging from the maw of the subway at Blackfriars. Throughout these investigations the wedding portrait balances delicately in the cradle of my fingers. I notice it as I flop down once more on the bed.

'Where did you get this?'

The voice, when it finally comes, is remote and preoccupied. 'I'm on it.'

'What do you mean, you're on it?'

'Like I said.' She sounds like a bored schoolmistress efficiently reciting tables to some numskull kid. 'I'm on it. Take a look.'

I gaze slowly across the creased polaroid. Me. Sondra giving an uncharacteristically snaggle-tooth smile. My mother looking distant but mildly benign; Greg prawnish and stupid. The Greatorexes fiery with discontent. An elderly couple, arm-in-arm and beaming. An odd girl in a patterned dress who might have been Sondra's sister.

'The girl in the patterned dress . . . Margy?'

'Got it in one,' Miranda says stonily. 'Me.'

'But you don't . . . Jesus, you don't even look like her.'

'Neat, isn't it?' Miranda says. 'Of course, the hair's easy – just dye and bob – but the rest . . . Do you know I had each cheekbone smashed and reset half an inch nearer the socket before I could get to come out here?'

'It sounds like an exam.'

'It is. Contrary to what you read in the papers, this is a professional organisation.'

Everything starts falling into place now. The anonymity. The fake IDs. The weird silences. The public humiliations. I snatch the picture back from her sinewy grasp.

'Why me? What did I do?'

This surely is unanswerable. Miranda/Margy shrugs.

'You ever hear from Sondra these days?' she asks.

'A couple of times. Last time would have been three years back.'

'OK. You want to know what happened to Sondra after she walked out? Six months in a psychiatric ward on Long Island for starters. Towards the end they found she had brain damage.

210

Not vegetable level, but enough to slur her speech a little, forget the right words. "Injuries consistent with being thrown repeatedly against a hard surface" it said in the report. She spent another year in rehab before they let her out. Of course, the modelling was all messed up. Plus the research project – I mean, she could barely hold a pen. Mostly she just stays home with mom and dad right now.'

While I think about this Miranda/Margy starts pulling her clothes on: underwear scooped up rapidly from the floor, jeans and T-shirt swiped off a chair-back. Completing the task, she turns back with her hands on her hips.

'But I don't suppose you even remember. According to Sondra you were out of your head most of the time. I mean, it was probably just one of those things that passed you by.'

She's dead right. I don't remember any of it. Thinking about it in silent paralysing horror I stare back at her, seeing now with a kind of fearful clarity the traces of the girl in the photograph. She looks – and here I strain for the right comparison – she looks like the ghost of Margy, whom I met, as it happens, only two or three times before the wedding at tense social events and crowded family clambakes. The eyes and the tilt of the nose are the same but the face has widened out some, the chin somehow lost its point and declivities. Bewildered by the vast, fuzzy unguessables looming at the edge of all of this, I ask:

'But why the wait? I mean, you could have beaten my brains out the night we met.'

Miranda/Margy frowns. 'You don't understand. It's not that simple. The guys in the newspaper stories, they weren't just casual pick-ups. Everyone was in what he thought was a long-term relationship. RAM is about humiliation as well as revenge.'

'Three months is a long time.'

'Oh, there was another side to it – I mean, I kind of liked you. No, even when I met you with Sondra I kind of liked you. That aloofness. So it wasn't any big deal. There are some girls, you know, have to take counselling, go and see therapists and so on, before they can bring themselves to go through with it. But that wasn't ever any problem for me.'

'I suppose not.'

'And then I tracked you down. It wasn't so hard. Those New

211

York consultancies keep big databases. In the end I spoke to that guy Hassenblad you used to work for. He didn't have your number but he had your brother's in Montana. That fixed it.'

'And then you were going to bust my head in half?'

'Sure,' says Miranda/Margy matter-of-factly. 'Then I was going to bust your head in half. For Sondra.'

'And the sisters.'

'Between you and me I don't go for that universal sisterhood rap. But I wasn't going to let you get away with what you did to Sondra.'

Another silence. I pull my own clothes on, somehow more embarrassed by my nakedness than by what has passed between us.

'The question is,' Miranda/Margy goes on, 'what happens now? I mean, I just tried to kill you with an five-pound steel hammer. Now, you could call the cops – which might cause a lot of trouble, for you as well as me – or you could just let me walk right on out of here. What's it going to be?'

For a second I hesitate, but Miranda/Margy is already brushing past on her way to the door, bag clutched in her fist. The light falls again on the claw hammer, hard and inert on the carpet, and suddenly rage supervenes. I grab hold of her arm, get a kick in the knee-pan that makes me loose my grasp. When I recover she's half-a-dozen paces gone into the lounge. Springing forward I collide with a chair ostentatiously flicked into my path by some departing extremity. By the time I make it downstairs into the street, down into the cold, alien moonscape of the Fulham Road where a single car lurches by, the silent, loping figure is twenty yards away, off in the direction of the Broadway and the cab rank. For some reason – some very obvious reason – I decide not to follow.

For a long time afterwards, as the gas fire burns on and the room finds its old, silent patterns once more, I sit wondering what to do. Where has she gone? Will she come back? Most important of all, is she what she says she is? My hand, hovering for a while over the telephone, does no more than hover. No conversation I can imagine, whether with cop, lawyer or journalist, is likely to expose me to anything but the vilest humiliation. In the intervals of establishing this reluctance to act, I pad silently across the room and restore some of its disarray. The claw hammer rests on the carpet. I stare at it once or twice, then pick it up. It weighs more than one could ever anticipate a foot-long slab of steel and metal could weigh. I take it through to the kitchen and junk it, in the sink, destroying whatever forensic interest it might possess.

Everywhere around there are traces of her presence. I gather them up, note resentfully how sparse, how sadly unincriminating is their cumulative effect: spent tissues, a pair of sneakers in the corner of the lounge, a little bundle of torn old papers. Eventually I do just about the only thing I can do in the circumstances. Taking a sheet of paper from the drawer, I sit down and compose a letter to Henry and Myra Greatorex, reminding them in dispassionate and neutral terms who I am and enquiring, unexcitedly, if they have any news of their daughter Sondra. Glancing up from the final sentence at the uncurtained window, I note the first, faint upward beat of the early traffic, but the impulse is uncontrollable and I sidle out into the Broadway to post it. The cars, lashed and jockeyed by their grinning drivers, surge forward into the dawn.

Later on in the day, aided by a copy of the *International Consulting Directory*, I try calling Danny Hassenblad. Coopers' switchboard in Manhattan thinks he might be off on vacation, but eventually I get a client number way out in upstate New York. A dozen rings and then a bored and hopelessly neurotic-sounding Jewish voice says: 'Daniel J. Hassenblad.'

'It's Scott Marshall, Danny. You remember?'

There is a pause down the line, and I try to visualise Danny stuck in his cramped consultant's dug-out down under a broking house or a giant computer warehouse, smoke trickling out of his cigarette, white, tonsured scalp shining up beneath the ash-grey curls.

'Guy who almost died on me in a fish restaurant. Could I ever forget?'

As ever, the fake jauntiness is undermined by deep-seated unease. Danny starts saying something else, but the words are swallowed up in a surge of mechanical crepitations.

213

'You out on a contract someplace?'

'Maintenance scam for a dairy farm is all. They got us twenty feet down in the control station fixing the grid for these automated milking machines. Every half hour or so some asshole forgets we're here and turns the generator on.'

'Uh huh. How's business?'

'Can't complain. Sixty g's and a medicare package. Plus I get to crap in the executive consultants' john.'

'Creature comforts?'

'Hey.' Danny's voice narrows. 'There's this Puerto Rican chick I met on the Staten Island ferry, OK?'

During the course of the ensuing rhodomontade, which for Danny carries an odd weight of conviction, I try to estimate what kind of take he might have on the business in hand. I'd come across Danny in the early 1980s, two or three years before I started working for him; he'd come to the wedding – a lone, brooding presence, looking dangerously out of place amid Greatorex retainers and my father's Pederson relatives – and his bourbon-soaked camaraderie had helped sustain me in the days after Sondra quit.

'Danny,' I say, breaking into an X-rated monologue about his exploits in a motel hot-tub in Kansas City, 'you get a call from a girl called Margy Greatorex recently?'

'Sister of that chick you were married to? Yeah as it happens. Three, four months back. Wanted your number too.'

'You give it to her?'

'Gave her your brother's. Any reason why I shouldn't?'

'Only she just missed splitting my brain in half with a cleaver.'

Danny quietens down a touch after this, and I manage to glean the essentials of Margy's enquiry, principally an innocuous-sounding request to convey some 'message' from Sondra. Further details about Margy's dainty ways have him gurgling with terror.

'Don't tell me about it, Scott. Just don't tell me, OK? Like, we got these feminist gangs over here too. You ever hear of the Lesbian Avengers, or the Dagger Dykes? Last month they cornered this guy in a parking lot outside of Huntsville and . . .'

'Listen Danny,' I interject again. 'Do me a favour, will you? Old times' sake or whatever, but just do it. Check out Sondra for me. Where she is. What she's doing. Whether she's OK. And then call me.'

Somewhere down the wire there is a clatter of voices. The generator roars. 'Listen Scott,' Danny says, 'I have to go right now.'

'But you'll do it for me? For old times' sake?'

'OK I'll do it,' he says hastily. 'But not for that.'

'What?'

'*Fuck* the old times, Scott,' Danny shoots back, with a proud, unwonted savagery. 'Just fuck them OK?'

A couple of weeks later. I separate the slim airmail letter with its Massachusetts frank out of the strew of bills and circulars in an instant and tear it open. Henry Greatorex's handwriting.

Dear Scott,

It would be dishonest of us not to say that we were surprised and distressed by your letter. In the circumstances we had not expected to hear from you again. Neither can we imagine what you hope to achieve by writing in this way. In answer to your question, Sondra is currently working in Seattle as a volunteer in a community drug rehabilitation project and when we last saw her seemed positive and happy. As you did not ask it, we have not told her of your letter; nor shall we. We would be obliged if you did not attempt to contact us again.

Yours sincerely

Henry and Myra Greatorex

And what about your other daughter? What about poor mad Margy? There is another letter to be written here, but I'm not the guy to write it. I convey the Greatorexes' reply – an exquisite Massachusetts liberal reply, it strikes me – to a cardboard box in the back room to lie alongside a tourist map of Upstate New York, some motel bills, a grainy studio print of Sondra in an Armani swimsuit, a handful of maple leaves picked up from some New England forest floor years ago.

PART THREE

And Quoodle here discloses
All things that Quoodle can.
G.K. CHESTERTON – *The Song of Quoodle*

13

A present from London

On a bright spring morning I go to meet him at the airport. Sunlight sparkles off the walkways and grids; pennants flap in the breeze. In the arrivals lounge I notice him immediately: a spry, distinguished figure in smart yet winningly casual clothes. Luggage lies drawn up around him: hand-grips and cameras and sleekly expensive suitcases. When he catches sight of me easing across the teeming plain, he gestures gladly. Surrounded by touched, approving faces we silently embrace. Striding proudly in tandem with his baggage towards the waiting cab, I glance back at him, noting and savouring the tanned skin, the calm, watchful eyes. Outside sharp, shiny light floods the outbuildings and storage halls. In the cab, rolling back along the wide, empty highways to central London, we sit in mute but cheerful amity. Finally, as the city's bulk looms towards us, my father turns towards me, hand clasped fervently in my own. 'It's been a long time, Scott,' he says at length.

Let's play that one again.

On a stormy spring afternoon I go to meet him at the airport. Rain spills over the unwelcoming tarmac; the planes keel crazily through the murk. In the arrivals hall I strain to recognise him amid the clamouring Asian families and the Yankee tourists in their stretch-slacks and shell-suits, a bent, bewildered figure in a pair of faded dungarees and a cotton jacket. A couple of winded K-Mart carriers, broken open and disgorging their contents over the floor, lie at his feet. When he catches sight of me, slowly responding to the windmilled signals from a yard or so away, he stares blankly for a while before giving a faint simpleton's nod. Surrounded by sullen, indifferent faces we nervously contemplate each other. Struggling laboriously in single file with his baggage towards the empty cab rank, I glance back, deprecating the worn declivities of his skin with its cross-hatch

219

of wrinkles, the weak, rheumy eyes. In the cab, labouring back along the choked, narrow highways, we sit in mute but uneasy embarrassment. Finally, as the city's bulk looms towards us, my father turns sideways, hand clasped anxiously within my own. 'I'm not feeling so good, Scott,' he says at length.

Above the throb and whine of the bunched traffic we bicker helplessly. 'How do you mean, you're not feeling so good?' 'I don't know. Kind of sick in my stomach.' 'You want me to tell the guy to stop?' 'No.' The old man is taking in great gulps of air, noisily inflating his caved-in cheeks like Hoover bags. 'And I have this pain in my head.' 'How bad?' 'Pretty bad. Say seven point five on a scale of ten.' The cab nudges forward for a quarter mile or so, then snarls up in a mass of cones and reversing trucks. 'You want me to get the guy to stop?' 'It's no big deal,' says my father vaguely. Fetched up in a layby beneath the disapproving eye of the cab driver I watch him curl forward on the tarmac, clutching his stomach. Peering short-sightedly around him, tendrils of greying hair plastered across his forehead by the rain, he looks like an exceptionally frail and elderly turtle. From afar comes the rattle of thunder. Eventually he retches a couple of times, inconclusively, then straightens up. 'You feel any better?' 'A little maybe.' As I help him back the cab driver turns suddenly solicitous. 'All right mate, all right,' he chides as my father's hand slips on the door. The meter by this stage is way over the £20 mark.

Back in the car he grows more animated. 'You take time off work to come down here?' 'Uh huh.' 'I appreciate that, Scott.' Steam rises from his sodden clothes: an odd smell of rivery deliquescence. Half-a-mile further along the road one of the K-Mart carriers spills open across the seat. Gloomily I marshal its contents: a pack of See's chocolates, a wodge of paper tissues, a bunched pair of sneakers. At the bottom of the pile is a porn mag called *Asian Babes*. I flick through a couple of pages and come across a picture of a disdainful muscleman sodomising a doleful-looking Filipino girl. 'You just walked straight through Customs with this?' 'Oh they're tolerant guys back there,' says my father. I put *Asian Babes* back in the carrier along with a sheaf of Greyhound bus tickets, a three-week-old copy of the *Washington Post* and a couple of Snickers bars.

220

The cab charges on towards the West London hinterland of
Brentford and Chiswick. Somewhere near Chiswick he feels sick
again. Pulled up at the side of the road, with the traffic curling
angrily around us, he finally throws up in honking, implacable
spasms. The cab driver looks on impassively. 'Is he your dad
then?' 'He sure is.' 'Not too healthy is he, mate?' 'I guess not.'
The meter by this stage has reached £35. Manoeuvred back into
his seat he looks white and exhausted. Staring sightlessly at the
cellphone ads and the No Smoking sign he dabs at his mouth
with a tissue. 'How far is it?' he asks at one point. 'How far to
where we're going?' 'A couple of miles. You think you can hold
out till then?' 'I guess so.' Nearing Hammersmith Broadway he
stares wonderingly at the huddled crowds and the blighted
storefronts. 'Are we in London yet?' he asks. 'We sure are.' A
moment later, as the cab surges forward over the bridge, he
says, 'And would this be the old Thames river?' 'It would.' Long
after the cab is caught up in the tumult of the Fulham Road he
sits twisted up in his seat, gazing back along the trail.

The cab drops us outside my apartment. I flip the driver a £50
note. ('Cheers mate. Anytime.') Hustled indoors, K-Mart
carriers clutched anxiously to his chest, he flops down uneasily
on the lip of an armchair, knees rising to his chin like a winded
grasshopper. 'Are you OK?' 'Sure I'm OK. Flight took it out of
me is all.' 'You want me to get you anything?' 'What you got?'
asks my father critically. 'Coffee. Juice. Beer. Bourbon.' 'Beer,'
he says throatily. I grab him a can of Budweiser out of the
chiller, watch him take a sip or two and then wedge it
awkwardly between his feet. 'Nice place you got here,' he says
without looking up. 'I like it.' 'Greg now, I went to stay with
him one time and he was living in a cardboard box up in the
woods someplace.' 'Is that right?' 'Haven't seen Greg in a while
though.' 'I guess not.' Desperately seeking some respite from
this sitcom dialogue, I gaze round the room. Here and there are
tiny remembrances of Miranda – cassette tapes, marker pens, all
the detritus of a spent, anonymous life. The effect is highly
disturbing. 'You know,' says my father, managing to make the
suggestion sound an idea of mild originality, 'what I could
really handle is a liedown.' He takes three attempts to shift
himself out of the chair. Finally I haul him up two-handed,

221

misjudge the effort required, and he tumbles forward into a brief, slumping embrace. His body feels sparse and loose, troubled by these small, effortful manoeuvres. 'Are you OK?' 'Just a little tired is all,' he says humbly. In the bedroom, after taking off his jacket and making a cursory inspection of drawers and coverlets, he falls asleep almost immediately, hand held on one side in the crook of his arm. I draw a blanket over him, go back to the sitting room where I retrieve the seven-eighths full can of Budweiser, rescue vague, floating items of his personal paraphernalia – a leaky biro, a grimy pack of mints – from hidey-holes in the carpet or down the sides of the chair. Later I return to the bedroom and stand there for a minute carefully looking him over, eager to establish what the intervening years have done. In repose, keeled over on to his back now with his eyes half open, he seems only a strange, worn-down ghost of the guy I knew: hair turned grey-white and almost gone, chicken-wing arms drawn up across sunken ribs. Twisted up above his calf, the pants leg reveals a tracery of shot veins. On the bedside table, half-hidden under the discarded cotton jacket, there are bottles of pills. I haul them out and take a look: prednisolone, dialaudid aspirin. The memory of paranoid riffling through medical textbooks assures me that prednisolone are cortico-steroids, but dialaudid, unless I'm greatly mistaken, is synthetic heroin. I stow the bottles back beneath the jacket, and steal away.

An hour later Greg calls.

'He get in OK?'

'Sure.'

'Seemed OK?'

'Depends what you mean.' What does OK mean? I haven't seen him in ten years. OK could mean coughing blood. I explain a bit about the stuttering cab ride. Greg whistles down the line. 'Figures. Last time I saw him he got sick in a restaurant. Spewed all over a plate of anchovies.'

'Listen Greg,' I tell him. 'There's a bottle of prescription dialaudid on the table in the other room right now.'

'Fuck is dialaudid?'

'It's synthetic heroin. Morphine. They give it to terminal cases in New York Central.'

222

There is a silence. 'Look,' Greg says warily. 'Don't get me wrong, but there's a state congressman out there in the corridor wants to buy a timeshare ranch. Just keep me posted OK?'

'OK.'

He sleeps for a long time: five or six hours. Eleven has long gone by the time he shuffles blearily into the sitting room, wearing an old dressing gown I left hanging behind the door and massaging his scalp with the back of his hand.

'What time is it?'

'Midnight, near enough. You want anything to eat?'

'Guess not.' He slips the *Daily Mail* up off the davenport and starts flicking through the listings pages. 'Hey. You have cable TV over here?'

'This is England.'

I leave him peevishly installed in front of a Channel Four talkshow. At three, wrenched from a turbulent nightmare involving Miranda and a band of chainsaw-wielding harpies, I monitor the frail, pinkish glow burning beyond the bedroom door.

Waking at seven, the first thing I register is a smell of cooking fat. Outside, beneath blue-black clouds, rain blows in on the wind. In the kitchen the old man stands with his back to the door, hunched over the stove. 'I fried you some mushrooms,' he says. 'You want them now?' 'I usually miss breakfast.' 'These are good,' he enjoins. 'Go on. Eat them.' They are good as well. Awed by his level, domineering gaze I swallow half-a-dozen in quick succession. 'That's right,' the old man says benignly. He looks better this morning, like a zestful elderly pixie. 'How long you been up?' I enquire. 'Me? I never went to bed. Watched a couple of talkshows and then called Elizabeth. You don't mind?' I didn't know he was still in contact with Elizabeth, but I don't mind. 'No, I don't mind,' I tell him. 'You want some more to eat?' I shake my head and he conveys plate and utensils reverently to the sink and dowses them with water. At eight he hauls himself away to the bedroom, re-emerges a few minutes later in a plaid, lumberjack's shirt, Levis and open-toed sandals. Framed in the backdrop of bright check his face looks white and translucent, the eyes milky and remote. 'You have to go to work today?' he asks. 'I took the week off.' 'That's good,' he says vaguely. We have another cup of coffee and watch the breakfast news: tanks rolling over the Iraqi desert, Bush on the White House lawn, Major at the despatch box. 'Kind of like that guy,' the old man ruminates. 'Papers back home said he was a fruit, but I kind of like him.' The coffee lies cold and untouched in his cup. 'I never did . . .' he starts, but what he never did is gathered up and overrun in a noisy fit of coughing. I stare at the carpet while he hawks and whistles and honks into a wad of tissues. 'Are you OK?' 'I guess so,' he says disbelievingly, turning his head from side to side as if the room has somehow developed new planes and angles which he can't quite assimilate into his personal topography. 'No, I mean are you really OK?' The eyes are wary and unfocused now, lost in some private world of calamity and calculation. 'I'm dying, Scott,' he says.

Later I creep into the bedroom and find him perched on the mattress with his knees drawn up on either side of his chin like an old, frail grasshopper, drowsing over a book called *The Ecclesiastical Architecture of Surrey*. 'You mind if I ask you something?' 'No.' 'OK. What is it?' Getting only a blank stare, I stumble on: 'I mean, what are you dying of?' The old man makes a neat little wave with one forefinger – a courtier's wave, a dandy general's wave to his eager subalterns – and then taps it against his ribs. 'Cancer?' He pulls the finger away and looks at it curiously, as if it were newly grown. 'Uh huh. You ever hear of a thing called sarcoid?' I shake my head. 'Yeah, well neither did I until a year or so back. You know how a kettle gets furred up with limescale sometimes? Well, that's what sarcoid does to your lungs. It's not life-threatening, not usually. But me, they reckon there's something else going on in there as well. Some complication, I don't know.' 'You seeing a doctor right now?' 'Was doing.' 'You want me to fix you up to see one?' 'I'm OK,' the old man says suspiciously. 'You just leave me alone, OK?'

Several times over the next day or so I renew this appeal. The response is always the same. Sarcoid, as checked out in the medical dictionary in Fulham Library, is much as the old man describes it. Like tuberculosis or leprosy, the book helpfully

224

proposes, the difference being that there isn't a cure. He gets pills from somewhere: I don't bother asking how the rows of canisters are renewed. When he sleeps during the daytime I prowl round the apartment, call Terry Long, sit staring at the Walham papers, think about Slater, Farq and Quoodle, wondering vaguely, but with increasing desperation, what I'm going to do about it all.

In these early spring days the pattern of our lives settled into a calm, unhurried flow. We breakfasted late and cursorily. My father had no appetite now but it amused him to pretend that he had. For a morning or two I was deceived by his careful pretence of hunger: only a chance inspection of the garbage can revealed the succession of steaming dishes and the plates piled high with toast to be an elaborate piece of camouflage. Later we caught subway trains to the tourist landmarks: Westminster, the Palace, the Tower. If my father enjoyed these excursions he did not say so. Caught up in a tide of impressionable fellow-countrymen, his stance was that of the respectful ingénu who seeks in antiquity the whiff of moral excellence. He had a little game involving the waylaying of policemen before well-known public monuments. Was this, my father would enquire, standing as it might be on Westminster Bridge, his jaw irradiated by a hayseed's grin, the celebrated Big Ben of which he had heard so much? Was that, he would demand, reaching the end of the Mall half-an-hour later, the famous Buckingham Palace? The policemen were polite and informative, but there was a sardonic glint in his eye that made me writhe with nervousness.

My father was methodical in his approach. He had a tourist map of elderly vintage on which he recorded his journeys around the city; a slow, laborious trail that took him northwards as far as Regent's Park, south to the borders of Lambeth, west to Marble Arch, east to Brick Lane and the cockney street markets. Long years of study had raised his familiarity with the subject in hand to the level of arrogance. Like the professional oenophile obstinately demanding some prized vintage from a reluctant waiter, he would not be fobbed off by denial or prevarication. In this way, arriving some ten minutes after the cut-off point for entry, professing at first bewilderment, then outrage, then steely determination, he contrived to get himself privately escorted around the Tower of London long after the last of the Scandinavian tourists had gone marching off into the late-afternoon gloom. 'A fine building,' he told the elderly seneschal who had conducted him, 'I'm glad I saw it.'

But he was a discriminating visitor. Later on, when the centre of his map had disappeared beneath grids of red ink, we moved eastward to seek out forgotten City churches mouldering in flyblown squares hard by Puddle Dock and Victoria Street. Here my father proved unexpectedly knowledgeable on the subject of ecclesiastical architecture. 'Pretty good finial,' he would say as we stood in the vestibule of some gaunt, silent chapel where pigeons roosted above the aisle and mice tumbled over the worn altar furnishings, 'but I've seen better.' Where, I wondered? He had original views about design, marked Wren down as a misguided egotist and Hawksmoor as his naïve acolyte. 'What I like,' he told me, 'is something *snug*.' Obscure meeting houses, sunless porticoes reeking with the taint of river water, where no congregation had met for a century, were his delight.

Three or four days passed in this way. Occasionally, from phone boxes near Eastcheap or in the shadow of St Paul's, I called Slater. He was never there. His secretary reported him in meetings with John Birningside, with Farq and Quoodle, at presentations in remote Docklands conference chambers. I put down the receiver and searched for the small figure standing alone at the entrance to a subway station or hobnobbing over a newsvendor's stand. There were stories about Walham in the papers each morning, tales of Barry Mower's new Jaguar, its interior picked out in the club colours, of the two million pounds that Liverpool were supposedly offering for Jimmy Hood. I read these accounts without interest. They were despatches from a battlefield which in my absence had grown distant and illusory: it was my father, picking his way along the City pavements, who was real.

Our complicity grew. We ate lunch in cramped City winebars, in dim, subterranean restaurants where red-faced men talked excitedly about the war and the balance of payments. The Allies were bombing Baghdad, but it would not last, they said. There would be a settlement. Then, inexorably, the price of oil would rise. A rival consultancy firm laid off a hundred and fifty staff that week. Yet even this news, which might once have depressed or exhilarated me, struck no answering chord. I had slipped down beneath the waves, I felt, to an older, more elemental world.

For the first half of our week together my father kept silent. Occasionally, half-way up some stone staircase, marooned on the upper deck of some open-topped bus, I caught him looking at me with deep, lugubrious interest. Then, without warning, he grew voluble. 'Ever hear of a place called the Ritz Hotel?' he asked once. 'Sure.' 'I'd kind of like to have tea there,' my father admitted shyly. 'You think that's something we could do maybe?' 'I don't see why not.' 'Wouldn't have to dress up or nothing?' 'I don't think so.' It was impossible to tell in these exchanges whether my father was being wholly serious. 'Well then, I'd appreciate it.' And so we went to the Ritz and ate tea before a gazebo of artificial palm trees to the accompaniment of a string quartet. My father approved the atmosphere. 'This would be the place, would it not, where your nobility, your old aristocratic families, would stay when they came to town?' 'I guess so.' 'And the ornaments of your *beau monde*,' said my father, in the rich, sonorous voice that he sometimes used for declamations of this kind, 'they would surely come here for refreshment after an evening at the theatre?' I glanced sideways for the inevitable glint of irony: none came.

But there were more elaborate excursions in hand. Late one evening as we lingered over a Chinese meal ('It is a pleasure,' my father had pronounced, 'to dine in one of your traditional ethnic quarters') he said unexpectedly: 'You know where I really want to go?' 'No. Where?' 'Grimsby.' 'Grimsby?' 'Sure. You know where that is?' 'Sure I do. Why Grimsby?' Hunched over the table, a full bowl of noodles growing cold before him, he seemed gravely disappointed. 'Jesus, Scott, I have to go to Grimsby to see the postman.' For a second I thought he was mad. Then the memory of the cassette tapes and the faded newspaper clippings returned. 'You want to go to Grimsby to

227

see the Singing Postman?' I got *letters*,' said my father fiercely. Dipping clumsily into his tourist's money pouch he pulled out a couple of feathery A4 sheets. Each bore the address of a Salvation Army hostel. The first, signed by a Salvation Army captain, confirmed that a Mr A Smethurst was a hostel resident. The second was a photocopied timetable of visiting hours. They seemed doubtful inducements. 'You want to go to Grimsby to see a guy who made a few novelty records you bought twenty-five years ago?' 'I been writing to him,' my father said. 'A dozen letters maybe.' 'Sure. You ever get a reply?' 'Just these.' 'No way,' I said. 'Scott.' His voice rose to a high, pitiful quaver. 'You got to do this for me. You hear now? You got to do this for me.' 'No way.' 'You got to, Scott. You just got to.'

And so I went to a British Rail station and made the arrangements for my father to visit the Singing Postman.

The train bore us northward over a flat, alien landscape. At King's Cross my father had been curt and irritable, mislaying his ticket amid the detritus of his wallet, bristling up implacably in a line of travellers. Now, cheered by the warmth of the carriage, he grew confidential. In particular, he assumed a persona that dated from the earliest days of my childhood and which I had not seen for nearly twenty years, that of the garrulous Southern gentleman. This was an immensely subtle piece of character acting which in the hands of a performer less practised than my father would quickly have degenerated into pastiche. How many times at college, in New York, at dinner with Danny Hassenblad, had I not seen some Yankee wiseacre plant one thumb in an imaginary waistcoat pocket, use the other to flick back an invisible wideawake and declaim in an accentuated ante-bellum drawl that he was jest dah'en to mosey down to th'ole cottonfield to see how the nigras was faring? My father's assumption of this venerable role was entirely different. Rather than involving a simple imitation of some screen-sanctioned Southern archetype – old O'Hara, say, in *Gone With the Wind* – it began with a barely perceptible heightening of various aspects of his own speech and demeanour, continuing to the point when some stray inflection or gesture would suddenly betray that the translation had been effected. Even

228

now, after twenty years, instinct told me that the point had been reached when, after a discussion of the terrain through which we were passing, its livestock, cultivation and agricultural prospects – all perfectly reasonable topics, innocently proposed – I asked if he would take a cup of coffee, and my father replied that he would *admire to greatly*. I padded along swaying corridors to the buffet, aware that by the time I returned the performance would have moved up a gear. Sure enough, he was sitting with his arms folded high on his chest, one leg hoisted over the other, staring keen-sightedly into the distance. 'You take sugar in this?' I asked, thumping the container down on the flimsy surface. My father shot back a cunning yet vaguely alarmed look – the Virginia senator brought news of Appomattox? The plantation owner with a conscience? 'It don't rightly signify,' he said mildly, and there was the faintest imaginable stress on the final syllable.

At Doncaster we detrained across windy platforms to the smaller vehicle that was to take us eastward. Installed in the three-carriage sprinter, he grew suddenly reminiscent. 'Hey. You remember a kid called Artie Tripp?' I thought for a moment, not so much about Artie Tripp as of the likeliest ways in which the garrulous Southern gentleman's stooge might frame his reply. 'I declare I do.' 'No,' said my father sharply. 'Can cut out all that stuff now. You remember a kid called Artie Tripp?' 'Sure I do. Used to practise pitching out in the yard?' 'That's right,' said my father, mollified by the solidity of the memory. 'Little kid, but kind of determined.' 'Kind of hopeless too. Greg and me used to think he was a real fruit.' 'I recollect that,' said my father with the faintest hint of reproach. 'Anyway, you want to hear what happened to Artie Tripp?' I thought for a second. Too young to have become a congressman or to have achieved gubernatorial office. Baseball, in fact any kind of sporting prowess, was necessarily a closed door. Computer genius? Best-selling novelist? 'Sure,' I said. 'What happened to Artie Tripp?' 'Five years ago. Down south someplace. Montgomery maybe, or Memphis. Walloped this old lady over the head with a tyre-iron and stole her purse. A squad car starts tailing him so Artie lights out into some high school and holds up the Math class. Turns out he had an assault rifle. They staked the place out and negotiated, of course, but there was a kid of thirteen got shot through the lung before Artie figured he ought to give himself up.'

For a moment I imagined the scene, a spectacle made familiar by a thousand police serials and movie trailers: terrified, upraised heads, lights flashing in the near distance, the whirling blades of the helicopter, only the banal figure of Artie Tripp, moving clumsily at its core, managing to impart an unlooked-for resonance. In itself the news was not especially shocking. Walloping old ladies over the head with tyre-irons and stealing their purses or holding up Math classes with an assault rifle was not unprecedented among the West Virginia youth of my acquaintance. Even at college one had known guys who had gone on to manage credit-card frauds, peddle sulphate and answer larceny charges before a federal jury. Artie Tripp, with his GI crewcut, his frown and his nervous smile, seemed an unlikely addition to their ranks.

Something of this seemed to have occurred to my father. 'Upset me when I heard,' he went on, 'because I *favoured* that boy. But you and Greg, now, you reckoned he was a fruit. Now why was that?' Not for the first time in our journey I had a sensation of an innocuous-looking puppet jerked suddenly into malevolent life. 'Oh, it was just he tried too hard.' '*Tried too hard*?' My father sounded genuinely bewildered. I tried to recall once more the intent figure of Artie Tripp crouching in the shadow of the cypress tree as he prepared to pitch for the fiftieth time that morning at the chalked human outline on the garage wall. Something to do with the refusal to face facts, persisting when persistence was futile, a kind of epically presumptive folly bordering on arrogance, the dogged conviction that one was special in the face of evidence that one was actually less than ordinary. But it was impossible to frame this dislike in any way that would have been comprehensible to my father. 'Oh, you know. Just that he tried too hard and he wasn't any good. At least, you know, there were other things he could have done . . .' And this surely, it seemed to me, was something that my father could have grasped, had he cared to, the hint that it was the public display of what amounted to Artie Tripp's self-humiliation that caused Greg and me to

230

despise him, that harbouring secret extravagances concerning one's own worth was one thing, but that to parade those extravagances in front of one's neighbours was a kind of masochism that deserved outstanding rebuke, that there were other places where he could have gone through his pitching routine, eyes that he could have performed beneath other than our own who had the measure of his folly and presumption. But if my father appreciated this line of reasoning he took care not to show it. For a long time, seated there in the bouncing carriage with the rain breaking on the window, he seemed to be considering his put-down. 'There are worse things than trying too hard,' he said. Then he said: 'You know what Artie Tripp talked about that time I drove him over to Beckley?' 'No.' 'Seventy miles there and seventy miles back again, do you know what he talked about?' 'Tell me.' 'He talked about his mother,' said my father. 'About how she had a weak heart and he wanted to do something that she could be proud of him for.' I shook my head silently over what seemed to me the apotheosis of Artie Tripp's unfittedness for any kind of reasoning human life. 'There are worse things you can do than try too hard,' he said eventually. It was the gentlest of rebukes, but once again I saw the marionette jerk violently to life beneath his hand.

We took a cab to the Salvation Army hostel. Here, inexplicably, his high spirits returned. Hunched into his overcoat on the back seat bowling through the untidy streets, he took a lively and romantic interest in his surroundings. 'These, I take it, would be the homes to which, having conducted their Empire's business in lands afar, gallant seafarers would return,' he said as we passed a nondescript municipal block near the harbour. 'I suppose they would.' 'And where, surrounded by their listening children, they would recount their exploits on the Seven Seas?' 'I guess so.' In the centre of Grimsby we traversed a street of boarded exteriors, To Let signs and a single store advertising a closing-down sale. 'A hard life but a proud one,' said my father blandly.

The hostel lay in a side street not far from the sea. At the roadside gulls worried fish and chip packets: the tang of salt

231

hung on the breeze. Here he grew oddly diffident. 'You think I'm crazy don't you?' 'Why should I think you're crazy?' 'Seriously. Coming all this way to see a guy I never met before just because I used to collect his records.' Something seemed to strike him and he moved conspiratorially towards me, pressing his nylon travelbag up against my arm. 'Hey! I brought him a present.' 'What kind of present?' 'Take a look.' Turning the protruding flap to one side I discovered a miniature box of chocolates, emblazoned with pictures of Beefeaters and bearing the message A PRESENT FROM LONDON. 'You think he'll like it?' 'Sure to.' 'No, really. He won't think it's corny or nothing?' – in his excitement he pronounced it *nuthin'*, like a stage Southerner. 'No way.' By now it was raining quite hard.

We pressed on into the vestibule, where a number of venerable figures stared vacantly from chairs. Sepia portraits of General Booth hung on the wall. A grey-haired woman, to whom my father declared his purpose, raised no objection. And then, curiously, his courage failed him. 'Hey,' he said as we stood half-in and half-out of the doorway. 'You want to come with me?' But the flame of interest, which had flickered briefly over the box of chocolates, subsided. I shook my head. 'You're sure now?' 'Positive.' While he was gone I turned over the magazines and looked at the portraits of General Booth. The grey-haired woman busied herself opening letters. When he returned a few moments later he seemed vaguely put out. 'How'd it go?' My father thought for a while. 'Great,' he said at last. 'That well, huh?' 'Like a house on fire.' 'But it burned out pretty quick?' 'He's kind of an old guy,' said my father reprovingly. 'Didn't want a load of half-assed questions from some stranger just walked in off the street.' 'Did he like the present?' 'Sure,' said my father cautiously. 'He liked it fine. Hey, he gave me this.' I saw now that he was holding a crumpled piece of paper carefully between the fingers of one hand. 'Taken in 1969,' my father said proudly as I unfolded the creased black-and-white photo. 'On his Welsh tour. Signed too.' I glanced down. The signature was vague and anonymous. It suggested that the Singing Postman had a certain amount of difficulty in writing. 'That's great,' I told him.

Outside in the street rain fell silently across the empty

232

pavements. It was barely midday. 'You want to eat here?' I asked. 'See the sights? The homes to which' – I improvised gamely – 'the gallant seafarers returned after their Imperial sojourns?' My father shook his head. He looked fretful and subdued, with bulging, stroke-patient's eyes. Glancing at the flap of his travelbag I saw that the box of chocolates with its garish wrapper lay undisturbed. 'You want me to get a cab and go back to the station?' The old man nodded, not looking up. 'Thanks Scott, I'd appreciate that.'

The train dragged slowly back. For a while my father slept, chin drooping on to his chest. Then, as we turned south over the waterlogged Lincolnshire fields, he grew talkative once more. Curiously it was not the Singing Postman he wished to discuss, but that older world populated by Artie Tripp and his kind, boys who'd 'gone bad', cast off the restraining shackles of their West Virginia upbringing and exploded into bustling criminal life.

Juvenile delinquency was a great topic of conversation among the people of my parents' generation. Twenty years ago the Sunday night back porches had resounded to the exploits of 'Pretty Boy' Floyd and Steve 'Cadillac' McGovern, hulking teenagers who had scandalised the locality by spiriting Oldsmobile patrol cars out of the police parking lot at Ossawatomie Heights or being arrested for transporting minors across the state line. The Cook County hoodlums of my childhood siphoned gas out of their neighbours' automobiles and lit out east to the coast in pilfered Chevvies. Dragged back by knowing patrolmen from Brownsville or Shenandoah Gorge, they made tear-stricken court appearances, were sentenced to juvenile supervision orders and marched away by white-faced parents. Retrospect gave these misdemeanours a prankish, mitigating gloss.

'Pretty Boy' Floyd and 'Cadillac' McGovern's descendants ploughed a more determined furrow. They beat up old ladies, smashed up pool halls with machetes, carved people's guard dogs into fillets and strewed them over the porch, drove souped-up BMWs into shopping mall frontages and spent the proceeds on heroin and STP. And somehow, despite his twenty-year

233

absence, my father had kept up with this catalogue of depravity, somehow he had kept tabs on the hissing cauldron of delinquent youth, so that even now he might have been a solid West Virginia citizen pausing over the barbecue to regale his guests with the mundane horrors of smalltown crime. 'Jumped him on the back porch and . . . Took the old lady into the kitchen and . . . Grabbed hold of the chainsaw . . .' Nestled into my seat, I thought about Miranda's vengeful glare, Barry Mower's banking arrangements, Slater's schemes, Jimmy Hood's hamstring.

But there were other, less abstract reckonings at hand. 'Hey,' said my father, hastily concluding an account of the Cook County Mangler and his final entrapment (' . . . so they pulled the old guy's corpse out of the chiller, tried on the severed arm and, whaddya know, it fitted') 'you hear from Greg at all right now?' 'Uh huh. A while back.' 'Greg's an asshole,' said my father with sudden, penetrating shrewdness. 'Stuck in a log-cabin up in the hills thinking he can sell timeshares to Jane Fonda and Ted Turner.' I ventured some mild remonstrance. 'Last I heard he had an office in Bozeman.' 'I been up there,' said my father decisively. 'Last fall. It ain't nothing. Half of some trick lawyer's parlour is all. But that isn't what I meant. Greg now, Greg just wants to look the part.' 'He does?' 'Sure,' said my father, warming to his task. 'You been to Montana recently? They got Hollywood actors in Armani buckskins crawling down Bozeman mainstreet these days. Last thing I heard some NBC anchorman was organising a petition to bring back the wolf. Greg'll get a couple of good old boys come and set fire to his cabin one of these days, and serve him damn right.'

Not until the train was nosing into the empty platforms of St Pancras did he revert to the Singing Postman. 'I'm telling you, Scott, it was the weirdest thing.' 'How weird is weird?' The old man twisted the index finger of his right hand up against the temple in an ancient Marshall family gesture. 'Pretty weird. You remember how Greta used to get?' – Greta was one of his Marshall cousins who'd spent the last quarter-century staked out in a Philadelphia incurables hospital. 'Like that and then some. The weirdest thing was that he wouldn't say nothing.' 'Not anything?' 'Nothing at all. Just stared at me.' 'What did you say?' 'What would you have said? I told him who I was. Told him I had all of his records. Told him about some of the country stars we have backhome, you know, Waylon Jennings and Willie Nelson – I figured he might be interested in that.' 'And he still didn't say anything?' 'Nothing at all. Here,' said my father, flicking something negligently across the table-top between us. 'Can have this if you want.' It was the photograph.

Later, back at the apartment, I smoothed the picture of the Singing Postman down on a flat surface and examined it minutely. Presumably shot on some TV set, for there were bright studio lights in a row above his head, a glimpse of tangled flexes by his feet, it showed the Postman bent admiringly over his guitar, only his head raised turtle-like towards the camera. I studied his face for a long time: knobby, coy, eyes edging myopically over horn-rimmed frames. It was the kind of face you see fifty times a day, but with all the essential characteristics exaggerated: vacant, complacent, full of peasant artfulness. My early life, I realised, had been crowded with such faces, faces that belonged to delivery drivers out on the springy West Virginia backroads, to shy fatmen who owned the barbers' shops where my father took me to get my hair cut, bank tellers in flyblown Southern towns deserted for the harvest; perky, irresolute, hewn out of soap. For a moment I tried to imagine my father and the Singing Postman together. In what spirit, I wondered, had they regarded one another? In the Singing Postman's case, I supposed, indifference verging on hostility. In my father's, esteem tempered by the gravitational pull that he brought to every human encounter – a reluctance to be impressed. The Singing Postman had stayed mute, but might he not have chanced some nod of recognition, some welcoming gesture, some tiny acknowledgment of an eccentricity at least as great as his own? Side by side, the one frail and garrulous, the other silent and inert, perhaps both had experienced some faint tremor of kinship?

He had a bad night. Coughed into the small hours. Awake at dawn. When I went in to see him once he waved me hastily away: an irritable, preoccupied gesture.

Once, around this time, I asked him: 'Why did my mother quit

England?' Getting only a blank stare in return, I followed up with: 'Why did she come to America, I mean, time she married you?'

The old man shrugged, an ostentatious, sitcom shrug, an oh-my-God-why-won't-the-asshole-get-off-my-back gesture to an unseen audience. 'Why did I want to come here? Figured I wanted to see the place is all.'

I tried a different line. 'You ever hear of anyone called Jefferies? Or Borthwick or Anstruther?'

The old man nodded, a faint exasperated nod of recognition. 'I heard,' he said. 'Listen. You go looking for Anstruthers and Borthwicks, you won't find them. Not anywhere.'

'Why not?'

'Because they're all dead. Mostly. The Anstruthers all died in the war. Ain't heard anything of the Borthwicks in twenty years. Was an old lady used to write to your mom once in a blue moon, but she died years back. Hey,' the old man said, 'why you interested in all this?'

'I want to know . . . about why she came over to the States. About what happened.'

If I had expected any shattering revelation, it never came. 'You tell me,' the old man went on. 'She'd never say. Folks were dead: I knew that much. Might have been some guy walked out on her. Might even have been a kid someplace. English people took that kind of thing pretty seriously back then.'

'American people too.'

'Sure.'

'And didn't you ever ask?'

'Sure I *asked*.' For a moment the old man looked stupendously aggrieved. 'Naturally I *asked*. Then I stopped. Didn't seem to matter if I knew or not. Anyhow, there were times when she used to talk about it.'

'About what?'

'Old times. Place in Sussex she used to live. Her ma and pa driving her to school someplace. Horse she used to ride.'

'And she never wanted to go back?'

'Never. You know something?' the old man volunteered. 'Long time ago, before you were born, I bought her an anniversary present. Two airline tickets to London. Hotel

236

reservation in Knightsbridge. You know what she did? Tore them up then and there. Last time I tried a surprise vacation on her.'

A place in Sussex. The car journey to school. A horse. Nothing.

14

Controversy or not

But I had had another interest throughout these short winter days. Or rather I had another obligation, at once pressing and unavoidable. I hung out with Barry Mower. Barry liked company but he had to look hard to find it: the kids were gone; Mrs Mower languished in Essex; the guys at the club went in awe of him; the women were shy of his reputation and the stories of model girls and the magazine meathookers; Maurice and Lennie had their sham companies and their travel insurance scams to run; and so Barry idled sadly in his office through the grim January forenoons calling up people who were by turns proud or anxious or elated to hear his voice but somehow wary of accepting his offers of a drink or a meal or a trip Up West to see the girls. And perhaps this, too, was a factor in his isolation. For Barry, it must be said, had old-fashioned tastes in pleasure. He liked steak dinners in mundane restaurants off the A40 at Hillingdon or Greenford, monochrome TV movies with Ronald Colman and Gregory Peck, pompous dinner-jacketed excursions to showbiz haunts in town. Photographs were returned sometimes from these diversions: Barry flanked by a TV magician or a sitcom bit-parter or two, face radiant with bonhomie, jaw cracked open by serious laughter. But back at his office he complained about fairweather acquaintances, old allies who saw fit to ignore him, and in fine was about as unhappy as a rich man with no friends who is forced to pay for his pleasures can be.

And so, for want of anyone else, and not unwilling to vary settled patterns of existence, I hung out with Barry Mower. I went to Variety Club dinners with him and rubbed shoulders with frail old men who remembered Sid James and Tony Hancock and the faces out of my father's scrapbooks. In his company I attended race meetings in the Midlands, where Barry

239

hobnobbed with the sporting gentry and dropped whimsical £100 bets on horses whose colours had momentarily attracted his attention. But there were stranger places than these, and stranger company: early mornings in Soho with the dawn coming up behind shuttered windows and a roomful of pale faces shining under the lamp; weekend poker games in Dalston and Shoreditch with gaunt East End grandmothers bringing in jugs of tea; late-night boxing matches in Bethnal or the Isle of Dogs with Barry's car and its chauffeur idling in the dark sidestreets to ferry us back to civilisation. Barry favoured sport above all things. He liked soccer, rugby, didn't mind greyhounds or darts and would go fifty miles on a December night to see a wrestling bout between two broken-down old walruses, one of whom might have challenged for the British title in 1968. I once went with him to a bare-knuckle fight, held over a gym in Hackney, with fifty guys baying round a makeshift ring, and watched two vicious, dead-eyed teenagers hammer each other unconscious: Barry loved it. He thought it was 'real boxing, not like these fakers you see on the telly, Tyson and that.' Two hours after the fight one of the kids fell down in a coma and was removed to Homerton hospital to have a clot scraped off his brain: Barry sent him £50 and a bunch of flowers. It might have been possible to be scared of Barry at these times, scared of the slow clump and parry of the boxers and the little gasps of breathlessness they made between rounds, the dazed look on the kid's face as he went down for the final time (some of the crowd threw coins in the ring – they thought he was faking), but somehow fear was kept at bay by the thought of decline and degeneration. They were a disappearing breed, Barry and his mates, the raucous East End women and their bolstered consorts, and they knew it. There were black kids staring at them as they came out of their pubs (amazing places cluttered with gangland memorabilia), skyscrapers going up over the dockland tenements, and they didn't like it.

Sometimes these junketings took place at Barry's house in Essex. Barry Mower's house! What prodigies of brickwork were accomplished in its execution! What darling fantasies were incorporated into its design! Barry had it put up in the late 1970s on the back of his profits from the property boom. Barry's house! I never saw anything like it, not even Palm Beach and the monster retirement glades of the Florida coast: a savage edifice, built in red brick, with swirling gravel drives, jutting rococo towers and a rooftop eyrie for Barry's nest of satellite dishes. It had an astroturf lawn complete with 9-hole golf-course, a silent banqueting hall, and the neatest little library, stocked by messrs Waterstone, where Barry roamed disconsolately on wet Sunday afternoons, his eye occasionally alighting on the stout hard-backed volumes, and was very dull indeed.

It was here, early in January on a dismal Sunday afternoon, that Barry held a party in honour of the quarter-final victory. There was no sign of Mrs Mower. She was in London, in Le Touquet, off visiting her scapegrace son. In fact you would have fancied Mrs Mower not to exist altogether – there was no trace of her in any of the upstairs rooms – had it not been for a note I found on the kitchen table which read: *B – Extra milk for Sunday. Plus remember pay newsagent!* Did Barry remember to pay the newsagent? I don't know. He bought a sheaf of national newspapers every morning and worked his way painstakingly through them in search of his name. Such a variety of ill-assorted people assembled at Barry's party! There were family connections from the old West London days – formidable women with flossed blue-white hair dressed in the fashions of thirty years ago who with their silent husbands stood in the great reception rooms and smoked cigarettes and wondered at the arabesques and the Fragonard cherubs with which some interior designer had thought fit to garnish Barry's ceilings; dapper, demure acquaintances from the turf or the stadiums who looked very knowing at the extent of Barry's shagpile and the riches of his drinks cabinet. Lennie and Maurice and the others came up from their weekend hideaways in Hertfordshire and Suffolk and smoked cigars in Barry's kitchen or vanished into the library with their mobile phones. Melanie, stationed inside the door with one of Barry's teenage staff to run messages, gave confidential assessments of these arrivals to which I was charmed to listen:

'The old man in the suit is called Unsworth. He and Barry's dad used to run the Hillingdon Labour Party in the old days. You know, fix the planning permission deals and so on. Lost his

241

seat in one of the corruption crackdowns, but he's supposed to be making a comeback. The large woman in the blue is Maureen McWilliam. She used to be in the films Barry backed in the 1970s, *Barbiecutie, Manhunter*. Do you remember them? They say she was quite something in her day. Just behind her . . . You see the old lady in green? Mrs Bailey who used to live next door to the Mowers in West Drayton. When Barry's mum died that time and he locked himself up in his room with the photos and the Jim Reeves records – it was all in the papers – she was the only one he'd let in to see him . . .'

'Uh huh. Who's the black dude?'

'Leroy. Leroy's something to do with satellite TV. Did you know Barry was thinking of going into satellite?'

'What kind of satellite?'

'Oh the hardcore end.' Melanie frowned. 'He thinks the European Court of Justice are going to legislate against scrambling.'

Later, after the guests had gone, I wandered through brightly-lit chambers full of glasses of flat champagne and discarded dinner plates. Outside there was snow falling over the gravel drive and I stood and watched it for a moment as silent women in waitresses' caps came and began to clear up the leavings and Leroy, his white teeth gleaming through the shadow, crept off up the back staircase on some errand of his own. In the library, looking out over the white lawn, Barry slept with his arms sprawled out on the table and a copy of *Le Rouge et Le Noir* pillowing his head.

Barry's legendary paranoia, never very far from the surface, moved sharply to the front of his mind at this time. He thought the players hated him, he thought that the press were after him, that the League chairmen held him in contempt. Once I found him wandering in the labyrinth of passageways under the main stand, kicking at the piles of waste paper and rattling doubtfully at the locks of the burger stands. Next to the venerable graffiti on the black walls there were fresh splashes of crimson paint, contemplation of which had plainly disturbed Barry.

'Now who would you reckon done that?' he said sadly, tracing the curve of the letters vaguely with a fat hand.

242

I stared at the words – BARRY MOWER IS A CUNT in letters three feet high – with resolute dispassion. 'I don't know Barry. Some kid got in here at night.'

'Place is locked up and patrolled isn't it? . . . Has to be an inside job.' Barry brooded forlornly for a moment. Then without warning his mood moved up a gear. 'You mind if I ask you a personal question Scott?'

'I guess not.'

'Would you say I was a happy man?'

He was serious, too. I thought about it for a moment while he stared at me haplessly.

'That depends Barry . . . I mean, it's a relative thing.'

'No, seriously. Would you say I was a happy man?'

There was no way out. 'Jesus, Barry. You're the chairman of a club that's in the semi-finals of the Rumbelows Cup. You're the boss of a . . . You run a highly successful commercial empire. I can't speak for your private life but, well, just look at it all.'

The hard, thin furrows along Barry's forehead relaxed. 'You're a good lad Scott, and I appreciate what you're saying . . . It's just that sometimes, no, I'm not a happy man.'

'No?'

'People think just because you live in a big house and get your name in the papers you must be doing OK, isn't that right? Well, I could tell them a thing or two about that,' Barry went on fervently. 'Do you know what's in those letters that come in every morning to the office?'

'Tell me.'

'About half of it's just fanmail. Old blokes who think they remember seeing Walham in the 1930s. People who reckon they went to school with Tusker Holloway. But the rest . . . I got girls who want to be in the magazines sending bits of their fannies and pictures of them in the bath. There's some geezer in Cirencester, is it, writes to me every other day saying I'm the depraved symbol of a decadent society and he'd like to jump on my head.'

'Maybe he's the guy with the spray can.'

'No. Cirencester's too far away,' Barry said solemnly. 'But I'm not a happy man Scott, and I'd just like you to remember

243

that next time somebody sprays BARRY MOWER IS A CUNT on the wall of a place that I bloody well pay for.'

Poor Barry! He had the graffiti painted over that afternoon, and the security firm who patrolled The Dray were put on double time, but the words were back a couple of days later, not in the anonymous recesses beneath the stand, alas, but on the wall outside above the eulogies to Pat Arrowsmith and Tosh Mulligan.

Many of these anxieties surfaced in Barry's TV appearance a week before the first leg of the semi-final. They had him on one of those Channel Four talkshows, famous for controversy and the defiant inarticulacy of its protagonists, beamed out to a meagre collection of small hours insomniacs. As one cultural misfit gave way to another and the camera bulbs popped and fizzed in the background Barry sat at the side of the stage silently drinking gin out of a carafe and staring at his fellow-interviewees: he appraised the figure of the ex-porn queen in a kindly way, but the creations of the excremental sculptor left him unmoved. Finally, with ten minutes left and the studio audience desperate with boredom, they moved the cameras across and Barry's swaying, rhomboid frame loomed ponderously into focus.

Barry's performance was unique even in *Imbroglio*'s short and tarnished annals. Questioned about safe sex, he diffidently suggested that condoms were for teenagers and perverts. Pressed anxiously to deny these prejudicial inferences, he cheerfully admitted to dislike of homosexuals, Jews, negroes and Italians. As the baying from the floor grew louder (mixed with a sprinkling of presumably ironic applause) the interviewer turned hastily to the topic of Walham Town. Confronted with a forthcoming newspaper report to the effect that Jimmy Hood considered him dictatorial in outlook and was seriously considering withdrawing from the semi-final squad (BOSS IS LIKE HITLER SAYS WALHAM'S HOOD!) Barry vowed that he would personally rip the little bastard's legs off and those of anyone else who forgot who paid their wages. Asked his opinion of the League's management committee, he essayed a passionate attack on class prejudice ('the reason people hate me is because I was born in a council house, right?') and lamented the passing of Mrs Thatcher. By this stage there were warning lights flashing over the control panel above the interviewer's head; an earlier decision to take the show off the air, suspended at the point where Barry began with surprising coherence to discuss the advantages of the long-ball game, was hastily renewed at the moment in which Barry offered to tell a joke ('Not like the stuff you usually get on the telly, right?'). The last two or three minutes, the interviewer reduced to a state of craven subservience, cameramen gesticulating, the intrusive movement of security guards at the back of the theatre, were simply a succession of random questions and answers:

INTERVIEWER: Why don't you like Italians?

MOWER: 'Cos they don't play fair, of course. Always falling over and pretending they're hurt. Bastards!

INTERVIEWER: Who is the greatest love of your life?

MOWER: My mother.

INTERVIEWER: What do you think about feminism?

MOWER: What does a pig think about bacon slicers?

The last joke, by the way, was not of Barry's own devising. I had taught it to him in the hospitality suite half-an-hour before the show, watched by a Norwegian death metal musician named Count Grishnakh and the members of a lesbian mime troupe. They managed to get him off the stage after that, in a tangle of wires and tottering equipment, with a security gorilla pulling on each arm – Barry felled one of them with a tremendous karate chop to the neck – and the studio erupting into riot as Barry's personal bodyguard, Big Eamonn, fisted his way through the throng from the back. It made most of the next morning's newspapers – deplored by the *Guardian* as 'a parodic embodiment of the illiberalities of Essex Man', he was applauded in the *Daily Telegraph* as a contributor to the gaiety of nations – but Barry's resentment extended to a single minor detail. 'I shouldn't have mentioned me mum,' he said sadly afterwards. 'No?' 'No. Never does any good to talk about your mum.' 'No?' 'No. And she wouldn't have liked it neither.'

There was a photograph of Barry's mother, a grim old party arrayed in the fashions of the early 1950s, on Barry's office wall, and a white marble shrine on a private plot in Ealing cemetery, its floral cornucopia weekly renewed. The rest Melanie filled me in on: 'They were very close. But she didn't approve of the magazines. She was very religious, Barry's mother. And then she died very suddenly one year when he was on holiday in Tenerife. Barry was distraught. I mean really distraught. He went around saying it was a judgment, and there was talk of him selling the warehouse.' For a second I remembered my mother dying – of an aneurysm which nobody knew she had, triggered by diving into a motel pool outside Orlando – and the funeral, held in the Baptist church at Margaretsville where we'd gone as kids, burning letters on the porch while the real estate salesman measured up the house and Greg, who was banking on thirty thousand dollars for his restaurant business, whistled cheerfully at the window.

Three days before the semi-final – they'd drawn Manchester United, home leg first – a first division side bid a million pounds for Ashley Flack: Barry turned them down flat. All the seats had been sold a fortnight since. Two ageing pop stars and a sporting cabinet minister who applied in person at The Dray were refused. One of the commercial TV companies made a ten-minute documentary that appeared as *Walham's Glory Road*. Barry watched it uneasily on the set in the Barry Mower Lounge, the doors barred to all except me and Melanie. Pastiche sporting fanfare gave way to a shot of The Dray's worn exterior, then to pictures of Jimmy Hood and Ashley Flack doggedly unloading their sports bags from a parked car. *Fourth division Walham Town are not a fixture in football's hall of fame* a male voice solemnly intoned, over a glimpse of The Dray's fetid urinals, *yet theirs is a proud heritage.* Cut to a photograph of Tusker Holloway, and a knowing ancient who admitted to having once attended a Walham match before the Second World War. More sporting fanfare introduced footage of Jimmy Hood being dangerously assaulted by two of his colleagues after scoring the winning goal against Aston Villa. *Now, since their march to the semi-finals of the Rumbelows Cup, there are few football fans unfamiliar with giantkilling Walham* (shot of Walham High Street and an Asian bus conductor) *players like Jimmy Hood and Ashley Flack* (a startled-looking Jimmy and Ashley being waved through the foyer by a twinkling commissionaire) *and, most of all, their*

246

colourful chairman Barry Mower. Love him (pictures of Barry being mobbed by tearful pensioners) *or hate him* (close-up of threatening graffiti) *you can't ignore Barry.* While the voice descanted impressionably on Walham's path to the semi-final the camera dwelt on Barry patting the head of an infant mascot, being kissed on the cheek by an elderly woman to whom he had just presented a bunch of flowers, and nodding seriously over a sheaf of X-Rays proffered to him by the club physio. *Success has come rapidly* maintained the voice, *perhaps too rapidly* (cut to Darren talking nervously into a telephone while Barry peers sternly over his head). *So how are the team coping with this new-found celebrity?* There followed a succession of high-speed interviews. In the first, shot in an anodyne domestic interior, Jimmy Hood accepted a baby from a suspicious-looking woman, examined it disdainfully and admitted that being recognised in the street was a big problem. Subsequently Rickie Weller proposed that Barry could be an exacting employer but he personally had nothing but respect for him. After a brief swirl of footage from the early games, the voice continued: *Walham's success has been built on a fast, free-flowing game that the fans want to see.* Barry's face loomed up crazily to fill the screen. 'We play a fast, free-flowing game which the fans want to see,' he declared. 'I'm not naming any names, but it's a lesson that other sides could learn to their advantage.' *But for all these triumphs* (a picture of Barry exultant on the touchline) *this is still a club plagued by controversy. In particular, there are long-standing claims that Walham operate an unofficial colour bar. For a reaction to these allegations, I spoke to chairman Barry Mower.* Barry, seated in his office, stared sullenly at the camera.

INTERVIEWER: So how do you react to the allegations that Walham operate an official colour bar?

MOWER: It's not true that I'm prejudiced against blacks. Last three years we've had four, five black apprentices on the books.

INTERVIEWER: None of whom seem to have played in the first team. And two have alleged that you racially abused them in front of their colleagues.

MOWER: Well, they would do wouldn't they? I mean, it's always the same with that lot isn't it? They were good boys, but they couldn't take the physical style of play. Some of those blacks can't you know.

The camera held Barry in freezeframe for a second – a looming, gargantuan presence – before cutting to an aerial view of Wembley Stadium. *Controversy or not*, the voice concluded, *Walham's target is firmly within their sights.*

Another time – very close to the semi-final it was, a cold, windswept afternoon in late January – he installed me in the front seat of the Jaguar for a long and apparently purposeless journey through north London. There, as the light spilled and dwindled around us and the pylons marched off into an horizon of purest indigo, Barry drove doggedly through the pinched sidewalks of Cockfosters and Potters Bar, past clustered railway lines and gaunt, untidy thoroughfares to the A1. In the distance lines of trucks sped off towards the coast; pale hills stretched out into the shadows beyond. Near South Mimms, a mile past a sprawling service station, Barry pulled the Jag into a slip-road and lit a cigar.

'Been here before?'

There were road-signs pointing to Hatfield and Peterborough. 'Not uh . . . precisely. I did a weekend in Cambridge one time.'

Barry shook his head mournfully. 'No offence son, only it's not . . . It's not the same. I mean' – he flung his hand expansively to one side in a gesture that recalled TV conjurers summoning up white, trembling doves – 'just look out of the window. No, not back that way. Up there.'

Small houses, strewn on a hill, white stucco frontages glimmering out of the dusk, the whole drenched in a late-afternoon sodium glare.

'Used to come here when I was a kid, see,' Barry went on. 'Before all this was built. Estates and that . . . You have places like this in the States?'

I stared inquisitively at the low, bulging exteriors, the cheap cars parked at the side of the road in such a way as to suggest abandonment. They were the kind of houses where, back home, white trash families lived in huge, unhappy colonies: the trailer parked in the yard, men with slack, unruly faces idling, a dozen radios tuned to the Nashville country station. The old man had fetched up in one once, down in East Tennessee, after the loan bank collapse, until Elizabeth Schenectady had come and dug him out.

'Sure,' I said. 'We got places like this back in the States.'

Outside the ground was crisp with half-frosted mud. Barry strode through encroaching dusk, head down, over the road, odd fragmentary sentences winging back over his shoulder.

'All fixed of course, back then . . . Wasn't such a thing as planning permission.'

I had no idea what bygone rumpus room he was attempting to frame in these aphasic ramblings. We traipsed down a badly-lit street of mostly defunct shops, on through a weird erector set world of houses arranged in clumps of five or alone in solitary eminence, roads that led off into ditches or turned back on themselves. There was no one about. Barry stopped at a newsagent's and bought a Mars Bar.

'Used to be a farm not far away where y'could buy pails of milk. Great big pails they were . . .'

There was something pulling him down, I had divined by now, something weird and threatening that tugged at his coat as we trudged over the concrete, prospected a children's play area of breezeblocks and smashed glass, followed one road that ended in an un-negotiable pond, took up a second that returned us to the first. Barry turned back sharply, so sharply and with such an intensification of his features that I pulled up.

'Y'see . . . Y'see, *I built all this.*'

'All of it?'

'Not the Tudor-style mansions at the top, that was Lennie's lot . . . but, yeah, eighty per cent. Had some Mick over on the boat from Tipperary with an asphalt roller to do the roads, but, yeah, I was subcontracting to him.'

I watched a small, waif-like boy on a mountain bike come cycling down the road ahead of us – the first human being we had encountered – steer inexpertly past a network of potholes and then twist his front wheel on a stupendous rut. The effect was symbolic.

'Didn't anyone try to stop you?'

'Nah. This was twenty-five, thirty years ago. They didn't

have planning regulations then . . . Well, they did but . . . There was *compensation* and all,' Barry said fiercely. His features relaxed. 'Fucking Labour council, too.'

We passed back to the car through a final outcrop of silent, somnolent houses drawn up together in an arbitrary corral. In the distance, across the ploughed fields, traffic hummed and whined.

'There's some people,' Barry ventured, 'would be *glad* to live here.' I thought of Uncle Ponderevo, remembered *Tono-Bungay* read aloud by my mother long ago.

'I suppose,' Barry persisted, 'it's for the best.'

'I suppose it is.'

'That farm . . . where we used to buy the milk.'

The car had ceased to be a remote, amorphous shape and grown into something clear and tangible.

'When we got the contract, when Lennie had squared it with the planning department, I went down there and gave them fifty quid. Just like that. They didn't know me from Adam, but I just went and gave them fifty quid.'

There was a hole in the Jaguar's nearside rear window and a couple of long, curving abrasions on one of the doors. Barry stumbled over the brick that had made them as he rummaged stroppily for his keys. I inventoried the depredation – Barry's portable, a stack of magazines fresh from the warehouse, a package (contents unspecified) over whose absence Barry later got surprisingly agitated – while he stood gloomily to one side turning clods of earth over with his toes. Then we drove off, out of the pale shadow of the Hertfordshire hills back into the shoals of silvery, south-bound traffic, lights curving away into the bustling city, back into the real world.

15

The happiest day of my life

'This is the happiest day of my life,' Barry Mower says
confidently.

'As good as the quarter-final?'

Barry looks momentarily alarmed, as if this is somehow a
trick question, an invidious comparison set to expose him to
ridicule. He stands stock still for a second, closing his eyes and
opening them again before murmuring something noncommittal, but it's clear that the edge has been sanded off his
rapture. Beside him Melanie pouts routinely and tugs at his
arm.

'Don't let me interfere,' she says demurely, 'but there's a man
from *Midweek Sports Special* over by the door would like a
word. You want to see him?'

Barry nods gravely. Dressed in a capacious chalk pinstripe,
lemon-yellow shirt and tan Oxfords, sparse hair tossed into
ambrosial fronds by Dino of Berwick Street, he looks the
epitome of lordly self-possession, a legendary prince of darkness
prowling the Darklord's throne room. I watch him flap and
knuckle his way off through the crowd, which parts obediently
to admit him, catch sight of him again beneath the tangle of arc-
lights and the glamorous TV glare.

'Will they use it?'

Melanie shrugs, a kind of saucy, come-hither shrug which has
been oddly in evidence over the last couple of days. 'They might
do. The TV's been running shy of Barry after what happened at
the weekend – you know *Celebrity Squares* cancelled him? – but
it's semi-final night, they might use some of it.'

At 6.45 p.m. in the Barry Mower Lounge, three-quarters of
an hour before kick-off, there are sixty or seventy people milling
around the puny rows of chairs, fisting the complimentary
tumblers from the bar, gaping at the pictures of Tusker

251

Holloway and Biddy Biddlecombe: reserve players, awkward in their chainstore suits, reporters from the nationals, local hotshots. The Mayor of Walham, a black guy in a three-piece, stands alone in the centre of the room staring fixedly in front of him. Beefy security Joes look on benevolently. From afar, looming up from the tinted darkness beyond the window, comes the deeper baying of the crowd. Capacity audience again. They closed the gates fifteen minutes ago and the latest intelligence from below is that several hundred ticketless Manchester United fans were only narrowly repulsed from one of the perimeter fences.

Melanie saunters off in the direction of the bar. I accept a drink from a tuxedo'd flunky, take it to a tenantless chair in the corner, hoist one knee over the other and take a look at the match programme, lavishly constructed in Barry's most florid style. There are photographs of Barry exultant on the touchline as the quarter-final winner went in, Barry with one anaconda forearm draped around the shoulders of Miss Katrina Cerotti, a blowsy sixteen-year-old recently elected 'Squirrels Supporter of the Year', Barry applauding the team from the pitch at the conclusion of a recent league game. The players look strangely cowed and resentful, dwarfed by the clamouring presence of their saviour. Ashley Flack's 'Captain's Logbook' reflects the unstoppable, centrifugal force of Barry's temperament: *Talking to our well-loved chairman Barry Mower the other day, he asked me: 'Ashley, how is it since the cup-run that we've had so few injuries?' 'Search me, boss,' I replied, 'but I suppose our will to win helps us to overcome these obstacles.'* There are other scraps of homely intelligence in keeping with this humble urge to triumph: how Rickie Weller's grandmother is travelling down from Kirkcaldy to witness her boy in his glory, how the incubator of the child prematurely given birth to by Neil Paragon's wife five days ago (*Opinions are divided over the nipper's name but 'Barry' is a strong contender!*) is currently decorated with a black-and-white scarf and a squirrel mascot.

The hands of the clock on the wall have moved round to 6.55. Over by the door some *bon mot* Barry has unleashed on his interlocutor spreads out in a circle of sycophantic ripples; the heads loft upwards, gradually recede. Back at the apartment

252

the old man will be in bed by now, taking the radio with him. He hasn't been too well the last couple of days – each afternoon gathers up now into a fog of catnapping and fuddled bewilderment – but Walham's progress has seized his imagination. 'Guy like that,' he has remarked of Barry Mower, 'you reckon he's fixed the game?' 'What do you mean, fixed it?' 'What I say. Bribed the umpires. Promised a new auto to the other team's coach?' 'This is England, daddy. They don't do that kind of thing here.' 'Yeah, and then some,' the old man countered knowingly.

Thinking of the vast unsolved problem of my father brings me back, inevitably, to other equally pressing dilemmas, in particular what to do about Barry Mower and his financial sleight of hand, a subject as yet uncommunicated to anyone at KLS save Terry Long. So far I haven't told Slater (on the sensible grounds that Slater won't be interested and doesn't want a scandal with a KLS client at this delicate juncture, thanks very much). I haven't told Barry for reasons which it would be otiose to specify. Watching Melanie as she lingers by the bar, one hand stroking some fanciful cocktail (Melanie has exotic tastes in drink: on the last occasion we ventured into a smoke-drenched riverside pub she astonished a disbelieving barman by demanding an Alabama Slammer) the other neurotically smoothing down the lapels of a velvet trouser-suit from Harvey Nichols, I wonder about telling her. Because Melanie, so far as I can judge from the nods, winks and meaningful remarks, seems to have an agenda which is not, shall we say, entirely congruent with that of her employer. Would Melanie welcome this information and, if so, what would she do with it? I take another look at the small, inscrutable figure at the bar, run my eye down the programme's prize crossword ('*Not the worst Manchester United player you could have in your team (4)*') and settle down to brood.

From outside the startled whizz of a firecracker breaks through the dense roar of the crowd. Nearer at hand, impenetrable converse fizzes and whines. This, as Barry has not ceased to remind his staff and dependants since the day of the semi-final draw, is the Big Time. Not the FA Cup, or Europe, but big enough for a fourth division outfit with an average gate of 1,500. The BBC are doing live commentary; televised highlights will be shown later tonight. A camera crew has arrived from Paris to cover what I heard some diminutive Gascon describe to the microphone as '*un événement tres spectaculaire*'. The morning's papers echoed to the noise of oldster columnists recollecting their teenage years on The Dray's cheerless terrace, the Squirrels' proud history and the fate of Tusker Holloway, and a *Times* leader commended the existence of a competition which permitted '*the unsung heroes of W13 to succeed at a time when so much well-remunerated talent and ambition has fallen by the wayside. Of such feats does the romance of sport consist . . .*'

I have other things that bother me right now, though, compared to which Walham's performance out there on the cogged and rutted turf of the Dray is a minor sideshow. The first of these was a call the other morning from, of all people, Henrietta. In fact so long had been our severance – since the pre-Christmas party disaster, I calculated – that it took a second or two to establish the provenance of those crisply truncated vowels with their devious mingling of assurance and anxiety. Henrietta, I should add, has undergone an unprecedented character change since our last meeting, transformed from the nervous ornament of parties to The Woman He Left His Wife For, The Great Man's Mistress, all a consequence of Quoodle's startling decision to leave his wife and children in Onslow Square and relocate himself in her apartment. Slater filled me in on it a week or so back: 'Yeah, some Sloaney kid or something he met at a party. Apparently it's like standing in the paddock at Goodwood' (this I took to be a reference to Henrietta's splendiferous teeth). 'Word is he'll be dead of exhaustion within the month.' All of this, it transpires, has had a decisive effect on Henrietta's personality and demeanour. Gone, mysteriously, are the stricken silences and the phatic ripostes: in their place comes a steely determination to expose each successive intricacy of the Quoodle connection – the evening Quoodle arrived on her doorstep with a suitcase (well, a cab full of suitcases actually), what his wife said, what her friends said, the domestic consequences of life with Quoodle (they breakfast at six before the limo calls), how tearful Quoodle progeny flit impulsively towards her in Kensington Gardens. The latest word is that Mrs Quoodle's father, a legendarily officious ex-City gent, is putting pressure on his errant son-in-law through a line of disapproving company chairmen.

'So how are your parents taking it?' I interject at one point.

'Mummy and daddy? They're very relaxed. And of course Daddy and Q were in Pop together.'

'And, er, what about his wife?'

'Actually we get on *really well*,' Henrietta intones breathlessly. 'We had coffee the other day in Harrods as a matter of fact, and she told me she thought it was really all rather for the best.'

This is a bright, dazzling version of Henrietta come to dethrone the timid supplicant of the past. Bracing myself for further lavish confidences about Quoodle's temper and accomplishments, or at the very least a belated roasting for what happened at the party, I discover that she has another end in view.

'Actually,' Henrietta says, 'it's about that business thing.' Character transformations, of course, can only go so far. Henrietta may have wandered off with someone else's husband, redrawn her moral map and her conversational style, but what her paramour does in the City is still 'that business thing'.

'Which business thing?'

'The, er . . . thing with your boss chap. Salter . . . Sillitoe.' More decisive evidence of Henrietta's new vantage point on life: the wilful misremembering of people's names.

'Slater.'

'That's right. The thing is, I thought you ought to know that it isn't working out quite the way everyone thought it was going to.'

'How come?'

'Q hasn't said much about it. But nobody seems to know quite what's going to happen.'

'OK. Why exactly are you telling me this?'

'Well it's bound to affect you isn't it?' says Henrietta severely. 'Affect your job and everything. So I thought you ought to know.'

For an instant I was visited by the memory of the last time I slept with Henrietta: Laura Ashley furnishings, the Brompton Road glimpsed through chinks in the curtain, the chaste, sprigged nightgown, decorous twilit fumblings, Henrietta disdaining orgasm to pursue a phone ringing in the corridor. But these were thin, pale ghosts.

'It is. Thanks Het.'

That Henrietta has bothered to tell me all this, that Henrietta even knows about it, is faintly ominous. What are Slater and Quoodle doing? Or what are they failing to do? I tried calling Slater at KLS but found him gone, fixed up with Linda – a suspiciously alert and diligent-sounding Linda – to see him on the morning after the semi-final.

Another thing on my mind is last night's phone call from Danny Hassenblad.

'I got it,' he said, eschewing pre-emptive banter. 'She's cool.'

'Who's cool?'

'Sondra. I checked it out. I even spoke to her folks. You'll love this. Told them I was a security analyst from AMEX investigating a suspected credit card violation.'

'Did they believe that?'

'Seemed to. You want the details? Right now she's living in Seattle with a guy who teaches in the University humanities faculty. Got some volunteer job in a rehab unit, but does freelance research for a few brokerages. I called one of the brokerages. Said she was sex on two legs, but the thing with the professor boyfriend was serious.'

Not sure whether to confess to relief or unexpected, bitter jealousy, I listened to the urban noises which furnished a solid, up-tempo accompaniment to Danny's voice: distant sirens, a faint susurration of traffic. The effect was to produce an aching, overpowering nostalgia.

'Hey,' I said. 'What's it like in New York? Tell me about it.'

'What do you mean, what's it like in New York?'

'Tell me about it. I mean, what can you see out of your window, right now?'

'Listen,' Danny stridently intones, 'I'm sitting in a vault fifty feet under Trump Tower, so there isn't a window. The coffee machine's blown, and every three hours the partner calls up and bites my ass. You get the picture?'

256

'I get the picture.'

'And don't start talking to me about old times OK? The old times are fucked. Gone away and died someplace.'

Sure. That's what happened to the old times. They went away and died someplace.

The second thing to bother me is a conversation with the old man. Coming into the kitchen the other evening, I found him hunched up against the chiller coughing unhappily over a tumbler of water and a saucerful of purple pills. 'You OK?' 'Sure I'm OK,' said my father, retching inconclusively into the sink. 'Just a little breathlessness is all.' 'You want me to get you a doctor?' 'Not unless you want a heap of trouble on your hands.' I made a cup of coffee and watched the rhythmical shake of his shoulders for a while. He looked wrinkled and sad, like some immensely distressed and elderly dinosaur emerging from its place of concealment after a meteorite shower to find its friends gone and the landscape changed out of recognition. 'Maybe,' said my father, staring intently above him as if he were reading off some invisible autocue, 'all this was a big mistake.' 'Maybe all what was a big mistake?' 'All this. Coming here. Making you haul me around. After all,' he went on with surprising conviction, 'you don't like seeing me.' 'I like seeing you fine.' 'I know,' the old man went on more indulgently. 'You're busy with your job and stuff. Plus you got turned over by that girl. But . . . that thing with the Postman, that was a big mistake.' 'It went fine. You said so yourself.' 'I had it all planned,' he said wearily. 'All of it. Everything I was going to do. Back home, you know, I got this London scrapbook. Your guide to the sights. Places to see. That kind of thing. Elizabeth and me used to stick pictures in it from out of the papers on Saturday nights . . . And then you get here and it ain't nothing.' 'Nothing at all?' 'Seems like it sometimes. Hey,' he brightened suddenly. 'You lend me a thousand dollars?' 'I might do. What do you want it for?' 'That's not part of the argument,' the old man said. 'Just as an objective question now. Will you lend me a thousand dollars?' 'I might do. What do you want it for?' The old man looked up from the sink: an ageless, timeless look, the look of the young lawyer in his Legal Eagle suit in East Tennessee all those years ago, the look of the muse-stricken

257

poet labouring at the kitchen table back in Margaretsville, the look of the baseball impresario monitoring Artie Tripp's progress on the parched lawn. 'I want to go home.'

Back in the Barry Mower Lounge it's 7.05 and the press of bodies grows ever thicker. Outside on the pitch the skirl of the Dagenham Girl Pipers has given way to the gun-cap patter of fireworks. On the far wall a video screen plays highlights of the campaign so far: hand-held camcorder shots of the opening round taken from high up in the stand so that the players seem to be moving in random flights and patterns quite independent of the ball; the team, sheepish and dogged posed in front of the dug-out; Ashley Flack staring inanely at the coin spun and shown to him by a sardonic-looking referee; the whole suddenly cancelled out by the superimposition of Barry Mower's face, which rears up out of a throng of other faces and, presumably owing to some mechanical fault, hangs there, eyes staring, jaw agape. A few feet away, meanwhile, the real Barry Mower is talking into a microphone held up to his face by an interviewer from the local hospital station. Caught up and obliterated by the wider blare, the words come out in scrambled half-sentences.

'They're good boys, all of them, and I'm right behind them . . . Anyone who scores, that's a car all right . . .? Night like this I'm conscious of our heritage, I mean that's what it's about isn't it, Tusker and that . . . There when he had his heart attack . . . Worst afternoon of my life . . . Tusker . . . A great honour to have the trust of our supporters and the local community . . . No truth in the rumour that the club will be put up for sale . . . I reit . . . reit . . . I say it again . . .'

Melanie moves determinedly into view leading by the hand a stocky, elderly guy in a serge suit and a stretched off-white shirt through whose folds and crevices grey chest hair busily curls.

'Scott. I'd like you to meet Tosh Mulligan.' She pauses. 'Mr Mulligan played left back in the 1958/59 cup run side.'

Tosh and I shake hands. He looks faded, creased, worn away, eyes sunk back in his head, cheeks a crosshatch of veins.

'It's a great honour, Mr Mulligan.'

'Great honour for me too son. Nice gesture of Mr Mower to ask me. Appreciate it.'

258

Melanie smiles encouragingly. Is that another wink? Emboldened, I press on: 'It must bring back a few memories. Tusker and so on.'

Tosh's glaucous eyes narrow. 'Between you and me, son – and I'm sure this young lady here won't mind me for saying so – Tusker was the stupidest old bastard I ever come across.'

'Is that so?'

'Straight up. I seen him choose teams by picking the names out of a bleeding hat.'

Whatever further revelations Tosh might be disposed to convey about Tusker Holloway and his methods of team selection are halted by the sight of Barry wheeling into focus, arms outstretched. Melanie beams. Struck by an odd feeling of elation, the clatter of the fireworks resounding in my ears, I beam back. Somehow I'm going to work it all out, as Uncle Lou might have said, what to do about Slater, the old man, Barry and the money. Somehow I'll cruise over these minor bumps and imperfections, wheel away towards the stars. The bodies are disappearing now, off towards the gangways and the executive boxes. In the midst of their flight a waitress twists sideways between us and shoves a tray of canapés into the unoccupied space. As Barry hovers solicitously and Tosh Mulligan prods sourly with his thumb at a lump of cheese, I pick up a square of pastry and start ingesting what tastes notionally like prawns and mayonnaise, Melanie laughs, and then a wisp of something freewheeling around in the back of my throat plunges inexorably downward. I try to repel boarders but it's too late, way too late, and all that emerges is a vague yet sinister hissing noise. Immediately an horrific clarity super-venes. 'Wos going on?' Barry enquires in tones of amicable interest. Tosh Mulligan stares woodenly ahead. I take a few faltering steps forward, still striving for that wondrous sense of purchase which won't come, it just *won't* come, stare around me but find only the image of Balaraj's restaurant set against the Manhattan skyline, the slow stare of the two corporate monsters, the pale, anxious face of Danny Hassenblad. Melanie is saying something, something sharp and urgent which I can't make out. I'm down on one knee now, hands clawing at my throat. Tosh Mulligan's mouth has fallen open in disbelief, the corners of the room curl up in leaves of yellow and brown, gather themselves together in pinpoints of shiny amber light and everything goes dead.

'You looked pretty bad back there,' Melanie says evenly.

'I don't remember much about it.'

'There was a moment when we thought your heart had stopped beating. But then just after they'd cleared the obstruction the man from the ambulance brigade found a pulse.'

Staring around the walls of Barry's office from the vantage point of its cornerbound couch, conscious all the while of an unsupportable agony somewhere beneath my ribcage, I nod gratefully at remembered artefacts, Barry and Princess Margaret at the charity show, the pouting calendar girls. Beyond, the noise of the crowd rises dramatically and then fades away to a murmur. Within, a clock on the wall says 8.03. According to Melanie's level testimony, I owe my salvation to the timely intervention of a paramedic from the St John Ambulance Brigade, summoned (by Melanie) from the first aid post near the foyer at the first hint of trouble.

'You were in shock for about twenty minutes,' Melanie goes on. 'Barry thought you ought to go to hospital, but the paramedic said you'd be fine after you'd had a rest.'

I don't feel fine, though, as various internal soundings are quick to confirm. The spot where someone, presumably the paramedic, punched me in the stomach hurts like fuck. Plus there is a searing pain, like the rapid buzz of static electricity, behind my eye.

'You know something?' Melanie says. 'I'd say you'd done this before. I once saw a man nearly choke himself to death and he was almost demented. Ran round the restaurant falling over tables. But you just sort of stood there, as if you almost accepted it.'

There is a strange excitement in Melanie's voice that makes me glance across at her. Seated on Barry's king-size office chair, hands pressed down into her lap, face glowing, she is clearly quivering with suppressed emotion. As it happens, I'm familiar with this phenomenon. Danny Hassenblad, whose mangled form had once been pulled from the wreckage of a convertible on the New Jersey turnpike beneath the gaze of a female insurance broker on whom he had designs, maintained that the surest way of raising yourself in a woman's estimation was nearly to die in front of her: 'Yeah, I'd swear by it. Even when I was lying there on the stretcher I could see her having a rethink. As soon as I was out of intensive care she was in to visit. Made her the day I got discharged.'

Outside the blare of noise whips up to crescendo. Melanie shrugs.

'You haven't missed anything. They're three-nil down.'

The news has a fatal resonance: frost, long-anticipated, fallen on frail blooms preserved beyond their season. 'Already?'

'That's right. Ashley Flack put through his own goal in the fourth minute. Since then it's turned into a rout.'

'So that's it then?'

'Oh, that's it all right,' Melanie nods vigorously. 'Barry'll sell the club now. He's made enough out of the cup run to cover this year's losses. Probably make a bit more selling on one or two of the players. Everton are interested in Jimmy Hood. Some Italian side are supposed to be coming in for Rickie Weller.'

Something in the matter-of-factness warns me to exercise care here. 'He tried to sell it before, didn't he?'

Melanie grinds her hand even deeper into her pelvis. 'That's right,' she says affably. 'He bought Walham at the start of the property boom because he thought he could sell it on for development. Not the whole ground – even Barry didn't think he could get away with that – but perhaps the north stand and the track behind it. Put in luxury flats or a fitness centre. In fact we had KLS do a study recommending just that. Barry spent a year trying to fix the planning permission, only then along come the local council elections, Labour gets in and slaps a preservation order on the place. Barry's left with a white elephant that costs him a million pounds a year and nobody wants to buy.'

'But I thought he was Mr Walham? Running the Squirrels was supposed to be his childhood ambition?'

'Oh *that*?' Melanie allows herself a generous smirk. 'That was just PR. Between ourselves, Barry's not terribly interested in football. And he hates the players, absolutely hates them.

Says they're a load of working-class tossers. As for all that stuff about seeing Tusker Holloway die of a heart attack, well, it's a good tale and Barry tells it very well.'

Such breath-taking duplicity demands some kind of comment. 'He's not stupid is he, Barry?' I venture, judging that this remark will commend itself to our joint sense of superiority.

Melanie simpers and darts another demure little look across. 'No, he's not stupid. Did you know Barry made a fortune out of traded options in the 1987 crash? God knows how he did it – went along, I suppose, when the market was falling. That's quite an achievement for someone who looks as if he'd have trouble adding up his lunch bill.'

'How much do you think he'll make out of selling the club?'

'Half a million. A million perhaps. All the players are worth a bit more now, you see. There's some American lawyer who grew up here in the 'fifties supposed to be interested.'

'Even with the state of the accounting systems? Surely that's going to put off a potential buyer?'

'That's right.' Is this a complicit smile? A come-on? At any rate Melanie shifts her chair – Barry's chair – a foot or so closer. 'Actually that's something I've been wanting to talk to you about for a long time. In fact there are several areas where I think your views would be . . . valuable.'

'Like the payments into the promotions fund?'

'Exactly. Like the payments into the promotions fund.'

Outside, a drop in the volume level indicates that half-time has been reached. Below, two or three thousand feet moving in search of coffee, burgers or the bathroom give the illusion of a giant centipede curling and recurling beneath the stand. Trapped by Melanie's rapt, encouraging gaze, mesmerised by the sound of her fingers drumming on the velvet cloth, reckoning up the pleasures of this newly-minted alliance, I explain about the promotions money and the overpayments. Something – an habitual caution? A desire to keep something in reserve? – allows me to temper the uncharitable speculations about the cash payments to Lennie and Maurice, but I can see Melanie nodding as I make them, and no doubt the point's gone home.

At the end of this considerable recitation Melanie sighs

comfortably, like a child who has completed some demanding task in the expectation of lavish reward.

'That's really interesting,' she says. 'Finding out all that. In fact if there wasn't another half-an-hour of the game still to go I'd go and tell dad about it right away.'

It takes a second or two to work it out. Only a second or two, mind.

'You mean Barry . . . ?'

'That's right.' Melanie smiles seriously. 'Barry's my dad. I nearly told you ten minutes ago, but then I thought I'd hear what you had to say about everything – I liked all the stuff about him not being stupid, by the way. And, you know, thinking about it, I'm glad I did really.'

'So all the stuff about Natasha who ran off with the photographer and broke her daddy's heart was . . .'

'A lie. That's right. Actually when I was eighteen I did run off with a photographer. But I came back. And so did the photographer when he found out Barry was after him.'

'And what about the brother? The brother who was in Pentonville on a drugs rap?'

'Raymond?' Melanie frowns. 'He really is inside. Been there three years now. Barry hates him. But then he always did.'

' . . . ?'

'Because he's a boy. It's very simple really. You see, Barry always worshipped his mother. And I mean *worshipped*. You remember me telling you about the memorial garden? Well it's all true, all of it. And then when she died he decided to worship me. Raymond never got a look in. There were other reasons, of course – Raymond's not too bright, actually, and all he really likes doing is drugs – but being a boy was the main one.'

Another rabid crescendo of cheering bursts across the conversation and stifles it. Mildly interested, Melanie looks up. 'Four-nil, I'd say . . . The thing is, I was amazed you fell for it. I mean, you're a conceited little prick, Scott, even by American standards, but I mean, I don't talk like Barry and I don't look like Barry, thank God, but where on earth did you think I got my data from?'

I glance up as she says this, caught under the harsh, angular

263

light, perched on the lip of Barry's chair, the door a couple of feet away. The door. Strung out as I am on fear and fury, stomach incandescent with pain, I get the feeling that puzzled civility will be the only way out of this one.

'Was . . . ah . . . was all this really necessary?'

'Oh I think so,' Melanie says. 'I mean, we could tell you were up to something. Even Barry could tell. Funny, really, because all the other accountants we've had in here never did anything. Just sat there and pretended to add up a few figures. We could have been running Kalashnikovs and they'd never have noticed. Now, obviously you weren't going to tell Barry what you'd found out, and you certainly weren't going to tell a member of his immediate family, but we thought you might confide in someone else who seemed to be as concerned about it all as you were. And we were right.'

'Weren't you worried I'd guess? Talk to someone who knew you?'

'It was high-risk, but not *that* high-risk. I mean the people here – here at the club – don't know anything about Barry's family. Except what he tells them, that is. I'll admit I was worried at that party, the one last month, but not *that* worried. After all, I haven't worked for Barry that long and I haven't hung around his friends, so not many people know who I am. In any case Maurice and Lennie were already in on it.'

The light seems stronger now, for some reason, and Melanie only a blurred, dissolving fragment at its centre. I think of Barry perched in his eyrie beneath the roof of the stand or prowling the sodden touchline, Tusker Holloway dead on the pitch, the graffiti proclaiming BARRY MOWER IS A CUNT! 'The thing is,' Melanie goes on, 'now we've had this conversation I really don't know what to do about it. I could tell you to get lost and not come back and, well, you might do. I could give you five grand and tell you not to bother us again and, well, you might not. Barry could give you a job, I suppose, but then he's going to be selling the club next week so that wouldn't suit. And even though you're a conceited little American prick you've probably got every integrity button in your head going off right now.'

'Melanie,' I say, playing for time. 'Did you really go to Durham University?'

Fortunately she seems to regard this as a perfectly routine enquiry. 'Oh yes. Oh God yes. The worst three years of my life. Corridors full of middle-class kids from Chertsey. Barry came up to see me once. Can you imagine that? Wearing one of his kipper ties, calling all the girls "darling" and saying "pardon" every time he coughed. I hated him for being Barry, but I hated them a whole lot more for despising him. Anyway' – a quick glance downward – 'there's a quarter of an hour left, so I think I'll just take some soundings about where we go from here.'

In normal circumstances, that is, without the sensation of iron fingers scrabbling around in my stomach, I might have stopped her. As it is, I go sprawling over Barry's chair – cunningly steered into my path – and haven't yet reached the door handle before Melanie's on the other side of it and the key is turning in the lock. High-heeled footsteps go speeding away along the corridor and then clatter down the metal staircase.

Alone in Barry's office, supine on the carpet with my head cradled against the fallen chair, I take stock. After the ruckus of the last half minute, the place has a winded, untidy feel, the couch sunken, a gilt-framed photograph of Barry with some dead-eyed Barbie dislodged by Melanie's fleeing elbow. A row of telephones in bright colours rests on Barry's desk, but somehow I don't think calling the police is an option. Pulling myself cautiously up off the floor, I try the door with my shoulder a couple of times: it doesn't so much as shiver. Beyond the window the ball lofts suddenly into view: gazing out for a moment I watch the scurrying figures and the amphitheatre of faces. In the distance, aloft in the giant tower blocks, lights pulse on and off. Nervously I start rummaging through the topmost drawer in Barry's desk – unfastened, oddly enough – but find only two packs of playing cards, empty cigarette cartons and a 1987 Licensed Victuallers' Association diary. The second drawer, though, yields up a much more salient item – a nasty little jack-knife with a long, rusted blade. Once, fifteen years ago, luxuriating in expertise derived from an apprentice teenage hood of his acquaintance, Greg taught me how to shoot a lock with a knife blade. I tweak away at the tooth for a while, give an extra, wrist-rolling twist for good measure and miraculously the door snaps open.

Beyond, the corridor is drenched in soft grey light. Twenty feet away a harsher beam shines over the staircase. Keeping close to the wall, still clutching the jack-knife (a vainglorious gesture but one I don't feel like foreswearing) I pad off. From below noise echoes through the dead air: in a kitchen somewhere out of sight, the sound of manhandled dishes. As I reach the lower floor and sidle left into the Barry Mower Lounge a waitress hovers into view carrying a mound of plates stacked on a tray and we nod as if my presence there clutching my stomach, knife packed under my elbow, is the most natural thing in the world. The lounge looks ancient and devastated: abandoned glasses lie over the empty tables; ash stains the carpeting. Gaining the further door I halt for some reason and lurch over to examine the picture gallery, half-lit now and bathed in shadow, with its portraits of Tosh Mulligan, Les Parrott and Tusker. Looming up out of the half light Tusker seems wholly unreal, an angry, bespectacled presence, the team drawn up alongside him no more than attendant wraiths waiting uneasily on his command, the turf before them a sinister spectre's promenade leading down into eternal gloomy dungeons. Sharp, hasty movement at the end of the lounge breaks in on this reverie: another waitress. Gathering speed again I hustle down a final flight of stairs, emerge into the silent foyer – empty except for a tremendous commissionaire nodding over a paper – and on into the welcoming darkness.

Outside it takes a second to get used to the mute, crepuscular world thrown up by the streetlamps' imperfect illumination: the broken-backed dinosaur swung out over the further kerbside turns out to be a line of burger vans, lights extinguished and shutters drawn up; the giant forest leaves underfoot a carpet of discarded newspapers. Cowering beneath the grey brick wall of The Dray I stare across the road. Graffiti gleams out of the night: VOTE PAT ARROWSMITH; MOWER IS SATAN'S FRIEND; INTER-CITY FIRM. Eastward, where the far end of the ground meets the line of the park, a taxi circles invitingly. As I hurry along the wall an early departee claims it and is sped away. Behind me the crowd, silent for the last minute and a half, groans, inhales and then explodes with fury. I look at my watch. Five minutes to go. The temptation is to loiter down by the

266

entrance gates and mingle with the hordes. But there are footsteps pattering vaguely behind me and I don't feel like lingering. A quarter of a mile away through the park, its open gates rearing up out of the sodium glare, lies the subway station. I head off into the dark.

Fifteen minutes later I'm seated in a train heading east. Lissom, strap-hanging teenage girls rove back and forth across the carriage. Next to me a guy of about my own age in a dark suit scribbles furiously away on a notepad. A procession of question marks parades urgently through my head. What do I do about this? Whom do I tell? Do I tell the old man? Slater? The police? The ethics committee of the Institute of Chartered Accountants in England and Wales? More important, what are Melanie and Barry going to do about it? Call up Linda and ask if they can fix a meeting? The train forges on through the shaft, breaks out momentarily across a bridge where below the reflected moonlight shines up from the surface of the river, burrows back into the dark. Six inches to my left a page of sprawling copperplate catches my eye:

Short-term objectives
Nikki
Catch up with friends
Marketing course (funding from O&M?)

Negatives
Break in career progression
Salary (flat)
Self-esteem etc

A swift re-read cracks it. *The guy has just been fired*! Not only that but, encouraged by the wily managerial handbooks, he has steeled himself to create what the gurus call an action plan. As I watch, more words spill out across the page. *Lessons learned: Q. Interactive skills satisfactory? Value of teamwork? Need to enhance market awareness*. Modern capitalism is a wonderful thing. They kick you out into the street on the pretext of falling sales or overstaffing, but their hold on your sense of yourself, on what the old man used to call your personal myth, is so profound that your only reaction is guilt.

267

Seeking corroboration of these surmises I cast my gaze slowly downward. There, sure enough, nestling on the dusty boards between the pair of shiny Gucci loafers is a black refuse sack, doubtless containing the contents of a couple of desk drawers. For a second I think about shaking the guy's hand, commiserating with him in some way, only to reject it in favour of wondering what Nikki did after she got this afternoon's anguished phonecall. Had her bags packed and was waiting by the front door for a cab, experience tells me. I was working in New York when the firm fired half-a-dozen bachelor analysts, all of whom were in steady relationships. Three of the guys' partners walked out immediately; the fourth had the grace to wait until she'd spent the guy's redundancy cheque; the fifth, who'd had the prudence to obtain her boyfriend's signature to a cohabitation agreement, simply sued.

The guy gets off at Earls Court, dragging the refuse sack behind him, like a bruised and battered mediaeval knight hauling his shield back defeated from the tourney. The teenage girls go skittering past towards the elevator: *they* don't have to worry about refuse sacks and *salary (flat)* bless them. Quitting the carriage at Fulham Broadway I stare anxiously at the loiterers on the stairs, the bony boys with macaw haircuts, the moody older guys in donkey jackets, all the gaunt flotsam of the West London night: there is no glint of recognition. Back at the apartment the old man is hovering in the lounge, hands stuck deep into the pockets of a borrowed bathrobe. Before him on the flickering screen film credits spin rapidly by. 'Too bad about the game, huh?' 'I left before the end. What was the final score?' 'Five O,' the old man pronounces, as in *Hawaii Five-O*, 'and one of yours got railroaded for slugging a guy. Hey, and some girl just called you.' 'What girl would that have been?' My father thinks seriously about this while on the screen a sleek roadster with whitewall tyres bursts through the gate of a Tuscan vineyard. 'She didn't say. Just to tell you it was urgent was all.' 'OK.' We stare at each other. I register that he looks marginally improved on this morning: at any rate there is a shred of colour in his cheeks and the voice seems more direct. Been out, too, as there is a copy of the evening paper face-down on the carpet. 'You OK?' I ask. 'Yeah, I'm OK.' The old man looks as if he might go on but then unexpectedly clams up. I pick up the paper and flick suspiciously through to the City pages. Halfway down the second page is a headline that says KLS CONSULTANCY BUY-OUT, with pictures of Farq, Quoodle and John Birningside. I read the story gravely a couple of times, only then becoming aware of its ominous discrepancy, its beguiling absence. No mention of Slater. I read it through again. No mention of Slater. At all.

The phone goes off twice during the night. I don't get up. The second time the old man rises to answer it and I hear him shuffling through to the hall to conduct some laboured and indecipherable colloquy. Five minutes later the light goes on and I find him standing in the doorway, face gathered up in shadow. 'Was that girl again for you.' 'Uh huh. What did you say?' 'Told her you hadn't come back.' 'OK. Thanks.' But the old man seems disposed to linger. Inching forward into the room he starts rooting through the rubbish banked up on the clothes chest: boxes of tissues, stray cufflinks. The room's only sound is his stertorous breathing and the rub of his fingers on the laminate surface.

'Hey,' he says as if the thought has only just occurred to him, 'you in some kind of trouble?' 'Could be.' 'I figured so. You want to talk about it?' 'Later maybe.' 'Fair enough.' The old man nods. 'Listen. Was something I meant to tell you about.' 'That's OK.' 'No, I mean really tell you about.' 'Go on.' 'Might not be things you'd care to hear.' 'I'll stop if I get tired. You want to sit down?' He shakes his head in a quick but preoccupied way like a horse trying to shake off a fly. 'Thing is I got a letter this morning. From Elizabeth. Wrote to her after I got sick and now she's written back.' 'Saying what?' The old man blinks, not without all ostentation. 'She's saying she wants me to go back and she'll nurse me.' 'Is that good or bad?' 'Good, mostly. I always did favour Elizabeth.' His hands, I notice, have taken on a life that is all their own, crawling dexterously up the front of his gown, winding themselves into a kind of Gordian knot of clove-hitched veins and exposed knuckles. I scoop my watch up from the bedside table and inspect the dial. It reads 3.15.

269

'Hey,' I say, 'you mind if I ask you something?' The old man looks curious, curious and somehow remote, as if whatever he gazes at exists on the further side of a cellophane sheet and has thereby forfeited its lustre. 'No, I don't mind.' The question forming in my head is *What happened between you and my mother?* or *Why did you quit?* but somehow it fractures in my mouth, thuds up against back-tracking synapses and comes out as 'How do you remember me as a child?' The old man takes this in his stride. 'You were a superior kid,' he says, not unkindly. 'Nose in the air, that type. Seen it before. Had a brother – Uncle Duane – who was that way. Can't have been much fun.' There is an ominous silence. 'Anyhow,' he goes on, 'how do you remember me? How do you remember me when you were a kid?'

I sift through the memories of the days back in Margaretsville, tall cypress trees, kids playing by the car ports. 'I don't know. Getting the English magazines. Watching Artie Tripp practising his pitching.' 'Artie Tripp,' says the old man doubtfully. 'Don't rightly recollect anyone of that name.' 'Artie Tripp. Who wanted to play in the major leagues. We talked about him on the train that time. Kid that practised pitching every morning.' The old man's eyes glint. 'Yeah, I remember. Artie Tripp. You and Greg now, you didn't like him?' 'No.' 'So why was that then?' 'Oh we thought . . .' And here, just as during the train ride, I stop, intensely bewildered by the prospect of trying to justify my dislike of Artie Tripp, his criminally foolish self belief, his pitiable integrity, his willingness to go on cultivating those ridiculous and unsustainable myths around himself. 'We figured', I end up tamely, 'that it was kind of stupid. Trying that hard at something you were so bad at.' The old man looks on drily. 'Like I said, you were a superior kid.'

For some reason I can feel my face burning with shame at this rebuke – and under-exposed as I've been to the old man's parched irony in recent years, I take it that it is a rebuke. I feel like slamming back *So what makes a superior kid if not his parents?* Not at 3.30 in the morning though, with the light livid and sickly and the old man standing at the foot of the bed looking somehow argumentative and overheated, eager to justify the most flagrant of his transgressions.

270

'I mean,' the old man goes on. 'Let's say you're Artie Tripp out there practising your pitching.' And extraordinarily he starts to make sharp, agile little movements, bringing out a phantom ball and hauling it up to his ribcage. 'OK, so you know you're never going to be Babe Ruth or Huntz Hall. So what are you going to do with yourself?' He draws the arm back and pitches into space. 'Give up? Stay in bed? If everyone felt that way there wouldn't be a whole lot of baseball teams.'

'There's a difference,' I say, 'between knowing your limitations and acting like an asshole.'

'Oh yeah, and you'd know all about that wouldn't you?' the old man shoots back. He turns to one side, suddenly weary and disillusioned. In the distance a siren starts wailing. 'Phone rings again, I'll let it go,' he says, shuffling towards the door.

I listen to the noise his feet make on the carpet, a kind of soft, rhythmical abrasion, like some small creature of the woods prowling determinedly through piled leaves. When the noise stops I listen on, realising that the effect of its absence is somehow greater than the sound itself. Fear rises up from the street, moves easily through the square and shuttered windows, spills out over the darkling floor.

271

16

Panama City motel

'What really pisses me off,' Slater says mournfully, 'what *really* pisses me off is that I never saw it coming.'

'Not any of it? Not ever?'

'Not a thing. Even when they were weekending with Birningside at that fucking stately home Quoodle rents out for his PR do's I was sitting back here with the portable in my lap thinking OK, let them sort it, let them do the work if they want to.'

'And there's nothing you can do about it?'

'There's fuck all I can do about it. Think about it Scott. Gentleman's agreement. Not a line in writing. Go and see a lawyer about this one and he'd just, he'd just . . . I suppose I should have taped the calls, but, well, it's not something you ever think about is it?'

Slater's office, 10.15 a.m. Somewhere beyond St Paul's a helicopter buzzes east over the City. Overflowing with freshly filled ashtrays, lights glowing palely against the murk, the room has the air of some gaunt foxhole at dawn, its occupant bruised and winded by the sorties of the previous night, and now braced against final attack.

'You spoken to them since?'

'Have I *fuck*?' The cigarette smoke pours out of Slater's nostrils in a bifurcated stream, like a dragon exhaling. 'Some lawyer rang me up the other day and offered me a hundred grand in severance. I told him to fuck off.'

The exact details of the scam worked on Slater by Farq and Quoodle continue to elude me. Their essence, however, is painfully clear. Used as a frontman to gain an entrée into the elevated portals of the KLS consultancy division, employed as the bridge between Farq and Quoodle and Birningside's august satrapy, Slater has now been ceremoniously dumped.

273

Footsteps clack outside in the corridor.

'What's Birningside up to?'

'John? He's sitting pretty isn't he? Chairman, maybe, for a couple of years – you know, getting pissed in the hospitality box at Wimbledon – and then back to his farm in Surrey with a pension.'

I've had these conversations before, of course: conversations in tense, smoky chambers with shattered businessmen the day the roof fell in. With the head of the New York systems team on the morning the New York systems team ceased to exist, with Danny Hassenblad when the bank foreclosed. What distresses me is that Slater – wild, pugnacious Slater – should react in the same way, not quite in the Hassenblad style (Danny had threatened suicide, then violence against the bank's president, then burst into tears, then gone and got drunk) but with a kind of fanatic, morose bewilderment.

A copy of the *Daily Mail* face down on the edge of Slater's desk discloses the sports page. A picture of Barry Mower, head in hands, crouched in the dug-out rides beneath DREAM ENDS FOR PLUCKY WALHAM. I read idly on as a wedge of sunlight suddenly breaks into the room, dazzles against the metal door-frames and sends the motes of dust cascading down its back. '*Despite a sterling performance it was a rude awakening for the Fourth Division's gallant band of cut-price heroes in last night's torrid encounter at The Dray. But even in the hour of defeat colourful chairman Barry Mower was putting on a brave face. "Five goals is a big deficit," he told reporters, "but there's another 90 minutes left and I can assure our fans that Walham will go down fighting. You ain't seen nothing yet."*' This statement seems so transparently deranged and puerile that I think about it for a while as the sun fades and recedes and Slater burrows his spine deep into the back of his chair, lights another cigarette off the butt of its predecessor and affects to study what I deduce is actually a blank sheet of paper in his in-tray.

'What are you going to do?'

'What am I going to do? Right now? Tomorrow? Next week? *Right now* I'm going to clear my desk, which between you and me means chucking most of it in the bin. *Then* I'm going to ring up the editor of *Accountancy Age* and tell him about it. *Then*

274

I'm going to go and have lunch at Simpson's. Steak and kidney, roast potatoes, bread and butter pudding, the works. *Then* I'll probably go off and get pissed at the Wig and Pen.'

'And what about me? What do I do?'

The look Slater shoots back is not unkind, just uninterested, neutral, dispassionate. 'Well, you can take it from me Scott, as far as this place is concerned you're fucked.'

'Badly?'

'Point of no return. Did you know Quoodle's going to marry that Henrietta? Straight up. Mrs Q's sitting in a cottage in Faversham right now ringing up all her mates and telling them not to go. Of course, isn't anyone these days doesn't buy damaged goods – it's not like when I was a kid, you knew what you were getting then – but I don't reckon Quoodle's going to want you hanging round the place and simpering every time someone mentions his wife, do you?'

A foot away the picture of Barry Mower stares up from the desk. I wonder about telling Slater about Barry, Melanie and the events of the previous night, reject the idea immediately. It's not Slater's problem. Slater's agenda is calling the editor of *Accountancy Age*, having lunch at Simpson's and going off to get pissed at the Wig and Pen, followed by grey, semi-penurious retirement in a London suburb. Henrietta is marrying Quoodle. Quoodle is marrying Henrietta. My relations with Barry Mower and his daughter, my telephone calls and my anxious stares down the street aren't anyone's concern but mine.

'Cheers then, Scott,' Slater says in that curiously generic way in which humbled captains of industry bid farewell to their employees, the way Danny Hassenblad stared up that sullen morning in Manhattan when the Hassenblad Consultancy hit the deck. 'All the best.'

'All the best.'

Outside in the corridor I check my watch: 10.30. So far the morning has proceeded without incident: early breakfast with the old man, the latter ostentatiously inert and uninquisitive, listening for phonecalls that never came; slipping out of the apartment unmonitored in the grim sunrise; anonymous sub-way journey; straight in here to see Slater. But what to do? Sit here and hope they don't get back to me? Go somewhere else and hope they don't follow? Still pondering fearfully I tread back to my office, turn into it without looking up. Unvisited these last weeks, it has a pallid, twilit air: wads of unopened post, old coffee cups growing mould, film of dust over the desk-top. Not untenanted, though. A scrawny junior consultant, face narrowly recognisable, sits at the work table, head down over a strew of papers. As I breeze in he jerks up cravenly.

'I'm sorry, I didn't . . .'

'Fuck off,' I tell him seriously. 'No I mean it. Just *fuck off*.'

He heads off without even looking back, papers wedged under his arm. At the door one of them flutters down. I pick it up and hurl it into the corridor after him, turn back to the desk and light a cigarette. The phone rings almost immediately. I give it six or seven rings before I pick it up. Melanie's voice. Calm, not unironic.

'Hi Scott. Too bad you couldn't hang around last night.'

I don't say anything. She strides on. 'As you probably know I rang you a couple of times at home, but there was only some old man. Very polite but unhelpful. Your father I take it? Anyway, to cut a long story short I've talked it over with Dad, with Barry, and we think you ought to come in for a chat. This morning. In fact now.'

'And what if I don't . . . What if I don't want to?'

'You've got a riverside view haven't you? Well, look out of the window. Far side of the road.'

I look down at the spot she advises. A black woman wheeling a baby buggy. A spindly teenage girl. Finally my gaze falls on a pair of inordinately large guys in black raincoats, one of whom might be Barry's driver, Big Eamonn.

A prolonged teenage diet of cop serials reconciles me to the fact that one invariable says something stupid at times like these.

'Is that a threat?'

'Gracious no. Eamonn and Gary just happened to be passing and thought you might like company on the trip. Don't think you have to hurry by the way. They'll be there all morning. Afternoon too, if you like.'

'I get it.'

The line goes dead. I look out of the window. An old guy on crutches labouring towards the bus-stop, a shell-suited jogger,

Eamonn and Gary in their raincoats, cigarettes on, feet scuffing the paving stones.

Some questions that need asking are: how do I get out, and can they stop me? I wonder for a long time if Barry and Melanie know where I live, and then assure myself that they don't; they just have a phone number that gestures at habitation somewhere in Fulham but can do no more. They could find out, though. Inspired by this thought I call personnel and briskly inform them that if anyone comes through in the guise of an insurance company, say, wanting to confirm personal details, they can safely give them the cold shoulder.

I sit in the chair for twenty, thirty minutes smoking cigarettes, thinking about the events of the past twenty-four hours. It occurs to me that I haven't eaten in that time so I hike up to the canteen – deserted except for Caribbean waitresses – buy a sandwich and feed it circumspectly down a still fantastically painful pharynx. Eventually I pick up the receiver and dial home, wait a dozen rings before the old man hauls it up.

'You OK?'

'Sure I'm OK.' He sounds uncharacteristically – or rather characteristically – belligerent. 'Was fixing my medication in the bathroom. How's it going?'

'Pretty bad. I won't go into details but . . . you doing anything this morning?'

'I guess not.'

'OK. You got any money?'

'I got cards. Amex. Diners. What you want?'

I hesitate for a moment, trying to establish in my mind exactly what I want him to do and the chances of him wanting to do it. 'Are you set on going back? Going back soon I mean?'

'How soon is soon?'

'How soon is now? There's a travel agent on the Broadway. Between the Pizza Hut and the chemist. That way. You with me?'

'I get it.' The old man sounds absorbed, pleasantly interested in whatever little game I might have contrived for his amusement.

'Get on down there in the next half-hour or so and book a

277

couple of flights to JFK. Earliest available. This evening if they're there. Then call me back OK?'

'OK.' He doesn't sound in the least discountenanced by the urgency of this request. 'Catch you later.'

'Catch you later.'

It's 11.15. Five minutes later the phone rings again. I pick it up sadly aware that it's too soon to be the old man. Melanie says:

'By the way, Scott, I forgot to say we've got the back entrance covered too.'

'You have?'

A voice that might be Barry Mower's crashes on in the background bawling something that might be *let me fucking talk to him* OK before Melanie supervenes. 'Yes, just in case you feel like going out the back way.'

'Fine.'

I sit in the chair for five or ten minutes. An unfamiliar head stares through the door, catches sight of me, moves away. Later I pull the Mac keyboard towards me, activate the screen and start on the letters. Minor variations on a single theme. One to the KLS senior partner, a doddering sexagenarian named Armitage who won't know what's hit him. A second to the editor of *Accountancy Age*. A third to the President of the Institute of Chartered Accountants in England and Wales at Moorgate Place. A fourth to the Chief Executive of the Football Association at Lancaster Gate. A fifth to the Fraud Squad. With some of these I enclose copies of documents ferried with me this morning in my briefcase. The letter to the Fraud Squad gets duplicated to the City editors of the *Telegraph, Times, Guardian* and *Independent* and, just for good measure, the *Sun*. It takes an hour and a half. Halfway through, the old man calls.

'I did what you said.'

'Uh huh.'

'Two seats on the 7.30 to JFK.' There is a pause. 'You OK Scott?' He sounds steadier than for some time. 'I mean, are you in some kind of trouble?'

'Tell you about it later . . . Listen, you think you can fix our stuff?'

'What do you mean, "fix our stuff"? You aiming on taking the whole apartment back or what?'

278

Eamonn and Gary have moved off a little way down the street now. I watch them come idling back, lit cigarettes dangling from fat fingers, as I spin out details of what to pack and where to find it. He listens in silence. When I finish he says, not in any sense of bewilderment or wonder but with the calm circumspection of one who wishes to complete a task with maximal efficiency:

'What about the rest? You figuring on coming back here?'

'Could be. Could be not. I make it twelve right now. When you've finished the packing just sit tight OK? I'll be back late afternoon sometime. Say four-thirty or five. And when I say sit tight I mean sit tight OK? Don't go out. And if anyone rings on the doorbell don't answer it.'

'You got it.'

Finishing off the letters, clipping the neat rows of incriminating data to their cover sheets, I wonder what the old man makes of this, what he thinks is going on. I picture him for a moment roaming through the apartment and uncovering its secrets – the pile of condoms, say, in the bedside drawer, the boxful of old letters and *billets doux* – cast the image aside, unalarmed and even gratified, somehow, that his curiosity about me should match mine about him. By 2 p.m. the letters are complete. I lope out into the corridor and junk them into the mail tray, go back into my room and smoke another cigarette, feet up on the table, eye fixed vaguely on the street. There remains the problem of how to spend the next two or three hours. Still thinking about this I stand up, twist my raincoat off the hook, cast a long look round – at the world map on the wall, the dusty flip-charts, the row of phoney management primers – switch off the light. Outside the corridor is deserted, abandoned in the lunch-hour scurry. Slater's office is empty, the door half-open, a reek of cigar smoke hanging in the air. Padding off towards the elevator I reflect that while Barry and Melanie might be smart enough to have the front exit and the back exit covered, the chances of them knowing anything about the side entrance, a rank culvert from which catering supplies are occasionally unloaded, are remote in the extreme. At ground level a few purposeful looking twenty-three-year-olds hang about in the space between the elevators. An elderly audit partner, umbrella hooked over his

279

forearm, goes mincing by. I head east, past the mailroom, past a cavern full of computer hardware, past the translucent doorways of the training room where whey-faced inductees look up sadly from their desks, into a warren of passageways and service elevators strewn with mounds of janitorial supplies and stationery. A fat, bolstered figure with what looks like a bizarre head-dress but is actually a frizzy mass of unusually styled hair, moving at speed from around a corner, nearly collides with me and I shift backwards against the wall.

'Linda!'

Linda comes to a halt, breathing noisily, regards me with a kind of scared abandon, takes a second or two to establish my identity and then smiles sternly.

'Hello Scott.'

It occurs to me that someone, at least, ought to know about my impending departure from KLS. Pressed up against the wall, the surge and croak of Linda's breathing gradually subsiding, I offer a sanitised explanation of my sudden exit involving a deceased grandparent and the prospect of a job back home. When I get to the end Linda says, quite sharply for her:

'That's a coincidence.'

'What is?'

'Actually I'm leaving as well. Today as it happens. Didn't you get my note about the leaving do?'

The note about Linda's leaving do. A dim memory of some dogged circular glared at a fortnight ago strays into my consciousness, speeds away again.

'I guess it must have got lost in the mail.'

'I put it on your desk actually . . . Anyway, the party's tonight so you wouldn't have been able to come.'

There is an unusual intransigence about Linda as she says this, a sort of confident anger that I don't recall experiencing before. I take a closer look at her dull, jowly face – that peculiarly English kind of face that stares up at you eternally from bus windows and store doorways – but it stays impassive. Still mesmerised, I nod back.

'So why are you leaving Linda? You got another job maybe?'

This, clearly, is too much. Linda tosses her head, so that a mass of dun-coloured hair waves uneasily behind her.

280

'Actually, Scott, I'm going to university.'

This is so wholly unexpected, so extraordinarily unbelievable, that I don't say anything. Taking her cue from the silence, Linda goes on:

'English Literature. At Goldsmith's College. You have to be quite clever to go there, Scott, did you know that? Of course it's not Harvard or Yale or anywhere like that but, still, you have to be quite clever to go there. If Dalton hadn't persuaded me I wouldn't even have tried.'

'And does Dalton . . . Does Dalton go there too?'

'Actually,' Linda says, in the tone of one administering a stupendous put-down, 'actually Dalton's doing a part-time degree in Biophysics, we're gong back-packing for six months before the courses start. Is that good enough for you Scott?'

The slow, steady gaze can be readily decoded, telling as it does of a year's subtle or not so subtle patronage, the new world gaily come to expose the presumed inadequacies of the old and so on. What to say?

'Congratulations Linda.'

'Thanks Scott. I hope it works out for you as well. You once told me all your grandparents were dead, but never mind.' She smiles. 'Oh, and if you were thinking of asking me some stupid question about American politics the answer is *I don't bloody know.*'

We shake hands. At least I imagine we shake hands. Dazed and chastened, I trip my way past the obelisks of jotter pads and Post-it notes and the stacked roller towels into bright cold air. Outside in the tiny concrete courtyard, shielded from prying gaze by a looming support wall and the flank of a delivery truck, I ponder my options. The sight of Linda, for all its unwelcome exposure of condescension and contempt, has given me an idea, dredged to the surface an elderly ambition ripe for fulfilment. Emboldened, I start threading my way cautiously out of the courtyard into the shadow of the neighbouring building. Here, where the grey back of a tower block rises in the distance, I hail a cab.

'Where to mate?'

'Penge.'

'Anywhere special in Penge?'

'I don't know. What do they have in Penge? A main street? A rail station? Someplace like that.'

I let an almost forgotten Southern twang stray into my voice for the final sentence and the cab driver brightens. Just some mad Yankee tourist, some mad American he can wheel round in circles for half an hour for fifty quid.

'Cheers then mate. Be my guest.'

The sharp, crystalline air disappears on the instant, cancelled out by a warm, human stench of dead smoke, leather and fast food. The first time I climbed into a London cab, back in 1988, I used to think there must be some special aerosol they handed out to the drivers, compounded of cigarette ash, pizza fragments and prohibitively cheap perfume. I settle back grandly against the shiny upholstery, one foot braced against the tip-up seat, as the cab wheels violently down a slip-road toward Waterloo, where grim, grey buildings – pubs and tenements and welfare offices – huddle together in the shadow of the tower blocks. A flock of pigeons goes whirling off like scraps of burnt paper rising into a chimney flue and the cabbie goes back to the rinky-dink of his commercial station, the rough South Circular voices, the perky phone-in callers and the record requests for Darren and Sharon. Seen from beyond the glass, looming into view from the mouth of tunnels, receding above the hunched rooftops, the city has a distressed, alien quality. In the distance familiar landmarks – clock towers, spires, the sprawl of the South Bank – fade into concrete. The cab carries me on, deep into the South London sprawl, past arid commons where broods of children roam, old grave high streets full of burger joints and junk stores and antique emporia where light gleams behind the stacked furniture. Kennington. Camberwell. Dulwich. Friends of Henrietta's, thrown out of their jobs or on bad terms with their parents, sometimes ended up here. These reluctant emigrants – the ex-guardee living above the Deptford garage, two or three girls apartment-sharing in Brixton – were referred to by Henrietta in tones of semi-amused disparagement as a kind of going native in one's own country.

The cab charges on into Sydenham, through leafy inclines dominated by the distant telecom tower, past rows of identikit stucco villas. Once or twice I cast an eye back along the street, find only a stalled transit truck, a skimming milk float, a fleet of bicycling schoolkids. I wonder how the old man is, back in the Fulham Road, laying out the empty suitcases, prying into the secrets of my cluttered English life. The cabbie fiddles the radio dial, sends it at a leisurely pace through a political talkshow, a football round-up (I listen half-interestedly for a mention of the Walham game, but none comes) and a black rap band commending the joys of some 69 bonin', switches it off. Cigarette crooked between his fingers, a long, delicate trail of ash suddenly descending to the floor, he half turns in his seat.

'Over here on business are you mate?'

'That's right.'

'Your first time is it?'

'It sure is.' And then for some reason I sketch out an elaborate fantasia – rather in the manner of my father but without his attack – of myself as an innocent abroad. I make myself the finance director of a textile firm from Chattanooga ('It's a pretty neat set-up we have down there'), gravely bewildered by unfamiliar social usages ('Was at dinner last night and this cat got up and sashayed along the table just as cool as fuck OK?'), naïvely picking a path through the brushwood of the tourist trail, conscious all the while of how the old man would have done it – the barely perceptible emphasis, the fine line between plausibility and pastiche adumbrated but never crossed – conscious too of his daunting superiority in the fields of irony, pattern and design. The cabbie listens meditatively for a while and then launches off – an interruption that my father would not have permitted – into an anecdote about an American tourist who had offered him a hundred-dollar bill and demanded to be taken to a store that sold bagels.

Outside the grey frontages of another high street crowd the kerb: laundromats, McDonald's, winded paper shops with Marlboro ads above the door. Sustained by patched brick arches, the trains thunder overhead. The cab idles in mid-lane, noses through the timid, suburban traffic to the sidewalk.

'Penge,' the cabbie says at length. He pronounces it sadly, hoarsely, like the name of a lover found on the doorstep with her suitcases packed or stepping from the limo with a grinning, tuxedo'd quarterback. Looking at him closely for the first time,

I see what resembles a beaten-down yet cunning walrus: fair, straw-coloured hair, a couple of yellowing 'taches curving down a gloomy, pockmarked face. In New York the cab drivers are all skinny Ricans, scarred Vietnam vets twitching under the methamphetamine blanket. Here in London they seem to be sombre, brooding guys in their fifties slowly bulging out to fill the vacuum of their cabs, alone with their fags and their phone-ins. A gleaming family triptych is propped up on the dashboard, curling under the incline of the scummy window.

'Those your kids?'

The cabbie frowns at the picture, sideways on. 'Come off it mate. Grandchildren.'

'How old?'

'Donna's thirteen. Maxine's eleven. Little Paulie'd be four . . . no, five.'

For some reason I couldn't begin to fathom, I find myself wanting urgently to prolong this interrogation.

'You get to see them a whole lot?'

'A bit. My eldest's kids. Bastard who married her tooled off after Paulie was born, so they come round the house and that.'

Donna, Maxine and Paulie. Those English names! In the States they'd be called Lee-Ann, Maddy and Jackson, have wired teeth and bold, confident, street-sharp grins. Donna and Maxine look pale and tired, hunched down into the collars of what are presumably school uniforms – blue sweaters, white shirts, Neapolitan ice-cream ties – as if the demands of early adolescent life here in the thin suburban hinterland with its teeming playgrounds and rainy dawns are already a tad too much for them. Maxine has her hair constrained by an Alice band; Donna's nondescript locks are gathered up in a risible bubble perm. Below, wan skin sags. The cabbie looks up mildly.

'Don't mind my asking mate, but how long you staying in Penge?'

How long am I staying in Penge? 'Half an hour. Three quarters maybe.'

'Uh huh. And then you'll be wanting to go back to town I take it?' That 'I take it' is characteristic, a tiny fragment of formality picked up from the soaps to adorn these conversational breezeblocks.

284

'I guess so.'

'Righty ho. Well, there's a cab rank up there. Up near the bookies.' He waves a hand upstream, where a brace of trucks lies stalled at the roadside. 'If I go and have a cup of tea and you like to walk up there in half an hour or so then I could drive you back couldn't I?'

'Why not?'

The dial, by this stage, is hovering around the £20 mark. At first he makes an anguished display of refusing money ('Cheers mate, but they all come back'), in the end gamely consenting to take £15 on account. Deposited on cracked flagstones by a derelict store whose doorway is stacked with refuse bags, I watch him go sailing past towards the truck halt, a fat hand waving from the window. I pad on down the high street, jinking through the clogged baby buggies and the lumbering children. At a clutch of phone booths, where crop-haired ten-year-olds stand trading cigarettes, I stop and call the old man. A dozen rings before he answers, then a fit of exasperated coughing.

'You OK?'

'Crumb stuck in my throat is all . . . I did what you said. Packed up a couple of cases just fine.' The old man sounds galvanised, nearly babbling in his excitement. He lowers his voice a second. 'Hey. You own this furniture and such?'

'It's a furnished apartment, Dad. All comes with the lease.'

Unappeased, the old man reels off a list of salient items currently reposing on the lounge floor: books, cassettes, magazines, thick KLS report files, managerial vade-mecums. I listen for a while, gazing aloft towards the rooftops. In the distance, out towards the English home counties, the grand, sequestered fiefdoms of Kent and Sussex, the sky darkens.

' . . . Yeah, and a pile of feasibility studies for United Bank of Switzerland.'

'Junk them,' I say. 'Throw them away.'

'Are you serious about this?' the old man wonders. 'I mean really serious?'

'Of course I'm fucking serious. Do you think I'd have got you to fix those tickets if I wasn't serious? Anybody call?'

'Someone rang the doorbell an hour back. I didn't answer.'

'OK. I'll be back in a couple of hours. Sooner, maybe. If

anybody calls, I left town.'

'Scott,' the old man quavers, 'what you done boy?'

What you done boy? It was what he used to say a quarter of a century ago back in West Virginia whenever I sent one of my remote control model airplanes spinning into an apple tree in the backyard or Greg slapped Cyrus Fuller in the mouth and old man Fuller came complaining. It was how, too, he used to invoke delinquent local politicians or public figures whose depravities were exposed by the county newspaper; welfare assessors gone down under embezzlement raps, DAs busted for corruption. *What you done boy?* For some reason I put down the phone and burst into tears, made scared and wretched by how stretched out and frightful everything feels, the traffic streaming up the hill before me turned into hulking metal monsters, the storefronts endless and gaping. Beyond the sentry-post of the phone booths the road falls away again into stacked housing. Here parkland runs in parallel with the cluttered terraces, and I wander down a serpentine asphalt track, fence-posted by dying elm trees, past drab grass, with sharp photographic prints from twenty-five years ago running hurriedly through my head: Reagan and Nancy hosting some gubernatorial clambake, the day Bobbie Kennedy died, the aerial picture of Woodstock with the crowd rolling away for ever, swamping the tiny stage like scurrying ants. And dominating it all, pushing this fractured landscape beneath him so that he strode above it like a Colossus, the old man.

A hundred yards away, down where the trees flank a tiny, dried-up pool and a ramshackle boathouse, something stirs. A guy in a trenchcoat, cigarette sending up a file of wispy grey smoke, starts moving quickly towards me. Big Eamonn, not a doubt. Frozen to the path, whose whorls and crevices rear up before me like the wounded topsoil of an earth tremor, I stare at him with a kind of resolute dispassion. What can he want with me, here in a park in London SE25, in a part of my life that is over, cancelling itself out before my eyes? Big Eamonn shouts something that the breeze takes and hurls away and I start running back up the hill, past the stunted trees, over the grass and the piles of dogshit into the brumous road. The cab rank is another hundred yards on. Not pausing to check on the pursuit,

286

I head on up past the phone booths and tatty stores, stumble into a fat guy carrying a stack of brown paper parcels, spin round, put my head down and batter my way forward again.

There are half-a-dozen cabs pulled up on the rank. I flap round them for a moment peering at the unfamiliar forms, until a yard or two beyond I find Walrus-face drowsing over a styrofoam coffee cup and the racing page of the *Standard*.

'Cheers then mate. OK if I just . . .'

'Listen. I have to get out of here.'

The cabbie stares ponderously. 'You're the boss.' He swings the cab out towards the road, where it immediately snarls up behind a couple of buses and a truck. In the distance sirens break out of the traffic's growl. Eventually the buses move on.

'Where to then?'

'Fulham Road. *Fast.*

'How fast?'

'Look, I think I'm being followed OK? *Fucking* fast.'

Walrus-face looks interested. 'Oh yeah. You a copper or something?'

'No.'

'All right. All right mate. No offence. Only I once ended up carrying some copper, some plain-clothes bloke, after some armed robbery suspect. Of course I didn't fancy that much but, well, when you've got some eight-foot gorilla waving an ID at you there's not much you can do.'

Back down the street a fusillade of horns is sounding. A red Metro, snagged up in a crush of vans and courier bikes, is trying to push its way forward. Walrus-face glances over his shoulder.

'Well, he isn't going anywhere in a hurry is he? So why don't I just – *whee*' – he jabs the front end of the cab out into the flow of oncoming traffic, which screeches and concertinas to a halt – 'and then *whoosh*.' It turns on a nickel and is gathered up immediately in the thunder. As we spin past the stranded Metro I can see Big Eamonn and the other guy, heads down over the wheel.

The cab bowls on, back towards Upper Norwood and Crystal Palace. Animated by the events of the previous five minutes, Walrus-face discourses on the vagaries of the cab-driving trade and the idiosyncrasies of cab drivers. 'Of course .

287

. . *dadadada* . . . You have to, I mean you have to have the head for it. 'It snot. It snot just a driving job is it? I mean, I mean I've never come across a thick cabbie all right, and I . . . *whee*! There's been blokes with university degrees tried to drive cabs in their time and . . . *just fuck off all right* . . . ? They can't, they can't . . .'

We're getting back on towards Clapham, the prospect behind us is grey asphalt emptiness, just a bus or two or a hard-hat cyclist pedalling furiously in mid-lane. As Walrus-face descants on memorable fares past and present ('This old girl, see, with seven dogs, used to want to go to Potters Bar every Sunday morning. Didn't know if she was coming or going. And then one Sunday morning we start driving back, right, and there's only six of them . . .'), I contemplate the tangled, overgrown pathway that lies ahead: inhospitable, jobless America. The States are full of out-of-work consultants, guys who worked for Kinseys, guys who oversaw government-funded dam programs in the Third World until the government decided to spend the money on tax cuts. And what about the old man? Does he go off to live (and die) someplace with Elizabeth Schenectady or with me? I have a vision – to be accurate I have a renewed visitation of a vision that has been beguiling me for days – of the old man and me sharing an apartment, in Chicago say, or Miami, or someplace where they still need systems analysts, and the old man getting weaker by the day, taking his meals in bed, lying there watching the TV with the covers drawn up and the thermostat full on, and his face falling in on itself more and more, until one day I come home and find him dead, jaw agape over the bedspread, the body pressed into my anxious grasp no more than a bag of sticks. Like something out of a movie except that this time it's for real, and you can smell the sickroom cloaca, weigh the morphine capsules in the palm of your hand.

I start crying again now as the cab slews over Chelsea Bridge and turns west along the Embankment and the cabbie, ostentatiously quiet, stares fixedly ahead at the unravelling tarmac. To the left container barges float cumbrously by, battered by the heavy swell of the mid-stream current. A helicopter chugs busily down river into the distant wall of mist. All of us drifting away on a grey tide: Barry Mower back to his old furtive life, Henrietta to a rectory someplace with Quoodle and a decade of social ostracism, Miranda/Margy to a vagrant, anonymous existence in some of the gaps and spaces of the turning world, the old man and me back to all the uncertainties we had looked to escape. In the Fulham Road the street lights are going on; dusk steals up over the tacky storefronts, the 24-hour diners and the florid amusement arcades. The old man's head cranes out of the door as I hasten up, like a gaunt, elderly bird, wisps of hair straggling over his crown like moulting plumage. His eyes are sunk deep back into his skull, but he retains the morning's glint of interest.

'You OK?'

'Sure I'm OK.' He makes a quick, self-deprecating gesture which turns into a tug on the door-frame. The door falls open to reveal a pile of cases and hand-grips. 'Say, a guy called for you an hour back. Came on really strong.'

'Uh huh. What did you say?'

The old man coughs, pauses between dry, leathery intakes of air, and croaks: 'Told him if I saw him I'd bust his head.'

Silently I load the gear into the taxi. Inert behind the glass, features obscured by the gusts of cigarette smoke, Walrus-face stares at us. The dial stands at £45. Moving from the doorway down into the booming corridor of the street the old man stumbles, one leg collapsing in on the other like a snapped stalk or a high-grade impersonation of Charlie Chaplin. I reach him just before he tips over on to the kerb, lock my hands on to his elbows.

'Sure you're OK?'

'Lost my balance on the step is all . . .' Decoding my nod as a rebuke he yells, 'Look Scott, I just lost my balance on the step!'

'OK. Just sit quiet there for a minute. I'll be right back.'

Winging back up the staircase I take a final look around the apartment. Box files lie piled up on the davenport; cutlery gleams from the sink. In the main bedroom I find a tower of shot trash: old albums, credit counterfoils, a copy of *Time Out* from October 1988. I look at it for a second or two, then prowl back to the front door, step outside and slam it shut.

In the cab ('Heathrow is it mate? Well, you're the boss') the old man sits tensed up against the far window, feet splayed sideways over a suitcase. His whole face is bloodless, the eyes blank and unseeing.

'Hey,' he says suddenly. 'Where are we going?'

'Home,' I say sharply. 'We're going home.'

'No,' he comes back, less urgently. 'It's OK Scott, I'm not . . . I'm not . . .' I watch him search for the right words. 'I mean, I'm OK in my head you know. It's just . . . I mean, when we get off the plane at JFK where are we heading?'

'We'll find somewhere . . . Where's Elizabeth right now?'

'Someplace Texas way. Fresno. El Paso.'

'OK. We'll check into some hotel and then we'll call her up.'

That seems to satisfy him. When I glance up again he's fallen asleep huddled up against the glass, lower lip drooping down to expose the yellow pegs of his teeth. The cab surges west through the late afternoon and England floats by, this lost kingdom in the mist with its stretched suburbs and grainy streets, its little Queen with her white face. The old man lists into consciousness once more and I say: 'You mind if I ask you something?' 'Sure. What about?' 'Something personal.' He thinks about this for a moment, lower lip moving in palsied circular motion. 'Go ahead. Ask.' The neon from the lights overhead bounces around us. 'OK. Why did you leave?' The old man looks puzzled. 'What do you mean, why did I leave? I'm here ain't I?' 'No. That time back in Margaretsville. Time we came back and you'd walked out on us. Why did you do it?' 'What kind of question is that?' I wonder whether to leave it, but something jerks me on. 'Jesus, you're my father. You walked out on us when we were kids and never came back. Why?' He coughs a couple of times in a way that mimics glue boiling in a pot, waves a hand in front of his mouth and staunches whatever lurks inside with a tissue. 'I want to know,' I go on, feeling an extraordinary glow of bravado, a quite visceral satisfaction in articulating the words. 'Was it us? Jeannie and Greg and me, I mean? Was it Mom? Something else we never knew about? I mean, just what on earth happened?'

Through the darkness of the cab's interior, with its background pattern of street signs, the low humps of terraced houses, I can see the old man's eyes gleaming. He looks craven, scared, confused. 'Fear,' he says finally. '*Fear*?' 'That's right. At least,' he hurries on, 'that's what it amounted to time I sat and thought about it.' 'And when was that? I mean, when was the time you sat and thought about it?' 'Back in Miami, a week or so later.' 'What do you mean, fear?' 'Shit, I don't know. Was OK when you were kids. Little kids I mean. I could handle that. And your mom, now, I could handle her. But then . . .' 'But then what? Didn't we turn out how you wanted?' 'No, you were fine. Jeannie now, she was kind of *scholarly*.' He pauses to give the word full weight. 'I like that in a kid. Greg, he was never going to get a citation from Harvard but he was a kid any father could be proud of.' I stare at him through the gloaming, searching for a radium-glimmer of irony: none emerges. 'And what about me?' 'Like I said,' the old man blinks, 'you were a superior kid.' 'So why couldn't you handle it?' 'Hey now,' the old man says quietly, 'it was a long time ago.' 'I know it was. Why couldn't you handle it?' The old man shimmies his hand up and down in front of his face. 'I don't know. You ever found you did something and couldn't work out why you did it?' 'Sometimes.' 'Sure, well, I liked your mother – no, really liked her – but I never figured out how I got to marry her.' 'No?' 'No. Just woke up one morning in a hotel outside of Birmingham and found I'd done it. Same with you and Greg and Jeannie. One moment we're talking about starting a family – and let me tell you Scott, if ever you get married . . .' He pauses. 'If ever you get married again . . . that's one of the things you talk about. The next there's five of us sitting round the table at Thanksgiving and you're upgrading your car. Isn't anything you can do about that. It just happens.' 'And?' 'And you turn around one day and find you've lost control of your life.' 'You do?' 'I wouldn't say I was a selfish kind of a guy,' says my father sententiously, 'but . . .' 'And I wouldn't say you were a particularly original one either.' 'No' – and the look here is withering – 'I don't suppose you would. But that's what happened anyhow. I don't expect you to festoon me with flowers on account of it, but that's what happened. And another thing.' 'Uh huh?' 'You won't hardly credit it, Scott, but I was always going to come back.' 'Always?' 'Ten, fifteen years. I used to sit there in Miami, Key West or wherever and I'd plan it all out. Sell up, kiss goodbye to Gabby or Denise or whoever and just go back to my old life.' 'So what

291

happened?' 'What happened? Something always got in the way. One time Gabby got pregnant. Another time . . . Hey, you remember that time I was staying in the trailer out near Orlando? Time you came and visited?' 'Sure, I remember.' 'I was going to quit it all then. Had everything planned. Go back to Margaretsville, you and me. But it didn't work out.' 'Why not?' 'Don't know,' the old man says thoughtfully. 'Could see you reckoned I was turning into a real cracker. You know, guy walks in wearing a Fox Brothers suit and his old man lives out of a trailer down in the boondocks. So I thought, what the hell?' Uncle Hervey's rapt, weaselly face bad-mouthing Teddy Kennedy steals into view: I beat the ghost away. 'So I thought, what the hell,' he ends up lamely and I stare at him open-mouthed, winded by irritation, guilt, a furious sense of missed connections, of how things might have been throughout twenty years of fractured, unreal life.

'What happened the time Gabby got pregnant?'

'Uh huh. She was going to keep it at first. Talked about getting married. But then she decided she couldn't go through with it. Had a Hoover job one day without telling me. We split up soon after that.'

'I'm sorry.'

The airport lights are only a mile or so away now. Traffic flows noisily by on either side. The old man shifts nervously in his seat, hands crawling over his upper torso. 'I'm not feeling too good, Scott,' he says. 'You got any medication you can take?' He nods ambiguously. 'Hey, you got to do something for me Scott?' 'What's that?' 'When we get to JFK you got to get me a doctor.' 'Sure, anything you want.' 'When we hit JFK, promise me you'll get me a doctor.' Watching the ripple of his shoulders against the glass I divine that he is shaking with terror, hands knotting and re-knotting in the bony cradle of his lap. 'It's OK,' I say. 'It's OK. We'll fly to JFK and I'll get you a doctor.' 'Not a hospital,' he says wildly. 'Not a fucking hospital. Just book me into a motel someplace, someplace where they don't mind you taking sick, and have a guy come round, you know.' He closes his eyes after this. Emboldened by God knows what stirrings of affection, pity, resignation and terror I steal across the seat and hoist my arm across his shoulders. He smells old and stale, the sweet grim smell of decay.

The road pans out, veers right and left into a long, empty stretch of tarmac where the moon breasts into view between rows of huddled houses, glints off the surface of distant water. And for some reason I remember seven or eight years back being in Panama City, off on some forgotten journey, a day spent prowling back streets that stank of gasoline and watching the red, sump-stained river, buying cigarettes out of a dwindling store of dollars and then haggling for a room with some crabby motel owner, where I lay all night reading from a pile of Spanish auto magazines before escaping at first light on to the freeway and a trail that led back into the bright, mysterious future.

That's all.